"My job seems glamorous, but it's not. It's a tough business involving ridiculous amounts of money, people with tremendous egos, extreme stress and short deadlines," he explained.

Geneviève wore a thoughtful expression on her face. "Then why do you do it?"

"Because when I was in high school an entertainment attorney came to speak to my class for career day, and the moment she started talking I was sold. I knew it was all I wanted to do. Some people enjoy reading magazines, but I enjoy studying law books and old court transcripts, and after seven years of practicing law I'm still eager to learn more."

And I enjoy studying you, Geneviève thought, admiring his face over the rim of her cocktail glass.

For the first time in months, Geneviève felt relaxed, at ease, and she was in no rush to return to the hotel. Roderick was the most fascinating man she'd ever met, and if she didn't have a six o'clock interview at a local radio station she'd spend the rest of the day with him.

Pamela Yaye has a bachelor's degree in Christian education. Her love for African American fiction prompted her to pursue a career in writing romance. When she's not working on her latest novel, this busy wife, mother and teacher is watching basketball, cooking or planning her next vacation. Pamela lives in Alberta, Canada, with her gorgeous husband and adorable, but mischievous, son and daughter.

Books by Pamela Yaye

Harlequin Kimani Romance

Visit the Author Profile page
at Harlequin.com for more titles.

PAMELA YAYE
and
SYNITHIA WILLIAMS

*Pleasure at Midnight &
His Pick for Passion*

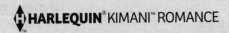

HARLEQUIN® KIMANI™ ROMANCE

ISBN-13: 978-1-335-43303-9

Pleasure at Midnight & His Pick for Passion

Copyright © 2019 by Harlequin Books S.A.

The publisher acknowledges the copyright holders of the individual works as follows:

Pleasure at Midnight
Copyright © 2019 by Pamela Sadadi

His Pick for Passion
Copyright © 2019 by Synithia R. Williams

Recycling programs for this product may not exist in your area.

Printed in U.S.A.

CONTENTS

PLEASURE AT MIDNIGHT

Pamela Yaye

Dear Reader,

Anyone who knows me knows I'm a music aficionado who enjoys watching iconic videos and documentaries and reading biographies about legendary singers. The idea for *Pleasure at Midnight* came to me last summer while attending a music festival. The artists gave thrilling, exciting performances, but as I watched fans demand autographs and pictures, I wondered about the downsides of fame. What happens when an artist gets sick of the business? Can they quit without repercussions? Or would they lose everything they'd worked so hard for if they walked away?

Jennifer "Geneviève" Harris is a superstar whose fun, catchy pop songs are burning up the charts. After decades of being in the spotlight, Geneviève needs a break, but her record label won't hear of it. Roderick Drake comes to her aid just in the nick of time. The entertainment attorney with the chiseled features is more than just a handsome face. He's sincere and loyal, and after several sightseeing excursions around Madrid, Geneviève *loves* the idea of escaping with him forever.

As you've already figured out, I enjoy writing novels with glitz and glamour set in exotic locales, and *Pleasure at Midnight* has everything you've come to expect from my Kimani romances. I'd love to hear from you, so connect with me at pamelayaye@aol.com or on my social media pages. Happy reading, friends!

All the best in life and love,

Pamela Yaye

Chapter 1

Entertainment attorney Roderick Drake stood in front of the bathroom mirror inside his eighteenth-floor hotel suite at the legendary Hotel du Lugo in Madrid, Spain, rehearsing his speech. Speaking in a quiet, soothing voice—the one he reserved for his most difficult clients—he smiled and nodded, as if he were addressing a room full of people rather than his reflection. His boss, Vincent Welker, didn't call him "The Closer" for nothing, and Roderick wanted to live up to his reputation.

Carefully inspecting his attire, he adjusted his metallic gray tie. Hired fresh out of law school at Welker, Bradford and Davidson, Roderick had had a seven-year career full of memorable moments. Visiting the White House during Obama's tenure, attending the Super Bowl with the senior partners and delivering the commencement speech at his alma mater were cherished memories, and Roderick felt fortunate to be working at the prestigious Manhattan law firm. Determined to become partner at Welker, Bradford and Davidson, he'd do anything to achieve his goals, and wasn't above breaking the rules to make it happen.

Grinning at the thought, Roderick leveled a hand over the lapel of his tailored Hugo Boss suit. He looked sharp in his designer attire, and there was no doubt in his mind that he'd get the job done. And once he did, he was heading back to New York. Roderick had a meeting with a rock band next week, and if he wanted to convince them to sign with Welker, Bradford and Davidson, he had to prepare. He had ten days to fix Geneviève's problems, and he would, no matter what.

Pleased with his appearance, Roderick turned off the light and stalked into the living room. Decked out in scrumptious furnishings, gilded chandeliers and mirrors, and floor-to-ceiling windows that offered striking views of the city, the Grand Prestige quarters were worth every dime, and after his meeting, he was going to take advantage of the in-suite massage service. Last night, at his boss's request, he'd boarded the private company jet for Madrid, and although he'd napped during the eight-hour flight from New York, he was still exhausted.

That's what I get for partying with my family on New Year's Eve, Roderick thought, yawning. Three days later, he was still beat, but duty called, and he wasn't going to let his boss down. Proud to be a senior attorney at one of the oldest and most successful law firms in the state, Roderick gave 100 percent to his clients.

Noting the time on the bronze clock hanging on the alabaster wall, Roderick put on his leather shoes, then grabbed his briefcase off the chestnut desk. He had a lot riding on his one o'clock meeting with Jennifer "Geneviève" Harris, and hoped the pop star would be receptive to what he had to say. The former child star and award-winning singer was one of the greatest voices of the twenty-first century. Blessed with remarkable talent, Geneviève had six platinum-selling albums, more endorsement deals than an NBA superstar and avid followers. The total package, she had an angelic voice and a fun-loving personality people couldn't get enough of. Everyone from Drake to the royals were huge fans of her music, and these days Geneviève couldn't go anywhere without being mobbed.

A troubling thought came to mind. What if, despite his best efforts, he couldn't reach a settlement agreement with the injured fan? What if Geneviève made good on her threat to cancel the rest of her European tour, and returned to Philly in the morning? Roderick feared what would happen if he blew it. Millions of dollars would be lost, the media—and her fans—would turn against her and Roderick could kiss his promotion goodbye.

Roderick gazed out the window. When he'd arrived at the hotel that afternoon, he'd been shocked to see hundreds of reporters, photographers and locals camped outside on the sidewalk, chanting Geneviève's name. He shouldn't have been surprised. Not after what happened on New Year's Day. A video had surfaced online of Geneviève slapping a young man outside Madrid-Barajas International Airport, and the damning footage had gone viral. The "fan" claimed he was emotionally, physically and mentally scarred, and the twenty-eight-year-old singer was being crucified by the local media for being an "Ugly American." Upset about the negative attention, Geneviève had lashed out at her critics, and threatened to cancel the rest of her tour. Mr. Welker had asked Roderick to travel to Madrid to meet with the fan and offer him a cash settlement.

And that wasn't all. His boss wanted him to persuade Geneviève to finish her lucrative, blockbuster tour. Inwardly seething, Roderick had gritted his teeth. He'd rather have a root canal than travel four thousand miles to babysit a spoiled pop star. Sure, he'd worked successfully with Geneviève in the past, but he preferred working with athletes, not entertainers. In fact, Roderick wanted to be transferred to the LA office in March to manage the athletic division. Working with the biggest names in sports would increase his profile and popularity, and he loved the idea of representing his favorite athletes. He'd started to suggest his boss send one of the associate attorneys to Madrid, but Mr. Welker had interrupted him.

"The Diversity Committee wants to elect an African American partner this year, and I think you're the perfect person for the job," he'd said, with an earnest expression on his round, wrinkled face. "You're a brilliant attorney, and I have high hopes for you."

Eager to hear more, Roderick had leaned forward in his leather-padded chair.

"Geneviève makes this firm truckloads of money every year, and if you persuade her to finish her European tour, I'll personally put forth your name for partner in May," he'd promised, nodding his shiny, bald head. "I have faith in you, Roderick. You can do it. I know it."

Fired up, Roderick had returned to his Hamptons bachelor pad, packed a suitcase and headed to the airport. He had to turn things around on Geneviève's world tour, aptly named *Total Drama*, before the pop star made good on her threat and skipped town. The Philadelphia native was a handful, and if she wasn't the firm's richest and most famous client, he'd drop her from his caseload. Welker, Bradford and Davidson provided legal counsel on business, corporate and entertainment issues, and was the first and only law firm in the nation to report a billion dollars in annual revenue. Heralded as the "Gold Standard for Law," employees prided themselves on always being available to their clients, and although Roderick had initially balked at traveling to Madrid, he was glad he'd made the trip.

Pocketing his cell phone, Roderick left the suite. He strode through the corridor, greeting everyone he passed with a broad smile. Life was good, and it was about to get better. There was no doubt in his mind he'd be named partner in May, and just thinking about the life-changing opportunity made his chest puff up with pride.

Roderick stopped in front of suite 1812, knocked and waited for someone to answer. Geneviève and her team had booked twelve rooms on the eighteenth floor, and the hotel manager had let it slip that the group was a loud, rowdy bunch. Said that other guests had repeatedly complained about the noise. Roderick wanted to speak to Geneviève alone, without any interruptions, and hoped he wouldn't have to compete with her entourage for her attention.

The door swung open, and a dark-skinned woman with doe-shaped eyes, red lips and honey-blond twists stared at him. For a moment, Roderick didn't recognize her, but when she spoke he remembered Geneviève's fun-loving kid sister with the wicked sense of humor. Not only did Demi oversee all aspects of Geneviève's personal and professional life, she designed all the costumes for the tour, and also managed her sister's social media accounts. Every day, her posts racked up millions of views, and Geneviève credited her sister for the staggering success of her brand and her worldwide appeal.

"Roderick? Oh my goodness, you look like a completely different person!"

He cocked an eyebrow. "Is that a good thing, or a bad thing?"

"It's a *great* thing." Whistling, Demi fanned her face. "You've always been handsome, but now you're sexy as hell, and if I wasn't head over heels in love with my boyfriend, Warner, I'd be *all* over you."

Roderick chuckled and regarded the twenty-six-year-old personal assistant with amusement. He couldn't believe how bold she was. Demi was right; he'd changed drastically since last year. Nine months ago he'd been out of shape. Happy in love, he'd quit working out, and started partying with his fiancée, Toya Janssen, and her socialite friends. He spent thousands of dollars wining and dining the New Hampshire native, lavishing her with expensive gifts and affection. All for naught. Three months before their wedding, she'd betrayed his trust, and their engagement had imploded.

Painful memories darkened his thoughts. He'd coped with their breakup by downing shots at his favorite bar, and things had gotten so bad his brothers had pressured him to go to rehab. Duane was a brilliant software engineer with a wife and four sons, and Morrison was an esteemed judge with a feisty fiancée, and even though they had busy lives, they'd harped on him nonstop about seeking professional help.

To get his siblings off his back, he'd quit drinking, hired a personal trainer and adopted a healthier lifestyle. His hard work had paid off. He'd lost weight and regained his confidence, his swagger. Roderick enjoyed the Hamptons nightlife and being in the company of beautiful women, but he refused to let his mom set him up on blind dates. His father, Nathaniel, was a retired Supreme Court judge, and his mother, Viola, a talented interior designer, but Roderick often joked she should have been a professional matchmaker. His mom was obsessed with finding him Ms. Right, but Roderick didn't want to settle down. Love sucked, and he wanted no part of it.

"How's life?" Demi asked with a bright smile. "Still killing it at that fancy law firm?"

"You know it!" Roderick laughed. "How are things with you? Having fun on tour?"

Demi groaned. "Don't ask. These days I'm so busy I don't know if I'm coming or going."

"I hear you. I was so tired I crashed as soon as I boarded my flight last night, and if the stewardess hadn't woken me up when we landed I'd *still* be sleeping soundly on the plane."

"It sounds like this trip came at the perfect time." Demi waved him inside, then closed the door. "I love Madrid, and you will, too. The museums are incredible, the people are friendly, the food is to die for and the architecture is enchanting."

"Sounds like my kind of place." Having done his homework, he knew Demi was one of the few people Geneviève trusted, and if he hit it off with the personal assistant, she could help his cause. In many ways, Demi reminded him of his sister. Emmanuelle had been gone for years, but not a day went by that Roderick didn't miss her. He tried not to think about the tragic pool accident that ended Emmanuelle's young life, only the good times, and pushed the memory of her funeral to the furthest corner of his mind. Emmanuelle's daughter, Reagan, was a college freshman, and Roderick cherished their monthly dinner dates at the teenager's favorite sushi restaurant in Manhattan.

"I'm only here for a few days, but I plan to do some sightseeing before I return to New York next week. Where do you recommend?"

"You have to check out the Royal Palace of Madrid. It's stunning." Her eyes lit up as she spoke about sightseeing with Geneviève the night before, and it was obvious Demi adored her older sister. "Madrid is one of the coolest places I've ever visited, and every time I'm here I find something new to love about the city."

Bubbly and energetic, Demi spoke in an animated way. Chatting with the Philly native about her favorite spots in Madrid and her new YouTube channel, he thought about his sister again. It wasn't until she'd died that he'd realized how important his family was, and he'd vowed never to take them for granted again.

"Roderick, can I interest you in something to drink?"

"No, thanks." Following Demi through the luxurious suite, he searched for Geneviève, but couldn't find her. Hearing loud voices, his gaze strayed to the balcony, and he listened closely.

"If you cancel the tour we'll lose hundreds of thousands of dollars, and your reputation will be toast. Is that what you want? For people to think you're a spoiled, ungrateful pop star who doesn't care about her fans? Who'd rather lay around than fulfill her contractual obligations?"

Roderick winced. He couldn't believe that Geneviève's mother, Althea Harris, could be so mean and hoped she didn't upset Geneviève.

"Mom, you don't understand—"

"No, *you* don't understand. You're being paid remarkably well for the European tour, and I won't let you throw everything away just because you're upset. You can't let a deranged fan and a little bad press stop you from performing. The show must go on."

"But, I'm physically and mentally drained—"

"Stop whining," Althea snapped. "Your European tour only has twenty-five dates. Beyoncé and Taylor Swift did twice as many shows last year, so you have no right to complain."

"You have no idea what it's like being me. I'm tired and stressed, and I haven't had a good night's sleep in months," Geneviève confessed in a quiet voice. "I can't keep living like this."

"You have to. You have four sold-out shows in Madrid, then stops in Paris and Dublin…"

Roderick and Demi shared a look. His first thought was to leave, to return in an hour, but before he could speak, Althea gestured for him to join her on the balcony. Statuesque, with heavy makeup and dark curls, the single mom was in her fifties, but dressed like a college student. Her ruffled tank top showed off her cleavage, her denim shorts were skintight and her chandelier earrings jingled every time she moved.

"Roderick, I'm so glad you made it." Rising from the table, a cigarette dangling from her lips, Althea greeted him with a hug. "It's good to see you again, son."

I wish I could say the same, he thought, forcing a smile onto his mouth. He'd met Althea twice, and both times the momager had rubbed him the wrong way. He knew from past conversations with Geneviève that her mom had been her manager from day one, and Roderick pitied her. Althea was a momager of the worst kind—

selfish, bossy and shortsighted—and if Roderick wasn't worried about making waves at the law firm, he'd tell Geneviève to fire Althea and hire someone educated and experienced who'd support her wholeheartedly, not a calculating momager who was driven by the almighty dollar.

You're a fine one to judge, said his conscience. *You're driven by the almighty dollar, too!*

"Roderick? What are *you* doing here?"

His gaze landed on Geneviève, stretched out on the striped chaise lounge chair in the corner of the balcony, and his thoughts scattered. She looked glamorous in her silk headscarf, oversize sunglasses and flower-printed dress, but he couldn't help noticing her woeful disposition. And that wasn't all. Her mocha-brown skin looked lifeless, and her curvy, voluptuous figure was a thing of the past. He was shocked by her drastic weight loss, and feared the stress of being Geneviève—one of the biggest pop stars in the world—was affecting her health. Was she eating well? Did she have time to rest after concerts, or was her schedule jam-packed with meetings, rehearsals, costume fittings and interviews?

"I came to see you, of course. The opening night of your European tour received rave reviews and I wanted to see the show for myself," he said. "I'm your biggest fan ever. Think you can hook me up with some front-row tickets?"

Geneviève's eyes narrowed, and a scowl pinched her lips.

"You're not here to see the show," she said. "My mom called your firm in a panic and summoned you here to talk some sense into me, and you came running. Isn't that right?"

Geneviève stared him down as if they were mortal enemies, but Roderick wasn't intimidated by her piercing gaze; he stared back at her.

Althea raised her iPhone in the air. "I have some calls to make, so I'll leave you two alone to discuss business. Make the right choice, Gigi. I'm counting on you."

"Mom, it's my life, my career, my decision, and I don't need your permission to cancel the tour."

"That's not how it works in the music business, and you know it." Althea sounded exasperated, as if she was at her wit's end. "If you cancel the tour and return to Philly, there will be serious consequences."

"Geneviève, don't worry," he said smoothly. "We'll figure something out."

Stepping past Roderick, Althea jabbed him in the side with her elbow, then whispered, "I don't care what it takes. Convince Geneviève to finish the tour."

Roderick nodded in understanding. "Ms. Harris, I'll try my best—"

"No," she snapped. "Make it happen, or you're fired."

Chapter 2

Geneviève inspected her French manicure. She pretended to admire her nails, but she was listening in on her mother's conversation with Roderick. As usual, Althea was up to her old tricks. Her mom wasn't happy unless she was calling the shots, and it was times like this—when Althea was plotting and scheming—that Geneviève wished she could fire her. But she couldn't. Wouldn't. She felt guilty for even having the traitorous thought. She owed her success to her mother, and if not for Althea's drive and tenacity, Geneviève wouldn't be an international pop star. Her mom didn't wait for things to happen, she made things happen, and even though Althea didn't have a business degree from Harvard, she acted like she did, and could outwit anyone, including record executives, event promoters and seasoned professionals.

Her ears perked up. *Convince Geneviève to finish the tour, or you're fired?* Geneviève scoffed. As if she'd let

Althea fire Roderick. Before retaining his counsel last year, she'd done her homework about the popular, New York attorney. She'd searched the internet for information about him. And the more articles she read about the Columbia University graduate, the more Geneviève was intrigued by him. Success was sexy, and Roderick was an overachiever destined for greatness in the legal world. His clients included actors, singers, bestselling authors and artists, and everyone he represented raved about him.

The first time Geneviève met him she'd drooled all over her Gucci pantsuit, but what impressed her most about Roderick Drake wasn't his good looks, or his smooth-as-silk baritone; it was his confidence, how he carried himself, his strength. Unlike everyone else who worked for her, Roderick wasn't afraid of her mother and didn't back down when Althea lost her temper.

"Bye, honey," Althea said with a smile and a wave. "See you in a bit."

Geneviève was annoyed with her mom but she bit her tongue—for now.

"Let's discuss the incident at the airport," Roderick said, sitting down at the table.

Glad she was wearing dark sunglasses, she admired the attorney's good looks. His low-cropped hair, his neatly trimmed goatee, his blinding-white teeth and flawless pecan-brown complexion. *Damn, he can rock a suit!* A year ago, Roderick was an out-of-shape groom-to-be, but today he was chiseled, dapper and fine. *Why are all the good guys taken?* she thought. *Why can't I meet someone as successful and charming as Roderick-fine-ass-Drake?*

He smelled of spices, and his scent was intoxicating.

Over the years, Geneviève had met some of the biggest names in the entertainment business, but none of them excited her. Not the way Roderick did. It was hard to be in his presence without gawking at him, and every time their eyes met she had to remind herself to breathe.

Wetting her lips with her tongue, she fingered the ends of her wavy, shoulder-length hair. *Gosh, I wish my mom had told me we were having company*, she thought, crossing her legs at the ankles. *If I knew Roderick was stopping by I would have done my hair and makeup, and put on something cute.*

Roderick clasped his hands together. "Let's talk."

"Let's not, and say we did." Geneviève acted as if she couldn't be bothered to discuss her problems, but deep down she was glad Roderick had made the trip to Madrid. Her interactions with him had always been positive, and she could count on him to tell her the truth even if she didn't agree.

Her thoughts returned to last year. She hadn't seen Roderick since he'd attended her post-Grammy celebration party in Philadelphia. He'd arrived at her estate with his fiancée, a perky blonde with a fitness trainer's body, and she'd reluctantly posed for a picture with the happy couple. "Congratulations on your marriage," she said now. "How was the wedding?"

His face darkened, and his shoulders tensed. Why was he mad? Had she crossed the line by asking about his personal life? Was he having problems at home? Seconds passed before he spoke, and when he did his voice was so low Geneviève had to strain to hear him.

"My engagement ended."

Boy! Spill. The. Tea! For some reason, she wanted to cheer, but resisted the urge. She didn't know Toya, or have anything against her, but Geneviève never thought the socialite was good enough for him. Sure, she was pretty, but Roderick should be with someone who was ambitious and successful, not a woman who spent her days shopping, waxing and Tweeting.

For the second time in minutes, Geneviève gave Roderick the once-over. Took in his stoic demeanor and rigid posture. Is that why he'd lost weight? Why he wasn't his usual playful, jovial self? Because he was bummed about the demise of his engagement? Roderick was her attorney, not a friend, but Geneviève wanted to hear more about his breakup. Before she could ask him, though, he changed the subject.

"I know you're busy, so I won't take up too much of your time." Roderick opened his briefcase, took out a yellow notepad and a gold-plated fountain pen. "Tell me what happened at Madrid-Barajas International Airport on New Year's Day. I saw the footage online, but I want to hear your side of the story."

Geneviève dropped her gaze to her lap, and fiddled with the charm bracelet at her wrist. It was a Christmas gift from Demi, and every time she looked at it a smile warmed her heart. Geneviève didn't want to talk about the frightening incident at the airport days earlier; she wanted to discuss the legal ramifications of canceling the rest of the European tour. She'd been in the public eye ever since she landed her first TV commercial at eight years old, and after two decades in the entertainment business, Geneviève needed a break.

And now was the perfect time. Yesterday, her sixth studio album was certified triple platinum, and her singles, "Savage," "Salty Girl" and "Don't Tweet Me, I'll Tweet You," were burning up the Billboard charts. She'd amassed a fortune beyond her wildest dreams, and she would never have to worry about going to bed hungry again. Tired of living out of suitcases and being hunted by the paparazzi, Geneviève was ready for the next chapter of her life. She didn't want to just sing about love; she wanted to experience it for herself. But first, she had to shake her mom, and the record label.

"Why did you slap the fan who asked for your autograph?"

The sound of Roderick's voice broke into her thoughts. His question irked her, set her teeth on edge. *He's not a fan! He's a jerk!* She had a loyal fan base, nicknamed *G Posse*, and every day they flooded her social media pages with well-wishes and concert pictures. They supported her endeavors, and unlike the creep who'd grabbed her outside Madrid-Barajas International Airport, they respected her as a person.

"He's lucky that's *all* I did," she said. "I wanted to slap the taste out of his mouth, but my bodyguards grabbed me before I could."

"Why did they let José Sánchez get so close to you?"

"They didn't. The crowd was out of control and that creep used it to his advantage. He attacked me when my bodyguards had their backs turned, but I handled it—"

"Attacked? What did he do? The video shows you slapping him, and that's it."

Geneviève leaped to her feet. "Of course I slapped him. He grabbed my ass!"

"But there were thousands of fans there. How can you be so sure it was him?"

"Because the creep had the nerve to wink at me. He's lucky security confiscated my pepper spray at the Portugal airport because I would have sprayed his ass." Geneviève wanted to say more, to tell Roderick about the downsides of fame, but since she didn't want him to think she was another ungrateful celebrity, she held her tongue.

"Geneviève, I'm sorry that happened. That must have been awful for you," Roderick said, wearing a sympathetic expression. "Now I understand why you want to cancel the rest of the tour and return to Philly."

Her eyes widened. "You do?"

"Yes, of course. You were sexually assaulted, and instead of being comforted and supported, you were vilified in the press. You're the victim, and you shouldn't be criticized for defending yourself," he continued. "And now that I know the facts of the case, I'll arrange a meeting with your attacker and his attorney first thing tomorrow."

"Earlier, you mentioned the kid's name. Do you know anything else about him?"

Roderick consulted his notepad. "His name is José Mateo Sánchez, and he's a nineteen-year-old college student from a small town near Barcelona. He has no living relatives, and was raised in an orphanage in one of the poorest neighborhoods in Madrid—"

"I don't care if he was raised by wolves!" she thundered, pacing the length of the balcony to blow off some steam. "He had no right to put his hands on me."

Geneviève couldn't read the expression on Roderick's face, but she sensed his disapproval and regretted yelling at him. It wasn't his fault that she felt overworked, unappreciated and disrespected as an artist. "Roderick, don't get me wrong. I love my fans, and I'd be nothing without them, but people are always touching me and grabbing me, and it's infuriating."

"Geneviève, you have rights just like everyone else. No one has the right to touch you without your consent, and the law permits you to defend yourself against all harm." Roderick wrote on his notepad for a few seconds. "I know you've decided to leave town, and in light of what happened at the airport, I don't blame you, but have you ever stopped to consider all the people who'll be out of work if you cancel the rest of the tour?"

His words gave her pause, and she listened to his argument closely.

"The people who sell refreshments and souvenirs in front of the arena, the *viejos* who drive the buses and taxis that bring the fans to your concerts, and the local musicians you hired will be adversely affected if your tour abruptly ends," Roderick explained. "I don't care about the concert promoters or scalpers. I'm thinking about the folks who are just getting by, living paycheck to paycheck and desperately need the income generated from your shows."

Guilt overwhelmed her, making Geneviève feel low. She'd been so busy thinking about herself and what she wanted that she'd never stopped to consider the hardworking locals who helped behind the scenes of her shows.

"I don't want you to get burnt out, but—"

"Too late for that, counsellor. I was fried before the tour even started," she confessed. "I don't have any downtime. Every minute of every day is accounted for, and it's exhausting. I have photoshoots to do, interviews, dress fittings and fan meet and greets lined up."

A frown darkened his face. "Cancel them. You need a break."

"Tell that to my mother."

"I will. You're a musician, not a machine, and it's imperative you take time for yourself."

"That's easier said than done. You don't know my mom, or the executives at Urban Beats Records." Geneviève rubbed her hands across her chilled shoulders. "They're hard on me."

"It's obvious you need a vacation, so finish up the rest of the tour, then take a month or two off," Roderick advised, returning his notepad and pen to his briefcase. "And that's an order."

"I wish I could, but I can't. The record company arranged for me to shoot the music video for 'My Bae' in Santorini, and I have several movie auditions lined up in Paris, as well."

Roderick stood, and joined her at the balcony. Geneviève held her breath. She could smell his aftershave, and the clean, subtle scent made her think of turquoise-blue water, ice-cold cocktails and skinny-dipping after dark with him. To regain control of her wayward thoughts, she gave her head a shake. Geneviève didn't know why she was fantasizing about Roderick. He was her lawyer, not a love interest, and she'd never hook up with someone who worked for her. *I learned my mistake the last time.*

"Mind if I give you a piece of advice my grandmother gave me when I was deliberating over going to law school or joining the marines?"

Afraid he'd hear the desire in her voice if she spoke, Geneviève simply nodded.

His eyes twinkled, and a grin dimpled his cheek. "Live your life without worrying about pleasing others, and if they don't like your choices, screw them and keep it moving!"

A giggle tickled her throat. "I don't believe you. Your

sweet, old grandmother did not say that. You're just trying to make me laugh."

"She sure did! And just so you know, there's nothing sweet about my Grandma Edith. She smokes cigars,
drinks Jamaican rum like it's water and swears more
than a gangster!"

Geneviève cracked up. It felt good to joke around with
Roderick, and for the first time in forever she could see
the light at the end of the tunnel. She'd finish the tour, then
take six months off. *Or more*, she thought, but didn't say
out loud. It wasn't the right time. Geneviève didn't want
anyone to know about her plans to quit show business—
for fear they'd talk her out of it—and hoped that when the
time came for her to retire, Roderick would be an ally, not
a foe. Signed to a multi-album contract with Urban Beats
Records, she needed legal advice about how to renegotiate her contract, and made a mental note to speak to him
about her future before he left for New York.

He squeezed her hand, and goose bumps rippled
across Geneviève's skin.

"Urban Beats Records is lucky to have you signed
to their label." He wore a broad smile. "And thanks for
being so easy to work with. Last night, I dreamed that
you whacked me upside the head with your purse, but I
was worried for nothing. You're a sweetheart."

Geneviève smirked. "There's nothing sweet about
me. I'm impulsive, stubborn, and I drink mai tais like
they're water."

"Just like my granny!" Chuckling, Roderick grabbed
his briefcase off the table. "I'll be in touch. Once I meet
with Mr. Sánchez and his attorney, I'll give you a ring."

"I look forward to hearing from you, Roderick.
Thanks for coming by."

"It was my pleasure. You're my favorite client, *and* my favorite singer, too."

Geneviève rolled her eyes skyward. "Sure, sure. I bet you say that to all your clients."

"No, beautiful, just you."

Roderick nodded, then turned and stalked inside the suite, whistling one of her songs.

Slumping against the railing, Geneviève watched him with keen interest. Everything about the chiseled, brown-eyed attorney appealed to her, and even though he was off-limits, that didn't mean she couldn't fantasize about him.

Chapter 3

Demi burst into Geneviève's bedroom suite, snatched the iPhone out of her sister's hands and stuck the device in the back pocket of her striped leggings. "Gigi, get up," she demanded, in a no-nonsense voice. "You've been cooped up inside here all day, and it's not healthy. You have two choices. You can come with me to the hotel's rooftop gym, or we can go for a walk around the city center. What's it going to be?"

Geneviève groaned. Leaving the suite was out of the question. These days, she couldn't go anywhere without being recognized, and even though she appreciated her fans, she didn't feel like posing for pictures, signing autographs or snapping selfies. Fans talked her up in the streets, invaded her personal space and followed her, even when she asked them not to, and Geneviève didn't have the energy to interact with pushy strangers on the busy city streets.

"None of the above, so give me back my cell and bounce. I want to be alone."

"No, you want to clap back at the internet trolls who posted negative comments on your social media pages, and it's a complete waste of time." Demi grabbed her arm, pulled her up off the king-size bed and gripped her shoulders. "You're Geneviève Harris, one of the most successful artists of all time, not some wannabe singer seeking affirmation."

Deep down, Geneviève knew her sister was right, but it bothered her what people said about her online. She knew it shouldn't, that it didn't matter what anyone thought about her or her music, but for some strange reason it did.

"Girl, what you should be doing is sexing your fine-ass attorney, Roderick Drake."

"Oh brother, here you go again."

"What do you expect me to do? I have to do something before it's too late. You should be dating, not hanging out in your hotel suite with your vibrator."

"Keep your voice down," Geneviève hissed, glancing at the bedroom door. "I don't want Mom to hear you and start asking questions."

Demi smirked. "Oh please. Mom has a pink buzz buddy, too, named Big Willy, and she never leaves home without it!"

Laughing, Geneviève grabbed her hoodie off the suede armchair, put it on and stuffed her feet into her gold Nike sneakers. "One hour. That's it."

"Great! Let's go." Demi linked arms with Geneviève, then patted her hands. "Now, back to Roderick. He's the perfect man to bring you out of your funk, and I'm going to get him for you."

"Get him for me?" Geneviève repeated, wrinkling her nose. "He's a man, Demi, not a dog."

"Gigi, you can say *that* again. He's a dark-chocolate hottie with a killer body, and if I wasn't committed to Warner, I'd be all over that hot New York attorney with the brick-hard butt."

Geneviève pressed her lips together. Turning toward the window so Demi couldn't see the amused expression on her face, she willed herself not to laugh. She didn't want to encourage her sister, but she struggled to keep a straight face. Demi loved to crack jokes, and derived great pleasure from shocking Geneviève with titillating stories about her sex life. Demi and her boyfriend of six months, Warner Erickson, couldn't keep their hands off each other, and when they weren't making out they were planning their next romantic weekend.

"I'm worried about you. You've been single for over a year, and it's time you started dating again. You don't have to marry the guy, Gigi. Just go out and have some fun for once."

"What makes you think he's even interested in me?" Geneviève asked.

"Isn't it obvious? He dropped everything and flew thousands of miles to see you."

Demi led Geneviève through the suite, gushing about how smart and handsome Roderick was. Her sister was right. He was a catch, exactly her type, but Geneviève would never get romantically involved with him. Roderick was her attorney, and she didn't believe in hooking up with her staff. Even worse, he was still hung up on his ex. She saw it in his eyes, heard it in his voice, and didn't want to be with a guy who was pining for someone else.

Painful memories darkened her heart. Years earlier,

she'd fallen head over heels for one of the executives at the record label, and thinking about the talented music producer from North Philly made her heart ache. In the beginning, Joaquin Moreno couldn't keep his hands off her, but five months into their red-hot affair he became distant, treating her with disdain, as if she didn't matter. If she hadn't trolled him on social media during the Christmas holidays and found pictures of him vacationing in Bali with his estranged wife, Geneviève wouldn't have even known he was married. She'd put on a brave face in the studio, but she'd been heartbroken, devastated that the man she loved belonged to someone else.

Emotionally distraught, she'd shut herself away in her Chestnut Hill mansion. To ease her pain, she'd written dozens of songs, and when the album was released it had skyrocketed up the charts, but the accolades and awards made Geneviève feel worse, not better. The album was a painful reminder of the love she'd had and lost. *Had he ever cared for me, or was it all just an act?*

"Keep it a hundred," Demi implored. "You like Roderick, just admit it."

Do. I. Ever! Opening her mouth, a lie fell off her lips. "You're wrong. I don't."

"Oh stop, it's the twenty-first century, so quit playing hard to get and ask Roderick out."

"Ask him out? I don't even know him!"

"Exactly!" Demi wore a toothy smile. "Invite Roderick to have drinks with you tonight at the hotel bar, and once you get to know each other better, do what comes naturally."

Geneviève sniffed the air. The suite smelled of spices, and she guessed her mom was cooking in the kitchenette. Sure enough, Althea was standing at the counter, chopping vegetables, and hearing her mother hum the chorus of "Salty Girl" brought a smile to Geneviève's lips. They had adjoining rooms, and it was times like this that she loved having her mom nearby. Althea wasn't perfect, but she was the only parent Geneviève had, and she appreciated everything her mother did for her.

Sunshine streamed through the windows, warming the room with natural light. Filled with plush carpet, contemporary furniture and decorative lamps, the suite was as lavish as it was inviting, and even though it was a beautiful, comfortable space, Geneviève still missed her home in Philly. Last year, she'd built her dream house in one of the most affluent neighborhoods in the city, and she wanted to finish decorating the posh, six-bedroom estate.

Geneviève spotted her Versace luggage set beside the couch and sighed. Twenty-fours hours ago, she'd been determined to leave Madrid, but after thinking about what Roderick said, she'd had a change of heart. People were counting on her, and she didn't want to let them down.

"I was beginning to wonder where you girls were," Althea said, glancing up from the wooden cutting board. "Gigi, did you have a nice talk with Roderick?"

Starving, Geneviève grabbed a banana from the glass fruit bowl, peeled it and took a bite. A light flashed, temporarily blinding her, and she swatted her sister's shoulder. She hated when Demi snapped pictures of her when she wasn't looking and hoped she didn't post the unflattering photograph online. "Knock it off."

"Bite me!" Demi stuck out her tongue, then laughed at her joke. As usual, her eyes were glued to her iPhone, and she was typing furiously. Last week, she'd launched her lifestyle website and YouTube channel. Obsessed with attracting viewers and sponsors, Demi posted dozens of videos, pictures and beauty tutorials a day.

Geneviève was proud of her sister and glad she'd found something she was passionate about, but she was tired of being the object of Demi's attention. To Demi's delight, and Geneviève's dismay, her candid posts always received millions of views. Geneviève was annoyed, but her sister was over the moon that her YouTube channel was trending, and she didn't have the heart to rain on her parade.

"Mom, I've decided to finish the rest of the European tour, but—"

Althea dropped the knife on the counter, then danced around the kitchen to an inaudible beat. Throwing her hands in the air, she shouted, "Praise Jesus! There *is* a God."

Demi and Geneviève shared a look.

"Gigi, I'm so proud of you." Althea cupped Geneviève's face in her hands and kissed her on both cheeks. "I knew you'd make the right decision. You always do."

"Mom, you didn't let me finish. I'll continue the tour, but I'm not working on my days off, so cancel everything you've scheduled for the next two weeks."

The smile slid off Althea's face. "Y-y-you can't do that," she stammered. "I've already made arrangements for the photoshoot, the music video and a magazine interview in Barcelona."

"Roderick said I'm not legally bound to anything besides the tour, so cancel everything."

"Oh, he did, did he?"

"Yes, and he also offered to contact Urban Beats Records to revise my current schedule."

Propping her hands on her hips, Althea spoke through clenched teeth. "He. Did. What?"

"I'm not attending the state ceremony dinner at the Royal Palace on Saturday night either." Geneviève finished her banana, tossed the skin in the trash can and washed her hands in the sink. "I'm going to stay here and kick it with the band."

"Honey, you have to go. This is a big event, and I'm excited about meeting the president."

"Then go. No one's stopping you."

"I can't attend the state ceremony dinner without you. I'm *your* plus one."

"Mom, I'm tired, and I really want to relax this weekend."

Althea clasped her hands as if in prayer. "Please, Gigi. I'm begging you. Think about what this could do for your career, about the doors it could open for you in the future. This could be huge for us… I mean, for you."

Geneviève bit down on her bottom lip. Deliberating over what to do, she considered her conversation with Roderick that afternoon and remembered his advice. Or rather, his grandmother's words of wisdom. *Live your life without worrying about pleasing others—*

"Gigi, don't do this. You're making a mistake," Althea continued. "Please reconsider."

Determined to stick to her guns, Geneviève straightened her shoulders and spoke in a confident tone of voice. "Mom, I'm not going. The band has been busting their butts for months, and I want them to know how much I appreciate them, so on Saturday night I'm treating everyone to dinner and cocktails."

Demi waved her cell in the air. "And I'll be there to capture every scandalous moment!"

"Oh, no you won't!" Geneviève quipped, plucking the device out of her sister's hand. "And now that I have your iPhone, I won't have to worry about you ruining our fun."

"That's *your* cell, not mine." Demi laughed. "Mom, we're going to the gym. See you later!"

Exiting the suite, Geneviève put on her baseball cap and pulled it down past her eyebrows. She released a deep breath, then another. She'd done it. Stood up to her mother, and it felt good. For some strange reason, she wanted to call Roderick, to tell him what she'd done, but she dismissed the thought.

"I wish he'd quit calling," Demi fumed, sucking her teeth. "He's so annoying."

Geneviève glanced at Demi's iPhone, saw the name D.D. on the screen and rolled her eyes to the ceiling. She wanted to press Talk and curse him out, but she didn't want her dad to know he'd gotten under her skin. His name was Dwight Dellamarre Jr., but they'd nicknamed him Deadbeat Dad when they were kids, and the moniker stuck.

A lump formed in her throat. Geneviève had always dreamed of reconciling with her estranged father, but he'd dashed her hopes and dreams when she was eighteen years old. Once her debut album was released, everyone she knew was trying to cash in on her fame—distant relatives, music teachers, and her good-for-nothing father. For a handsome, six-figure fee, he'd given a tell-all interview to a national magazine, and not only revealed embarrassing secrets about Althea's past, he'd released family photographs from Geneviève's childhood that she'd never seen before.

Her thoughts returned to weeks earlier, and anger coursed through her veins. Over the holidays, Dwight had emailed her, begging for money. He didn't care about her; he cared only about her bank account, and she didn't want anything to do with him. Althea was stubborn and bossy at times, but Geneviève couldn't imagine her life without her. Her mom worked tirelessly as her manager, and she loved her with all her heart.

Born and raised in the Badlands, a neighborhood in North Philadelphia known for its street gangs and drugs, she'd experienced difficult times as a child, and Geneviève would never forget the sacrifices Althea had made for their family. To pay for vocal lessons, dance classes and theater camp when Geneviève was a child, Althea had remortgaged their home—twice—and if not for her mother's unwavering faith, she wouldn't be a successful singer with fans all over the world.

A suite door opened at the end of the hallway and a petite brunette dressed in a crisp hotel uniform emerged, holding a beige travel bag. Gasping, Demi clutched Geneviève's forearm. "Damn, he's fine!" she gushed, panting her words. "Check out his package."

Geneviève held her breath. Roderick was standing in the doorway in a pair of black Nike shorts, and the sight of his bare chest made Geneviève moan inwardly. Swallowing hard, her gaze slid over his broad shoulders, down his flat-board stomach to the bulge in his shorts. Her thoughts spiraled out of control, and heat flowed through her body.

"Good evening, ladies." Leaning against the door-frame, he folded his arms and nodded his head in greeting. "Where are you headed?"

Geneviève wanted to speak, but her tongue was twisted inside her mouth like a rope. She was attracted to him, and staring at his muscled biceps and dark, round nipples made her pulse pound in her ears.

"We're going to the rooftop gym," Demi said. "Want to join us?"

"I'll take a rain check. It's been a long day, and I was just about to jump in the shower."

Need some company? Geneviève pressed her lips together to avoid speaking the words.

"Geneviève, I'll call you in the morning after my meeting with Mr. Sánchez and his attorney."

Ordering herself to get a grip and to quit fantasizing about him, she dragged her eyes away from his chest and said, "I'm going to the stadium in the morning to run through my set for next Friday's show, and I won't have my cell, so if I don't answer leave a message and I'll call you back when rehearsal's done..." Geneviève knew she was rambling, but she couldn't stop herself. Felt as if she'd lost control of her mouth. She wished her voice wasn't shaking, and hoped Roderick didn't notice she was a quivering, blabbering mess. *Unbelievable!* she thought, scolding herself for losing her composure. *I can perform in front of thousands of people but I can't talk to Roderick without breaking into a sweat! Go figure!*

"Sounds good," he said with a nod. "Enjoy your workout, ladies. See you tomorrow."

You can bet on it! Geneviève boarded the elevator. The doors closed, and she slumped against the wall. Demi chatted a mile a minute about her rabid social media followers, but Geneviève wasn't listening. She was fantasizing about the man in suite 1824.

Roderick worked for her, but that didn't stop her from lusting after him. Geneviève wished she could spend the rest of the night with Roderick, and as the elevator rose to the twentieth floor, her body ached for the dashing New Yorker with the ripped physique. Try as she might, she couldn't stop her X-rated thoughts about him, and wondered how long she'd be able to resist the needs of her flesh.

Chapter 4

Roderick took one look at the Madrid Law office and had second thoughts about entering the weathered brick building sandwiched between a youth hostel and a dilapidated liquor store. Garbage littered the sidewalk, and tattooed men in soccer jerseys and shorts were chugging beers. Roderick feared the business was a front for illegal activity and glanced over his shoulder as he exited his rental car, clutching his briefcase. Madrid Law was located in one of the worst neighborhoods in the city, but Roderick knew better than to judge a book by its cover. From what he'd read online, the company had a great reputation, talented attorneys and a winning record.

Activating the alarm on the Ferrari 488 Spider, he noticed several pedestrians eyeing the vehicle, and considered moving it around the corner. He had insurance on the sleek black sports car, but he hoped it wasn't stolen while he was inside the law firm, meeting with Mr. Cabrero.

Roderick gave his head a shake. Dismissing the thought, he adjusted his tie, then smoothed a hand over his tan Armani suit. He opened the front door, stalked inside the reception area and took off his aviator sunglasses. A rancid odor was in the air, but he resisted the urge to flee, and nodded in greeting at the slender woman standing behind the desk in the fuchsia dress.

"Welcome to Madrid Law," she chirped in a thick, Spanish accent. "How may I help you?"

With her blond bob hairstyle, oval-shaped face, she looked like an older version of the rapper Cardi B, and had the squeaky, high-pitched voice to match.

"Hello, I'm Roderick Drake, and I'm here to see—"

"You're American!" The receptionist stuck out her chest and fluffed her hair. "I've always wanted to visit America. I heard there are celebrities everywhere!"

Amused by her naivety, Roderick returned her smile. "Is Mr. Cabrero available?"

"Are *you* available?" A grin curled her lips. "This must be my lucky day. First, I find fifty euro in my *abuela*'s purse, then I meet you, a handsome, successful man from America."

Roderick glanced at his Rolex watch, hoping she'd get the hint, but she continued flirting with him. The phone rang on her desk, but she didn't answer it.

"It was nice meeting you, but I'm really pressed for time. Is Mr. Cabrero around?"

Ignoring his question, the receptionist chatted about her desire to find love, get married and relocate to the United States. Roderick knew *Madrileños* were friendly, outgoing people who loved shooting the breeze, but he'd never met someone with such a bold personality. Her honesty was a turnoff, and her shrill voice was giving him a migraine. The receptionist was cute, but it took more than a pretty face to capture his attention. Furthermore, Roderick had no desire to settle down. Not after everything his ex-fiancée had put him through.

Anger stabbed his heart. He'd been single for nine months, but every time Roderick thought about what Toya did to him, his hands balled into fists. Initially, he'd hoped she'd come to her senses and return to his estate, but when he heard about her engagement to a hedge fund manager fifteen years her senior, his feelings for her died. She'd humiliated him, made him the laughingstock of the Hamptons, and if not for his brothers, he never would have survived her bitter betrayal. Roderick would never date someone like Toya again. He wanted to date someone who was humble and sincere—*like Geneviève*, offered his inner voice. *She's independent, mature and classy too.*

Roderick booted the thought from his mind. No way, no how. Dating a client was out of the question, and if he crossed the line with the pop star he could lose his job, and nothing mattered more to Roderick than becoming the first African American partner at his firm. He was attracted to Geneviève, but he'd never act on his feelings. He couldn't risk upsetting Althea, or worse, his boss.

"Are you free tonight? I know the best places to party, and I would love to show you around Madrid," the receptionist said, sticking out her chest.

"Thanks for the offer, but I'm busy." Roderick took his cell phone out of his pocket and raised it in the air. "Should I call Mr. Cabrero, or can you show me to his office?"

Her face fell, and her shoulders caved in.

A dark-haired man in an ill-fitted black suit and checkered tie appeared at the front desk, and the receptionist hopped like a rabbit in a meadow.

"M-M-Mr. Drake just arrived," she stammered in a wobbly voice. "I was going to bring him to the conference room, but we got to talking and, ah, lost track of time."

Roderick scoffed. *Is* that *what happened? More like you held me hostage!*

"Mr. Drake, it's a pleasure to meet you. I'm Bautista Cabrero."

The men shook hands, and the short, stocky attorney led Roderick through the corridor.

"Sorry about that," he said, with an apologetic smile. "My sister is a chatterbox, but if I fire her my *madre* will disown me, and I can't live without my mother's cooking."

Roderick chuckled. He was a good judge of character and liked Bautista's jovial personality and warm smile. He heard telephones buzzing, people speaking in Spanish and boisterous laughter. The carpet had coffee stains, but the colorful oil paintings of the Spanish countryside hanging on the cream walls brightened the space.

Entering the conference room at the end of the hallway, Roderick noticed a slim, clean-cut man standing in front of the window, and frowned. This was Geneviève's attacker?

Roderick scrutinized the stranger's appearance. He'd expected her attacker to be a street thug, someone with piercings, tattoos and baggy clothes, but in his navy blazer, V-neck shirt and dark, crisp slacks, José Sánchez could pass for one of the interns at Welker, Bradford and Davidson.

"Mr. Drake, thank you for coming," Mr. Cabrero said, gesturing to a chair at the round table. "Please have a seat. I know you're a busy man, so let's get down to business, shall we?"

Roderick sat down and opened his briefcase. He remembered every detail of his hour-long conversation with Geneviève yesterday—how her voice shook as she spoke, the sadness in her eyes, her subdued demeanor—but he still opened his manila folder and consulted his notes. "I spoke to Ms. Harris at length yesterday about the incident that took place outside Madrid-Barajas International Airport on New Year's Day, and she was very forthcoming about what happened."

"Oh good, so she admits to striking José repeatedly in the face."

"No," Roderick said in a firm voice. "He grabbed her, and she slapped him once."

José made his eyes wide. "That's a lie. I wanted to take a picture of her, but her bodyguards were shielding her from the crowd, and I couldn't get close enough to her touch her."

Roderick believed Geneviève. Had no reason not to. She wasn't a hothead who got off on attacking people, and during her twenty-year career she'd never been sued or accused of assaulting anyone. "Then why did she slap you? Just for the hell of it? That doesn't make any sense, Mr. Sánchez, and you know it."

"Beats me." Shrugging a shoulder, the teen wore a sad smile. "Maybe she was having a bad day, or was cranky after her flight from Portugal. I don't know, and I don't care. All I know is Geneviève hit me, and she needs to pay for what she did."

Inside, Roderick was seething. He suspected the college student had set Geneviève up, and wanted to wring his neck for putting his hands on her, but he exercised self-control. Told himself to relax. Not to lose his temper and give his enemy the upper hand. One way or another he'd uncover the truth, and when he did, José Sánchez would be begging him for mercy. The thought heartened him, and his anger waned.

"My client wants a million euros for his pain and suffering," Mr. Cabrero announced.

What pain? What suffering? Roderick thought, forcing himself not to laugh out loud.

"Since the attack, I've had crippling headaches, constant neck pain and horrible nightmares." Wincing, José massaged his temples with his fingertips. "I can't stop reliving the beating in my mind, and every day it gets worse."

"Beating?" Roderick repeated, unable to bite his tongue. "You grabbed Geneviève, and she struck you once. That's it. End of story. There was no beating, or ongoing assault."

"No, she struck me multiple times, and I have witnesses to corroborate my story."

Yeah, paid *witnesses, who'll lie through their teeth for the right price.*

José spoke in a somber voice, as if he was fighting back tears, but mischief glimmered in his eyes. "I want a million euros, and a public apology from Geneviève. It's the least she can do after everything she's put me through. I'm a good guy, and I didn't deserve to be attacked."

Roderick leaned back in his chair. He had to give José credit; he was one hell of an actor.

"I'll speak to Ms. Harris and contact you by the end of the week."

Mr. Cabrero scratched his pencil-thin mustache. "That's not good enough, Mr. Drake. My client is anxious to put this traumatic incident behind him and get on with his life…"

No, Roderick thought, *he's anxious to get a settlement, and spend every last dime of it.* He wanted to slap the smug, slick expression off José's face, but kept his hands to himself. If he lost his temper he'd probably be charged with assault, and the only thing worse than being hauled off to jail was going on a blind date with one of his mother's friend's daughters.

Roderick tapped his pen on his notepad. His cell phone buzzed inside his pocket, but he ignored it. He guessed it was his boss on the line, calling for an update on the "Geneviève situation," but Roderick didn't have anything to report. José was a well-spoken kid, but Roderick wasn't going to let the college student get the best of him. Not today, not ever.

"You have forty-eight hours." The lawyer gave a curt nod. "If we don't hear from you by Friday, we're proceeding with our legal case. I like Geneviève, and my daughters are huge fans of hers, but if she doesn't pay up I will make her life a living hell. *¿Entendido?*"

Glaring at his nemesis, Roderick realized he'd pegged the attorney all wrong. His jovial demeanor was an act, a facade. He was a snake in an ill-fitted suit, and if Roderick wasn't careful, the crafty Spaniard would eat him alive.

"I'll be in touch." Reluctantly, Roderick shook hands

with the scheming twosome, exited the conference room
and marched out of the building. Putting on his sunglasses, he heaved a deep sigh. Outside, locals were
gawking at the Ferrari like wide-eyed fans at the Madrid Auto Show. They were reclining on the hood, snapping pictures and selfies, but when he deactivated the
alarm the group scattered.

Roderick unbuttoned his suit jacket and loosened the
knot in his tie. Anxious to speak to Geneviève, he slid
inside the front seat and sped out of the parking lot as if
his life depended on it. And it did. If he didn't convince
Geneviève to finish the European tour and reach a settlement with José Sánchez, he'd lose favor with his boss,
and Roderick couldn't stomach the thought of losing his
fiancée and his promotion in the same year.

His cell phone rang, and he grabbed it from the center console. Roderick didn't recognize the number, and
couldn't think of anyone in Madrid who'd call him, but
he pressed Talk, and put his iPhone to his ear. "Hello.
Roderick Drake, attorney at law."

"Where do you get off telling Geneviève what to do?
That's *my* job, not yours!"

Roderick cringed. Althea was yelling so loud his ears
throbbed in pain. Moving his cell phone away from his
ear, he listened to the momager rant and rave about his
private conversation with Geneviève. "I came to Madrid
to convince Geneviève to finish the tour and reach a settlement with José Sánchez, but after speaking with her
at length yesterday, it's obvious she's unhappy, and I felt
compelled to help her. She needs a break, Ms. Harris—"

"Says who!" she shouted. "You don't know what she
needs. I do. I'm her momager, and I know what's best
for her. Got it?"

Roderick wanted to argue, but knew it was pointless. He'd have more success trying to subdue a steer in a bull-fighting ring than convince Ms. Harris that her daughter was on the brink of an emotional breakdown. Besides, he didn't work for Althea. He worked for Geneviève, and he was going to do everything in his power to help her, whether her mother liked it or not. "My apologies, Ms. Harris. I didn't mean to upset you, or—"

"Did you reach an agreement with Mr. Sánchez? The kid is a nuisance, and I'm sick of seeing his face on TV, lying about my daughter attacking him."

Damn, Roderick thought, gripping the steering wheel. *Is she ever going to let me finish a sentence?* He wanted to turn up the radio, to drown out Althea's voice, but he remembered what was at stake and kept his hands off the stereo system. "I haven't reached a suitable agreement with Mr. Sánchez, but I'm working on it."

"Working on it?" she repeated, her disappointment evident in her tone. "What's taking so long? I summoned you here to help us, not to sit around in your cushy hotel suite maxing and relaxing. Do your job, and resolve this matter today."

"Ms. Harris, I'm afraid that's impossible. His settlement demands are outrageous, and I have to discuss the situation with Geneviève before I contact his attorney to renegotiate."

"Don't bother. Give him what he wants. I'll arrange the payment within twenty-four hours."

"But he's demanding a million euros, and a public apology from Geneviève."

Althea scoffed. "He can have the money, but that's it."

At a loss for words, Roderick couldn't speak. He didn't want to make an enemy out of Althea, but he couldn't

betray Geneviève's trust. Not when she needed his guidance now more than ever. Her rags-to-riches story was
inspiring, making her easy to root for, and he didn't want
her to get scammed. He liked her, respected her ambition
and tenacity, and contrary to what her mother thought,
he wanted the best for her. Furthermore, he was an attorney, not an errand boy, and there was nothing Althea
could say to change his mind about settling the Sánchez
case. "With all due respect, Ms. Harris, I work for Geneviève, not you."

"Like hell you do!" she quipped. "Gigi doesn't do anything without my approval, and that will never change. I
am the law, the be-all and end-all, and what I say goes.
Now, contact Mr. Sánchez for his banking information
or I will."

Unaffected by her brisk tone, Roderick stood his
ground. "I need to speak to Geneviève first. It's her career, her reputation, on the line and she has the right to
make her own decisions."

"I never should have asked you to come to Madrid.
You're useless."

And you're a control freak! Roderick thought, clutching his cell so hard his veins throbbed in his wrist. He
wanted to set Althea straight, but before he could give
her a piece of his mind, the line went dead.

Chapter 5

WiZink Center was one of the largest concert venues in Madrid, and as Roderick entered the darkened arena and strode down the aisle a voice filled the air, seizing his attention, and he sank into the closest chair. Geneviève was standing in the middle of the stage clutching a microphone, and the expression on her face was so intense, Roderick feared she was going to cry.

The hair on the back of his neck shot up. Her vocals were flawless, her background singers moved in perfect sync and the mood was thrilling, more electrifying than a championship soccer game. Geneviève hit so many high notes, Roderick lost count. The tempo picked up, a blue haze drifted across the stage and a piquant aroma tickled his nose.

Leaning forward in his chair, he bobbed his head and tapped his feet to the music. Roderick recognized her smash hit, "Savage," and hummed the lyrics. The song was fun and catchy, and set to a thumping, infectious beat. The all-female band danced alongside Geneviève while deftly playing their instruments, and Roderick whistled when the group executed the splits. Dozens of pictures flashed on the overhead screen, and the candid, behind-the-scene images of the pop star made him feel closer to her.

His stomach grumbled, cuing him it was time for lunch, but Roderick would rather starve than miss a second of Geneviève's rehearsal. Her personality shone onstage, her undeniable wit and charm, and the more he watched the Philly native, the more impressed he was with her stage performance. Dressed in a tie-dye hoodie and denim jean shorts, Geneviève moved in such a provocative, seductive way, Roderick couldn't take his eyes off her.

A million thoughts raced through his mind, and each one was X-rated. Feeling guilty for fantasizing about Geneviève, he pressed his eyes shut to regain control. It didn't help. The vision grew stronger, brighter.

"This a pleasant surprise."

His eyes flew open. How long had Demi been watching him? Was it obvious he'd been fantasizing about Geneviève? Was the truth written all over his face? Straightening in his seat, he wore a polite smile. "Hi, Demi. It's good to see you again."

"Enjoying the show?" she asked, batting her thick, extra-long eyelashes.

"Immensely. Your sister's an outstanding performer, and her vocals are out of this world."

"I know, right? I've been touring with Gigi for years, but she never ceases to amaze me." Cocking her head, she studied him for a moment. "She likes you, you know."

"I bet she likes a lot of people."

"Excuse me?" Demi hitched a hand to her hip. "Are you calling my sister a ho?"

"No. Never. She's witty and down-to-earth and I bet she makes friends easily," he explained.

"That's true," she conceded. "But you're the only guy she's romantically interested in, and I think you two should hook up while you're in town."

Roderick choked on his tongue. His heart was beating so loud it drowned out the music in the arena. Excited about the prospect of hooking up with his secret celebrity crush, his mouth dried. Rules were meant to be broken, and Roderick could think of a half dozen rules he'd like to break with Geneviève in Madrid. "She told you that?"

"She didn't have to. I'm her sister, her bestie, and it's obvious Gigi wants you. She's just too scared to admit it."

"But I'm her attorney—"

"So what? You're single, she's single, and you're in one of the most romantic cities in the world." Demi squeezed his shoulder. "Make the most of this opportunity, Roderick."

"I don't believe in mixing business with pleasure, and neither does my law firm."

"Okay," she trilled, cocking her head to the right. "But don't blame me when someone else wins Gigi's heart, and you're left out in the cold, wondering what went wrong."

Sweat drenched his palms. Thinking about Geneviève getting cozy with another man made his stomach churn. Was Demi right? Was the pop star worth breaking the rules for, or cut from the same cloth as his ex-fiancée?

An idea sparked in his mind. "Demi, I need you to do me a favor," he said, eyeing her Bedazzled iPhone. "Reach out to your social media followers and ask them to post any videos they have of Geneviève arriving at Madrid-Barajas International Airport last Sunday."

Lines wrinkled her forehead. "Why? The incident is old news."

Roderick told Demi about his early morning meeting with José Sánchez.

"He's lying. He grabbed my sister and she had every right to defend herself. It's a good thing he didn't touch me, because I would have whupped his ass up and down the airport terminal!"

For the first time all day, Roderick laughed. He had a plan, and hoped Demi would come through for him. Feeling his cell phone vibrate against his leg, he took it out of his pocket and stared at the screen. Mr. Welker was on the line, but Roderick made a mental note to call him back when he returned to his hotel suite.

"Please, Demi? I could really use your help."

"Roderick, don't worry. I'm on it. Just call me Columbo!" Demi laughed at her own joke. "I'll reach out to my social media followers right now."

"Sounds good. Thanks a million, Demi." Roderick glanced at the stage, noticed it was empty and heaved a deep breath. He'd been so busy talking with Demi, he hadn't noticed Geneviève leave the auditorium, and wondered where she was. Demi must have read his inner thoughts because she said, "We're having lunch at a nearby tapas bar, and if you promise not to bore us with stories about your bougie Manhattan law firm, I'll save you a seat next to Gigi."

Chuckling, Roderick nodded in agreement. "Pretty lady, you have yourself a deal."

Taberna de Mármol, the bar around the corner from WiZink Center, was decorated with bullfighting gear, cheap wallpaper and fake flowers, but Geneviève liked the secluded location and the quiet ambience of the establishment. The patrons either didn't know who she was, or didn't care, and that suited Geneviève just fine.

Settling into one of the padded leather booths, Geneviève took off her sunglasses and rested her tote bag at her feet. Spent after a grueling two-hour rehearsal, she was ready to cut loose with her band, Divalicious, and hoped no one ruined their fun. Her bodyguards, two burly brothers with ponytails named Salvador and Felipe, sat at a nearby table, keeping watch.

"Gigi, your dreamy, fine-ass attorney is headed this way, so perk up, sis!"

Geneviève lowered the menu from her face and scanned the restaurant. Her heart lurched inside her chest, and her mouth was so dry she couldn't swallow. Roderick strode into the bar, and silence descended across the room. She had no words. Couldn't stop gawking at him. With his soulful features, commanding presence and athletic physique, Roderick deserved a billboard in the heart of the city center.

Suddenly short of breath, Geneviève fiddled with her charm bracelet. She was glad she'd taken a few extra minutes to do her hair and makeup. Frowning, she inclined her head to the right. Come to think of it, she'd had no choice. Demi had insisted—no, demanded—that she dress up. Feeling confident in her yellow jumpsuit, cropped, bomber jacket and high heels, Geneviève met

Roderick's gaze. Deep down, she was glad that Demi had invited him to lunch, and was secretly thrilled to see him again. He was smart, intelligent and hot, and Geneviève wanted to know more about him.

Last night, she'd scoured the internet for personal information about Roderick and his illustrious family. She'd read dozens of articles about the Drake family, even watched a decades-old interview about his father, but it wasn't enough. It only increased her curiosity about him, her interest.

"Roderick, what are you doing here?"

He patted his stomach, drawing her gaze to his chest, and her mouth watered at the memory of his abs. The man was a force, a six-foot-four ebony god, and if Geneviève wasn't afraid of getting hurt she'd invite him back to her suite, and ride him until sunrise.

"I'm here for the paella, and the half-priced drinks."

"We're going to the bar, so keep Gigi company while we're gone." Demi stood, grabbed Roderick's hand and forced him to sit down in the booth. "Laters! Be back in a few."

To Geneviève's surprise, everyone surged to their feet, grabbed their cell phones and followed Demi to the bar. What the hell? Geneviève shot daggers at her so-called friends. So much for her girls having her back. Without her band around to run interference with Roderick, she was liable to put her foot in her mouth, and Geneviève couldn't imagine anything worse than embarrassing herself in front of the suave, sophisticated attorney from the Big Apple.

"I sat in on your rehearsal and it was outstanding," Roderick praised, an awestruck expression on his face.

"Your vocals, your choreography and your energy are second to none."

"Nicely played, Counselor. Flattery will get you everywhere."

"It's the truth," he said, with a broad smile. "I have no reason to lie."

A waiter strode by, carrying a tray of sizzling appetizers, and Roderick wet his lips with his tongue. "If the food tastes even half as good as it looks, I'm going to be a very happy man."

Geneviève moaned inwardly. *I wish you were licking me, instead of your lips!*

"I know you've had a stressful week and you're trying to relax, but if it's okay with you I'd like to spend a few minutes discussing my meeting with José Sánchez and his attorney." Roderick took off his suit jacket, draped it over the booth and rolled up the sleeves of his pale blue dress shirt. "I know you're eager to put this ugly incident behind you, but I'm going to need a bit more time to resolve this matter."

"What happened? Are they still threatening to sue?"

Leaning forward in her seat, Geneviève listened to Roderick with rapt attention. He told her about his impression of the college student, and his strategy to outwit him.

"I hope your plan works, because I'm not giving that creep a dime of my money."

"Trust me, you won't have to. I've got this."

"Are you always this confident?"

"Yeah, except when I go up against my brother in the ring." Roderick shuddered and shook his head. "Morrison is insanely competitive. The last time we faced off

he gave me two black eyes—and it was a charity boxing match!"

Geneviève gasped at the thought of Roderick being
bruised and battered, but his lopsided grin made her
laugh. Crossing her legs, she settled comfortably into
the booth. Dropping her gaze to the table, Geneviève
scooped up the laminated menu and perused the lunch
specials.

A waitress arrived to take their orders. Wearing a
toothy smile, she promised to return promptly with their
appetizers and a complimentary bottle of wine. The owner
appeared, cap in hand, and bowed at the waist. His accent
was thick and it was hard for Geneviève to understand
him, but she nodded politely as he welcomed her to his
family-owned bar.

"Bienvenido!" Bending down, he clasped her hands
in his calloused ones and shook them as if he was playing maracas. "We're honored to have you at Taberna de
Mármol, Ms. Geneviève, and if there is anything me or
my staff can do to make your dining experience more
comfortable please don't hesitate to ask. We are at your
service, and…"

Geneviève glanced around the room, noticed the other
patrons watching them and cringed. Every muscle in
her body tensed. *So much for a quiet lunch.* Releasing
a deep sigh, she tried not to let her aggravation show.
Geneviève knew why the owner was making a fuss over
her, and she didn't like it. He wanted her to rave about
his bar on her social media pages, but her iPhone was
in the bottom of her Chanel tote bag, and that's where
it was going to stay.

The owner left, and Geneviève sighed in relief.

"So, what do you do when you're not thrilling audiences and shooting music videos in exotic locales half-way around the world?" Roderick asked, reaching for his glass of ice water.

"I love hiking, snowboarding and skiing, and if I wasn't a singer-songwriter I'd probably be a ski instructor, or a tour guide in Alaska."

"I can't ice-skate to save my life, but I'm a beast out on the slopes."

"Really? Then you should check out Baqueira-Beret, in Northern Spain. The trails are impressive, and the landscape is breathtaking." Fond memories filled her mind, warming her heart. "It's my favorite place to ski, and if I could I'd rent one of the cozy log cabins in Vielha and spend the entire winter up there."

The waitress returned, set the appetizers down on the table and left. As they ate, Roderick entertained Geneviève with stories about his family, his clients and his favorite vacation spots. Personable and charming, it was easy to open up to him, and Geneviève spoke freely about her twenty-year career in show business. She was having so much fun with Roderick, she didn't care that the bar was noisy, the drinks were bland and the food was mediocre. They clicked on every level, and time flew by as they relaxed in their corner booth, talking and cracking jokes.

"Your turn. What would you be doing if you weren't an attorney?" Geneviève asked.

"Working my ass off to become one."

"I'm not surprised. I bet you love schmoozing with your famous clients."

"My job seems glamorous, but it's not. It's a tough business involving ridiculous amounts of money, people with tremendous egos, extreme stress and short dead-lines," he explained.

"Then why do you do it?"

"Because when I was in high school an entertain-ment attorney came to speak to my class for career day, and the moment she started talking I was sold. I knew it was all I wanted to do. Some people enjoy reading magazines, but I enjoy studying law books and old court transcripts, and after seven years of practicing law I'm still eager to learn more."

And I enjoy studying you, Geneviève thought, admir-ing his face over the rim of her cocktail glass. She spot-ted Demi exiting the lounge with the band and wondered where they going. Demi was on her cell phone, laugh-ing outrageously, and Geneviève guessed her sister was chatting with her boyfriend, Warner.

Frowning, she wondered how long they'd been at the tapas bar. Deep in conversation with Roderick, she'd lost track of time and forgotten all about her friends. For the first time in months, Geneviève felt relaxed, at ease and she was in no rush to return to the hotel. Roderick was the most fascinating man she'd ever met, and if she didn't have a six o'clock interview at a local radio station she'd spend the rest of the day with him.

"Where did the name Geneviève come from?" Rod-erick asked, reaching for his wineglass.

"A Seychelles actress from the late fifties. My mom thought the name sounded exotic, and insisted I use it as my stage name when I signed with Urban Beats Re-cords."

"Is that what you wanted?"

Geneviève shrugged. "I was a teenager at the time. I didn't know what I wanted."

"And now," he prompted. "Do you know what you want now?"

You mean besides a night with you*?* Surprised by the thought, she felt heat singe her cheeks. Images of them kissing flashed in Geneviève's mind, arousing her, and she hoped she didn't say or do anything to embarrass herself.

The waiter returned, giving Geneviève a moment to organize her thoughts, and when the wide-eyed brunette left with the empty plates, she answered his question.

"I know this is going to sound stupid, but I want to be a regular person for a while," she confessed, toying with her napkin. "Not Geneviève the pop star, with fans around the world and dozens of number-one hits, just Jennifer, the chill, fun-loving girl from North Philly."

Roderick touched her hand. "I don't think that's stupid."

Geneviève wet her lips with her tongue. For the second time in minutes, thoughts she had no business having about her attorney consumed her mind, and her gaze zeroed in on his mouth.

"You can't be anybody but yourself, and pleasing yourself is all that matters…"

He spoke with an air of authority, like a therapist with decades of experience. Jazz music filled the air, drawing Geneviève's attention to her handbag. Recognizing the ringtone, she knew her mom was on the line, but she decided to let the call go to voice mail. It stopped, then started up again, and Geneviève considered turning off her phone but she didn't want to waste time looking for her cell in her purse.

"This was fun," Roderick said, with a devilish grin. "We should do this again sometime."

His voice was silky smooth, and his smoldering gaze filled her mind with explicit thoughts.

"Do you have plans on Saturday?"

"Why? What's on the docket?"

"A law joke. Cute. Did you come up with that all by yourself?"

Geneviève smirked. "No, your mama helped me!"

"Keep it up," he jeered. "One more mama joke, and it's *on*."

Laughing, she wiped her fingers with a napkin, then dropped it on the table.

"I'm going hiking next Saturday. You should come." Roderick fished his wallet out of his back pocket, opened it and took out several crisp dollar bills. "You deserve a break, so let's ditch that fancy hotel and spend the day in the great outdoors."

"I can't. I promised my mom we'd go to Barcelona, and I don't want to disappoint her. She's been looking forward to this mother-daughter shopping trip for weeks."

"No worries. Another time."

His words floored her. Another time? What made him think she wanted to see him again? Could he sense her desire? Her need? Were her feelings for him *that* obvious? Or were his words nothing more than wishful thinking?

Geneviève dodged his gaze. Pretended to admire the framed black-and-white photographs hanging above their cozy, corner booth.

The waitress appeared. "Can I interest you guys in chocolate churros?"

"Nothing for me." Geneviève was stuffed to the brim, and just thinking about eating the sweet, decadent dessert made her stomach groan in protest. "I'm going to use the ladies' room before we leave."

Standing, Roderick took Geneviève by the hand and helped her to her feet. His aftershave tickled her nose, and his touch aroused every nerve ending in her body. He was a gentleman with impeccable manners, and Geneviève appreciated his chivalrous ways. The fact that he was a great human being with a big heart made him even more appealing.

Geneviève strode through the restaurant and into the washroom at the rear of the bar. Small but clean, it had pendant lights and vintage wallpaper. Geneviève entered the corner stall, then hung her purse on the metal hook behind the door.

"Where are you? I know you're in here. Come out, come out, wherever you are."

Geneviève froze. She heard footsteps on the tile floor, and the stench of cheap cologne polluted the air. A dark silhouette in faded blue jeans and muddy sneakers filled the space in the door. The stranger banged on the stall, then spoke in a low, sinister voice.

"I know who you are. You're that rich American pop star worth millions."

Her heart jumped into her throat, stealing her breath.

"Give me your purse, *now*," the voice thundered with rage. "Or I'll break down this door and bash your pretty face in."

Chapter 6

Geneviève's limbs were shaking, and her high heels were glued to the floor, but she pressed her body flat against the wall, out of sight. A fat, blistered hand appeared under the door, swatting at the air, but she dodged each swipe. The stranger panted, as if he'd just finished running the fifty-yard dash, then cursed in Spanish. Did he have a weapon? Would he use it if she didn't comply with his demands? Was he acting alone, or did he have an accomplice?

"I'm not playing with you. Give me your purse, or you'll be sorry."

Perspiration dotted her forehead, and panic coiled inside her chest. Her stomach churned, pitching violently back and forth, and Geneviève hoped she didn't get sick. Over the years, fans had done crazy things to get close to her—they'd chased her tour bus, scaled the fence at her gated mansion, broken into her cars and dressing rooms—but for the first time in her twenty-year career Geneviève feared for her life. Something told her the stranger wasn't making idle threats, and she didn't want to be his next victim.

"Perra Americana," he rasped. "Don't make me come in there and mess you up…"

Geneviève cocked her head to the right. *Who's he calling an American bitch? Is he on drugs?* Anger consumed her, and her hands balled into fists. She wanted to confront him, to ask him who the hell he was talking to, but Geneviève decided to stay put. Remembering her bodyguards were nearby, she reached into her purse, took out her cell phone and punched in her password. She had several missed calls and text messages from her mother, but she typed a group text message to Salvador and Felipe, and hit the send button.

"Geneviève, it's Roderick. Is everything okay in there?"

"No!" she shouted, cupping her hands around her mouth so he could hear her outside the bathroom. "Someone's harassing me!"

Glad she wasn't alone, Geneviève yanked open the stall door just in time to see Roderick confront the short, potbellied stranger. Salvador and Felipe arrived, grabbed the goon by his wrinkled shirt collar and dragged him out of the bathroom, kicking and shouting.

"Geneviève, what happened?"

Tears pricked the back of her eyes, and her mouth was so dry she couldn't speak.

"Are you okay? Talk to me. I need to know that you're all right."

"I'm fine," she said, wanting to reassure him. "How did you know I was in trouble?"

"I didn't. I got worried when you didn't return to our table, so I decided to check on you."

Relief flowed through her body. "Thank God you did. That guy was scary, and he spooked me pretty bad."

"I bet, but you're safe now, and I won't let you out of my sight."

His hands closed around her waist, enveloping her in a hug, and Roderick pulled her so close to his chest she could feel his heart beating through his shirt.

Caught up in the moment, Geneviève brushed her mouth against his. It was supposed to be an innocent peck on the lips, a simple act of gratitude for her hero, but when their lips touched desire flooded her body and she deepened the kiss. Passion burned inside her, thrilling her flesh. His mouth was warm, flavored with spices, leaving her desperate for more.

Roderick pulled away, abruptly ending the kiss, and dropped his hands to his sides.

Wow, that was some *kiss!* Geneviève thought, struggling to catch her breath.

"It's getting late," he pointed out, gesturing to his designer watch. "I should take you back to the hotel so you don't miss your radio interview at Hits 100 FM."

Geneviève was worried about facing her attacker, but nodded in agreement. Gathering herself, she raised her chin and pinned her shoulders back. Her heart was beating in double time, racing out of control, but Geneviève put on her game face. Willed herself to be strong. She couldn't let anyone know she was shaken and scared. Forcing a smile, she exited the washroom with her head held high, blinking away the tears in her eyes.

Geneviève marched through the sliding glass doors, projecting confidence. Favored by dignitaries, foreign diplomats and British royalty, the five-star hotel in the heart of Madrid had world-class amenities, a rooftop track and picturesque views of the cosmopolitan city. Trendsetters, tourists and hand-holding couples packed the main floor, but when Geneviève entered the lobby she spotted Althea pacing in the waiting area, and groaned inwardly. Dressed in ivory from head to toe, she looked smart and sophisticated in a fitted business suit, ruffled blouse and patent pumps. Geneviève liked Althea's designer attire, and wished her mom would wear more age-appropriate clothes.

Geneviève glanced at the bronze wall clock hanging above the reception desk. The radio interview was in two hours, giving her ample time to shower and change, but Geneviève could tell by her mom's furrowed eyebrows and pursed lips that she was upset, and hurried across the lobby toward her.

Her insides quivered at the memory of the incident at the tapas bar. She'd driven back to the hotel in Roderick's sports car, and although her bodyguards had followed behind them in a Hummer, she'd feared the goon from the bar would run them off the road. It was an irrational thought, but Geneviève couldn't help thinking the worst.

Geneviève increased her pace, reaching her mom at last. "Mom, is everything okay?"

Relief washed over her face. "Where have you been? I must have called your cell a dozen times. Didn't you get my messages?"

Stepping back, Geneviève wrinkled her nose. Althea smelled of nicotine and hard liquor. She used to have a couple glasses of merlot with dinner, but these days it was one bottle after another. Althea was ranting and raving like a table-flipping housewife from New Jersey, drawing the attention of the distinguished-looking guests seated in the waiting area, but Geneviève spoke to her in a quiet, soothing voice.

"Mom, calm down. I was having lunch with Roderick, and as you can see I'm perfectly fine."

As if noticing him for the first time, Althea's eyes narrowed and her nostrils flared. She made a noise in the back of her throat, a cross between a snort and a growl, and Geneviève feared her mom was going to make a scene in the lobby.

"What's the matter with you?" Althea jabbed Roderick in the chest with an index finger. "I told you to stay away from my daughter, and I meant it. Leave her alone, or I'll fire you."

"Ms. Harris, it's obvious you're upset, but this isn't the time or the place to air your frustrations," Roderick said in a stern voice. "And I'd hate for you to embarrass yourself, or your beautiful daughter in the most expensive hotel in Madrid."

Impressed, Geneviève raised an eyebrow. He'd successfully defused the situation with Althea, which was no simple feat. Her mom was being mean, and if they weren't in the hotel lobby, surrounded by the upper crust, Geneviève would put Althea in her place.

"I'm staying in suite 1824," he continued. "Feel free to stop by anytime to discuss my performance, the settlement case or anything else troubling you."

Althea flinched as if she'd been slapped, then dropped her hands to her sides.

Geneviève wanted to give Roderick a high five for going toe-to-toe with Althea and winning. Her mom could intimidate someone with just one look, and had once reduced a record executive to tears after a blistering tongue-lashing. But not today. Roderick held his ground. Didn't buckle under her dark, withering stare.

Geneviève smiled at Roderick. She hoped he didn't take offense to what Althea had said. Geneviève needed him. She valued his advice and his legal knowledge, and trusted him to tell her the truth. "Thanks for everything, Roderick. I owe you one."

"No worries. I'm just glad I could help."

The sympathetic expression on his face touched her heart. From time to time, Geneviève liked to disconnect from the world and leave everyone and everything behind, but she wished she could hang out with Roderick alone in her suite. Her jam-packed schedule, the incident at the bar and her fears about the future weighed heavily on her mind, and she wanted to vent to Roderick without her mom listening in. Deciding to text him later to arrange another lunch date before he left for New York, she met his gaze.

"Knock 'em dead at Hits 100 FM." Roderick gave a thumbs-up. "I'll be hard at work in my suite, but I'll make sure to tune in to your interview at six o'clock."

"Thanks for the support, and for lunch. I really enjoyed your company this afternoon."

"Likewise, Jennifer…"

A dreamy sigh fell from her lips. Hearing her legal name come out of Roderick's mouth gave Geneviève butterflies.

"Hanging out with you was the highlight of my day, and I'm looking forward to doing it again soon. Just say when, and I'm all yours."

A nod, a wink and Roderick was gone. Oblivious to the world around her, she followed him with her gaze through the gleaming, sun-drenched lobby. Watching him march into the lounge with the air of a king, Geneviève couldn't help thinking about that kiss they'd shared at the tapas bar. *Had he enjoyed it? Wanted more? Or did he regret it?* She didn't. It was magical and, given the opportunity, Geneviève would do it again.

"I don't trust him—"

"Mom, you don't trust anyone."

"And for good reason. In the last three months alone, I've had to fire two vocal coaches and your personal trainer for selling fictitious stories about you to the tabloids, and my intuition is telling me that Roderick Drake is an opportunist." Althea sucked her teeth. "You know how attorneys are. They're liars who'll say and do anything for the right price."

Eager to return to her suite, Geneviève gestured to Salvador and Felipe, and followed them to the private elevator, adjacent to the spa. She noticed people staring at her with wide eyes, and spotted guests shooting videos and snapping pictures of her. Feeling like an animal on display in a pet store window, Geneviève dropped her gaze to the floor and shielded her face with her hands.

"Geneviève, I love you! Can you take a selfie with me? *Please?*"

Hearing a small, fluting voice, Geneviève glanced over her shoulder. A chubby girl with pigtails was standing directly behind her. "Of course, sweetie," she said brightly, waving the child over. "Come here."

Geneviève took a selfie with the girl and her British nanny, then signed their Real Madrid T-shirts. In a blink, she was surrounded by a loud, cheering crowd. Geneviève signed autographs, gave out hugs and posed for dozens of pictures. A teenager belted out the chorus of "Savage", and Geneviève sang along. Laughed out loud as toddlers skipped and danced around. Snapped pictures of the crowd with her iPhone. Geneviève adored her fans, and it was times like this, when she was surrounded by them, that she loved her life. Appreciated and valued everything she'd accomplished, and the people who'd helped her along the way.

If you love your fans so much, then why did you threaten to cancel the rest of your tour? questioned her inner voice. *And why are you itching to leave the music business behind?*

Geneviève swallowed hard. She thought for a moment, realized the truth was too painful to admit even to herself and buried the answer in the depths of her heart.

"Gigi, let's go. You have an interview to do in an hour, remember?"

Tugging on her forearm, Althea urged her to board the elevator, but Geneviève moved closer to the crowd. Her mom was being jealous and controlling, and Geneviève was tired of arguing with Althea. It was her life, her decision. Besides, she needed something to cheer her up after her run-in with that madman at the tapas bar, and being with her fans instantly bolstered her spirits.

"Bye, everyone! Gigi loves you! Thanks for the support!" Althea shouted above the noise.

Reluctantly boarding the elevator, Geneviève smiled and waved at the cheering, animated group. The doors closed, and she leaned against the wall. A text popped up on her iPhone, and reading Roderick's message made her giggle.

Let's hook up later. Swing by my suite after your radio interview for cocktails, dessert and an Antonio Banderas movie marathon. Come on! You know you love *Shrek*!

"Quit playing on your phone, and listen to me," Althea snapped. "This is important…"

Frowning, she studied her mother. Althea was losing it. Getting worked up over nothing. She gestured wildly with her hands, and was speaking so fast Geneviève couldn't get a word in.

Blocking out her mother's voice, Geneviève took a moment to consider Roderick's offer. Hanging out with him sounded fun. They'd had a great time at lunch, and she wanted to hear more about his family, his background and his past relationships. Why not kick it with her handsome attorney after dark? She had nothing else to do, and liked the idea of spending time with him—and getting away from her mother for a few hours. Althea was having an attitude, and Geneviève feared what would happen if they were alone in her suite for the rest of the night.

Feeling playful and giddy, she answered his text.

Just make sure you have sweet and spicy wasabi popcorn, or I'm out!

"Roderick has to go. I don't like him," Althea continued in a curt voice.

"You don't have to. He's my attorney, not yours, and I trust him. He's good people."

Her eyes bugged out of her head. "Oh really? You've had lunch with him, and now you think he's the best thing since fat-free cheesecake. Well, he's not. I know his type, and if you confide in him he'll burn you just like all the others."

"Or not. It's my decision, and I want to keep Roderick on staff. And if you fire him or call his law firm to complain, you'll be looking for someone else to manage."

Althea gasped. "Jennifer Tyesha Harris! How dare you speak to me with such disrespect! Have you forgotten everything I've done for you over the years? How much I sacrificed to make you into the star you are today? Do I need to remind you of where we come from?"

Geneviève stared down at her high heels so she wouldn't have to see the pained expression on Althea's face. Guilt made her feel low, and she deeply regretted disrespecting her mom.

"When the applause fades and your fans disappear, I'll still be here. Don't ever forget that…"

The doors slid open, and Geneviève followed behind her bodyguards. A pregnant woman waddled by, rubbing her baby bump, and the bearded man at her side pushed a pink stroller.

Geneviève stared longingly at the couple. *When is it going to be my turn? When am I going to find love and happiness?* she wondered, admiring the family. *Am I ever going to have a child, or am I just fooling myself? Wishing and praying in vain?*

"We're a team, Gigi, and if you disobey me, you'll live to regret it, so get rid of Roderick and hire someone else. Someone trustworthy and reliable who'll do what they're told."

At the sound of her mom's voice, Geneviève abandoned her thoughts and raised an index finger in the air. "Give me one good reason why I should replace Roderick."

"Just one? Where do I begin?" Smiling triumphantly, Althea made her case. She complained about Roderick's unprofessionalism, his cocksure attitude and his deceitful ways. "I told him not to bother you about the settlement case, but he went behind my back and contacted you anyways. Can you imagine? Such disrespect!"

The wheels turned in Geneviève's mind as she unlocked the door and marched inside the sunny, lavender-scented suite. Now she understood why her mom disliked Roderick. Why Althea was giving him a hard time. Why she wanted to fire him, and ship him back to New York on the red-eye. It wasn't because Roderick was incompetent or unprofessional; it was because he'd dared to defy her. And that made Geneviève like Roderick even more.

Chapter 7

Cheers exploded inside the arena on Friday night, and Geneviève was so moved by the outpouring of love from the fans chanting her name all across WiZink Center that she didn't want to leave the stage. She considered debuting her new song, "Hands on You," even though her voice was hoarse, but she remembered that the chorus needed work, and decided against it.

Waving at the crowd, Geneviève reveled in the moment, soaking in their praise and adoration. Children were crying, couples were dancing in the aisles, teenagers wearing I Love Geneviève T-shirts were screaming at the top of their lungs, and cell phones flashed all over the arena. Geneviève was proud of her performance and her kick-ass, all-female band. They'd wowed the audience, given them one hell of a show, and she planned to reward them for their hard work when they returned to the States.

Glancing over her shoulder, she spotted Demi and Roderick waiting in the shadows, and wondered what they thought of her performance. As usual, her sister had her eyes glued to her iPhone, oblivious to the world around her. Roderick flashed a broad grin that made his eyes light up, and butterflies swarmed Geneviève's stomach.

Damn, he's sexy! His denim shirt was open at the collar, enhancing his sex appeal, and his slim-fitted jeans and casual shoes complemented his stylish appearance. The attorney had the wow factor, and his inherent charm and charisma were undeniable. But what stood out most about Roderick was his kindness. And what a dynamic kisser he was. That's why Geneviève had been flirting with him on the phone every night. And why she'd been sneaking around with him for the past five days.

Fond memories warmed her heart. All week, she'd been hanging out with Roderick, and aside from Demi, no one knew about their secret rendezvous. Geneviève would have been perfectly content relaxing in his suite, eating junk food and watching telenovelas, but Roderick insisted on taking her out on the town. At his request, she'd ditched her bodyguards, her iPhone and her beloved baseball cap.

Every date with Roderick was a thrilling adventure, and an opportunity to experience something new. On Tuesday they'd explored museums filled with historic masterpieces and sculptures, on Wednesday they'd strolled through markets and high-end boutiques buying souvenirs and, last night, they'd traveled from one tapas bar to the next, drinking, socializing and sampling the local cuisine. That morning, Roderick had persuaded her to join him in the hotel restaurant for breakfast, and what should have been a quick meal lasted three hours.

If Demi hadn't come calling, she'd probably still be sitting on the deck with Roderick, discussing pop culture and the music business.

The sound of foreign languages yanked Geneviève out of her thoughts.

"Geneviève, *te amo!*"

"Tu es le meilleur!"

"Du bist ein star, Geneviève!"

"Encore, encore, encore! Give us one more song!"

Exhausted and thirsty, Geneviève was anxious to return to her private dressing room, but she decided to spend a few more minutes with her fans. Crouching down in the first row, Geneviève signed T-shirts, magazine covers bearing her image, homemade posters and even ticket stubs. She posed for pictures and selfies, and the crowd lost its mind, cheering louder than ever before. It was the perfect way to end the show, and when her band members whisked her offstage, Geneviève thought her heart would burst with joy.

After two decades in the spotlight, she was ready for the next chapter of her life, but Geneviève was going to miss connecting with her fans, hearing them sing her songs and seeing their faces light up every time she took the stage. She'd never reveal the truth to anyone, not even Demi, but she wanted to disappear to a private island where no one—including the paparazzi *and* her mother—would ever be able to find her.

"Gigi, you were amazing!" Looking sporty and athletic in a white, knee-length dress, canvas sneakers and a baseball cap, Demi swiveled her neck and snapped her fingers in the air. "I've seen you perform hundreds of times, and I didn't think you could outdo yourself, but the acapella version of 'For All the Wrong Reasons' was fire!"

Roderick kissed Geneviève on the cheek, then handed her a bouquet of carnations. "I agree."

Desire warmed her skin. She wanted to kiss him, to hold him close, but since Geneviève didn't want her band or anyone else backstage to know she had a crush on her attorney, she said, "Thanks. I'm just glad there were no mishaps during the show. I hate when that happens."

"Let's celebrate with a sister selfie!" Demi lobbed an arm around Geneviève's shoulder, raised her iPhone in the air and snapped multiple photographs. "Smile, Gigi! You should be happy. You killed tonight, *and* you looked fierce doing it!"

Geneviève blew out a deep breath. "Don't post these. I'm sweaty and gross—"

"Sis, relax, they're pictures, not stickers," Demi said, giggling. "No one can smell them."

Roderick chuckled, much to her chagrin, and Geneviève playfully swatted his shoulder. "Enough of that. You're my attorney, not hers, so don't laugh at her jokes."

Clutching the flowers to her chest, Geneviève closed her eyes and inhaled the sweet, fragrant aroma. She marched down the hallway, listening to Demi and Roderick praise her show, and pride flowed through her veins. All of the planning, rehearsals and late-night meetings with her band in her hotel suite had been worth it; they'd delivered the performance of their lives, and Geneviève couldn't be happier.

"Allow me." Roderick opened the dressing room door. "After you."

Geneviève went inside, sank into the red, velvet sofa and kicked off her studded pumps. The space was bright, decorated with designer chairs, ornate chandeliers and mirrors, and a walk-in-closet so plush it would make the Duchess of Cambridge green with envy.

"There's my talented, amazing daughter!" Althea stood in front of the wall-mounted TV with a bottle of Cristal in her hands. Pretty in a tie-waist dress and silver accessories, Althea sauntered across the room with a pep in her step. "Gigi, I am so proud of you I could weep! You were sensational, baby girl…"

Bending down, Althea gave her a hug and a kiss. Her mom smelled of strong liquor, and Geneviève suspected Althea had made several trips to the concession stand during the concert. Or had a miniature flask in her clutch purse.

"You brought your songs to life, and left your fans begging for more. Well-done, Gigi!"

Touched by her mother's words, Geneviève hugged her tight.

"Roderick, please excuse us," Althea said, straightening to her full height. "I'd like to have some quiet time with my daughters. You understand, don't you?"

"Absolutely. It's no problem at all, Ms. Harris." Roderick gave a polite nod. "Ladies, enjoy the rest of your night. And Geneviève, congratulations again on your show. You were incredible."

Roderick left, closing the door behind him, and Geneviève strangled a groan. She wished he'd stayed, and her mom had left. Experience had taught her that when Althea said she wanted to spend "quiet time with her," it was never as innocent as it seemed, and Geneviève wanted to relax, not discuss her career.

"Gigi, I have great news!" Althea announced, in a

shrill, animated voice. "Cosmic TV Network is giving you your very own reality show!"

Geneviève scoffed. "And that's good news?"

"Of course it is. It's an opportunity of a lifetime."

"Mom, if you think it's such a good idea then *you* do it."

"I wish I could, but I'm not one of the hottest pop stars on the planet. *You* are, and the network is willing to pay big bucks to sign you."

Althea's eyes lit up like a casino slot machine, and Geneviève knew her mom was thinking about the financial terms of the deal. What else was new? These days that was all Althea cared about, and Geneviève didn't understand why. They had more money in the bank than they could ever spend, but it was never enough for her mom. Althea was always on the hunt for the next multimillion-dollar deal, and her quest for more fame and fortune—often at Geneviève's expense—was frustrating.

I wish things were the way they used to be. Cherished memories came to mind, warming Geneviève's heart. Over the years, she'd had wonderful times with her mom—collecting seashells at Asbury Park, perusing music stores for vinyl records, participating in their first Mother-Daughter Charity Walk and attending the Essence Music Festival in Durban, South Africa. Her mom used to be easygoing and agreeable, but the more successful Geneviève became, the more demanding Althea was, and they hadn't been on the same page for years.

The same page? quipped her inner voice. *You're not even reading the same book!*

"Filming starts in June, which coincides with your break, and that's not all. The network is willing to fly you out to LA, put you up in a five-star, boutique hotel and provide you with a chauffeur during your stay." Althea popped the cork on the champagne, strode over to the mini fridge and filled three glasses to the brim. "The show is tentatively titled *One Night with a Pop Star*, and the network thinks it could be the runaway hit of the summer!"

"One Night with a Pop Star?" Demi repeated, glancing up from her iPhone. "That's a dumb title. The network needs to go back to the drawing board. They need to come up with something fun and playful like *Geneviève Gets a Man* to entice viewers."

"That's brilliant!" Althea whooped for joy. "I love it! Way to go, Demi."

Geneviève glared at her sister. "Thanks a lot, Judas."

"What? Don't get mad at me. I'm just being honest." Demi stretched her legs on the coffee table then crossed them at the ankles. "Forget I said anything. It's none of my business."

"Good, because I'm not doing the show."

"Yes, you are," Althea insisted. "I've worked hard on this deal, and I won't let you ruin the plans I've made. You're doing the show whether you like it or not, and that's final."

"No, I'm not. We've talked about reality TV before, and my position hasn't changed. I have no desire to do a reality show, so kindly tell the network thanks, but no thanks."

Anxious to take a shower, Geneviève stood, stripped off her accessories and dropped them on the coffee table. For the first time since entering the dressing room, she noticed all of the glass vases were filled with carnations. *Did Roderick do this? Had he arranged to have the flowers delivered, and displayed around the room?* Admiring the colorful, vibrant arrangements, Geneviève asked, "Where did the carnations come from—"

"Forget about the stupid flowers," Althea snapped, tapping her high-heel-clad foot impatiently on the ivory carpet. "You're a star, Gigi, a global icon in the making, and we need to capitalize on your celebrity before time runs out."

"Mom, I'm still not interested—"

"Why not? Lots of singers have done reality TV with great success."

"Good for them, but it's not for me, so forget it."

Anger flashed in her mom's eyes, and her face wrinkled like a prune in the sun. "Why are you being difficult? For once, why can't you do what I ask without giving me attitude?"

"Because I'm not a little girl anymore. I have dreams and aspirations and they don't include being on a pathetic reality show, or touring ten months out of the year, either." Geneviève wanted to say more, but thought better of it. There was no use talking to her mom; once Althea got an idea in her head there was no reasoning with her, and Geneviève didn't have the energy to argue with her mom. Not after a two-hour show. "I don't want to talk about this anymore. It's a waste of time."

"Not so fast," Althea said, sliding in front of her with more finesse than MC Hammer. "We have to iron out the details of this deal tonight because we have a phone conference with network executives in the morning, and it's important we're on the same page."

Geneviève raised an eyebrow. "But we're going sight-seeing tomorrow."

"We'll go another time. When we're less busy."

"No," she said, drawing out the word to emphasize

her point. "It's my day off, and we're going shopping in Barcelona. *You* said you'd clear my schedule."

Althea shrugged. "Things change. Deal with it. We have several meetings scheduled after breakfast, and a magazine photoshoot, so you really need to bring your A game, Gigi…"

Like hell I do! This is my life, not yours, and it's high time you realize it!

Geneviève stared at the dressing room door. She heard footsteps in the hallway followed by boisterous female voices, and guessed her bandmates were waiting for her in the corridor. After each show they usually went to a lounge to critique their performance over cocktails and appetizers, but arguing with her mom was draining, and now all Geneviève wanted to do was sleep.

Liar! argued her conscience. *If Roderick called and asked to see you, you'd go running!*

"I almost forgot to tell you," Althea said. "You have a vocal lesson tomorrow, as well."

"No, it's my day off, so cancel the plans you've made, because I won't be there." Geneviève pulled her hair back in a bun. "I'm going to take a shower."

"All right, baby, you do that." Wearing a sympathetic smile, Althea reached out and rubbed her shoulder. "I know you're tired, so we'll talk about the TV deal later."

Is she for real? Didn't she just hear what I said? Realizing there was no getting through to her mom, Geneviève threw her hands in the air and entered the bathroom. She locked the door, then slumped against it. She could hear Demi and Althea whispering, and wondered whose side her sister was on. It didn't matter. She wasn't signing on to do the reality show, and there was nothing anyone could say or do to change her mind.

Geneviève glanced at her watch. She wanted to see Roderick, to vent about her argument with her mom, but it was too late to call him, and going to his hotel room after dark was out of the question.

A grin curled her lips. Excited about the plan taking shape in her mind, she turned the water faucet on full blast, then stripped off her costume.

Althea knocked on the bathroom door. "Gigi, I'm returning to the hotel," she said in a cheerful voice. "Sleep well, honey. See you bright and early in the morning."

No, you won't, Geneviève thought, *because by the time you wake up I'll be long gone!*

Chapter 8

Roderick awoke with a start. Squinting, he waited for his eyes to adjust to the blinding sunlight streaming through the windows, and stretched his arms in the air. Yawning, he glanced at the digital clock on the mahogany side table. It had been years since he'd slept in, and Roderick wondered if he was tired because of the change of scenery or because of the explicit dreams he'd had last night about Geneviève. In it, they'd made love in her dressing room—twice—then chartered a private jet to a secluded Caribbean island.

Roderick cranked his head to the right. No, he hadn't imagined it. Someone was definitely banging on the door. Clad in a white, ribbed undershirt and Nike basketball shorts, he rolled out of bed and stumbled into the hallway. Curious about who it was, and why they were interrupting his sleep, Roderick asked, "Who is it?"

"It's me. Hurry up before someone recognizes me and tips off the press."

His eyes widened. What was Geneviève doing at his suite? Had someone upset her? Every muscle in his jaw tensed. Had José Sánchez put his hands on her again? The deadline for the settlement agreement had passed, and he feared the college student had hassled her in the hotel lobby. Mr. Cabrero had called him yesterday threatening to sue Geneviève for millions, but Roderick wasn't worried. He'd find a way to outsmart Dumb and Dumber before he returned to New York. Had to, or he wouldn't be named senior partner in May.

"Roderick, open up, it's your favorite pop star."

Deciding to have fun with her, he joked, "Rihanna, is that you?"

"Ha, ha, very funny," she quipped, her voice thick was sarcasm. "Now, open the door and let me in before I fire you and replace you with a *real* lawyer."

Roderick stared down at his clothes. He considered returning to the bedroom to get dressed, but since he didn't want to keep Geneviève waiting, he yanked open the door and smiled. "Good morning, Ms. Harris. To what do I owe this honor?"

"Finally," she drawled, emphasizing each letter. "I thought you'd never wake up."

"It's not my fault. I need my beauty sleep."

"Slacker! I've already worked out, had breakfast *and* blogged about last night's concert."

Frowning, Roderick glanced up and down the hallway. "Where are your bodyguards? You shouldn't be walking around by yourself, especially considering what happened at the tapas bar. It's dangerous, and I don't want anything bad to happen to you."

"I gave them the day off," she answered. "I needed some space. Relax. I'll be fine."

Geneviève marched past him, then stopped abruptly. "Are you alone?"

"No." A grin curled his lips. "Adele and Lady Gaga are on the balcony drinking cocktails."

"You are so silly. Are you *sure* you're an attorney and not a comedian?"

"Positive. I passed the bar my first try with a perfect score," Roderick boasted, plucking at his cotton undershirt. "Don't believe me? Ask my mom. She framed the results!"

Roderick laughed, but Geneviève didn't. He could tell by the pensive expression on her face and her stiff posture that something was bothering her. Her smile was fake, lacking warmth and happiness, and she looked more stressed than a college student cramming for finals. "So, what brings you by this morning?"

"You invited me to go sightseeing with you today, remember?"

"Yeah, but you turned me down. If memory serves me correctly, you were going to Barcelona with your mom to enjoy some retail therapy."

"Well, my plans fell through, so here I am." Fiddling with the straps of her nylon backpack, she shifted her sneaker-clad feet. "I just need to get away for a while, you know?"

"Geneviève, what's wrong?"

"Everything," she grumbled, her lips twisted in a scowl.

"Talk to me." Roderick wanted to take her into his arms, to caress her flawless brown skin, but remembered Geneviève was his client, not his girlfriend, and folded his arms across his chest. He'd made the mistake of kissing her once, but it wasn't going to happen again. "Tell me what's bothering you. I want to help."

Seconds ticked off the wall clock, but Geneviève didn't speak; she paced. It was moments like this, when she was quiet and introspective, that it was easy for Roderick to forget that she was one of the biggest pop stars in the world. She never fussed or threw a tantrum when she was upset, and he appreciated her levelheaded approach.

Watching her, he noted her hostile gaze. Still, she was breathtaking. A stunner. Drop-dead sexy. Her sleeveless turquoise shirt was tied in a knot at the side, and her mesh leggings fit every curve and elongated her toned legs—legs Roderick wished were clamped around his waist.

Scared he'd cross the line, Roderick tore his gaze away from her fit and toned body. He felt it—the familiar pull between them, the electricity crackling in the air—but he'd never act on his feelings. Knew if he did he could lose his job, and Roderick didn't want to be the laughingstock of the law firm.

His thoughts returned to last year. He'd seen something special in Geneviève the first time they met, but over time her light had dimmed, faded under the glare of the spotlight, and Roderick feared she'd crack under the pressure if she didn't take a stand against her record label—and her mother. He wanted to share his concerns, but Geneviève spoke, seizing his attention. Her confession made his temperature rise. Roderick didn't want her to know he was upset about her TV deal. He hated the idea of Geneviève being the star of a dating show.

You want her all to yourself! jeered his conscience. *Just admit it!*

"My mom's pressuring me to sign on, and even though I've told her a million times I'm not interested, she keeps badgering me about it," she complained. "I don't know what else to do."

Leaning against the back of the couch, stroking his jaw, Roderick considered every option.

"If not for the tour, I'd pack my things and head to the mountains for some R&R."

"Geneviève, you don't need to run away. You need to face your problems head-on."

"And how do you propose I do that? My mom won't listen to me."

"Then call the network and speak to them directly. Tell them what you just told me."

"You make it sound so easy. My mother's been my manager from day one, and if I go behind her back and contact the network she'll be hurt, and that's the last thing I want."

"Do you want me to call the network on your behalf?"

"No, I'll figure something out," she said with a sad smile. "But thanks for the offer."

Roderick reached out, took her hand in his and squeezed it. He knew touching her was a mistake, that it could push him over the edge, but he wanted Geneviève to know that he supported her. "*We'll* figure it out together. Don't worry. I've got your back."

Her eyes lit up when she smiled, and Roderick felt proud, as if he'd accomplished a death-defying feat. Geneviève was more than just a pop star; she was a beautiful, intelligent woman and everything about her appealed to him, especially her lush lips. The urge to kiss her was overpowering. It was all he could think about, all he wanted.

Roderick frowned. A voice blared in his head, and it sounded like Mr. Welker. *Don't do this, man. You're asking for trouble!* Heeding the warning, he released Geneviève's hand and moved away from her. Scolding himself for acting like a horny teenage boy on prom night, he wiped every explicit thought about her from his mind.

It was hard to do the right thing, especially after the conversation he'd had with his brother last night. Duane had called while Roderick was jogging on the rooftop track, but after five minutes of conversation he'd ended the call. He didn't want to hear about his ex-fiancée returning to the Hamptons days earlier with her beau, and wished his friends and family would stop blowing up his cell about his no-good ex. Roderick didn't care about Toya. Not anymore. He hadn't thought about her in months, not since he heard she was engaged, and he wanted nothing to do with her. Toya wasn't the woman he thought she was, and she'd done him a favor by dumping him.

"If the invitation still stands I'd love to go hiking with you. It's gorgeous outside, and I don't want to be cooped up inside the hotel arguing with my mother about that stupid TV deal."

Roderick surfaced from his thoughts and straightened to his full height. On the outside he remained calm, but on the inside he was pumping his fists in the air. There was no one he'd rather spend the day with than Geneviève. There was nothing fake or pretentious about her, and they always had great conversations about life. "Sounds like a plan. Give me ten minutes to get ready, and we'll be on our way."

Her face brightened. "What's the plan? Where are we going?"

"The Spanish countryside, of course. Every once in a while, when I need to recharge my batteries, I jump in my car, put the top down and cruise for hours."

"Sounds like my kind of trip. I can't wait!"

"I love sightseeing, but when I need to escape the crowds, and the noise I head to the mountains. Hiking is the ultimate stress reliever."

"Be careful, Counselor. It might be so relaxing I won't come back!"

Roderick gestured to the kitchenette. "Feel free to make yourself a coffee while you wait."

"Thanks. That's very kind of you. I think I will."

"Cool. I'll be right back. In the meantime, make yourself at home."

"Don't dawdle," she quipped, wagging a finger at him. "I'm eager to get going, so hurry."

Roderick saluted. "Yes, ma'am. I'll be back before you even notice I'm gone."

"Ma'am?" Geneviève winced as if she were in pain. "*Please* don't call me that. It makes me feel old, and I'm twenty-eight not eighty-eight, so knock it off, Roderick!"

Chuckling, he turned and strode through the living room, marveling at his good fortune. For the first time since his engagement imploded, he felt a rush of excitement—and an erection inside his basketball shorts—and his feisty, sassy client from North Philly with the bodacious body was the reason why.

Geneviève stood on the steep hillside, shielding her eyes from the sun, basking in the beauty of her surroundings. She heard birds chirping, saw them skipping and hopping on tree branches, and appreciated being in the great outdoors. Geneviève loved feeling the sun on her face, the wind in her hair and the fresh air blowing against her skin.

Inhaling, she enjoyed the peace and tranquility of the world around her. Snuggled in the mountains that surrounded Madrid, the town was quiet, isolated and serene. Picturesque, with clear blue skies, sweeping views and radiant sunshine, it was the perfect escape from the chaos in her life, and Geneviève loved everything about the small, charming city.

Raising her bottle to her mouth, she took a sip of ice water. The ground was uneven, rocky and full of tree roots and broken branches, but Geneviève relished being in the forest. There was nothing more relaxing than being at the Spanish countryside, and as she reflected on her day trip with Roderick, she smiled.

They'd done it all—visited the cathedral, strolled the narrow streets, bought souvenirs and relaxed for hours at a tavern-style restaurant with scrumptious appetizers and drinks. No topic was off-limits, and chatting with Roderick had helped Geneviève forget her problems for a few hours. He was a remarkable guy on every level, and spending the day with him confirmed what she'd known all along: she wanted him more than she'd ever wanted anyone. Making the first move wasn't her style, but Geneviève was tempted to throw caution to the wind and kiss him until he saw stars.

"Excuse me, miss, do you mind taking a picture?"

Geneviève spun around, spotted a group of college-aged women in tank tops and denim shorts standing behind her, and forced a smile. She wasn't in the mood to take pictures, but Geneviève reminded herself she had nothing to complain about. Thankfully, no one had recognized her while she was with Roderick that afternoon and she'd enjoyed blending in with the crowd during their outing. "Sure, no problem."

"Thanks so much!" A slender woman with braces stepped forward and handed Geneviève a Nokia camera. Frowning, she glanced from the camera to the brunette, unsure what to do.

Appearing at her side, Roderick leaned over and whispered, "They want you to take a picture of *them*, not with them. Think you can handle that, Ms. Harris?"

"Oh, my bad." Heat warmed her cheeks, and she giggled. "Say cheese, ladies!"

Geneviève snapped the picture, returned the camera, then retightened her loose ponytail.

"I told you no one would recognize you here." Roderick draped an arm around her shoulders. "The locals are too busy farming and horseback riding to notice celebrities, so cut loose while you're here. No one will ever know."

His cologne washed over her, arousing her flesh. Hiding a girlish smile, she snuggled against him. Roderick made her feel safe and secure, as if she was important to him, and it was a great feeling. Better than winning a Grammy award. Leading her along the winding trail, he educated her about the history of the city, the culture and its most notable residents.

"I represent a Latin songwriter who grew up here, and he said everyone's so chill and laid-back that he had his first glass of wine at a wedding when he was nine years old. Crazy, huh?"

No, she thought, gazing at him. *What's crazy is how dreamy you are!*

"Growing up, my parents were cool, but they weren't *that* cool," he said with a chuckle.

Soaking up every word that came out of his mouth, she committed pertinent details about his family, his upbringing and his career to memory. Every day she learned something new about Roderick, and when he wasn't making her laugh, he was educating her about Wall Street, world affairs and the American justice system. It was hard to think straight, to focus on putting one foot in front of the other when Roderick touched her, but she willed her knees not to buckle.

Their eyes met, and tingles rocked her spine. Geneviève allowed her gaze to linger on his lips even though she knew it was a mistake. Dangerous. Playing with fire. Tempting fate. She'd never met a man of his caliber before, never connected with someone in such a real, profound way in such a short period of time, and the more Geneviève tried to fight her feelings for him, the stronger they became. Her inner voice tormented her, telling her she didn't stand a chance with him, but she ignored the taunts. Refused to believe he wasn't attracted to her. Not because Geneviève thought she was the most beautiful woman in the world, but because they were kindred spirits who had a lot in common, and never ran out of things to talk about.

Gathering her courage, Geneviève found her voice and spoke with confidence, even though her heart was hammering inside her chest. "Roderick, can I ask you a personal question?"

"Sure," he answered with a shrug. "As long as you don't mind me asking you one, too."

"Ask away. I'm an open book. I have nothing to hide."

"I know your mom raised you and Demi alone, and that you're exceptionally close, but why does her opinion and happiness matter more to you than your own?"

A lump the size of a grapefruit formed in her throat. Needing a moment to catch her breath, Geneviève sat down on a wooden bench and drank some water. She'd never told anyone the truth about her childhood—for fear they'd run straight to the tabloids and sell her story—but she wanted Roderick to know about her background, even though she felt tremendous shame about her formative years in North Philly. Geneviève didn't know where to start, but when she opened her mouth the words fell out, surprising her.

"My dad left when Demi and I were very young, and what hurt more than anything was that he didn't even have the decency to say goodbye to us," she confessed, kicking a rock across the trail. "He left for work one morning, drove off in his pickup truck and never returned. To this day, I still don't know why he walked out on us."

Geneviève took several deep breaths to steady her erratic heartbeat. Glancing around to ensure the other hikers weren't listening in on her private conversation with Roderick, she waited until the coast was clear before she resumed speaking about her absentee father. "Soon after Dwight moved out, life got worse."

"It must have been hard for your family without your dad at home."

"That's an understatement," she said, warding off bitter memories. "When Dwight left, everything fell apart, and despite my mother's best efforts we lived in poverty for many years. Teachers took pity on me and would bring me food sometimes, but dinner was often my only real meal of the day. I know my mom can be difficult, and hard to please at times, but she means everything to me, and I could never repay her for everything she's done for me."

Geneviève took off her Chanel sunglasses, wiped her eyes, then put her shades back on.

"Thanks for confiding in me about your childhood. Now everything makes sense."

Roderick stretched an arm along the bench, and his fingers brushed against her neck. Electricity shot though her body, and Geneviève struggled to keep her hands in her lap and off his smooth, chiseled face. She craved his kiss, longed to feel his gentle caress against her skin, but she was determined to maintain her composure during their outing.

"Your mom is a tenacious, ambitious woman who helped you achieve your dreams, but she isn't responsible for your success. *You* are. *You* put in the hours, *you* practiced tirelessly, *you* wrote incredible songs..."

A dreamy sigh fell from her lips. It was one of the nicest compliments Geneviève had ever received, and hearing Roderick praise her work ethic, her professionalism and her talents made Geneviève want to jump up and skip along the trail. The entertainment business was cutthroat, more grueling than military boot camp, and after years of being knocked down she'd lost her voice, her power, but Roderick had reminded her how strong she was. Geneviève believed every word he said. He was right. She needed to live life on her own terms; she was her own woman, her own boss, and from now on she wasn't going to let anyone bully her.

"Thanks, Roderick. I don't know what I'd do without you."

"No worries," he said, inclining his head toward her. "I'm just doing my job."

I know, and you're brilliant at it, but I wish you'd do me instead!

"Earlier you said you wanted to ask me something. What is it?"

Geneviève dismissed his question with a wave of her hand. "It was nothing. Forget it."

The wind picked up, and thick clouds threatening rain darkened the sky.

"We should head back to the car. It looks like a storm is coming, and I'd hate for us to get caught in the middle of it." Roderick zipped up his hoodie. "Where should we go next?"

"Anywhere but the hotel." They'd been hiking for ninety minutes, and even though the temperature had dropped, Geneviève didn't want to leave. All afternoon her mother had been blowing up her cell with angry text messages and voice mails, and Geneviève dreaded seeing Althea when she returned to her suite. Her mother meant the world to her, and she didn't want to hurt her feelings, but she was tired of living a lie. She was ready to start the next chapter of her life—one that didn't include doing press, performing around the world or starring in a reality TV show. "I'm still full from lunch, but I'd love a cold drink."

Standing, Roderick offered Geneviève his hand. "I know just the place."

Chapter 9

Cócteles Clásicos, a trendy restaurant-lounge near the Royal Palace of Madrid, attracted a youthful, energetic crowd, and as Roderick pulled up to the front entrance in his sports car, Geneviève had second thoughts about having drinks at the most popular lounge in the city. Patrons in bling and designer threads were lined up around the block, and Geneviève felt out of place in her lightweight tracksuit, neon-pink sneakers and windswept hair.

"Roderick, I think we should leave," she said, gesturing to her clothes. "I'm a mess."

"No, you're not. You could wear a brown paper bag and *still* look sexy."

"There's no way we'll get into the VIP area dressed like this, so why even bother trying?"

Squeezing her hand, he wore a reassuring smile. "Of course we will. Just watch."

"I wish I had your confidence, but I don't. We don't look the part, and I don't want to be publicly humiliated when the bouncers reject us."

"Don't worry, Geneviève. I'll handle it."

Always smooth and never in a hurry, Roderick exited the vehicle, strode around the hood and opened the passenger side door. Geneviève hesitated; she wanted to have drinks with Roderick, but she didn't want to leave the car. What if someone recognized her and took pictures? Or worse, recorded a video of them being turned away from Cócteles Clásicos and posted the embarrassing video online?

"Geneviève, trust me," Roderick said in a quiet voice. "I've got this."

Against her better judgment, she took his hand and followed him toward the entrance of the bi-level brick building. Tourists in hats and T-shirts were strolling the streets, posing for pictures in front of landmarks and sampling the local cuisine in nearby bars and restaurants. In Madrid, people made time for friends, conversation and leisure, and the city was vibrating with energy. Geneviève could hear techno music, boisterous laughter and conversation, and the delicious aromas in the air made her mouth water.

You're not hungry for food, quipped her conscience. *You're hungry for Roderick!*

"You're going to love Cócteles Clásicos," he promised, rubbing the small of her back. "They don't allow cell phones or cameras in the VIP lounge so you don't have to worry about anyone secretly filming you. For once, you can drink and relax like everyone else."

One of the tuxedo-clad bouncers in front of Cócteles Clásicos spotted them and beckoned them to follow him.

Wearing a broad smile, the bouncer abandoned his post and hustled them through the main floor. Packed with revelers, it was the size of a football field, with a mile-long bar, candlelit tables and cushy, padded booths. The dance floor had lasers and disco balls, and vibrant lights bounced around the room, illuminating the faces of the people in the crowd. Living it up in style, patrons were drinking, toasting and laughing without a care in the world.

"As requested, the VIP lounge is yours for the rest of the evening," the bouncer said with a nod. "If you need anything, just press the red table buzzer for your hostess."

Glancing around the space, Geneviève took in her surroundings. Low-hanging lights, leather armchairs and vintage mirrors created an inviting ambience, and the glitzy chandeliers reeked of elegance.

The hostess appeared, put drinks and appetizers on the round, copper table, then left. Deep in thought, Geneviève tapped her foot on the floor. Roderick must have called the lounge when they'd stopped for gas on their way to Madrid, because her music video for "Salty Girl" was playing on the mounted, flat-screen TV, glass vases were filled with carnations and decorative candy bowls had her favorite Swiss chocolate.

From where Geneviève was standing, she could see the dance floor, and enjoyed watching partyers execute the latest dance moves. "Savage" blasted out of the sound system, and the crowd cheered. Worried someone would recognize her, Geneviève backed away from the balcony and faced Roderick. "It never gets old," she said with a sheepish smile, swaying to the music. "It doesn't matter how many times I hear one of my songs playing, it always gives me a rush. I should be used to it after all these years in the music business, but I'm not."

"That's probably what keeps you humble." Roderick sat down on the couch, picked up his glass tumbler and tasted his rum and Coke. "You've had a long, illustrious career with plenty of highlights, but what would you say is your most cherished memory?"

Geneviève took the seat beside him. "That's easy. The day I handed my mom the keys to her gated mansion in the Hamptons. She was so excited she fainted *twice!*"

"Really? I expected you to say winning your first Grammy, breaking Billboard records, your blockbuster American tour or singing the national anthem at last year's Super Bowl…"

Feeling her eyes widen, Geneviève hoped she didn't look as foolish as she felt, but his words surprised her. Caught her off guard. Roderick knew a lot about her career, more than her deadbeat dad did, and she couldn't help wondering if his interest in her was strictly platonic.

Her gaze zeroed in on his juicy lips. *I've never been this attracted to anyone, and I want to spend the night with you.*

"All of those things are great, and I'm proud about everything I've accomplished over the years, but nothing compares to fulfilling a lifelong dream," she explained, reaching for her cocktail glass. "When I signed with Urban Beats Records at sixteen, I promised my mom I'd buy her a mansion one day and I did. Nothing beats that."

"Come on, be honest, filming your cameo in *Fast & Furious 6* was mad cool, wasn't it?"

"You know what's mad cool? Visiting sick kids at the Children's Hospital of Philadelphia with my band, Divalicious, and throwing an impromptu concert in the game room. Seeing them smile and sing is the best feeling in the world, and I wouldn't trade it for anything, not even for a cameo in a blockbuster action movie."

He stared at her for a long moment. "You're some kind of woman, Geneviève Harris. If all of my clients were like you, my job would be a walk in the park and life would be golden."

From the comfort and privacy of the VIP lounge, Geneviève ate caviar, drank cocktails and danced with Roderick to her favorite songs. He took her hand, twirled her around the room, then pulled her to his chest, holding her close. He smelled of soap, clean and refreshing, and inhaling his scent caused explicit images to fill Geneviève's mind—images of them kissing, and caressing each other's bodies. Slow dancing with Roderick turned her on, almost as much as his kiss, and feeling his hands along her hips made her nipples strain against her bra, and her sex tingle. Geneviève wished she were wearing a loose, flowy dress instead of a tracksuit, but she matched him step for step, moving against him to the beat of the music blaring in the restaurant-lounge.

Hours passed, and as the night wore on, Geneviève felt herself loosen up. Relax. Speak freely, and flirt boldly. And she wasn't the only one. Roderick held her hand in his, kissed her palm as he praised her inner beauty and played with her hair. Seated side by side on the couch, they chatted and flirted. He shared hilarious stories about his most outrageous clients, his colleagues and his siblings, causing Geneviève to shriek with laughter. It had been a long time since she'd met someone she was excited about, and Geneviève was excited about Roderick. Who wouldn't be? He was charming, ridiculously smart, thoughtful and kind.

From the moment he'd arrived in Madrid, he'd gone above and beyond his job description, and Geneviève appreciated everything he'd done for her. He made her feel special, as if she mattered to him, and he was so easy to talk to, she'd confided in him about her tumultuous childhood. Roderick had everything Geneviève wanted in a partner—the personality, the character, the intelligence and the good looks—but could they have a successful relationship? Or would he end up betraying her like everyone else in her past?

"Yesterday, I read in the local newspaper that you're dating a Real Madrid soccer player," Roderick said, raising an eyebrow. "Is it serious?"

"Boy, please. We took a picture together at my show, I signed a poster for his daughter and we hugged. End of story." Realizing she sounded bitter, she softened her tone. "Don't get me wrong, I'd love to settle down and have a family, but most of the guys I meet would rather hook up than get to know me as a person, so for now I'm happily single."

The wide-eyed expression on his face puzzled her, but Geneviève didn't ask Roderick why he was gawking at her. She was dying to know more about his personal life, and hoped he'd answer her questions truthfully this time. "What about you? Are you dating anyone special right now?"

Roderick scoffed. "Not if I can help it, but my family is making it hard for me."

"What does that mean?"

"My mom and my sister-in-law, Erikah, are determined to find me a wife ASAP, but since I refuse to go on blind dates with the women they choose, they've taken to sending females to my office damn near every day, and it's infuriating."

Gasping, Geneviève cupped a hand over her mouth. "No way! Are you serious?"

"At first, I thought it was amusing, but now I just want it to stop."

"I'm not trying to be insensitive, but most men would love to have that problem."

"Not me," he grumbled, cracking his knuckles. "I'm tired of females showing up at the law firm with home-made cookies, tickets to sporting events and dinner invitations—"

"Have you ever dated one of your clients?" she blurted out, her curiosity finally getting the best of her. The question had been on her mind all week, ever since Roderick had showed up at her hotel suite to meet with her, but she didn't have the courage to ask him—until now. The cocktails she'd had, and the gritty hip-hop song playing in the lounge, made Geneviève feel bold, and when Roderick met her gaze she said, "Go on, Counselor, answer the question. Don't worry. Your secrets are safe with me."

"I don't have any secrets. Furthermore, I've never dated a client, and I never will."

Disappointment filled her, but she forced her lips to move. "Why not?"

"As an attorney, I'm subject to codes of professional responsibility and ethics," he explained. "And the law firm has a strict conduct policy. I'd never want to do anything to humiliate them, myself or my family. Welker, Bradford and Davidson expect me to be a good steward of the firm, and I don't want to disappoint them."

"I'm surprised. You strike me as the kind of guy who likes to break the rules."

"I do, but only when I'm in the boxing ring with Morrison." Chuckling, he clasped his hands behind his head and crossed his legs at the ankles. "Ask anyone. I'm practically a saint."

Her eyebrows shot up. "A saint? I find that hard to believe. You have the words *bad boy* written all over your face, and I bet you've broken hearts in all fifty states."

"Contrary to what you think, I'm not a dog who mistreats women. I like to party, but nothing beats going home at the end of a long, grueling day to a woman I love, who loves me, too. Nothing at all. Not even courtside seats at the Knicks game."

Geneviève sucked in a breath. *Is Roderick serious? Does he really mean that? He'd rather be in a committed relationship than play the field?* His confession boggled her mind, but thinking about how caring and gentle he'd been toward her after that frightening incident at the tapas bar proved he was telling the truth...or was he? Geneviève cocked her head to the right. Something he'd said minutes earlier replayed in her mind, renewing her doubts. "If you're such a relationship guy, then why are you dead-set against your mother setting you up?"

"Would you date someone your father handpicked for you?"

Geneviève shivered at the thought. "God no! Dwight doesn't know anything about me. Hell, I love my mom, but I wouldn't let her hook me up either—"

"My point exactly. I'm a grown man. I can find my own wife, and when I'm ready, I will, but it won't be anytime soon."

"No? How come?" Geneviève asked, trying to sound nonchalant, even though she was secretly bummed by his confession. She wanted to date Roderick, but only if he was ready for a serious relationship. Her biological clock wasn't ticking, it was ringing louder than the Liberty Bell, and if she didn't do something about it soon she'd never fulfill her dreams of being a mother.

"Right now I'm focused on my career, and I don't want anything to distract me from achieving my goals." His brow was arched, his chin was set in determination and his voice was strong, full of conviction. "I'll do anything to become the first African American partner at Welker, Bradford and Johnson, and I have to put all my energy into fulfilling my dreams..."

Geneviève's iPhone rang. Glancing down at the table, she saw her mom's name and picture pop up on the screen, but decided to let the call go to voice mail. She sipped her cold, fruity drink. Eyeing Roderick over the rim of her cocktail glass, Geneviève listened as he spoke about his career, his long-term goals and his upcoming trip with his brothers to Los Cabos for Morrison's bachelor party in March. Their conversation turned to their favorite travel destinations, and when Roderick promised to take her bungee jumping in Nepal for Valentine's Day, she burst out laughing.

"Not on your life," she quipped, waving her hands furiously in front of her face. "I'm as adventurous as the next girl, and I love trying new things, but there's no way in hell I'm jumping headfirst off a cliff, so find another travel partner, homey."

"Don't be like that." Roderick winked. "You know I'll take good care of you."

His breath tickled her ear, and heat flowed through her body. Geneviève enjoyed hearing about his life, and wished he wasn't leaving for New York in three days. She was having such a good time joking around with

Roderick, she'd lost track of time, and if not for Demi blowing up her cell phone with dozens of text messages, demanding to know where she was, Geneviève would have stayed in the VIP lounge with Roderick until closing.

He was an open book. Transparent. Real. Sincere. And Geneviève liked that. Roderick was the kind of man other men wanted to be, and women wished they had at home—including Geneviève—and it blew her mind that he was still single.

"I've been on a lot of dates in my life, but I've never been on one that lasted twelve hours, across two cities, in one of my favorite countries in the world."

Lines wrinkled his forehead, and confusion darkened his eyes.

Realizing her mistake, her cheeks burned with shame. "I'm sorry. I shouldn't have said that. You're my attorney and nothing more. I know that."

"Don't apologize. It's not every day I get to kick it with an international pop star, and I'm enjoying your company. You're charming, and I'm fascinated by you."

I feel the same way about you. Her gaze zeroed in on his mouth, and when he licked his lips, Geneviève moaned inwardly. "It's not every day I meet a man who likes foreign films, winter sports and wine tasting, so you're definitely a keeper."

Roderick chuckled, and his deep, throaty laugh filled the lounge.

A waiter with blond dreadlocks swaggered into the room, stared right at her, and dread coursed through Geneviève's body. Stopping in front of the couch, he claimed to be her biggest fan, then flashed a toothy smile. She knew what was coming next, what he was about to say, and held her breath. He asked for her auto-graph and two tickets to her concert on Tuesday night. His behavior was unprofessional, but not unusual. Ser-vice people routinely asked her for favors, and normally she obliged, but Geneviève didn't want anyone to intrude on her time with Roderick, and asked the waiter to leave. "Not right now, but if you come back in an hour I'll see what I can do."

Mumbling under his breath, he sucked his teeth, then stalked out of the lounge.

"Do you want another cocktail, or something else from the bar?" Roderick asked.

"No, I'm good. I've had plenty tonight, and if I keep downing mai tais you'll be carrying me back to the car *and* tucking me in at the end of the night."

"With pleasure. I've always been a sucker for a beauti-ful woman, and you're a stunner." Roderick's phone rang, and he swiped it off the table. Frowning, he raised it in the air. "It's your mom. What do you want me to tell her?"

Geneviève waved her hands in the air. "Don't answer it. I'll talk to her later."

"I need to take you back to the hotel before Althea calls Madrid's finest and has me arrested for kidnap-ping," he joked, pulling his car keys out of his pocket. "Let's go, Geneviève."

No, Geneviève thought, downing the rest of her cock-tail. *What you* need *to do is take me back to your suite, rip off my clothes and make love to me!*

Chapter 10

The private elevator at Hotel du Lugo opened on the eighteenth floor, and Geneviève clutched Roderick's forearm. He stood tall, like a man who was proud of his body and comfortable in his skin, and his self-confidence was a turn-on. Made Geneviève want to kiss him all over. Her gaze slid down his physique, and she appreciated every hard, muscled inch.

"I had fun today, Geneviève. You're great company and you tell the best stories."

His charm was endearing, and his smile was so warm it melted her heart. Desire flooded her body, momentarily paralyzing her, but Geneviève forced her legs to move. Her feet ached, but she strode through the dimly lit corridor, humming the Boyz II Men song playing in her mind—the iconic hit about making love all through the night—and wondered if Roderick had sex on the brain, too. He squeezed her hands, and Geneviève suspected they shared the same thought. Every time he touched her, her emotions went haywire, spiraling out of control, but tonight her symptoms were worse. Her mouth was dry, her palms were wet—her panties, too—and it took every ounce of control Geneviève had not to back him into the wall, grab his shirt collar and plant one on him.

Slowing, Geneviève peeked around the corner. She hoped her mother didn't jump out of her hotel suite, ranting and raving about what an ungrateful daughter she was. Geneviève didn't want to upset her mom, but she refused to feel bad for taking a day off and spending it with Roderick. They'd had a great time together in the VIP lounge, and Geneviève wasn't ready for their marathon date to end. Their friendship was safe, unlike anything she'd ever experienced, and every time Roderick gazed into her eyes, she felt desirable, as if she was the only woman he wanted.

"I'll walk you to your suite. It's late, and I don't want anyone to bother you."

Stopping in front of suite 1824, Geneviève glanced at her gold diamond watch and tapped the glass. "It's only nine thirty. You're not turning in now, are you?"

"No, I'll probably watch a movie, or the rest of the Arsenal game."

"Good, I'll join you. I'm great company."

His eyebrows shot up. "You will?"

"Yeah, you're welcome." Winking, Geneviève plucked the hotel key card out of Roderick's hand, slid it into the slot beneath the metal door handle and pushed it open. "And since I'm your guest I get to choose the movie, got it?"

Roderick chuckled. "Knock yourself out. The remote's on the side table, beside the lamp."

Entering the suite, he flipped on the lights and closed the curtains. Geneviève flopped down on the couch, stretched her legs out on the coffee table and crossed them at the ankles. Using the remote control, she turned on the TV, accessed the movie app and selected a Japanese chick flick she was dying to see.

"You can't watch a movie without your favorite snack," Roderick said, with a lopsided grin. "Wait right here. I know just what you need…"

No you don't! If you did, we'd be making love.

Geneviève admired his profile. He carried himself with an air of authority, like a commander-in-chief, and she couldn't help staring at him. Her gaze followed him into the kitchen. The movie started, but Geneviève was more interested in watching Roderick than what was on the screen. She'd never made the first move on a guy, but if life had taught her anything, it was to live in the moment, and for the second time in minutes Geneviève was tempted to pounce on her devilishly handsome host.

"One bag of sweet and spicy wasabi popcorn coming right up."

Geneviève noticed the plastic bag in his hands, and shrieked. "No way! Where did you find this? I've looked everywhere for it, but I couldn't find it anywhere."

"They carry it at a tiny specialty store in Segovia, so when my web conference wrapped up yesterday I jumped in the Ferrari and made the trip."

"I can't believe you went all that way just to buy me my favorite snack. That's so sweet."

"I'd do anything for you. You're more than just a client. You're also a friend."

"Roderick, I'm crazy about you." Feeling free, as if

a weight had been lifted from her shoulders, she wore a girlish smile. "There, I said it."

"I think you've had too much to drink—"

"And I think you're scared of getting hurt." Geneviève rested a hand on his cheek and caressed his smooth brown skin. "It's understandable, considering everything your ex put you through, but you have to put the past behind you and move on. That's what survivors do. They get up, dust themselves off and walk boldly into their future."

Geneviève couldn't fight her feelings for him anymore, couldn't resist the desires of her flesh, and traced his lips with an index finger. Her attraction to him was so intense her body vibrated uncontrollably, and when Geneviève spoke she heard the need in her voice, the hunger. "All I can think about is kissing you, and touching you, and undressing you…"

It started with a long, lingering gaze that set her body on fire, then snowballed into something fierce—a passionate, sensuous kiss that Geneviève never saw coming. Their bodies collided, pressing hard against each other, and it was perfect. Everything Geneviève wanted. Needed. Desired. Craved. Feeling his mouth against hers, probing and teasing, proved he was desperate for her, too, and the realization bolstered her confidence. Made her feel sexier than a Playboy Bunny. The spicy flavors on his tongue aroused her taste buds, and his gentle caress along her shoulders was as welcome as a cocktail on a hot summer day.

Doubts assailed her mind, but his kiss soothed her fears. Their relationship had gone from zero to one hundred in minutes, but everything about being intimate with Roderick felt natural, right. And his fervor thrilled her. He acted as if he wanted every inch of her. As if he was desperate for her, and Geneviève loved it. His hands were in her hair, along her neck, shoulders and hips, stroking her quivering body through her clothes.

Nibbling on his bottom lip, Geneviève marveled at how good he tasted. His touch was everything, turning her on, and Geneviève couldn't get enough. Wanted to skip first base and hit a home run. She wished his hands were on her breasts, rubbing and tweaking her nipples, and she willed him to undress her, right then and there on the couch.

Her thoughts ran wild, and so did her hands. They moved through his hair, across his jaw, down his muscled shoulders, arms and chest. Climbing onto his lap, Geneviève cradled his face in her palms and pressed soft, light kisses against his lips. She rubbed her body against his, moving her hips in circles. Although she sang racy songs and wore revealing costumes onstage, Geneviève didn't have a lot of experience with the opposite sex, and wanted to know what Roderick liked in the bedroom. "Tell me what you want," she whispered against his mouth. "Does that feel good? Do you want more?"

Mischief twinkled in his eyes. "Yes, please!" he said, grabbing her ass.

Roderick brushed his lips against the hollow of her throat, then licked it with his tongue, sending shivers careening down her spine. Draping her hands around his neck, she sucked his earlobe into her mouth. Roderick pressed his eyes shut, gripped her hips roughly in his hands. She heard his groans, his heavy breathing, could feel his erection pressed against her inner thigh, and wished it was buried between her legs. She'd never met a sexier, more confident man, and making out with

Roderick was more exhilarating than performing to a sold-out crowd.

Kissing him, Geneviève gently tugged on his lower lip with her teeth, playfully nipping it. Lost in the moment, her vision blurred and she was breathing so loud it drowned out the TV. Kissing Roderick was a total-body experience, one that had no equal, and as they desperately explored each other's bodies, Geneviève realized she was in over her head. Out of control. Losing it. But that didn't stop her from stroking his forearms and rubbing her sex against his crotch.

Eager to make love, Geneviève undid the button on his pants, yanked down the zipper and slid a hand inside his boxer briefs, capturing his long, thick erection in her palm. Roderick covered her hands with his, and Geneviève froze. Stared up at him in confusion, wondering what she did wrong. She saw the troubled expression on his face and noticed his lips were moving, but her brain was so fuzzy she didn't understand what he was saying. Geneviève held her breath, waiting for the moment to pass. Her gut was telling her that something was wrong, and alarm bells rang in her ears, but Geneviève didn't want to leave her cozy spot on his lap. "You're a great kisser," she praised, pressing her lips against his collarbone. "The best I've ever had."

"Geneviève, this is wrong."

She licked his earlobe. "If sexing you is wrong, I don't want to be right."

"I'm serious," he said, sliding her off his lap. "I don't have any protection—"

"Then we'll go down to the hotel gift shop and buy some."

Roderick gripped her shoulders, and she stopped caressing his chest through his shirt.

"We can't do this."

"Why not?" Geneviève hated herself for not grabbing her things and marching out the door, but she didn't understand why he was suddenly giving her the cold shoulder. "You're attracted to me, and I feel the same way about you, so why are you pushing me away? What did I do wrong?"

Silence enveloped the room. Dropping his gaze to the floor, he rubbed his forehead with his hand.

"If I wasn't your attorney I wouldn't give a second thought to making love to you, but I don't want us to do something we're going to regret in the morning."

Her intuition told her he was lying, but before she could question him he spoke.

"It's late," he said, his eyes glued to the wall clock. "I'll walk you to your suite."

Geneviève rested a hand on his cheek and forced him to look at her. "Roderick, you're overthinking things. It's just one night. One incredible, passionate night with no strings attached, and no drama. What could be better?"

"Geneviève, you don't understand…" Shaking his head, he trailed off. Roderick grabbed the remote control off the couch, turned off the TV and stared at the blank screen.

"You're right, I don't understand, so talk to me because none of this makes sense."

"For me, it could never be one night. I'm just not wired that way."

The pained expression on his face spoke volumes to her. He was upset, and Geneviève felt like an ass for ruining his good mood. An hour ago, they'd been laugh-

ing and flirting in the VIP lounge, and now he looked
as if his dog had died. Had she made a mistake inviting
herself to his suite? Did he regret making out with her?

"I'm not a one and done kind of guy. I've never had
a one-night stand or…"

*Good! Me neither, but I'm willing to make an excep-
tion for you!*

"When I fall for someone I'm all in, 100 percent committed, and I expect the same from the woman I'm dating," he explained, with a sad smile. "But I can't date
you."

The earth stopped rotating on its axis. A cold breeze
blew into the room, chilling Geneviève to the bone. Unable to believe what she was hearing, she gawked at him.
Narrowed her eyes and studied him like a painting in a
museum. For a moment she thought he was teasing her,
trying to lighten the mood with a joke, but there was no
mistaking the vulnerability in his voice, or the emotion
behind his words.

"Geneviève, I'm attracted to you, and I think you're
an incredible woman, but if I hook up with you it could
have serious consequences for my career, and I don't
want to lose the best job I've ever had. I've worked too
hard for too long to let that happen."

His confession was a painful blow, but she found her
voice and spoke her truth.

"Don't I get a say in any of this? Doesn't it matter
what I want?"

"I hope you'll respect my decision."

"Let me get this straight. You want to be with me, but
you're worried about getting fired?" Geneviève spotted
her backpack at the foot of the couch, snatched it off the
floor and searched inside for her cell phone. "I'm going

to call Welker, Bradford and Davidson and request another attorney, effective immediately. Problem solved."

"Geneviève, please don't. The senior partners will think I'm ineffective and incompetent."

"Then I'll just have to convince them otherwise." Her mind made up, she took her cell phone out of her bag and punched in her password. She had dozens of text messages and missed calls from her mom, but she ignored them. Searching online for the number for the law firm, Geneviève rehearsed what she was going to say to Mr. Welker when they spoke, but a text message popped up on the screen from Demi, and every muscle in her body tensed.

Gigi, I hope you're not in Roderick's suite because mom is on her way there!

What! Her stomach churned, and panic drenched her skin. Geneviève surged to her feet, marched into the bathroom and studied her reflection in the mirror. Shocked by her disheveled appearance, she cringed at the image staring back at her. Her eyes were sad, her lips swollen and her ponytail a crooked, sloppy mess. Althea would take one look at her and know exactly what she'd been doing in Roderick's suite, but Geneviève didn't care. She was a grown woman, not a kid, and she wasn't going to apologize for living her life. She was an accomplished, successful woman, not a puppet, and she deserved to be treated with respect.

Someone banged on the door, and the noise shattered the silence. Thinking fast, Geneviève rushed into the living room and yanked Roderick away from the door. She couldn't think of anything worse than her mom dragging her out of the suite, and pressed a finger to her mouth to prevent Roderick from speaking. Geneviève feared what would happen if he opened the door, and sighed in relief when the pounding stopped and footsteps faded into the distance.

"Have you ever met the right person at the wrong time?" Roderick asked in a quiet voice.

Ignoring him, Geneviève snatched her bag off the couch, slung it over her shoulder and spun on her heels. Roderick caught her forearm and pulled her to his chest. Gazing up at him, her anger waned. There was so much she wanted to say, but Geneviève kept her feelings to herself. Her confession wasn't going to change anything, so why risk being vulnerable? He'd made his position clear, and Geneviève wasn't going to beg for his affection. Instead of fretting over Roderick—a man who obviously didn't want her—she was going to wait patiently for Mr. Right to come along. Geneviève only hoped that he'd be as thoughtful and chivalrous as Roderick, because even though she was disappointed in him, he was one of the kindest, sweetest people she'd ever met.

"I didn't mean to upset you." He released her hand.

"What did you *think* would happen?" she demanded, cocking her head. "You know what, Roderick? Just forget it. Forget I was here, forget we kissed and forget you know me."

"Geneviève, don't talk like that. We're friends, and I'd do anything to help you."

"Good, then get out of my way." Shocked by the bitterness of her tone and bothered by the pained look in his eyes, Geneviève considered apologizing for snapping at Roderick, but deleted the thought from her mind. He'd hurt her feelings, not the other way around, and she didn't owe him anything. "I'm out of here. Have a nice life."

"I meant what I said. I had a great time with you tonight—"

Geneviève barked a laugh, drowning out the rest of his sentence. "I'm confused. Was that before or after you rejected me?"

"You make it sound sinister, as if I willfully and intentionally set out to hurt you."

"Don't sweat it, Roderick, it's your loss, not mine," she whispered in a sultry voice, leaning forward to brush her mouth against his lips. "I was going to rock your world *all night long.*"

Geneviève smirked. The look on his face was priceless. His mouth sagged open and his Adam's apple bounced inside his throat.

"Good night, Counselor." Stepping past him, Geneviève yanked open the door and marched into the hallway. She felt a pang of guilt and paused, glancing over her shoulder to say, "I won't see you before you leave on Wednesday, but have a safe flight to New York."

He called out to her, but Geneviève continued through the corridor, even though the weight of his rejection felt like an albatross around her neck.

And if that isn't bad enough, I have to sneak into my suite without my mom catching me!

Chapter 11

Roderick stared at the bleak, cloud-covered sky as he strode toward the rooftop gym. Exercise was a great stress reliever, and staying fit was an important part of his image, so he jogged every day, rain or shine. And, after working in his suite for hours, he needed a mental break. Before rolling out of bed that morning, he'd checked his work emails, his voice mail and his social media accounts, and discovered that several of his clients were spiraling out of control. His first task of the day had been to negotiate a contract for an aging R&B singer, and arguing with the Cleveland native had given him a migraine. His job was to advocate for his clients and teach them how to evaluate contracts for benefits and pitfalls, but she wouldn't listen to him, arguing that she deserved more money from her record label. When he returned to New York, he'd meet with her face-to-face, and explain his point of view.

The blustery morning breeze whipped through the air, and the clouds were darker than night, but Roderick wasn't worried about the impending rainstorm; he was worried about Geneviève. Had been ever since she stormed out of his suite on Saturday night. She'd knocked him off his game, and now he couldn't think straight. Couldn't think of anything but her, even though he had tons of paperwork to do. Every time Roderick closed his eyes, he saw Geneviève glaring back at him. Forty-eight hours later, her words still played in his mind, tormenting him. *You're attracted to me, and I feel the same way about you, so why are you pushing me away?*

Roderick yawned, then stretched his arms across his chest to loosen his sore muscles. His brain wouldn't shut off long enough for him to sleep, and last night he'd tossed and turned until his alarm clock went off at 5:00 a.m. He'd replayed every moment of his sightseeing excursion with Geneviève—their marathon lunch, their afternoon hike, flirting and dancing at the VIP lounge, hanging out in his suite—and wished he'd never asked her out. Not because he didn't like her, but because he couldn't control his feelings for her. It was hard to look at her and not think about kissing her…touching her…licking every inch of her delicious body.

Hooking up with Geneviève was risky. Reckless. Stupid. He knew the firm's rules, knew what was at stake, and he didn't want to do something he'd regret. Geneviève was a distraction—a five-foot-nine temptress with ridiculous sex appeal—and nothing good could come of them being lovers. He had to guard his heart against her. Sneaking around with Geneviève would be career suicide, especially if things went sour, and Roderick didn't want history to repeat itself. The last time he'd let his guard down he'd been burned, and he wasn't going down that road again.

Roderick bent down, tied his shoelaces, then set the timer on his Apple watch for one hour. The U-shaped rooftop track was his favorite amenity at the five-star hotel, and even though the weather was gray and gloomy, the outdoor gym was filled with dozens of other guests.

Putting on his wireless headphones, he adjusted the volume, turning it up loud to block out the noises around him. Rap music played in his ears, and the song made him think of Geneviève. They'd danced to it at the restaurant-lounge, and he remembered how they'd talked and flirted in the VIP area for hours. What struck him about Geneviève was how smart she was. Outspoken and animated, she enjoyed discussing social issues, world history and hot topics. Her stories were fascinating, her laughter infectious and her impressions of Althea and Demi made him chuckle long and hard.

Roderick ran full speed on the track, vigorously pumping his arms, but he couldn't outrun his thoughts. He had a soft spot for Geneviève, had since the day they met, and he wanted to make things right with her before he left Madrid. He'd reached out to her several times over the past two days, but she hadn't returned any of his calls or text messages. Thankfully, Demi did, and gave him daily updates about her sister. She'd invited him to Geneviève's concert and the wrap party afterward in the hotel lounge, and he'd accepted. He wasn't missing Geneviève's last show in Madrid for anything. Roderick didn't know what to expect when he saw her that evening, and hoped she wouldn't shut him out again.

Feeling energized by being outdoors, Roderick mentally reviewed his schedule for the rest of the week. He spent most of his day speaking to clients, managers, agents and record studio executives on the phone, and although he was thousands of miles away from New York, his agenda was jam-packed. He juggled dozens of business deals at one time, and when he wasn't writing, editing and reviewing contracts, he was advising his clients about the pitfalls of the music industry.

His first order of business tomorrow was a nine o'clock meeting at Madrid Law, but Roderick wasn't worried. The story of Geneviève assaulting José Sánchez was old news, and now Mr. Cabrero was sweating bullets because he didn't have any leverage. To make them disappear once and for all, Roderick would offer the scheming twosome a six-figure cash settlement, and he was confident they would take the money and run.

"I figured I'd find you here, running your ass off, but slow down, man. I'm out of shape!" Demi appeared, holding her cell phone in one hand and a water bottle in the other. "How is my favorite attorney doing this morning?"

"Hey, Demi." Stopping, he wiped the sweat from his brow with his wristband and dropped down on a metal bench. He needed a pick-me-up, something to take his mind off his troubles, and Demi was the perfect distraction. Moreover, he wanted to know how Geneviève was doing. Was she still mad at him? Had she read his text messages? Had she changed her mind about doing the reality TV dating show? She'd mentioned it on Saturday, and now it was all he could think about. Roderick worried Geneviève wasn't strong enough to stand up to her mother and would eventually agree to the offer. "How's it going?"

"Great! I just finished having brekkie, and it was so good my mouth is *still* watering!"

"Did you eat with Geneviève?" he asked, curious about his favorite client. "Where is she?"

"Rehearsing at the arena, of course. She's been at it nonstop since yesterday." Demi beamed. "Tonight's the big finale, and Gigi's pulling out all the stops for her Madrid fans."

"I need to see her, Demi. I have to apologize for the other night."

Leaning over, she patted his cheek. "You'll see her. I promise. Be patient."

"I'm trying, but I feel like an ass, and I want to make things right with her."

"You should!" she quipped. "Gigi's crushing on you big-time, and you blew it, man!"

Adorable in a hot pink crop top, leggings and sneakers, the personal assistant looked like a college freshman, and her bright outfit attracted the attention of the other guests at the gym.

"Demi, you're wrong. We're just friends—"

"Sure, sure, and this is my natural hair color!" Giggling at her joke, she gave him a shot in the ribs with her elbow. "Roderick, you don't have to pretend with me. I know you have feelings for my sister, and I think you're just the kind of man Gigi needs, so don't screw this up. I'm counting on you."

A bitter taste filled his mouth. He hadn't done anything wrong, but he felt guilty about what had happened in his suite with Geneviève on Saturday night. He'd lied to her about not having any condoms, and even though he'd had to take two cold showers after she left, he didn't regret his decision. He couldn't risk losing his career, or jeopardizing his promotion. To turn her scowl into a smile, he joked, "Demi, are you sure you're a personal assistant and not a therapist, because you sure sound like one."

"A therapist?" she repeated, with an amused expression on her face.

"Yeah, from now on I'm going to call you Dr. Demi, because you love to give advice—"

"I almost forgot, I have to show you something." Moving closer to him on the bench, Demi crossed her legs and raised her iPhone in the air. "Check this out."

Groaning, Roderick shook his head. "No more cat videos. I know you and Geneviève think they're hilarious, but I don't, and the one you showed me yesterday was downright creepy."

"It's not. I promise. A woman from Cádiz just posted this video to my social media page, and I think it's the footage you've been looking for."

Demi gestured to her iPhone with a flick of her head.

"Just watch," she said, in a stern voice. "Trust me, you want to see this."

Roderick took off his sunglasses and peered at the screen. The video was grainy and the sound was poor, but he recognized the Madrid-Barajas International Airport—and Geneviève.

At the sight of her, his mouth dried and his heart swelled. Clad in a denim blouse tied at the waist, slim-fitted white pants and pointy heels, she'd moved through the airport terminal with inherent grace, smiling and waving at the crowd. Outside, she'd stopped to blow kisses, sign autographs and take pictures with her pint-size fans.

Intrigued, he grabbed the iPhone from Demi's hands and moved it closer to his face. His teeth clenched, and if his pulse were beating any louder he'd be deaf. The video proved that Geneviève was telling the truth about the incident at the airport on New Year's Day. José Sánchez *had* grabbed her. His first thought was to find the smug, slick college student and pummel him into the ground, but Roderick remembered he was an attorney, not a WWE wrestler, and shook his head to clear his mind. Now that he had the footage, he had the upper hand, and Roderick planned to use it to his advantage.

"Demi, you're a lifesaver. Can you email this video to me, and all of the other footage you have?"

"Of course. No problem."

"Thanks, I appreciate it."

"No worries. It'll give me something to do while I wait for my boyfriend to call me back." Standing, she wore an apologetic smile. "Roderick, I have to go, but—"

"Where are you rushing off to? You just got here," he said, raising an eyebrow.

"I know, but I have to pick up Geneviève's costumes for tonight's show at a nearby boutique, and if I'm not at the arena by noon she'll flip out."

"Really? That's so unlike her. She's so chill, and easygoing."

"Yeah, well, ever since you rejected her she's been a bear to live with." Demi punched him in the forearm. "Thanks a lot, Roderick."

Wincing, he rubbed at his upper shoulder. "Have you ever considered a career in boxing? You should because you have one hell of a jab."

"And don't you forget it. I think you're mad cool, but

if you hurt my sister again I'll give you the worst beating of your life," she warned, shaking a fist in his face.

At first, Roderick thought Demi was joking, but when her gaze narrowed and a scowl twisted her lips, he realized she was serious. "I thought we were friends."

"We are, but blood is thicker than water, and I'll do anything to protect my sister."

Roderick slowly nodded. "Point taken."

"Good!" Waving, her eyes brightened and her smile returned. "Adios, Roderick! See ya!"

Hanging his head, Roderick rubbed a hand along the back of his neck. He sat on the bench, deliberating over lifting weights inside the enclosed gym or returning to his suite to prepare for his one o'clock web conference with a country singer he represented. The petite powerhouse needed legal guidance, and Roderick was glad she'd reached out to him for advice after receiving her first spokesperson deal with a cosmetic company.

His cell phone rang, and Roderick stared down at the screen. Fear coiled through his body. It was his boss. Again. It was the third time Mr. Welker had called that morning, and although Roderick had nothing new to report since their last conversation, he knew if he didn't answer, his boss would be pissed. His mind returned to Saturday night, to the exact moment he kissed Geneviève, and every muscle in his body tensed. He knew why Mr. Welker was blowing up his phone, why his boss was desperate to speak to him. He'd bet everything he owned that Ms. Harris had called his boss to complain. She'd done it before, but this time, Roderick was guilty. He'd fooled around with Geneviève inside his hotel suite, and even though he doubted she'd confided in Althea about their argument, it wouldn't have been hard for the momager to put two and two together.

Roderick swiped his finger across the screen, then put his iPhone to his ear. "Hello, sir, how are—"

Before the question was out of his mouth, Mr. Welker cut him off. His voice was stern, colder than ice, and Roderick knew he was in trouble with his longtime mentor and ally.

"Roderick, have you been making sexual advances toward Geneviève?"

His thoughts scattered, and sweat drenched his sleeveless nylon shirt.

"I just got off the phone with Ms. Harris, and to say she's upset is an understatement."

"Sir, I've never harassed anyone. I'm a professional, and I act as such at all times." He paused, decided it was important to speak his mind and said, "Ms. Harris isn't upset at me. She's upset because Geneviève has a mind of her own, and won't be controlled or pushed around anymore."

"I figured as much but I thought it was important I touch base with you," he said. "I'm just glad you were able to convince Geneviève to finish the rest of her European tour. It would have been a nightmare if she'd made good on her threat and returned to Philly, but thanks to you, a crisis was averted. Good work, Roderick."

"Thank you, sir, but I was just doing my job."

Mr. Welker cleared his throat. "For the sake of peace, and to get Ms. Harris off my back, Elliot will handle all of Geneviève's legal affairs from here on out."

Old man Elliot? He can't work with Geneviève! He's senile, short-tempered and he hates pop music! The golf enthusiast wanted to retire but couldn't afford it, and the last time Roderick spoke to the silver-haired attorney, he'd admitted to being burned-out. "Sir, with all due respect I don't think that's a good idea. Geneviève needs an attorney who has the stamina to keep on top of her demanding schedule."

"Are you questioning my decision making?" he asked, raising his voice. "I hope not, because it would be a mistake on your part. This is *my* law firm, and you'll do as you're told."

Roderick stared down at his cell phone. Mr. Welker was unlike his usual calm, unflappable self, and he suspected that Althea had gotten under the senior partner's skin. It didn't surprise him. The momager was a force, and his aging boss was no match for the ballsy Philly native.

"We have a problem, Roderick..."

Another *one?* he thought, pinching the bridge of his nose. *What now?*

"I need you back here pronto, so pack your bags and head to the airport. The company jet is waiting for you, and I expect you to be on the aircraft within the hour."

His shoulders slumped. He wanted to see Geneviève's final show, and even though she was mad at him, he wanted to speak to her before he left Madrid. "Sir, what's going on?"

"An Italian fashion designer contacted Darla Day's agent about her being his celebrity spokesperson, and Darla wants you to handle the negotiations. You know just what to say, what strings to pull and buttons to press, and she's confident you'll secure another million-dollar deal for her," he explained. "The meeting is tomorrow morning at 9:00 a.m. sharp, so you'll need to go straight to the company's headquarters after landing at JFK."

"I thought Theodore was filling in for me during my absence."

"He is, but Darla says he's softer than a tissue and refuses to work with him…"

The joke tickled Roderick's funny bone, but he didn't laugh. Didn't want his boss to think he was making light of the situation, or rejoicing in his colleague's suffering. Roderick liked the single dad and thought he was a good attorney, even though he wore his heart on his sleeve.

"And Darla's not the only one who's complained about his lackluster performance. All of your clients are eagerly awaiting your return, so shake a leg. The firm needs you."

Roderick chose his words carefully. After being reamed out by Ms. Harris, his boss was in a bad mood, and he didn't want to antagonize him. "Sir, you can count on me," he said, nodding to underscore his point even though his boss couldn't see him. "Tell Elliot to hang tight. I'll meet him at the airport, and we can discuss the Sánchez case before I take off."

"Elliot's not in Madrid. He's here, hard at work in his office."

"Then who's going to meet with José Sánchez and his attorney tomorrow morning?" For effect, he spoke in a somber tone. "I shudder to think what will happen when Ms. Harris finds out we canceled at the last minute. As you can imagine, she's still upset about the video that was posted online, and anxious to have this issue resolved."

"Yes," he conceded. "She told me that when we spoke earlier today, among other things."

Roderick wanted to say more, to remind his boss that Althea had threatened to find another law firm several times, but held his tongue. He'd said his peace and needed to be patient, didn't want Mr. Welker to know he was desperate to remain in Madrid.

"It's imperative you strike a deal with Mr. Sánchez before you leave town, so stay put." Raising his voice, he spoke with authority, like the president addressing the Senate. "We can't afford to lose Geneviève as a client, so do whatever it takes to keep her mother happy..."

Roderick scoffed. There wasn't enough money in the word to make that happen, but he didn't tell his boss the truth. Didn't want to argue with his mentor. Making peace with Althea was a tall order, but Roderick was up for the challenge. Would do anything to get the job done.

Loud noises seized his attention. He saw couples laughing and tracksuit-clad seniors power walking around the track. He heard animated conversation and the distant sound of Spanish music.

"Also, meet privately with Geneviève to ensure you haven't done anything to offend her."

With pleasure. Roderick had two more days in Madrid, and he planned to make the most of it. A prisoner of his thoughts, he relived his argument with Geneviève, and wondered how she was faring at rehearsals. Smoothing things over with her was his top priority, and he would, even if it meant apologizing a hundred times.

"You're the boss," Roderick said, pleased that his plan had worked. "Once we get off the phone, I'll call Ms. Day and touch base with her about the spokesperson deal. If we can't reschedule the meeting for later in the week, I'll Skype in from my hotel suite."

"Excellent work, son. Keep it up and you'll be senior partner in no time."

Guilt stabbed his conscience, and his tongue was so heavy in his mouth he couldn't speak.

"Remember what I said about Ms. Harris. Losing her as a client would be a huge blow, and the firm would hold you personally responsible."

Gritting his teeth, Roderick gripped his cell phone so tight a sharp, searing pain shot through his hand. He couldn't believe Mr. Welker could praise him and threaten him in the same conversation, but instead of lashing out at his boss he said, "I understand, sir, and I'll do everything in my power to ensure that doesn't happen."

Ending the call, he pocketed his cell phone and stood. Raindrops were falling, splashing on his sweaty face. Exiting the rooftop gym, he couldn't shake the feeling that Geneviève was in trouble, and with each step Roderick took his fears grew.

Chapter 12

"*Geneviève! Geneviève! Geneviève!*"

The crowd at WiZink Center chanted, shouted and screamed Geneviève's name, and as Roderick glanced around the darkened arena, he was blown away by the love and adoration the Madrid fans had for the American pop star. The air in the arena was electrified, the noise deafening and the energy so infectious Roderick joined in the revelry.

Standing backstage beside Demi, who was furiously Tweeting, posting and blogging about the sold-out show, Roderick watched Geneviève rock the stage. Whip the crowd into a frenzy. Prove to everyone in attendance that she was an icon, one in a million. A dynamic entertainer and an equally incredible woman, it was impossible for Roderick to take his eyes off her. He'd been an entertainment attorney for almost a decade, but he'd never met anyone like her. Never heard thousands of people lose their collective minds over one woman—a vibrant, mesmerizing woman with jaw-dropping vocals and stellar dance moves. The special effects, the dazzling light display and the home videos and pictures playing on the JumboTron caused the crowd to gasp, then cheer. Geneviève was exciting her fans with every flip of her hair and twirl of her hips.

Roderick whistled. Her stage presence and her blinged-out costumes were eye-catching. There was no denying it—Geneviève was a legend in the making. Impressed by her performance, he decided to capture the moment on his cell, and took it out of his back pocket. Roderick didn't know how Geneviève danced around the stage in a frilly, one-shoulder dress, and heeled, over-the-knee boots, and was blown away by her stamina.

Snapping his fingers, he bobbed his head to the music and tapped his feet on the floor. The strong, pulsing beat made him think of making love to her, and the way she moved seductively across the stage caused an erection to rise in his boxer briefs. Having been to the previous three concerts, Roderick knew "Savage" was the last song on the set list, and when Geneviève bowed, Roderick cheered louder than anyone.

She was more than just a pop star with stunning looks; she was a humanitarian who wanted to change the world. She visited sick children in hospitals, took social issues to heart and used her platform to draw attention to worthy causes. Geneviève was the kind of person he'd love to bring home to his family. Smart, independent women, who cared about others, were hard to find, and everything about her captivated him.

"Good night, Madrid. I love you!" she said into the

microphone, waving at the audience. "Thanks for the support! I couldn't have done any of this without you—"

In a blink, a scrawny man with spiky hair grabbed Geneviève's ankle and yanked her toward him. Fear flashed in her eyes, and her lips parted in surprise. The microphone slipped from her hand and dropped on the stage with a bang. Her legs slipped out from underneath her, and Geneviève fell flat on her back.

Roderick lowered the camera from his face and shoved it into his pocket. Blood rushed to his brain, filling him with anger. He wanted to run to Geneviève and scoop her up in his arms, but her bodyguards slid in front of him, blocking his path. Security personnel rushed to Geneviève's side, helped her to her feet, then escorted her offstage.

Wanting to comfort her, Roderick stepped forward, but Althea pushed him aside and wrapped her arms around her daughter's hunched shoulders. Tears streamed down Geneviève's cheeks, splashing onto her designer outfit, and she was shaking uncontrollably. Her sadness was so profound it oozed from her pores, and listening to her cry broke Roderick's heart.

"Sweetie, don't cry," Althea said in a soothing voice. "You're okay. Mom's here now…"

Inclining his head, Roderick watched mother and daughter with growing interest. He couldn't believe what he was seeing. Althea wiped Geneviève's cheeks, then stroked her long, wavy hair, and slowly rubbed her back.

Maybe I was wrong about her, he thought, following behind them. *Maybe there's more to Althea than meets the eye.*

"Gigi, what do you need? What can I do to help?" Demi rushed to the dressing room, unlocked the door, then threw it open. "Come in, Gigi. I'll get you some ice for your head."

The trio disappeared inside the dressing room, and the door closed in Roderick's face. He wanted to settle the score with the overzealous fan in the front row, but people were filing out of the arena, and Roderick couldn't find the man in the crowd. He wasn't leaving until he saw Geneviève, even if he had to stay at the arena for the rest of the night. She had a week off before traveling to Berlin, and if he didn't have an important function to attend on Friday, he'd stay with Geneviève in Madrid. One of the artists he represented had written the lead single for the soundtrack to an Avengers movie, and Roderick wanted to support the rock singer at the LA première. He was expected to attend all of his clients' press conferences, parties and concerts, even if it conflicted with his free time, and often spent his weekends driving from one social event to the other.

Janitors swept the corridor, and staff cleaned the empty arena. Supervisors clutching wooden clipboards shouted orders, and security personnel marched about, glancing over their shoulders. Geneviève's band, bodyguards and crew members stood in the hallway, chatting while they waited for their fallen leader to emerge from her dressing room.

Leaning against the wall outside of Geneviève's dressing room, he blocked out the noises around him and listened to the conversation the Harris women were having inside. For the first time ever, Roderick agreed with Althea. The momager was right; Geneviève's fall was no big deal. In his seven years at Welker, Bradford and Davidson, he'd seen worse—bandmates fighting, drunken artists getting sick onstage, an indie singer de-

stroying her boyfriend's sports car with a baseball bat—
and knew in a couple days the story of Geneviève's fall
would die down and social media would find someone
else to hassle.

"Gigi, it's no big deal. Singers fall onstage all the time,"
Althea said, her tone matter-of-fact. "I know you're upset,
but I wouldn't be a good momager if I didn't tell you the
truth. Forget about what happened tonight, and move on.
It's not worth fretting over."

"That's easy for you to say!" Geneviève shouted.
"You're not the one being roasted online! Do you know
what people are saying about me?"

Demi spoke up. "No, and we don't care. Sweetie, you're
a star. Who cares what the haters think? Ignore them—"

"You guys don't get it. This isn't just about the fall,"
Geneviève said in a shaky voice. "I'm exhausted. I need
a break. Why can't you see that?"

Footsteps pounded on the floor, then a door slammed
and silence fell across the room.

Roderick yawned and rubbed at his eyes. After leaving the rooftop track earlier that day, he'd returned to
his hotel suite to prepare for his one o'clock web conference. He'd contemplated ordering room service, but
had decided to call Demi to check up on Geneviève. Her
sister had reported that Geneviève was good, and he'd
sighed in relief. All afternoon, he'd worked in his suite,
tackling every challenge that came his way, and even
though Roderick was tired, he couldn't leave the arena.
He went the extra mile for his clients, no matter what,
and would do everything in his power to help Geneviève,
to cheer her up.

Roderick took his iPhone out of his pocket and punched
in his password. To pass the time, he checked his email,

answered messages and surfed the internet. Several media
outlets had posted the video of Geneviève's fall, and the
comments posted were cruel and malicious. Two hours
ago, her Madrid fans were applauding her, and now they
were making fun of her online. Roderick couldn't imagine what Geneviève was going through, and hoped the
carnations he'd had delivered to her dressing room that
afternoon brightened her mood. It bothered him that she
was upset. Geneviève should have been basking in the
worldwide success of her sixth studio album and her sold-
out European tour, not hiding out in her dressing room.

An hour passed. Hunger pains stabbed Roderick's
empty stomach. He considered going to the concession
stand to buy something to eat, but worried if he left,
he'd miss seeing Geneviève when she emerged from her
dressing room. Roderick was on his cell phone, reading
an endorsement contract from a popular tech brand for
a heavy metal group he represented, but when he heard
Geneviève's voice he shoved his iPhone into his pocket.

"Mom, I'm not doing any press, and that's final."

The door cracked opened, and Geneviève shuffled
into the corridor, flanked by her mother and sister. Her
sunglasses were on, her head was down, and a Gucci bag
dangled from her wrist. She'd changed out of her costume and into a black cropped hoodie, wide-leg pants
and canvas sneakers. Her damp hair was in a bun, and
she smelled of tropical fruit. She looked melancholy, with
lifeless eyes and a hopeless disposition. Walking seemed
to require all the energy she had. He could see the stress
on her face, the anguish, and longed to take her into his
arms, but thought better of it. Althea was glaring at him,
and Roderick didn't want any trouble. Arguing with the

momager was mentally draining, and if he did, she'd probably call his boss to complain again.

"Geneviève, you were incredible tonight," he said, meaning every word. "I'm sorry about what happened at the end of the concert, and I hope you're not too upset. Are you okay?"

Her feet slowed, but she didn't stop. He walked alongside the trio, and when Demi paused to speak to the members of Divalicious, he moved closer to Geneviève.

"I'm fine, Roderick. Don't worry about me."

"I never worry about you. You're extraordinary. You always land on your feet."

Fine lines wrinkled her forehead.

"We'll talk at the wrap party," he said, raising his voice to be heard over the noise in the corridor. "Make sure you save me a seat at your table. I want to hear all about your—"

"I'm not going. I'm tired, and I need to rest."

Roderick checked his watch, saw the time and frowned. She was lying, trying to push him away. He knew from previous conversations they'd had that Geneviève was a night owl, who stayed up late writing songs, watching movies and playing word games on her iPhone, but he decided not to argue with her. Grateful that Althea was too busy on her phone to notice him, Roderick reached out and clasped Geneviève's hand. "Can we have lunch on Wednesday in the hotel restaurant?" he asked. "My flight's at four, but I need to talk to you before I leave. We have a lot to discuss."

Slinging an arm around their shoulders, Demi emphatically nodded and joked, "We'll be there or my name isn't Super Demi!"

Demi giggled, but Geneviève wore a blank expression on her face.

Althea glanced up from her cell phone and jabbed an index finger in Roderick's chest.

"Get away from my daughters," she hissed. "Celebrity attorneys are nothing but glorified babysitters, but Gigi doesn't need you. She has *me*, and I'm not going anywhere."

Roderick bristled at her insult, but he didn't speak. He knew who he was, and what he'd accomplished in his career, and he didn't care what Althea thought of him. Though he did care what she said to his boss. For that reason, he maintained his cool.

"Mom, stop it." Demi took Althea aside and spoke through clenched teeth. "Roderick's been great to Gigi, and we've loved having him here with us in Madrid. He outwitted that pervert who grabbed Gigi at the airport, saved her from a mugger at a tapas bar *and* persuaded her to finish the rest of the European tour when no one else could—"

Althea sucked her teeth. "Please, that wasn't his doing. It was mine."

Geneviève exited the front doors of the arena, slipped into the back seat of one of the three limousines parked along the curb and disappeared behind the tinted glass. Fans surrounded the vehicle, shouting her name, banging on the windows and snapping pictures with their cell phones. Her band and bodyguards filed into the other chauffeured cars, and the convoy sped off.

Exiting the arena, Roderick tossed a glare at the mob and shook his head. No wonder Geneviève was sick of the spotlight and eager to take a hiatus from the music business. He didn't blame her; in fact, he finally understood why she was at the end of her rope. Like the record label, her fans didn't respect her personal boundaries and seemed to think her feelings didn't matter. She'd been riding a wave of popularity for years, and was so relatable and down-to-earth people flocked to her everywhere she went, but it was obvious the nonstop attention was getting to her, wearing her down.

Heading toward the parking garage, he noticed street performers, chic bars and restaurants, and elegant shops. Friends, couples and suit-clad businessmen clutching coffee cups strolled up the block, their voices carrying on the cool evening breeze.

Roderick heard his cell phone ring inside his pocket, took it out and checked the number. It was a video call from Morrison, and the moment he heard his brother's voice he smiled. They used to butt heads constantly, used to squabble and fight nonstop, but these days they were closer than ever, and Morrison was his biggest supporter. He'd been there for him when Roderick needed him most, and if not for his brother coming to his rescue when he'd run into trouble with the Securities and Exchange Commission, there was no telling where Roderick would be. Morrison had loaned him the money he needed to pay the million-dollar fine, and the day he paid him back they'd celebrated with Duane at their favorite cigar bar.

"How are things going in Madrid?" Morrison asked.

"Great. I have a few loose ends to tie up tomorrow morning, then it's back to New York."

He raised an eyebrow. "Bro, where are you?"

"I'm just leaving WiZink arena," Roderick explained. Arriving at the parking lot, he searched for his Ferrari, found it sandwiched between two compact cars with foreign license plates and used the smart key to unlock the doors. "Tonight was Geneviève's final show in Madrid, and she blew me away. She's one hell of a performer—"

"Bro, are those tears in your eyes?" Morrison moved his iPhone closer to his face and stared intently at the screen, as if he was mystified by what he saw. "We'll, I'll be damned. You traveled to Madrid for work and fell in love."

"Morrison, knock it off. No one's in love." Roderick slid inside the Ferrari, slammed the door and put on his seat belt. "Geneviève's a client, and nothing more."

Karma came up behind Morrison, put her chin on his shoulder and waved frantically.

"Hi, handsome! I miss you. When are you coming home?"

"Never," Morrison said with a wry laugh, his eyes alive with mischief. "He's crushing so hard on Geneviève, we may never see him again, and that's a shame if you ask me. Who am I going to beat up in the ring when I need to let off some steam?"

Karma screamed so loud Roderick feared he'd go deaf, and rubbed at his ears.

"You're dating my shero? The pop star I've been obsessed with since I was sixteen? That's amazing!" Squealing, Karma plucked the phone out of Morrison's hand and danced around the room. "I'm so excited I could scream!"

Roderick winced. "You just did, *twice*, and it pierced my eardrum."

"Back to you and Geneviève. How did you guys meet? Are you serious about her? Was it love at first sight?" Giggling, she dismissed her words with a flick of her hand. "That's a dumb question. Of course it was love at first sight. She's a bombshell!"

You're right, she is, he thought, as images of Geneviève

onstage flashed in his mind, *but she's also fun and thought-ful and kind, and I love her outrageous sense of humor.*

"You *have* to get her to sing at our wedding," she continued. "It'll be your present to us."

Chuckling, he started the car and turned on the air condition. Karma Sullivan, his future sister-in-law, had the energy of three women, and every time he talked to the salon owner she made him crack up. Karma was easy to like, and everyone in their family loved her. She went on shopping trips with his mom and sister-in-law, cheered on the Yankees with his ailing father and helped Reagan with her college work. Best of all, Morrison had changed for the better, and after years of being a bachelor he was ready to marry and start a family.

"Karma, I'm not dating anyone. Geneviève's a client, who I happen to be good friends with but that's it—"

"Yeah, for now," she quipped, with a cheeky smile. "You're a Drake, and I know how you guys operate with the ladies, so it's just a matter of time before you and Geneviève are an item. And when it happens I want to be the first to know, so hit me up on my cell, got it?"

Cruising out of the parking lot, Roderick pretended not to hear her question. Karma was a popular hairdresser, with a high-end salon in the Hamptons, but she could out-argue anyone, and Roderick didn't want to be her latest victim. "Karma, I have to run, but tell Morrison I'll hit him up in the morning."

"No, call him before your flight," she instructed, twirling an auburn lock of hair around a finger. "We have wedding stuff to do after breakfast, and I don't want Morrison to be distracted when we're choosing flowers and sampling cake."

"Yes, of course, we can't have that now, can we?

Everything has to be perfect for the wedding of the century, or life as we know it will be over."

"Watch it, Ro, or I'll tell Ms. Viola you're teasing me, and she'll slap you into next week."

Roderick pretended to shiver. "Oohhh. I'm shaking in my Jordans."

"You should be. Your mama doesn't play."

"Tell me about it," he conceded, recalling his conversation with his mother days earlier. "The last time I spoke to her she threatened to give me a good, old-fashioned beat down if I didn't agree to take her friend's daughter to a charity gala next month."

Karma made her eyes wide, and spoke in an awe-filled voice. "And why would you when you have the lovely Geneviève firmly in your sights?"

He heard Morrison laughing in the background, chuckling as if he were watching a comedy special on HBO, and knew his brother was enjoying their conversation.

"Bye, Karma," he said, eager to end the phone call. "Have a good night."

"I will. Love you, Ro. Give my best to Geneviève, my future sister-in-law!"

Roderick ended the call, but he could still hear Karma's voice echoing in his mind. *You're a Drake, and I know how you guys operate with the ladies, so it's just a matter of time before you and Geneviève are an item.* He jacked up the volume on the stereo system, but as he drove along the freeway, Karma's words rang in his ears—and for some strange reason her bold, outrageous prediction excited him.

Chapter 13

Roderick took off his Ray-Ban aviators, boarded the hotel elevator and leaned against the wall. The space smelled of cheap perfume, and the fragrance overwhelmed his nostrils, causing him to sneeze. A brunette in a tangerine bikini and stilettos winked at him, but he lowered his gaze to his iPhone, punched in his password, then checked his work email. His meeting at Madrid Law had gone better than expected, and Roderick was in such a good mood he wanted to celebrate—with Geneviève.

He'd played the footage Demi had sent him for José Sánchez and his attorney, and once they watched the forty-second video they were sweating, and stammering. Ten minutes after arriving at the law firm, Roderick was out the front door. He'd emailed Mr. Welker the good news, and his boss had called him immediately, eager for more details. After giving a play-by-play about his meeting, he'd returned to the hotel. He wanted to shower and change before his lunch date with Demi and Geneviève, and worried if he was late they'd leave.

Yesterday, while buying souvenirs for his niece and nephews at the ABC Serrano shopping center, he'd also bought gifts for Geneviève, and planned to give them to her at lunch. Roderick was proud of her for continuing the European tour, even though she was desperate to return to her home in Philly, and hoped she loved the presents he'd bought her.

The elevator pinged, the doors slid open on the eighteenth floor and Roderick marched down the hallway, whistling a tune. He was feeling great, energized after his meeting at Madrid Law, and just the thought of seeing Geneviève again made him smile. Last night, after returning to his suite he'd texted her but she hadn't responded to any of his messages. The footage of her fall was all over the internet, but he hoped Geneviève had put the incident behind her and was in better spirits today.

A text message popped up on his cell phone. Reading it, Roderick pumped his fist. His day just kept getting better. He enjoyed developing his clients, derived great joy from helping the artists on his roster achieve their dreams, and the Bronx rapper he'd inked a multimillion-dollar contract last month was a superstar in the making. The nineteen-year-old had performed at a charity event that benefited victims of the nightclub shooting in Orlando, and his thirty-minute set had received stellar reviews.

"You bastard! Where is she? Where is my daughter?"

Roderick glanced up from his iPhone, saw Althea marching toward him and groaned.

What now? he thought, tempted to duck inside his suite and slam the door. *What is her problem?*

And why was she yelling? Her short, auburn wig was crooked, and she was breathing so hard her cheeks looked like puffed wheat. The momager was shouting and cursing, waving her arms wildly in the air as she spoke, with tears coursing down her cheeks. Listening to Althea rant and rave about him being an opportunist caused his head to throb and his curiosity to rise. He wondered if she'd had cocktails at breakfast, but didn't ask the question circling his mind.

Roderick spotted Demi and narrowed his gaze. She was pacing at the other end of the hallway, and Geneviève's staff were standing in a semicircle, speaking in hushed tones.

Everyone on her team looked crushed, as if they were mourning the loss of a loved one. Fear seized his heart. Something was wrong. He could feel it. Sense it. Heard it in Althea's voice and saw it in Demi's sullen demeanor.

"Where's Geneviève?" His pulse was racing and sweat drenched his black, Brooks Brothers suit, but he remained calm, told himself not to panic. "Is she okay? Did something bad happen to her?"

"Sh-sh-she's not with you?" Althea stammered. "I—I—I thought she was hanging out inside your suite."

"I've been out all morning and just returned to the hotel five minutes ago. I haven't seen or spoken to Geneviève since last night at the arena, but we had plans to have lunch today."

Joining them, Demi wiped her bloodshot eyes with the sleeve of her gray Bob Marley–themed sweatshirt and shuffled her sneaker-clad feet. "Roderick, she's gone."

"Gone?" he repeated, bewildered by her words. "What do you mean 'she's gone'? Where did she go? Who is she with? When will she be back?"

"I don't know. I woke up this morning and she wasn't in her suite."

"Demi, why didn't you call me earlier? Why am I just finding out about this now?"

Sniffling, she dragged a hand through her hair. "Sorry, Roderick. I wanted to, but my cell died and I couldn't remember your number off the top of my head."

Struggling to get air into his lungs, he loosened the knot in his black silk tie, then took a deep breath. "How long has Geneviève been missing?"

"I got up at nine o'clock, and there was no sign of her. Her luggage is gone, and so is the Fiat I rented last week. Gigi was in such a hurry she forgot her iPhone, tablet and computer on the bedside table…"

Geneviève didn't forget them, Roderick thought, releasing a deep sigh. *She didn't want you to track her location using the devices so she purposely left them behind.*

"According to the front desk clerk, she checked out of the hotel at the crack of dawn, and if that isn't bad enough, I also found this note on her bed."

Demi handed him a piece of white paper, and reading it chilled Roderick to the bone. A burning sensation coursed through his chest.

I quit. I can't do this anymore. I need a break, so the European tour is over.

Roderick hung his head. With a pang in his heart, he realized he'd failed at his job—and failed Geneviève—and hoped he found her before one of her overzealous fans did. She was the It Girl of the moment, one of the most recognizable stars in the world, and he didn't want anything bad to happen to her while she was alone in the city. "Don't worry. I'll find her."

"How?" Demi asked. "You're leaving for New York in a few hours."

"I'm not going anywhere until I know your sister's safe."

Demi bit her bottom lip. "Maybe we should call the police. They'll know what to do."

Althea shook her head. "No way. Absolutely not. It would be all over the news, and that's the last thing I want. We have to keep this quiet…"

An Asian couple approached, holding hands and shopping bags, and Althea trailed off.

Recognizing their need for privacy, Roderick reached into his suit jacket, took out his key card and unlocked the door. He gestured for them to sit on the couch, but they stood in the living room, wearing long faces. Roderick projected confidence, even though he was worried about Geneviève. Not because he didn't think she could handle herself, but because he'd seen firsthand how aggressive some *Madrileños* were when they came face-to-face with the talented pop star. Geneviève's net worth was higher than most African countries, and if she made friends with the wrong people, her life could be in danger.

Past conversations he'd had with Geneviève about her favorite places in the country came to mind. Had she returned to the hiking spot they'd visited last Saturday? Was she cruising along the countryside, enjoying the morning breeze? Or had she traveled hundreds of miles away to the luxury ski resort she loved? Roderick decided to check out all of the places she'd ever mentioned to him, even if it took the rest of the day. He'd call Mr. Welker from the car and explain to his boss why he couldn't leave for New York that afternoon.

Glad he'd packed that morning after breakfast, Roderick strode into the bedroom, grabbed his suitcase from the closet and returned to the living room, clutching his coat in his right hand. "Does Geneviève use any aliases when she travels?"

Demi closed her eyes and massaged her temples. "Yes, several. Why? Do you need them?"

"Please text me the names."

"I'm going with you." Short black curls tumbled around Althea's face as she fervently shook her head. "I'm her mother. I should be the one to find her. She's my baby."

"Ms. Harris, I don't think that's a good idea. You should stay here with Demi just in case Geneviève comes back. But if I hear from her, I promise you'll be the first to know."

Seconds passed, then Althea spoke in a solemn voice. "You're right," she conceded. "I'd probably kill you if we were alone in your car."

Or vice versa, Roderick thought, tearing out of the hotel suite.

Six hours after leaving Hotel du Lugo, Roderick parked his Mercedes GLE on a tree-lined street in Vielha and turned off the engine. Thanks to the GPS system in the rental car, he'd arrived at the popular tourist destination in one piece, despite the blowing snow and icy, treacherous roads.

Roderick stared out the windshield of the SUV, curious about the bearded stranger inside the rustic log cabin. A Spanish man with a long, dark ponytail moved

throughout the main floor, but there was no sign of Geneviève, and if not for finding Demi's rental car in the
driveway, Roderick would think he had the wrong address. He found it hard to believe that Geneviève had
made the trip to Vielha by herself… His body tensed.
Or had she? Had she traveled with the Spaniard? Were
they lovers? Did the stranger own the cabin? Questions
filled his mind as he considered what to do next.

His cell phone rang from inside the center console,
and he glanced down at the screen. He had missed calls
and text messages from Althea and Demi, but decided to
contact them after he found Geneviève. He didn't want
to give them false hope in case he was wrong about her
location, and made a mental note to update them once
he checked out the cabin.

Roderick took off his sunglasses, tossed them on the
passenger seat and rubbed his eyes.

It had been a long day, filled with stressful, nerve-
racking moments. That morning, as he was leaving the
hotel parking lot, Demi had called to tell him that Geneviève had used her credit card at a gas station five hundred miles away from Madrid. He'd had a hunch that
Geneviève had traveled to her favorite ski resort, and
after swinging by the rental car company to trade the
sports car for an SUV, he'd jumped on the expressway and
headed east. Baqueira-Beret was the most popular resort
in the country, and skiers flocked there for the manicured
slopes, premier restaurants and world-class amenities.
Though he suspected Geneviève had driven to the town
because of its serene, isolated location.

A door slammed, and the noise drew his gaze back
to the cabin. The stranger put on winter gloves, hopped

inside the black, late-model pickup truck parked in front of the house, then sped off.

Roderick exited the SUV. Clutching his iPhone in one hand and a flashlight in the other, he jogged across the street. Snowplows chugged up the block, teenagers whizzed by on yellow snowmobiles and neighbors shoveled. The cold, blustery wind cut through his wool, knee-length jacket. Snow clung to the bottom of his leather shoes, soaking his silk socks, and Roderick cursed himself for not changing before leaving the hotel. In his haste to find Geneviève, he'd rushed through the door, and now his clothes were soaked.

Roderick increased his pace. He didn't want the Spaniard to return, find him on his property and start throwing punches. Pulling up his jacket collar, he glanced around to ensure no one was watching him, and nodded in greeting at the female dog-walker. Deciding to have a look around, he climbed the steps to the wraparound porch and peered inside the cabin.

And there she was. Geneviève. The woman he desired and adored.

Relief coursed through his body. He'd done it, solved the mystery of the missing pop star, and it was the greatest feeling in the world. Sitting at the baby grand piano in the corner of the room, Geneviève looked youthful and pretty in her burgundy, scoop-neck sweater dress and moccasin slippers. Her eyes were closed, but her fingers danced across the keys with finesse. She sang with passion and conviction, as if she were rocking the Grammy stage, and Roderick was so moved by her performance he wanted to cheer. Her strong, powerful voice penetrated the walls, warming his chilled body from head to toe.

Roderick touched the window with his hand. He

wished he could hold her, kiss her, tell her how much he cared about her and apologize for upsetting her on Saturday night. Geneviève must have sensed him watching her, because she opened her eyes and glanced over her shoulder. She spotted him standing on the porch, and froze.

Roderick gestured for Geneviève to open the door, but she didn't move. *What the hell?* It was freezing outside, snowing heavily, and after driving around all day, Roderick wasn't in the mood for games. He needed to return to Madrid, and the sooner he got in his car and back on the freeway, the sooner he could fly to New York. Mr. Welker had called that afternoon, as Roderick was grabbing a coffee at a local café, and his boss had implored him to find the pop star or else.

"Please?" he begged. "We need to talk."

Geneviève stood, then crossed the room. "Let me in. This will only take a minute."

Yanking open the door, she planted herself in the doorway. "How did you find me?"

"You used your credit card, which was easy to track." His cell phone rang. Roderick checked the number on the screen, then handed it to Geneviève, but she wouldn't touch it. "It's your mom. Answer it. She's worried sick about you."

"I don't want to talk to anyone right now, including you, so please leave."

Roderick swiped his finger across the screen and put his cell to his ear. She had a million questions, but he interrupted her. "Ms. Harris, please, calm down. Geneviève's fine. I found her safe and sound in—"

Geneviève plucked the iPhone out of his hand, pressed the End button and crossed her arms. "I don't want anyone to know where I am," she said, glaring at him with narrowed eyes. "I need some space, so if you don't mind I'd like to be alone."

"You can't get rid of me that easy. I'm a New Yorker *and* stubborn as hell."

His cell phone rang, and Geneviève glanced at the screen. A frown darkened her face.

"Why is Demi calling you? Are you interested in my kid sister?"

"No, she's calling me for an update about you. She's concerned, and rightfully so."

"I know, and I didn't meant to upset them, but I had to get away." Geneviève bit her bottom lip. "I don't want to see them right now, and if you tell them where I'm staying they'll come running, and that's not what I want. I need some time alone, so please respect my wishes."

"I won't tell them where you are. You can trust me."

Silence fell between them, lasting for several seconds.

"Go back to Madrid. I don't need you here. I can take care of myself."

Geneviève tried to close the door, but Roderick stuck his foot between the wooden frame. "I drove for hours in a snowstorm to find you, and you're not even going to invite me inside for a cup of coffee?" Curious about her accommodations, he checked out the two-story cabin. It had vaulted ceilings, plush area rugs and furniture, and a stone fireplace. It was the perfect balance of comfort and elegance, and the log accents throughout the space were eye-catching.

"You don't deserve coffee or anything else. The last time I saw you, you threw me out of your hotel suite, so you can get the hell off my doorstep."

"Spoken like a true Philadelphian," he joked. "With tons of sass, and plenty of attitude."

"Kiss my—"

"With pleasure." Cutting her off, Roderick stepped inside the foyer, backed her up against the door and crushed his lips to her mouth. She smelled of lavender, but the tranquil aroma didn't calm him; it made his pulse pound. Her lips were the best thing he'd ever tasted, soft, lush and sweet, and Roderick was hooked. Needed and wanted more.

And he was going to have her.

Cupping her face in his hands, he inclined his head to the right and deepened the kiss. Lust barreled through his body, stealing his breath and his resolve. Their chemistry was explosive, impossible to deny, and her passionate kiss rocked him to the core. Geneviève let his tongue inside her mouth, tickled it with her own and a low groan vibrated inside the back of his throat. They'd crossed the line, passed the point of no return, and this time Roderick wasn't going to deny himself the pleasure of her touch.

Chapter 14

Nothing made sense. Geneviève thought she was dreaming, but Roderick's slow, sensuous kiss and his urgent caress were as real as her raging heartbeat. Caught off guard, yet instantly aroused, her knees buckled and she collapsed against his chest. The moment their lips touched, fireworks exploded behind her eyes. It was the most passionate kiss of her life, one she would never forget. Her emotions were overwhelming and confusing. Geneviève didn't know how to feel, what to think. She didn't understand why Roderick had followed her to Vielha, and why he'd barged into her rental cabin. Four days ago he'd rejected her, and now he was turning her inside out with his mouth and hands. Geneviève wanted to push him away, but being in his arms gave her a rush, and she was helpless to resist his touch.

Her eyes fluttered closed. His cologne washed over her, filling her nostrils with a spicy, woodsy scent, and his groans played in her ears like a song on the radio. Roderick made her feel alive, desirable, and Geneviève struggled to keep her hands to herself and off his toned physique. Her palms were damp with perspiration, and goose bumps pricked her skin. That's what Roderick did to her, how he made her feel every time he kissed her.

Excitement built, filling every inch of the room. His hands traveled down her shoulders, across her breasts and along her hips. Geneviève welcomed his touch, yearned for more. She fantasized about all the things she wanted Roderick to do to her, could almost feel his tongue between her legs, swirling and twirling around her clit. At the thought, tingles rocked her spine.

"Are you dating the Spanish guy with the ponytail?" he asked, pausing to look at her.

"Why? Are you jealous?"

"Of course not. I have no reason to be. I'm a Drake." He winked. "*And* one of the most coveted bachelors in New York."

"I'm not dating anyone. Mr. Narváez owns this cabin and he wanted to make sure the fireplace was working properly before he returned to his villa in Barcelona," she explained.

"Good, we don't have to worry about being interrupted." He kissed the corner of her lips. "Geneviève, I want you *so* bad—"

"Yeah, right," she said, unable to resist speaking her mind. "Where was all this passion and desire on Saturday night when you kicked me out of your suite?"

"Nothing's changed. I wanted you then, and I want you now."

"Then why are you playing hard to get?"

Roderick cocked an eyebrow. "Is that what you think I'm doing?"

"You're not?"

"No. We have a great relationship, and if we sleep together it could complicate things."

"Or not," she said with a shrug. "I'm a big girl, Roderick. I can handle hooking up with a suave, dashing attorney. The question is whether or not *you* can handle a strong, feisty woman from North Philly who knows exactly who she is and what she wants."

"I'm not intimidated by you, Geneviève. I'm intrigued by you." Roderick drew a finger across her cheek. "Your beauty shines from within, and your body is a masterpiece."

"It is?" A smile claimed her lips. "What's your favorite part?"

Roderick sucked on her earlobe. "Here." He pressed his lips the curve of her neck. "Here." He slid his hands over her bottom and squeezed it. "And *definitely* here."

Oh, yes! More please! Geneviève thought, closing her eyes. Her inner voice told her to end the kiss, to push him away, but instead of heeding the warning, she moved closer to him. Stroked every muscle on his hard, toned body. His touch was magic, instantly making her wet. There was no greater thrill than being in his arms, and kissing him gave Geneviève a high. A rush. He used his lips, his tongue and his hands to please her, and when Roderick whispered the word *beautiful* in her ear, happiness flooded her heart.

"I want you to spend the night," she confessed, pressing her lips against his throat.

"If I wasn't your attorney I'd carry you to the bedroom and—"

Geneviève put a finger to his lips. "I'm not your client anymore, remember? My mom requested another attorney to oversee my affairs, and the senior partners agreed, so you're off the hook, Roderick. You don't have to babysit me anymore."

He snapped his fingers. "You're right. I'm not. You know what that means, right? It's on!"

His smoldering gaze warmed her all over. Geneviève read the look in his eyes, knew they shared the same thought and draped her arms around his neck, pulling him close. He licked her ear with his tongue, and a shiver raced down her spine. He cupped her breasts through her clothes, squeezing and tweaking her nipples, just the way she liked. Geneviève wanted to tell Roderick she loved what he was doing with his hands, but she couldn't get her lips to move. Couldn't do anything but moan and groan.

Passion ignited inside her. She felt as if she'd known Roderick all her life, as if they were meant to be together, and the more he kissed and caressed her the more Geneviève desired him. He possessed all of the qualities on her Boyfriend Wish List, right down to his taste in movies, music and novels. Best of all, he listened to her and respected her.

He slid a hand under her dress. "You're not wearing any panties."

"I know. You're welcome." Stroking the back of his head, she licked and nibbled his lower lip.

"You're trouble, you know that?" Desire shone in his eyes. "Where's the bedroom?"

Geneviève stepped past him, sashaying into the kitchen with the confidence of a world-class supermodel, and hopped onto the granite breakfast bar. "Who needs a

bed when we have a strong, sturdy counter right here?"
she asked, beckoning him over with a crook of her finger.

"I couldn't agree more." Roderick crossed the room,
took her in his arms and brushed his lips slowly against
hers. "Geneviève, tell me what you need. What I can do
to please you?"

Taken aback by the question, and the sincerity of his
voice, she sucked in a breath. Geneviève thought her ears
were playing tricks on her. No one had ever treated her
with such tenderness, such warmth, and she was moved
by his words. They took turns undressing each other,
kissing passionately as their clothes fell to the hardwood
floor. Fulfilling her unspoken requests, Roderick caressed
and massaged her body. Moans spilled from her lips. Lost
in the moment, her breathing sped up and the muscles between her legs contracted. She quivered as their tongues
tickled and teased each other.

Overwhelmed by her emotions, Geneviève did something she'd never done before—she begged. She yearned
to make love to him, and could no longer deny the needs
of her flesh. "Roderick, I need you inside me…please
don't make me wait…it's torture."

Desperate to feel him inside her, Geneviève slid a
hand inside his boxers and stroked his erection with her
palm. She relished in the moment, loved pleasing him
with her hands. Her mouth watered at the sight of his
dizzying, mind-blowing length. She wanted to taste him,
to lick every inch of his erection, but Roderick covered
it with a condom, spread her legs open and slid his shaft
against her clit. Like a paintbrush, he moved his erection
back and forth, ever so slowly, thrilling her with each
delicious stroke.

Waves of pleasure crashed into her. Afraid she'd

scream and the neighbors would come running, Geneviève buried her face in the crook of his neck to stifle her moans. A warm sensation flooded her body, leaving her feeling weak and spent. Geneviève locked her legs around his waist, pulling him close. Exhilarated, she felt as if she were riding the wildest, fastest roller coaster ever. Kissing him, she ran her hands along his neck, his shoulders and across his back. To please him, she moved her lips over his smooth skin, and her teeth grazed his earlobe. Grasping the back of his head, she teased his flesh with her tongue. Melting and exploding at the same time, she closed her eyes and savored the moment.

Intense emotions coursed through her, taking her by surprise. Geneviève was floating, flying high in the air. Roderick kissed her as if he was in complete control, and he was. He knew how to pleasure her, how to excite her, and she loved feeling him between her legs. She wasn't shy about telling him what she wanted, and he fulfilled her every wish, over and over again. He thrilled her in ways she'd never imagined. Geneviève wanted to be with someone who cared about her, who had her best interests at heart, and Roderick was the only man she wanted. Her female intuition told her he was The One, her soul mate, and the thought of dating him exclusively made her heart sing. "This is amazing, *you're* amazing and I—"

Catching herself in time, she pressed her lips together to trap the truth inside her mouth.

Roderick hiked her leg in the air, and pressed kisses along her inner thigh. His breathing was labored, his thrusts hard and deep, so powerful they stole her breath. Stroking his muscles was a turn-on, as erotic as his French kiss. There was a difference between making love and having sex, and even though Geneviève was sprawled out on the kitchen counter Roderick made her feel cherished and adored. She'd never had such strong feelings for anyone, and couldn't think of anything better than making love to Roderick in the rustic cabin nestled in the woods.

"You take my breath away," he said in a throaty voice. "And I'm crazy about you."

He kissed from her chin to her collarbone, and a shudder passed through Geneviève's body. Her thoughts spun and her limbs quivered. An orgasm rocked her with such force she collapsed onto the counter, panting. Her mind was spinning, so hazy she wouldn't have been able to remember her name if Roderick asked her what it was.

Clenching his teeth, he tossed his head back and gripped her waist. Roderick moved, fast and furious, each thrust deeper than the last. He groaned, grunted and cursed. Seconds passed, and the scent of their lovemaking perfumed the air. Pressing his eyes shut, he kissed her hard on the mouth, as if he couldn't get enough of her lips. His body went completely still, then he let out a long sigh.

Geneviève stroked his face with her hands, tenderly caressed his skin as she admired his chiseled features. Everything with Roderick was easy, effortless. There was no drama when they were together, no stress, and Geneviève couldn't help imagining a future with him. What was he thinking about? Had he finally changed his mind about them dating, or was this just a one-time hookup that meant nothing?

His naked, glistening body was a sight to behold, and Geneviève drooled when he winked at her. Roderick strode over to the garbage, opened it and discarded the used condom. He had a flat, washboard stomach and a firm, hard ass her hands were itching to squeeze again. He pulled on his boxers, but that didn't stop Geneviève from lusting after him.

"Can I get you something to drink?" he asked, gesturing to the stainless steel fridge.

Standing despite the dull ache in her thighs, Geneviève found her sweater dress beside the decorative lamp, put it on and leaned against the sofa. "If anyone should be getting drinks around here it should be me, not you. You're my guest—"

Roderick cocked an eyebrow. "Are you inviting me to spend the night?"

"That depends on what you have planned for the rest of the day," she said with a coy smile.

"You mean *besides* making love to you in every room inside this cabin?"

Please do! she thought, suddenly breathless. *I'd love that.*

Roderick slid his arms around her waist and held her tight, close to his chest. "We'll have dinner at the best restaurant in town, and when we get home I'll have *you* for dessert."

"Or we can *start* with dessert," she proposed, draping her arms around his neck. Feeling his hard, muscled body pressed against hers was a turn-on, and Geneviève couldn't think of anything but making love to him again. "Follow me, Counselor. We have to get clean before we can get dirty."

A grin curled his mouth. "Lead the way."

Chapter 15

"Wake up, beautiful. Your breakfast is getting cold, and I don't want the tostadas to get soggy."

Geneviève opened her eyes, spotted Roderick standing at the foot of the sleigh bed holding a wooden tray in his hands and smiled. Stubble covered his chin, giving him a sexy, rugged vibe. His sleeveless T-shirt showed off muscled biceps, and his sweatpants were a perfect fit. Wanting to kiss him, she hungrily licked her lips. Images of his naked body consumed her thoughts, but Geneviève changed the channel in her mind. They'd made love twice last night, and although she yearned for him, she didn't want to give Roderick the wrong idea. She cared about him, and wanted to have an honest conversation with him about their future before he returned to New York.

The curtains were open, allowing sunshine to pour through the windows and fill the master suite with natural light. A delicious aroma filled the air, and her stomach growled at the scent tickling her nose. Warm and snug in the fluffy duvet blanket, Geneviève pulled it up to her chin and rolled onto her side. "What time is it?"

Roderick glanced at his stylish sports watch. "Quarter to one."

"No way." Geneviève yawned. "I haven't slept this late for years."

"I didn't want to wake you, but I got bored after my workout and wanted your company."

His words warmed her heart. Sitting up, she belted her purple satin robe and crossed her legs at the ankles. "Breakfast in bed is a cliché, don't you think?" she teased.

Roderick shrugged. "I wouldn't know. I've never done this before."

"But you were engaged for over a year."

The grin slid off his face. "I know. Don't remind me."

Roderick set the tray down on her lap. Geneviève loved listening to his stories about his family and his colleagues at the law firm, but she wanted to hear more about his ex-fiancée. Roderick was genuine and honest—except when she asked him questions about his broken engagement. His behavior troubled her, making her doubt their connection. Was he still in love with the perky blonde? Did he want her back? Geneviève didn't want to upset him, but she wanted to know more about his past relationships.

"How come you never cooked for your ex?"

"Because she was always on a diet, and basically lived off salads and protein shakes."

"I can't imagine. I love food too much to starve myself, and the last time Demi forced me to do the liquid diet I only lasted two days!" Geneviève said with a laugh.

"Good. You're perfect just the way you are."

She smiled her thanks. "Do you miss your ex-fiancée?"

"Yeah, about as much as I miss having chicken pox." His gaze darkened, and he spoke through clenched teeth. "I don't want to talk about her."

"Why not? Because you love her, and wish you were still engaged?"

The silence was deafening. He stared at the bedroom ceiling, as if the answers to her questions were written there, and spoke in a solemn voice. "No, because every time I think about her I get a migraine, and I don't want anything to ruin our fun-filled day in Baqueira-Beret."

Geneviève stared down at her plate, admiring the impressive spread, but she couldn't stop thinking about what Roderick had said about his ex—or rather, what he didn't say. But before she could question him, he spoke, and his genuine excitement quieted her doubts.

"It's a traditional Spanish breakfast," he announced, gesturing to the tray with a nod. "So dig in and tell me what an incredible cook I am."

"You made all of this? Wow, I'm impressed. I'm going to start calling you Master Chef."

He had the biggest smile Geneviève had ever seen. Roderick had a charming personality and a generous nature, and she loved having him at her private hideaway in the mountains. For months, she'd felt as if a dark cloud was hanging over her head, but now that Geneviève was in Vielha, she didn't have a care in the world.

Everything was better when Roderick was around, and it didn't matter if they were watching movies, playing cards or cuddling on the couch—they had a great time together. Opening up to Roderick about her fears and insecurities last night in bed had brought them even closer together, making her feel as if they were a team, and Geneviève was glad she had him in her corner.

"This is a lot of food, Roderick. I can't eat all of this right now—"

"You better. We have a full day ahead of us and you're going to need your strength."

"We do?" she said, tasting the spicy vegetarian omelet. "Where are we going?"

"We'll go skiing this afternoon, then enjoy a world-class zarzuela show at the…"

Geneviève forced a smile. She loved the cozy rental property, and was content being indoors with her favorite attorney. For the past three days, they'd been holed up inside the cabin, and if it were up to Geneviève they'd stay in bed for the rest of the week. She relished sleeping in, taking bubble baths, writing songs and making love to Roderick whenever she was in the mood.

"We're hitting the slopes at three, so eat up."

His lopsided grin made her skin—and her sex—flush with heat.

"And sharing is caring, so join me," she said, patting his side of the bed.

"If you insist." Roderick plopped down on the bed, kissed her cheek then picked up the utensils from the tray. He picked up a piece of quince with his fork, raised it to her lips and said in Spanish, "Open up, beautiful. It tastes almost as sweet as you."

His voice tickled her ears, and he smelled so good Geneviève had to restrain herself from diving into his arms. She parted her lips and tasted the fruit. Taking turns feeding each other, they discussed their plans for the weekend, their favorite places in Madrid and the worst dates they'd ever been on. Sitting side by side with Roderick in bed, Geneviève couldn't help imagining them living as husband and wife, and beamed when he brushed his lips against her ear. His touch was invigorating, his stories excited her and his jokes made her laugh out loud. They had shared values and interests, but above all she wanted to be with someone she could rely on, and Geneviève trusted Roderick explicitly.

Loud noises drew Geneviève's gaze to the window. Icicles dangled from the roof, clouds sailed across the sky and the fir trees surrounding the property were covered in snow. Geneviève heard shovels scraping against the sidewalk and the distant sound of male voices. Her heart stopped. Were there reporters outside? Were they spying on her? Had someone tipped off the local press about where she was staying? Geneviève dismissed the thought. She'd sworn Roderick to secrecy, and he'd promised not to tell anyone she was renting a cabin in Vielha and she hoped he kept his word.

Geneviève wondered how her mom and sister were doing. She loved her family, but these days she felt as if she was being pulled in a hundred different directions, and she needed time to figure out her next move. Spending time with Roderick made Geneviève think about her hopes and dreams, and she was determined to regain control of her career, even if it meant making hard, life-changing decisions. "I almost forgot. I have a gift for you."

Surfacing from her thoughts, Geneviève winked at him. "I bet you do."

"You have a one-track mind," he teased. "Do you ever think of anything besides sex?"

Not when you're around, she thought, her gaze sliding down his broad shoulders.

Roderick took the tray off her lap, set it on the mahogany side table then marched into the closet. He returned to the bedroom seconds later with a grin on his mouth and a white, oversize box in his hands. "I was planning to give this to you on Tuesday night, to celebrate the success of your final show in Madrid, but you wouldn't talk to me…"

Heat burned her cheeks as she lowered her eyes to her lap. Geneviève didn't want to discuss what happened at the WiZink Center, but she felt compelled to defend her actions. "Do you blame me?" she asked, even though her mouth was suddenly dry. "I fell onstage in front of fifteen thousand people, and I was roasted on social media for days. I always want to give my fans a thrilling, memorable show, and I did, but for all the wrong reasons."

"You're being too hard on yourself. A fan grabbed you. It wasn't your fault you fell on stage."

Taking her hand in his, he squeezed it, then kissed her palm. Feeling his mouth against her skin made Geneviève wish they were making love again, moving together as one body, but she restrained herself from acting on her impulses, and listened intently as he spoke.

"I've been to dozens of concerts, but you're the best performer I've ever seen," he confessed, with an earnest expression on his face. "You're likeable and relatable, and people root for you. *I* root for you, and I always will. You're important to me, Geneviève, and I care a lot about you. Never, ever forget that."

His voice, like his gaze, was strong, and his words heartfelt. It was hard to keep her head, to keep her wits about her when Roderick brushed his lips against her cheek, and she pressed her lips together to trap a moan inside her mouth. Roderick was part of her life now, and thinking about him leaving for New York next week made her heart ache with sadness.

"Go on," he prompted, gesturing to the gift box. "Open it. You're going to love it."

I can never love anything as much as I love you. The thought made her heart race, and her pulse pound.

Her hands were shaking, but Geneviève opened the box and pushed aside the colored tissue paper. There were art supplies, Spanish audio books, a jewelry-making kit and the largest container of sweet and spicy wasabi popcorn Geneviève had ever seen. "Wow, Roderick, this is great," she gushed, blown away by his thoughtfulness. "Especially the watercolor paints. Now I have everything I need for the class I'm taking next month at the Philly Art Center."

The grin faded from his lips. "You're going home? But you have concerts scheduled in Berlin, Paris, Rome and a half dozen other cities."

"No, I don't. I canceled the rest of the European tour, and I posted an official statement on my website and social media pages last night."

"Last night?" he repeated, an incredulous look on his face. "Why didn't you tell me?"

"Because it's my life, not yours."

Raking a hand through his hair, Roderick blew out a deep breath. "Can we discuss this?"

"There's nothing to discuss. I thought I could push through and finish the tour because I didn't want to disappoint my record label, my mom or my fans, but I can't. I'm exhausted, and if I don't take a stand now I never will."

"I wish you had talked to me first before you posted a statement online."

"Why?" Geneviève tossed aside the blanket, jumped to her feet and met his dark, troubled gaze with her own. "I don't have to consult you, or anyone else about what's best for me. Furthermore, you're no longer my attorney."

"You signed a contract, and it's legally binding."

"And," she prompted, "I'm not the first artist to cancel a tour, and I won't be the last. I already feel horrible for disappointing my fans, so please don't make me feel worse about it."

"That's not my intention. I know this can't be easy for you, and I don't want to upset you."

Really? she thought, rolling her eyes. *You have a funny way of showing it!* Geneviève yanked open the closet door, selected an outfit then slammed it shut. His words confused her. One minute Roderick was telling her to do what made her happy, and the next minute he was pressuring her to finish the European tour. Why wasn't he supportive? What had changed? Why was he making her feel guilty for finally taking control of her life?

"I only want the best for you," he said, his hands outstretched. "I hope you believe me."

Geneviève moved away from him. Roderick's opinion mattered to her, but she wasn't going to change her mind about returning to Philadelphia just because he disagreed with her. "I'm not going to apologize for putting myself first. This is long overdue, and I won't let you or my mom or anyone at Urban Beats Records make me feel guilty for listening to my body. I'm tired and overworked, and I need a break."

Lowering his head, he rubbed the back of his neck with a hand.

"Roderick, I'm disappointed in you."

He stared at her for a long, quiet moment, but he didn't speak.

"I thought you'd be more supportive," she confessed. "Since the day we met, you've been encouraging me to take control of my life, and I did, so why are you giving me grief about it?"

He touched her arm, but his tender caress didn't comfort her. *Maybe I don't know Roderick as well as I thought I did. Maybe he doesn't care about me like he says he does.* The thought troubled her, but she listened to him with an open mind.

"Geneviève, I'm sorry. I'm not trying to be an ass, but I don't want you to do anything to ruin your career—"

Annoyed, she cut him off midsentence. "I'm more than just a pop star, Roderick. I'm a talented songwriter, and if I decide to retire from music I can still earn a comfortable living."

His eyes widened. "Retire from music? Is that on the table?"

"I don't know," she said with a shrug. "Maybe. I'll decide in a few months."

"Please don't make any rash decisions." His cell phone rang, but Roderick didn't answer it. "Talk with your team before you post any more announcements on social media. You have a lot of great people in your corner, and they deserve to hear the truth from you, not online."

Geneviève stared at him in silence.

"How much time are you taking off?" Roderick asked, scratching his jaw.

"The rest of the year. I'll reevaluate my career once I've had some me time."

Roderick whistled. "Nine months is a long break. What are you going to do with yourself?"

"All kinds of things. Improve my French, take fitness and art classes, and volunteer at after-school programs." Giving his question more thought, Geneviève wore a sheepish smile. "I'd also love to meet Mr. Right, move to the suburbs and have a baby."

"A baby!" Roderick repeated, raising his voice. "You're joking, right?"

"No, I'm serious."

"But, I thought you loved being a pop star."

"I've wanted to sing and write songs since I was a kid, but I never longed for fame or fortune. It was never about that. For me, it's always been about the music."

Roderick wore a thoughtful expression on his face. "And now the music isn't enough."

"No, it's not. I want to settle down and have a family," she said, speaking from the heart. "Most of my cousins are either engaged or happily married, and I envy them."

"Why? I bet they'd trade places with you in a heartbeat."

"I love the idea of having one special person in my life, for the rest of my life. Don't you?"

He dodged her gaze. His cell phone rang, and this time Roderick took it out of his pocket and stared at the screen. "It's my boss. I have to take this call, but I'll be right back."

Sighing deeply, Geneviève watched Roderick leave the master bedroom. She cherished the memory of their first kiss, the night they made love and all of the great conversations they'd had, but questioned whether or not he was the right man for her. His actions didn't match his words, and Geneviève didn't want to be with someone who played games with her heart—not even a sexy, debonair lawyer with a big heart and a brilliant mind.

Chapter 16

"What the hell is going on?" Mr. Welker demanded, his anger evident in his sharp tone. "Where is Geneviève, and why did she cancel the rest of the European tour?"

Roderick swallowed hard. His tongue felt heavy inside his mouth, rougher than sandpaper, and the lump in his throat was the size of a golf ball. His first thought was to lie, because he didn't want to disappoint his boss, but he deleted the idea from his mind.

"Answer me, Roderick. I need to know what's going on…"

Wanting privacy, he strode into the spare bedroom and closed the door. His head was still spinning from his conversation with Geneviève about marriage and babies, but he cleared his mind, and said, "Sir, I'm sorry I didn't respond to your messages earlier, but—"

"Don't 'sir' me!" he shouted. "Ms. Harris has been calling me nonstop, demanding to know where her daughter is, and her incessant phone calls are driving me nuts."

Tell me something I don't know, Roderick thought, pacing the length of the room. Althea and Demi had been blowing up his cell phone for the past three days, and every time he spoke to the momager she sounded frazzled, as if she was at the end of her rope. She demanded to speak to her daughter, but Geneviève refused to take her calls. He sympathized with the single mom, but there was nothing he could do. "I know Ms. Harris is upset, but Geneviève asked me not to tell her family where she's staying, and I want to respect her wishes."

"The last time we spoke you assured me everything was fine," Mr. Welker said. "Geneviève was doing great, her concert reviews were outstanding and you'd outsmarted José Sánchez and his attorney, so what happened? How could things go so bad so quickly? And why didn't you keep me abreast of what was going on in Madrid?"

Roderick sank into the padded brown armchair in front of the window and massaged his temples. He told his boss about Geneviève's onstage fall on Tuesday night, her unexpected road trip and her present state of mind. "I advised her to finish the rest of the tour, and even offered to drive her back to Madrid, but she's adamant about remaining in Vielha."

"Vielha?" he repeated in a solemn tone. "The town outside of Baqueira-Beret?"

"Yes. Geneviève plans to stay here until the end of the month," he explained. "She's taking a break, and there's nothing I can say or do to change her mind."

"Roderick, how could you let this happen? I was counting on you to successfully resolve this matter, and so were the other senior partners."

"I know, sir, and I'm sorry I let you down, but this situation is beyond my control—"

Mr. Welker interrupted him, and Roderick trailed off. His cell phone beeped, cueing him that he had an incoming call, and he glanced at the screen. It was Duane on the line, but he decided to connect with his brother later. His parents were throwing a surprise birthday party for Duane in two weeks, and Roderick was looking forward to the family dinner at his childhood home. He'd mentioned the party to Geneviève days earlier, but now that he knew the pop star had marriage and babies on the brain, he had second thoughts about her being his guest.

"I need you back here to deal with the fallout of Geneviève canceling her tour."

A war waged in Roderick's heart and mind. He didn't feel comfortable leaving Geneviève alone in the secluded resort town, far away from her family and bodyguards. He wanted her to be safe, and worried about her when they were apart. He considered requesting a two-week leave from work, but when he remembered what Geneviève had said about wanting to start a family during her hiatus, Roderick knew he had to leave. Had to put as much distance between them as possible now that he knew what her future plans were. His goal this year was to become partner at his law firm, not a husband and father, and Roderick didn't want to give Geneviève the wrong idea.

They had everything in common, amazing chemistry and mind-blowing sex, and even though she was exactly his type, the odds were stacked against them, impossible to ignore. Geneviève wanted a family and Roderick wanted a promotion; Althea hated him, and worse still, the pop star was the firm's biggest client, and his boss would go ballistic if he found out Roderick had slept with Geneviève. "I understand, sir. I'll make the necessary travel arrangements on Monday."

"No, I want you back at the office within forty-eight hours."

Bewildered, Roderick stared down at the phone. He often attended work-related events on the weekends, and met with his colleagues to strategize about potential clients, but he never worked at the law office on Sundays. His boss was punishing him for screwing up in Madrid, but Roderick knew he wasn't to blame. It was Geneviève's life, her career, and he'd never stand in the way of her happiness. The truth was, Roderick was proud of her for standing her ground. Geneviève was a pop singer, not a machine, and she deserved to take a break from music.

"Your vacation is over," Mr. Welker announced in a stern voice. "You're having a grand ole time skiing, drinking fine wine and socializing with celebrities at the Baqueira-Beret resort, but your clients are going crazy without you here, so pack up and head home."

His body tensed, and his stomach lurched. Mr. Welker thought he was staying at the fancy five-star resort, but Roderick didn't correct him. He shuddered to think what would happen if his boss knew the truth. He wasn't Geneviève's attorney anymore, but it wouldn't matter to the senior partner, and Roderick didn't want to do anything to make waves at the firm. Until he achieved his dreams, he couldn't do anything to rock the boat— like tell his boss he was staying with Geneviève at her secluded rental cabin in the woods.

"I'll see you at the office first thing Sunday morning," Mr. Welker said. "Don't be late."

The line went dead, and Roderick pocketed his cell

phone. He rested his elbows on his thighs, then scrubbed at his face with his hands. What bothered him most about his conversation with Mr. Welker wasn't his cold, harsh tone; it was his boss implying that he was a screwup. He'd talk to him first thing Sunday morning and set him straight.

Roderick raised his bent shoulders and stared at the door. For a moment, he thought the radio was on, but when he heard a soft, angelic voice that swelled with emotion, he knew Geneviève was singing in the kitchen. Love filled his heart, and as he listened to Geneviève sing, Roderick realized he'd been fooling himself from day one. Despite his best efforts, he'd fallen hard for the vivacious pop star, and wanted to be the only man in her life.

Stunned by the realization, Roderick sank back into his chair. Geneviève's confession about wanting to be a wife and mother had spooked him, but he still desired her, adored her and wanted to date her exclusively. Roderick considered his options. He could bury his feelings, or embrace them, and as Roderick rose to his feet he knew what he had to do.

Exiting the spare bedroom, his mind returned to last night. Blindsided by lust, he'd grabbed Geneviève as she'd entered the walk-in closet, and made love to her against the mirrored wall. Eight hours later he could still hear her moans in his ears. Roderick couldn't think about Geneviève without getting an erection, and wondered how he was going to function when he returned to New York. He craved her kiss, and every time their lips touched his temperature soared. He had to do a better job of managing his emotions. Of maintaining control. He didn't want Geneviève to think he was weak, and as he entered the kitchen he chided himself to play it cool, to think, not lust.

It didn't work. Roderick took one look at Geneviève standing at the sink in her short satin robe, and drooled all over his white V-neck shirt. Marching toward her, he couldn't think of anything but ravishing her sweet mouth. She was singing in Spanish, swaying her body to the music as she washed the breakfast dishes. He was surprised to see she was still in her pajamas, and wondered why she hadn't showered and changed yet. Was she mad at him? Did she want him to leave? Was their secret rendezvous over?

His gaze crawled up her legs and along her hips. His palms itched to stroke her, to squeeze and caress her skin, and for the second time in minutes thoughts of making love to her ruled his mind. Roderick gave his head a shake. Making love to her again would be a mistake. They wanted different things out of life, and he didn't want to lead her on.

But when Geneviève glanced over her shoulder and their eyes met, every rational thought fled his brain and blood shot straight to his groin. He hadn't touched her yet, but electricity scorched his skin, and Roderick knew it was just a matter of time before he was buried between her legs, pleasing her with his tongue.

Overcome with lust, he came up behind her, slipped his hands inside her robe and stroked her flesh. Roderick showered her cheeks and neck with kisses. He pressed his erection against her bottom, grinding his hips against her flesh to excite her. It worked. Her head fell against his chest, and a sigh escaped her lips. Easy to talk to and laugh with, Geneviève was great company, and Roderick enjoyed being with her—especially in the bedroom.

Her confidence and unbridled enthusiasm were a turn-on, and Roderick loved the idea of sexing his favorite pop star on the granite breakfast bar.

"I'm surprised you're still here." Turning to face him, she wore a sad smile. "I was sure I'd scared you off with my confession, and figured you were halfway back to Madrid by now."

An awkward silence descended on the kitchen, and Roderick took a moment to consider his response. He decided to be honest, and hoped she wouldn't hold it against him. "Geneviève, I'm crazy about you, and I think you're a dynamic woman…"

"But you're not looking for anything serious," she said, finishing the rest of his sentence.

"Oh, so you're a mind reader now," he teased. "Go on, tell me more. I want to know what you think."

"If you insist." Geneviève clasped his hand, led him over to the beige couch and sat down. "Roderick, it's obvious you have a lot on your mind, so let's talk…"

His erection died inside his boxer briefs. *Talk? But I don't want to talk. I want to tear off your robe, bend you over the sink and thrust so deep inside you, you scream my name.* His disappointment must have been evident in his demeanor, because she wore a sympathetic smile.

"Don't give me that face," Geneviève scolded in a playful voice. "This is important, but don't worry after we talk you can rock my world."

Roderick chuckled. The pop star didn't mince words, always spoke the truth, and her honesty was refreshing. "I'm listening. What's on your mind?"

"I didn't tell you about my desire to get married to pressure you to commit to me…"

Sighing inwardly, he nodded in understanding. *Thank*

God. Roderick wasn't ready for a wife, let alone a baby, but he didn't want Geneviève to think all he cared about was making money and chasing women. His ex had ruined his faith in relationships, but he couldn't deny his feelings for the talented singer. He thought about Geneviève all the time, even when they were in the same room, and she was the best lover he'd ever had. They didn't have sex; they made love, and it was amazing every time—even when she woke him up in the middle of the night for a quickie. He loved her fervor, her spontaneity, and waking up to her mouth on his erection was more electrifying than bungee jumping.

"We have a strong connection, but I don't expect you to pop the question after a few nights of amazing sex," she continued. "I want to date you, but I'm not going to force you to commit to me."

"I understand, and I appreciate your honesty." Desperate for her, Roderick reached out and stroked her cheek with his thumb. He'd met the right girl at the wrong time, and worried their affair would cost him a partnership at the law firm he loved. Listening to Geneviève share her hopes and dreams had spooked him, made him consider all the things that could go wrong in their relationship if they dated, and no matter how hard Roderick tried he couldn't shake his doubts. What if Geneviève left him for someone else? Or worse, humiliated him like his ex had?

"Enough talk, Counselor. It's time for the main event."

The sound of Geneviève's low, sultry voice seized his attention, and he surfaced from his thoughts. Grinning, he nuzzled his chin against her face. "I like when you call me counselor."

"And I like when you kiss me."

Roderick pressed his lips against her ears, her cheeks,

then her mouth. His iPhone rang, filling the living room with hip-hop music, but he continued pleasing her. Caressing him through his clothes, she lowered herself to her knees and pressed her body against his.

Desire spiraled through him, flooding his skin. Roderick couldn't think of a better way to start the day than by making love to Geneviève, and loved what she was doing with her mouth and hands. Kissing him, she untied the drawstring on his sweatpants, slipped a hand inside his boxers and stroked his erection to life. She nibbled it, caressed and licked it, and Roderick feared their lovemaking would be over before it even started.

His eyes closed, and his head fell back against the couch as her lips worked their magic. She ran the tip of his penis over the outline of her lips then against her teeth, and his toes curled. He gripped the side of the couch to avoid jumping ten feet in the air. He was groaning, cursing, couldn't stop. It was too much, *she* was too much, and Roderick didn't know how much more he could handle. Geneviève was in control, calling the shots, and he enjoyed every minute of it.

"Do you like that?" she whispered in a sexy voice. "Does that feel good?"

He growled in response. The pop star wowed him, did things with her lips, tongue and hands that excited him, and Roderick realized he'd finally met his match in the bedroom. Aroused by her touch, he struggled to control his emotions. To stay in the moment. His head was spinning, his body was throbbing, and he couldn't think straight.

Sweat drenched his skin. Geneviève blew on his erection, then sucked it into her mouth, inch by inch, sending him over the edge. The move was a game changer, so erotic his eyes rolled back in his head. It was an instant jolt of pleasure, sending a thousand volts of electricity through his body. Every flick of her tongue pushed him closer to the brink of delirium. Clutching his penis in her hands, she used it to trace her nipples and brush it between her breasts.

Gripping his hips, she dug her fingernails into his skin. Roderick watched her intently. His mouth dried and he moaned. Her hair swung over her shoulders, and her big, beautiful breasts bounced as she moved. It was the sexiest image Roderick had ever seen. Geneviève had no equal in the bedroom, and her confidence made him desire her even more. She was doing everything right, and he was so turned on by her sexual prowess his erection swelled inside her mouth. His gaze zeroed in on her dark, erect nipples and Roderick wanted to suck them, lick them, squeeze them in his hands—

His cell phone rang, then buzzed. He wanted to take it out of his pocket, yank open the front door and toss it into the snow. There was nothing better than being intimate with Geneviève, and Roderick didn't want anything to interrupt their red-hot make-out session.

Geneviève reached into the pocket of her robe, took out a gold packet and ripped it open. Disappointment tempered his excitement, but he concealed his emotions. He'd never had unprotected sex before, but Roderick was tempted to break the rules with her. He didn't want any physical barriers between them, wanted to feel every delicious inch of Geneviève's body. After making love in the shower on Wednesday night they'd had an open and honest conversation about their sexual history, and even though they both had a clean bill of health, Roderick knew they had to use protection. He couldn't risk Geneviève getting pregnant with his child.

The sound of her voice captured his attention, and his thoughts faded into the background.

"I can't wait anymore," she said, kissing the corner of his lips. "I need you inside me…"

Geneviève rolled the condom onto his erection, climbed onto his lap and lowered herself onto his shaft. Biting her bottom lip, she moved against his body, ever so slowly. Enjoying the view, he committed every detail of their lovemaking to memory. Her feverish moans, the feel of her soft, delicate hands against his skin, her hair tickling his face, the scent of her perfume.

Roderick devoured her mouth, feasted hungrily on her lips. Geneviève was more than just his lover; she was his dream girl, and no one else would ever take her place in his heart. From the moment he'd arrived in Madrid, he'd been trying to resist his feelings for her, but he'd failed miserably. He was weak for her, and now that they were lovers his desires for her were stronger than ever, impossible to ignore or control.

Sunshine splashed through the windows, creating a halo around Geneviève's naked body, and he marveled at her beauty. Soaked it all in. Every sensation, every touch, every word. Geneviève was a vocal and enthusiastic lover, and he enjoyed her playfulness. They moved as one body, perfectly in sync, and it took everything in him not to blurt out the truth.

"I've fallen hard for you, Roderick, and I *love* making love to you," she confessed, lowering her mouth to his. "You make me feel so damn good…"

Conflicting emotions flooded his heart. On one hand he was happy that Geneviève cared about him, but he worried about the repercussions of dating Welker, Bradford and Davidson's most successful client. Roderick pushed his fears to the furthest corner of his mind, refused to let anything ruin the moment. Making love to Geneviève exceeded his wildest dreams, and as she poured out her heart his feelings for her grew.

"Roderick, I know you're scared of getting hurt again, but take a chance on me. You're the only man I want, the only man I need, and I believe in us."

He opened his mouth to respond, but the words got stuck in his throat. His muscles contracted, and his thoughts spun. Increasing his pace, he thrusted harder, faster, gathering her close to his chest. Spasms rocked his body, and seconds passed before his limbs relaxed and the haze lifted from his brain.

Roderick stretched out on the couch, and wrapped his arms around Geneviève. He played with her hair, kissed her forehead, her nose and her shoulder. His eyes grew heavy with sleep, but he teased her about rocking his world Philly-style, and she burst out laughing.

"I still can't believe we're lovers," Geneviève said. "I mean, I wanted it to happen, but you're a pro at playing hard to get."

"I wasn't playing hard to get, Geneviève."

"Yes you were. One minute you're totally into me, and the next you're pushing me away."

Roderick blew out a deep breath. He didn't want to talk about his broken engagement, but he feared if he didn't open up to Geneviève about it she'd think he was still hung up on his ex. And nothing could be further from the truth. "My ex didn't just break my heart, she publicly humiliated me, and after she walked out on me I swore off relationships. She ruined my faith in women, and over the past year I've refused to let anyone get close to me."

"That's understandable. You had your world turned upside down, and you needed time to heal." Geneviève caressed his face with the back of her hand. "How do you feel now? Are you still wary of the opposite sex?"

Shaking his head, he stared deep into her eyes. "No. I came to Madrid for work, and fell for one of my clients, and she could be The One—"

"The One, or one of many?"

"Trust me," he said, leaning over and nibbling on her neck. "You're more than enough woman for me!"

Geneviève winked. "Good answer, Counselor!"

Roderick didn't know how long they lay on the couch whispering and cuddling, but he must have dozed off for hours because when he opened his eyes the cabin was shrouded in darkness.

"I'm going to go shower," Geneviève said. "But I promise I won't be long."

Yawning, he locked his hands behind his head. "No worries. Take as long as you need."

"Really? But I thought you wanted to go out today?"

To make her laugh, Roderick scoffed. "Woman, please. After all that good lovin' you gave me it will be a miracle if I can walk again, let alone ski!"

Chapter 17

Prima Restaurant & Theater was known for its eclectic menu and signature drinks, but what impressed Roderick most about the five-star restaurant was the talented waitstaff in elaborate velvet costumes. They sang traditional Spanish songs and joked with diners, and Geneviève whistled, cheered and clapped every time a waiter rushed into the dining room, singing at the top of his lungs. The performers were exuberant, the choreography was top-notch and the silver-haired piano player was hilarious. Owned by a father-daughter duo from Barcelona, the restaurant was popular among foreign travelers. Bright and inviting, with high ceilings, dim lighting and an open kitchen, the restaurant was buzzing with music, conversation and laughter.

"This is delicious," Roderick praised, pointing at his plate with his fork. His entrée was flavorful, seasoned with spices and one of the best meals he'd ever had. "You have to try some."

Geneviève pursed her red-painted lips. "I'm not trying wild boar, so you can forget it," she quipped, shaking her head. "I'm quite happy with my Caesar *ensalada*, so thanks but no thanks."

"You're adventurous in the bedroom so I figured you were adventurous with food, too."

Her eyes lit up. "Nope. Just in the bedroom and *just* with you."

A grin warmed his mouth. Memories of last night overwhelmed his mind. After waking up from their nap they'd ordered in, lit some candles and relaxed in the living room. For hours, they'd chatted and drank wine. They'd made love again, and although he'd woken up that morning exhausted from their late-night sexcapades, he'd hustled her out the door after breakfast and drove straight to the resort.

All day, they'd skied and played in the snow. Upon returning to the cabin that evening, Geneviève had offered to cook, but he'd insisted on taking her to Prima Restaurant & Theater for dinner and was enjoying her company. It did his heart good to see her smile and laugh. She looked beautiful in a white, lace dress, and every time their eyes met desire shot through his veins. Roderick wanted to lean across the table to kiss her, but knew if he did he'd lose all self-control, and didn't want to give the other diners in the restaurant an X-rated show.

"I want to go snowboarding tomorrow," she announced. "I've never tried it before, but I'd love to learn, and since you're an expert at winter sports I think you should teach me everything you know."

His tongue went numb, and his heart was beating so

loud it drowned out the music inside of the restaurant. Roderick didn't want to leave Vielha or disappoint Geneviève, and racked his brain for a solution to this problem. He considered calling Mr. Welker and requesting a week off work, but he knew his boss would never agree to his request, and dismissed the thought. "I'm returning to New York tomorrow afternoon," he explained. "My flight is at three o'clock."

The light in her eyes dimmed. "Are you sure you can't stay longer? I have the rental cabin booked for a couple more weeks so there's no reason to rush back to the States. It's quiet and secluded and the perfect place for some R&R."

"I have meetings I can't miss, and several clients eagerly awaiting my return, as well."

"Roderick, you can't go. You're my tall, dark and devilishly handsome bodyguard, and I need you to stay here and protect me."

"From what? Raccoons?"

"Yup, and coyotes, too. They're savages!"

He threw his head back and roared with laughter.

"I like having you around, and I won't feel safe at the cabin without you here."

"You're certainly as talented as Whitney Houston, but I'm not as stealth as Kevin Costner, so that bodyguard angle isn't going to fly with my boss."

Silence fell across the table, and even the tuxedo-clad waiters dancing in the aisle couldn't coax a smile from Geneviève's lips. Spending the past few weeks with her in Madrid had built a lot of trust and closeness between them, and he didn't want anything to weaken their bond. He didn't know what to do to bolster her spirits, and worried he'd ruined their romantic dinner by telling her about his impending travel plans.

"When will I see you again?" she asked.

Roderick opened his mouth, realized he didn't have an answer and slammed it shut.

Geneviève sat across the table from Roderick, studying his face for clues. Tried to understand why he was dodging her gaze. He couldn't look her in the eye and tugged at his shirt collar, as if it were choking him. Geneviève wanted to make the most of their time together and didn't want to stir the pot by badgering him about their future, but she wanted to know how he felt about her—before he left for New York—and figured now was the perfect time for a heart-to-heart. The performance was over, the restaurant was half-empty and her glass of white wine gave her confidence, calmed her frazzled nerves.

"Did you know turtles retreat inside their shells when they're afraid?" she said quietly, even though her pulse was beating in triple time. "I used to be like that. I've had so many close friends, family members and employees betray me during my career that I've lost count, and when my boyfriend broke my heart last year I wanted to run and hide, too."

Roderick lowered his utensils to his plate and leaned forward in his chair.

"For weeks, I shut myself away from everyone and vowed to keep the opposite sex at arm's length. But I realized in life pain is inevitable, but I didn't have to let it consume me or steal my joy. Every day, I make a conscious decision to live life fabulously and you should, too."

His face paled. "What makes you think I'm afraid?"

Her throat was dry, but she parted her lips and spoke the truth, even though Geneviève knew it would be hard for Roderick to hear. "I see it in your eyes every time you look at me."

"That's not true—"

"Yes, it is. You're scared history will repeat itself, and I'll break your heart just like your ex did, but I won't. I'm not her, Roderick. You can trust me."

His cell phone rang, and he glanced down at the table to check the number. It stopped ringing, then started up again seconds later, but Roderick didn't answer it.

"Someone's desperate to reach you," she pointed out, gesturing to his iPhone.

"All the more reason to let the call go to voice mail. Now, where were we?"

Geneviève paused, took a moment to collect her thoughts. She knew what she was about to say was going to rock the boat, but she didn't mince words. "We were discussing our relationship. Or rather, your reluctance to claim me as your girlfriend."

Sadness flickered in his eyes and pinched his facial features. "Geneviève, don't say things like that. It's not true. You know how I feel about you—"

"Do I?" she asked, interrupting him midsentence.

"If my boss or one of the other senior partners find out about us, I could face disciplinary action, or worse, lose my job. I love the firm and my clients, and I don't want to disappoint them."

"I understand." She didn't, but Geneviève didn't force the issue. She wanted to remind Roderick that Welker, Bradford and Davidson needed him, and not the other way around, but she bit her tongue.

Roderick stood, moved his chair beside hers then

draped an arm around her. "Geneviève, you're everything I could want in a woman, but I'm not ready to get married or have children and I know that's something you desperately want."

"You're right. I want to be a wife and mother, but relationships take time, and since I think we have what it takes to go the distance I don't mind putting motherhood on the back burner for a while."

He raised an eyebrow. "You don't?"

"I adore you, Roderick, and I want to be with you."

Roderick covered her hands with his own.

"I think the world of you, but if at any point you decide to walk away I'll understand. All I ask is that you be honest with me."

"Walk away?" he repeated. "Fat chance of *that* ever happening. You're one of a kind, Jennifer Tyesha Harris, and I'd rather be with you than with anyone else, but don't tell my mom I said that. She'd be crushed."

A laugh tickled her throat. "I'm looking forward to meeting your family. You talk about them so much, I feel like I already know them."

"Then you should be my plus-one for my brother's wedding in August."

"Hmm, I don't know," she said, though she was excited about the unexpected invitation. "That's seven months from now. Do you think we'll still be going strong by then?"

"Most definitely, so don't make any other plans. And feel free to invite Demi, too."

"No way. The last time I attended a wedding with my sister, she forced me to sing at the reception, and I ended up doing a thirty-minute set with the calypso band." Laughing at the memory, she slowly shook her head.

"The Long Island couple recently had their first child and named her Geneviève, so it was definitely worth it."

"And I bet she's just as beautiful as her namesake."

"Of course!" she quipped, with a cheeky smile. "That goes without saying!"

The waiter returned, cooing a sultry Spanish song, and cleared the empty dishes from the table. Roderick said he was full, but Geneviève ordered dessert and another bottle of wine.

"How much do you charge to perform at weddings?" Roderick asked. "My future sister-in-law is a huge fan of yours, and she wants you to sing at the ceremony."

"You don't have to pay me. I love weddings, and it would be an honor to take part."

"August 14 can't come soon enough," Roderick said, picking up his wine glass. "I love my brother, and I'm glad he found Karma, but I'm tired of hearing about their premarital counseling sessions, flower arrangements and honeymoon destinations. These days it's all Morrison talks about, and it's driving me nuts."

"It must have been hard for you to be around your brother when your engagement fell apart."

"Not at all. Why would it? I have a great career, a fantastic family and a car collection that makes me the envy of all my friends," he boasted, flashing a broad grin. "And if that isn't enough, I recently met a young, energetic beauty from Philly who I'm absolutely crazy about."

Her heart inflated with hope. Roderick lowered his head and kissed her palm. She turned his words over in her mind, hoping he meant it. His touch soothed her fears, made her think his feelings for her were real. His gaze was piercing, strong and intense, and warmed her all over. They'd been on only a few dates, but Geneviève was weak for him and couldn't picture her life without him.

That's impossible, argued her inner voice. *You're in lust, not love, so don't make any outrageous, heartfelt declarations.* Geneviève didn't heed the warning, knew her feelings for Roderick were real. There was no doubt in her mind that he was the right man for her. He supported her wholeheartedly, and having him in her corner meant everything to her. She put on a show for her fans, the executives at her record label and her social media followers every day, but with Roderick she could be her true, authentic self.

Scared her emotions would get the best of her and she'd blurt out the truth, Geneviève picked up her fork and tasted her dessert. Chewing slowly, she savored the sweet, moist cake. As they ate, they discussed their afternoon on the slopes, their favorite parts of the dinner theater show and her plans in Vielha for the rest of the month.

The waiter returned and bowed at the waist. "Mr. Drake, I trust that you enjoyed the show, and that the food was to your liking…"

Her thoughts wandered while the men spoke. Would Roderick make time to see her when she returned to the States next month? Was he serious about her being his plus-one for his brother's wedding? And most important, was he seeing other people? Roderick was a force, a magnet who women were helplessly drawn to, and Geneviève didn't want to compete with anyone else for his heart.

She didn't know what was going to happen in the future, but she knew one thing for sure: when they returned to the rental cabin they were going to make love. And when Roderick leaned over and kissed her passionately on the lips, Geneviève knew they shared the same thought.

Chapter 18

Roderick zipped up his camel leather suitcase, picked it up off the bed then exited the master suite. Marching down the hallway, whistling Geneviève's hit song, "Savage," he glanced out the window. Fluffy clouds sailed across the pale blue sky, the wind battered the trees dotting the property and icicles glistened in the morning sunshine.

His cell phone buzzed and he fished it out of the back pocket of his faded blue jeans. Roderick raked a hand through his hair. Demi had sent another text message asking him to call her, but he had to leave for the airport soon or he'd miss his afternoon flight. Even though Roderick liked the idea of spending more time with Geneviève, he didn't want to upset Mr. Welker. He'd blown his Madrid assignment, and now he had to work harder than ever to prove to his boss and the other senior partners that he was the perfect person to manage the athletic division in the Los Angeles firm.

Roderick heard the familiar whirl of an exercise machine, and poked his head into the home gym. A grin curled his lips. Geneviève was running full speed on the treadmill, but when she spotted him in the doorway she pressed the stop button and stepped down. Her workout clothes were drenched in sweat, but she still took his breath away. Abandoning his suitcase, he leaned against the doorframe, then folded his arms across his chest. "There's my number one girl," he said, admiring her taut, toned physique. "You look incredible as usual."

"Yeah, but I stink." Laughing, Geneviève grabbed her towel from the cup holder and wiped her face. "Where are you going? Your flight isn't for several more hours."

"I know, but I have a few stops to make before I head to the airport. My niece just texted me, begging me to bring her a Real Madrid jersey, and I don't want to disappoint her."

"You're a good man, Roderick Drake." Geneviève stood on her tiptoes and kissed his lips. "Are you sure there isn't anything I can do to persuade you to stay longer?"

Draping her arms around his neck, she pressed her body flat against his and brushed her mouth across his ear. Lust consumed him, but he resisted the needs of his flesh. Knew that if he made love to her again he'd miss his three o'clock flight, and Roderick didn't want to infuriate the senior partners. "We better not. I don't want to get fired—"

"Stop, being dramatic," she teased, rolling her eyes. "Welker, Bradford and Davidson will never fire you.

You're the best attorney they have, and they're lucky to have someone of your caliber working at their firm."

"Yeah, but I blew it, and my boss is pissed at me. I was supposed to settle the lawsuit with José Sánchez and ensure you finished the rest of your European tour, and I didn't."

"Canceling the tour was my decision, not yours. There's nothing you could have said or done to change my mind, so don't stress about it."

"Tell that to my boss. I had a lot riding on this trip, and since I came up short there's no way in hell I'll be named senior partner in May…" Seeing her eyes widen, then narrow, Roderick trailed off. "What's wrong?"

Tension filled the air as seconds ticked by.

"Y-y-you used me to get a promotion?" she stammered, dropping her hands to her sides.

Fear struck his heart, and Roderick struggled to free the truth from his mouth.

"Now everything makes sense," she continued. "You didn't drive to Vielha to check up on me. You drove down here to protect your own interests."

Guilt washed over him, filling him with shame and regret. "That's not true. I came here because I was worried about you."

"You don't give a damn about me. The only person you care about is yourself."

"Geneviève, I wasn't trying to deceive you. I swear. I was just doing my job—"

Her harsh laugh drowned out the rest of his sentence, and his voice faded.

"And what about Wednesday?" she demanded, folding her arms across her chest. "And last night on the couch? And this morning in the shower? Was that part of your job, too?"

Turning her accusations over in his mind, he understood her anger, her outrage, and searched his heart for the right words to say to soothe her feelings. From the moment they'd met, they'd had a powerful connection, and Roderick didn't want their relationship to end on a sour note. He looked forward to seeing Geneviève every day, enjoyed talking and joking with her, and would do anything for her—including keeping her location a secret from her family. Before Roderick could explain himself, Geneviève stepped past him and marched out of the room, grumbling about him being a wolf in sheep's clothing.

"I was wrong about you," she raged, tossing a glare over her shoulder. "You're not thoughtful or considerate or honest. You're an opportunist, just like everyone else who's ever worked for me, and I never should have trusted you."

His chest deflated. "I'm sorry. Tell me what you want me to do, what you need from me to make this right, and I'll do it."

"Get out." Geneviève stomped into the kitchen, snatched his car keys off the counter and chucked them at him. "I don't want you here."

"You don't mean that," he said, shaking his head.

She pointed at the door. "Yes, I do. Now please leave. You're not who I thought you were, and I have nothing more to say to you."

Roderick reached for her, but she slid behind the breakfast bar, using it as a shield. Glared at him in disgust, as if she couldn't stand to be in the same room as him, and the expression on her face troubled him. Made him think they'd never talk or laugh or kiss again. The thought made his shoulders sag. Her friendship meant everything to him, and he didn't want to lose her. In his wildest dreams, he never imagined falling for Geneviève and—

Falling? repeated his inner voice. *Is that what you call it? Naw, man, you're in love!*

The doorbell chimed. In his peripheral vision, he saw Althea standing in front of the window, banging on the glass with her fists. Strangling a groan, Roderick pressed his eyes shut. His morning had just gone from bad to worse.

Geneviève was at a loss for words. Dazed and confused, she glanced from the window to Roderick and back again. Her mom and Demi were standing on the doorstep, staring at her, and if Geneviève thought she could pull it off she'd drop to her knees and crawl out of the kitchen. Dressed in Gucci from head to toe, Althea looked elegant and classy, but her demeanor was sad. Demi's, too, and seeing the pained expressions on their faces made Geneviève feel guilty for shutting them out.

Her tongue was numb, and her throat was dry. It would be easier to free herself from handcuffs than form a coherent sentence, and when Geneviève tried to question Roderick, nothing came out of her mouth, not a word, not a sound. Her hands balled into fists. He'd betrayed her trust, and the urge to punch him was so strong it was all she could think about. Geneviève wanted to throw her iPod at him, but shoved it into the pocket of her leggings instead of giving in to her impulse.

How could Roderick do this to her? How could he break his promise? His word? She'd let his attention go to her head, and instead of protecting her heart, she'd fallen hard for him, and he'd used her gullibility to his advantage. Their relationship had been doomed from the start, and she'd been a fool to think they could ride off into the sunset and live happily ever after. "You called my mom? But I asked you not to."

"I didn't. I swear." His cell phone rang but he ignored it. "I spoke to her yesterday, and Demi, too, but I never revealed your location."

"Then how did she find me? You're the only one who knew I was here—"

"I didn't say anything to your mom," he insisted, his voice strong and convincing. "I know you think the worst of me right now, but I'm a loyal person. I would never betray you."

Her intuition told her Roderick was lying—again—but the sound of her mother's shrill voice made Geneviève lose her train of thought.

"Open this door right now," Althea demanded, stomping her foot. "Or I'll break it down."

Afraid her mom would make good on her threat, Geneviève forced her legs to move and dragged herself into the foyer. Her mom had a Mike Tyson-like temper, and she feared Althea would kick the door in with her high-heeled leather boots and storm inside, spoiling for a fight.

Sighing, Geneviève reluctantly unlocked the dead bolt, then stepped aside. "Hi, Mom."

"My baby!" Althea threw her arms around Geneviève and rocked her vigorously from side to side. "Gigi, are you okay? Tell Mom what's wrong I'm here now. I'll make everything better."

"Hey, sis." Demi sniffed, but her smile was bright. "I missed you *so* much."

To make her sister laugh, Geneviève joked, "Yeah, right. You probably didn't even notice I was gone. You have your beloved iPhone, your followers, and Warner, of course."

"N-n-not anymore," she stammered, fiddling with the silver ring on her thumb. "Warner dumped me a couple days ago."

Geneviève gave Demi a hug, and slowly rubbed her back. "Sweetie, what happened?"

"He's embarrassed of me. He says my YouTube page is silly, and that he's sick of his colleagues at city hall teasing him about my frivolous posts."

Straightening, Geneviève wore a sympathetic expression on her face. She'd been surprised when her sister started dating the budget analyst months earlier, but Warner was a great catch and Geneviève thought they made a cute couple. "Demi, I'm sorry to hear that. I know how much you love Warner and how much he means to you—"

"The worst part about the breakup is that you weren't around to talk to. You're not just my sister, Gigi, you're my best friend and I need you…"

Biting the inside of her cheek, Geneviève dropped her gaze to the floor. The outpouring of love from her family touched her deeply, making her realize how fortunate she was to have people in her life who were 100 percent loyal to her.

"Why did you run off?" Demi asked. "You had to know we'd be worried about you. We love you, Gigi, and life sucks when you're not around."

Overcome with emotion, Geneviève felt tears spill

down her cheeks. Geneviève didn't know why she was crying, but once she started she couldn't stop. Her mom held her tight, whispering words of comfort in her ear. Looking back, she recognized that hooking up with Roderick was one of the worst mistakes she'd ever made, and Geneviève wished she'd listened to her mom. Althea said attorneys were cutthroat, manipulative and sneaky, and had warned her not to trust him. *If I had listened to my mom I wouldn't be in this predicament now. Her gaze drifted across the room, landing on Roderick, and her heart ached inside her chest. Their eyes met, but Geneviève turned to her family, giving him her back.*

"Oh great, we have company," Demi drawled, her voice dripping with sarcasm. Moving quickly, she rushed around the main floor closing blinds and drapes. "The photogs just pulled up, so if you don't want to be on the cover of the *National Enquirer* avoid the windows…"

At first, Geneviève thought Demi was joking, but when she heard car doors slam and footsteps on the porch, she realized her sister was telling the truth. She straightened her shoulders and wiped her face with her hands.

Someone pounded on the door, then the bell chimed repeatedly.

"Geneviève, open up!" said a male voice.

"I want to interview you…"

A woman shouted, "Let me tell the world *your* side of the story!"

Frowning, Geneviève slanted her head to the right. *My side of the story? What in the world is she talking about?* She moved over to the window, parted the curtains behind the chaise sectional and peered outside. Chills flooded her body. Photographers, reporters and camera crews jockeyed for position on the wraparound porch, clutching electronic devices in their hands.

"I can't believe this," she grumbled. "There's paparazzi everywhere."

"You tipped the press off about Geneviève's whereabouts, didn't you?" Althea spoke in a clipped tone of voice. "You'll do anything to draw attention to yourself and your fancy law firm, won't you, Roderick?"

"That's not true," Roderick argued. "I only want what's best for Geneviève."

Scowling, Althea slowly clapped her hands. "I have to give it to you, Roderick. You're one hell of an actor. You tricked my daughter into believing you were a stand-up guy, but I knew you were a fraud from day one."

Speaking through clenched teeth, Roderick vehemently defended his name. "I've never spoken to the media about any of my clients and I never will."

"Can someone please tell me what's going on?" Geneviève asked.

"Sis, I'll show you, but you have to promise you won't get upset."

Too late, she thought, her body vibrating with anger. *I'm so mad I could scream!*

Demi took her cell phone out of her leather Dior purse, swiped her finger across the screen then typed for several seconds. Wearing an apologetic smile, she raised her iPhone in the air with one hand and squeezed Geneviève's shoulder with the other. "This bogus story is all over the internet, and several of the local TV stations have picked it up as well…"

The room spun, flipping upside down on its head, but she read the damning headline on the popular gossip site out loud. "'American Pop Star Geneviève Has

Mental Breakdown and Escapes to Baqueira-Beret with Her Dashing New York Attorney.'"

Her heart ached. Seeing the online story not only raised more questions about Roderick's character, it reopened old wounds. Since she'd signed her first deal with Urban Beats Records, it had been one betrayal after another. Employees often took advantage of her kindness, relatives helped themselves to items from her house when she was out of town and so-called friends leaked personal information to the tabloids instead of keeping her secrets. A terrifying realization struck her as she stared at Roderick. He'd done it, sold her out to the press, and now that Geneviève knew the truth she'd have to sever all ties with him.

"You should be ashamed of yourself. You used my daughter to advance your career—"

Roderick reached for her, but Geneviève pushed his hand away. "I didn't. I wouldn't," he pleaded in a desperate voice. "You have to believe me. I'd never do anything to hurt you."

"Leave, or I'll put you out," Althea snapped. "And if you ever contact Gigi again, I'll file an official complaint with Welker, Bradford and Davidson *and* the New York City Bar Association."

The muscles around his eyes tightened, and Geneviève knew he was angry. Good. She wanted Roderick to hurt, just as much as she was hurting, and didn't mind her mother threatening him. Geneviève recognized she was being petty and spiteful, but she couldn't control her feelings—or forgive Roderick for deceiving her.

"Geneviève, I'll call you when my flight lands in New York." He picked up his suitcase then exited the cabin.

"Good riddance," Althea said, slamming the front door. "Gosh, I thought he'd never leave."

Geneviève peered out the window. The paparazzi pounced on Roderick like sharks circling their prey, but he strode through the crowd as if he didn't have a care in the world. Typical Roderick. No matter the situation, he was always cool, always collected, and his calm, unflappable nature was one of the things she loved most about him.

Geneviève pressed her eyes shut. Deleted the thought from her mind. Told herself to stop thinking about him. They were over, and the sooner she forgot about him the better off she'd be.

"Gigi, we have to return to Madrid." Althea opened her vintage-style purse, took out her leather-bound calendar and tapped her finger against it. "If we're going to salvage the rest of the tour we'll have to meet with concert promoters ASAP."

"Mom, there's nothing to salvage. I'm taking a break, and there's nothing you can say or do to change my mind, so please let this go."

"Honey, you can't be serious. You can't cancel the second half of the European tour—"

"I already did." Her limbs felt heavy, as if they weighed hundreds of pounds, and moving required every ounce of her strength Geneviève had, but she walked across the room. "I'm going to lie down."

Althea dumped her things on the love seat. "I'll come with you. We have a lot to discuss and there's no better time than the present, so we can catch up while you rest."

"Not now, later." Geneviève hurried down the hallway before her mom could protest, ducked inside the master bedroom and locked the door. The room was sunny and bright, but the faint scent of Roderick's cologne filled her with despair. Her eyes wide, she inclined her head to the right and inspected the sleigh bed. A bouquet of carnations, a box of luxury chocolates tied with gold ribbon and a red heart-shaped envelope were propped against her pillow. Her first thought was to toss everything out the window, but her curiosity got the best of her and she ripped open the card. Reading it, her legs gave way and she sank onto the bed.

> *You asked when we're going to see each other*
> *again and the answer is simple: anytime you want.*
> *I'm just a phone call away.*
> *Love always, Roderick*

Choking back tears, Geneviève held the card to her chest. She told herself not to cry, willed herself to keep it together, but for the second time in minutes her vision blurred and her heart throbbed in pain. Remembering all the times they'd talked and laughed, their romantic dates and late-night conversations cuddled up in front of the fireplace, Geneviève couldn't believe he'd betrayed her trust.

Geneviève vacillated over what to do with the gifts. Keep them, or dump them? It was a thoughtful gesture, but she didn't want any reminders of Roderick, wanted to forget they'd ever met. To prove it, she surged to her feet, scooped the presents up in her arms then marched across the room. Second thoughts rose in her mind, but Geneviève pushed them aside and dumped the unwanted gifts into the wicker wastebasket.

Chapter 19

On Saturday afternoon, Geneviève unlocked the front door of her mother's Southampton estate, dropped the spare key on the raised, marble table in the entryway then ambled through the foyer. Yawning, Geneviève struggled to keep her eyes open. She hadn't had a good night's sleep since returning to the States last week and if she didn't have to talk some sense into her mother, she'd still be at home in bed. Demi had a condo nearby, and she'd spent the past few days relaxing at her sister's bachelorette pad. Demi said she was over Warner, and acted as if their breakup was no big deal on her social media pages, but Geneviève could see through her sister's facade. Demi loved Warner with all her heart, and was devastated by his rejection. To cheer her up, Geneviève baked her favorite desserts and took her shopping, but nothing she did made Demi smile.

Geneviève heard her mother's voice in the distance,

guessed she was relaxing in the den and strode through the main floor. Her iPhone rang, and she checked the number on the screen. Her producer was blowing up her cell—again—but Geneviève let the call go to voice mail. Executives at Urban Beats Records wanted her back in the studio, and even though she'd told them numerous times that she was taking a break they hounded her at every turn, and Althea was no better. Her mom texted her nonstop about lucrative business opportunities, but Geneviève turned down every offer. Wouldn't reconsider, even though her mother begged her to.

The air smelled sweet, like a rose garden, and the fragrant scent instantly calmed her. Obsessed with Afrocentric art, her mom had decorated the mansion with espresso furnishings, zebra-printed ottomans and pillow cushions, carved masks and eye-catching ceramics. Framed photographs covered the ivory-painted walls, but seeing the pictures they'd taken in Madrid weeks earlier made her heart ache.

Geneviève thought about the last time she'd seen Roderick, and wondered if she'd overreacted. Was he telling the truth? Had someone else on her team contacted the press about her whereabouts? Did it even matter? Breaking things off with Roderick was the smart thing to do. He wasn't ready to settle down, didn't know if he wanted a family, and that was reason enough to stay away from him.

That was easier said than done, Geneviève thought, pocketing her cell phone. All week, she'd thought of Roderick and nothing else, and being in the Hamptons made her long to see him. He called and texted her every day, sent her hilarious messages and had even arranged to have carnations delivered to her sister's condo. Geneviève had a sneaking suspicion that Demi was helping Roderick, but her sister denied it. Getting over Roderick was going to be harder than anything she'd ever done, but Geneviève was determined to move on with her life.

"Geneviève's not at her estate in Philly. She's staying in the Hamptons with her sister…"

Frowning, she stopped outside of the den and listened closely. Geneviève knew eavesdropping was wrong, but her mom was talking about her, and she wanted to know why. The door was closed, but she heard every salacious word that her mother said. Geneviève didn't know what to think, what to do, and thought maybe she was dreaming. Had to be. There was no way her mom was in cahoots with the tabloids. It was impossible, unthinkable…or was it? A cold breeze flooded the hallway and Geneviève shivered.

"And if you want the address it'll cost you ten thousand dollars," she continued, her voice brimming with confidence. "Throw in an extra five grand and I'll tell you about Geneviève's red-hot fling with Memphis rap star Rashad J."

Geneviève inclined her head. *What in the world? This can't be happening.* Her stomach churned, and a million conflicting thoughts raced through her head. She considered all of the conversations she'd had with her mom in recent weeks and swallowed the lump in her throat.

It wasn't her staff selling her out to the press. It was her mom. Now she understood how the tabloids knew so much about her personal life, how the photographers always knew where she'd be and why her mom insisted on knowing her whereabouts.

Desperate to get to the bottom of things, Geneviève opened the door and marched inside the room. Althea was sitting in a velvet armchair with her legs propped up on the mahogany desk, talking on her cell phone. The scales fell from Geneviève's eyes as she continued listening to her mother's conversation. Althea erupted in laughter, but when she spotted her standing in the doorway she gasped, and her iPhone fell from her hands. The look on her face said it all: she was guilty. "G-G-Gigi," she stammered, rising to her feet. "How long have you been standing there?"

"Long enough to know that you're a liar."

"Watch your mouth. I'm your mother, and I won't let you disrespect me."

Geneviève exhaled. Her mother's behavior was impossible to ignore and hard to justify, but she governed her temper, didn't lash out at her. "Mom, how could you do this to me?"

"You're only as big as your next song, so to keep you relevant I sell stories to the press from time to time."

"But they're lies."

"Who cares? All that matters is that the tabloids print the pictures, and I get paid."

"Paid?" she repeated, her eyes widening. "You have luxury cars, several expensive homes and enough money in the bank to last you a lifetime. Isn't that enough?"

"It will never be enough." Sniffling, Althea shifted her slipper-clad feet. "I was a great singer with an aspiring music career, but I had to give it all up when I got pregnant with you at twenty-three…"

Her voice cracked, and seconds passed before she could finish the rest of her sentence.

"After your father left, I struggled for many, many years to provide for you and your sister, and deep down

I'll always be scared of losing everything I've worked so hard for."

Silence fell across the room, and Geneviève was glad to have a quiet moment to reflect on everything her mom had said. They were millionaires who could afford to buy anything they wanted, and even if Geneviève decided to retire from the music business they'd still live a comfortable life. She wished she could see inside her mother's head to understand her rationale, but Geneviève suspected her mom was afraid of history repeating herself, and sympathized with her. She'd single-handedly raised her two daughters with no financial or emotional support from her ex-husband, and for as long as Geneviève lived, her mom would always be her hero. But, that didn't mean she was going to let Althea control her, or sell lies to the press.

"Gigi, I'm sorry," she said with an apologetic smile. "I never meant to hurt you."

"Mom, you've been deceiving me for years. What did you *think* was going to happen?"

"I don't know. I guess I wasn't thinking."

"That's it? That's all you have to say for yourself?" Geneviève scoffed. "I broke up with Roderick because I thought he betrayed me, but he didn't. *You* did. *You* were the one who called the press in Madrid and told them where I was."

Stepping forward, Althea took Geneviève's hands in her own and squeezed them. "I'll stop selling stories to the tabloids. I promise."

Geneviève stared at her mom for a long moment, but she couldn't tell if Althea was telling her the truth.

"Mom, I love you, and I'm grateful for everything you've done for me over the years, but if you ever sell a fabricated story about me to the press again, I'll fire you."

Her eyes wide with alarm, Althea cupped a hand over her mouth. "You don't mean that."

"Yes, I do," she shot back. "You work for me, not the other way around, and if I find out you're in cahoots with the tabloids I'll replace you without a second thought."

"Gigi, you're blowing things out of proportion. I didn't do anything cruel or sinister…"

Her thoughts wandered, and images of Roderick flashed in her mind. *I have to see him, now, before it's too late. I was wrong, and I have to apologize for shutting him out.* The memory of their first kiss was burned in her brain forever, and thinking about that tender, romantic moment at the tapas bar caused her temperature to rise. She'd found love when she'd least expected it, and wanted to spend the rest of her days and nights with Roderick. But first she had to make things right with him.

Anxious to see Roderick again, she spun around, marched out of the den and rushed down the hallway. She took her cell phone out of her jacket pocket, typed her password and searched for his cell number.

"Gigi, come back here! We need to talk!" Althea pleaded. "Where are you going?"

Without breaking her stride, Geneviève glanced over her shoulder and flashed a cheeky smile. "To get my man, of course."

Chapter 20

"Damn, bro, you look like hell." Morrison clapped Roderick on the shoulder. "What's wrong?"

Roderick raised his flute to his mouth and drank some champagne, savoring the fresh, citrus taste. He was standing at the custom-made bar inside the great room of his childhood home in the Hamptons, surrounded by friends, family members and business associates. Roderick was supposed to be celebrating his brother's birthday, but his heart was so heavy he couldn't even smile. The estate was filled with black-and-white helium balloons, bearing heartfelt messages to Duane. Metallic streamers hung from the ceiling, party banners decorated the walls and tuxedo-clad waiters carrying silver trays offered guests appetizers and cocktails. "Thanks, Mo," he said sarcastically. "I can always count on you to cheer me up when I'm down."

Leaning against the marble counter, Morrison wore

a sympathetic smile. "Are you still bummed about your argument with Geneviève, or the meeting you had with your boss?"

Both. All across the room, people socialized, snapped pictures and danced, but Roderick didn't have the energy to mingle with the other guests. His thoughts were a million miles away.

The conversation he'd had with Mr. Welker yesterday played in his mind, and every time he remembered the things his boss had said anger coursed through his veins. Inwardly seething, Roderick gripped the flute so hard he was surprised it didn't shatter in his hands. Althea had made good on her threat and filed a formal complaint against him. To appease the feisty momager, Mr. Welker had given Roderick a written reprimand, revoked his transfer to LA and issued a three-month pay cut. During the meeting, he'd learned that Mr. Welker was the one who'd revealed Geneviève's location to Althea, but he still didn't know who'd tipped off the press about the rental cabin.

Initially, he'd planned to fight the disciplinary action, but after discussing the situation with his brothers last night while having drinks at their favorite Brooklyn pub, he'd changed his mind. Duane and Morrison had given it to him straight; he'd broken the rules, upset one of the law firm's richest clients and deserved to be punished. He'd been annoyed with them, pissed that they'd sided with his boss, but deep down Roderick knew they were right.

"I'll be fine." It was a lie, but he didn't want his brother to worry about him. To get Morrison off his back, Roderick jabbed him in the side with his elbow and asked, "How are the honeymoon plans coming along? Have you finally decided where to take Karma after you tie the knot?"

"No, and I'm running out of time. It's a toss-up between Tahiti and Amalfi Coast, but—"

"Oh brother, not again. Do you ever talk about anything besides your fiancée?"

Roderick turned around, took one look at Duane and burst out laughing. Chuckled long and hard. His brother was wearing a gold party hat tilted to the side, birthday-themed sunglasses, and a round, shiny button that said It's My Birthday was pinned to his suit jacket. "Happy birthday, old man," Roderick teased, giving Duane a one-arm hug. "How does it feel to be a year older, but not wiser?"

Duane popped his shirt collar. "Bro, don't hate, congratulate. I'm living the American dream, I'm fine as hell and I don't look a day over twenty-one."

"Are you high?" Morrison scoffed. "You must be, because you're talking crazy again!"

While his brothers traded jabs, Roderick finished his drink. Morrison and Duane were a riot, and listening to them crack jokes helped him momentarily forget his problems. Roderick reached into his pants pocket, clutched his iPhone and discreetly checked the screen. His shoulders slumped. He didn't have any voice mails or text messages from Geneviève. *Why hasn't she returned any of my calls? Doesn't she know I'm losing my mind without her?*

All week, he'd been tracking her social media pages, and last night she'd posted a series of cryptic Tweets about relationships, then added pictures of herself with an NFL quarterback at a trendy café. His mind had gone to a dark place, but when he remembered all of the good times they'd shared in Madrid—and their explosive, passionate lovemaking—he dismissed all thoughts of Geneviève hooking up with other men. To alleviate his fears, he'd reached out to Demi and learned that Geneviève was serious about taking a break from music, and was spending her time off writing songs, taking art classes and volunteering at inner-city music programs. The news had made him smile. There was no doubt in his mind that she'd be a hit with her students, and he was proud of her for giving back to the community.

Heaving a deep sigh, Roderick glanced around the room. Guests danced to the R&B music playing on the stereo system, and the iconic Lauren Hill song made Roderick think of Geneviève. It wasn't until he'd lost her that he realized how much she meant to him, how much he adored her. She'd put some spice into his life, excitement, spontaneity and adventure, and he wanted to create more wonderful memories with her.

A month ago, he'd been obsessed with becoming senior partner at his law firm, but now Geneviève—not Welker, Bradford and Davidson—mattered more to him than anything. Demi had agreed to speak to her sister on his behalf, but Roderick wasn't going to sit around and wait for Geneviève to contact him. Couldn't risk that NFL pretty boy stealing his place—and her heart.

Roderick checked his watch. He was anxious to leave, but decided to slip out the back door after dessert. Once the party ended, he was going to Geneviève's Philadelphia estate, and he wasn't leaving her gated mansion until she agreed to speak to him. Since his engagement ended, he'd avoided getting close to anyone, had purposely kept the opposite sex at arm's length, but her cheeky smile, exuberant laugh and spirit had won him over, and now he wanted her to be his girlfriend. He couldn't imagine his life without Geneviève. He pictured them dating long-term and hoped she could find it in her heart to forgive him. Roderick regretted pressuring her to continue the European tour, but the accusations Althea had made against him were false, and Roderick was desperate to clear his name. It took losing Geneviève for him to realize how much she meant to him, and if she forgave him he would never take her for granted again.

"Roderick, you're the best!" Karma gushed, throwing her arms around his neck.

A grin curled his lips. The salon owner was a spitfire, a ball of positive energy, and her crimson red, fit-and-flare cocktail dress complemented her bright personality. "It's good to see you, too."

"I can't believe Geneviève's going to sing at my wedding! It's a dream come true."

Morrison cleared his throat. "Your wedding?"

"I mean *our* wedding." Wearing a sheepish smile, Karma linked arms with Morrison and rested her head on his shoulder. "Sorry about that, baby. I didn't mean anything by it. This is *our* wedding, and it's going to be an incredible day because I'm marrying my one true love—"

Roderick interrupted her midsentence. "How do you know Geneviève agreed to sing at your wedding? I spoke to her about it in Madrid, but I never told you she agreed to perform."

"Duh," Karma said with a smirk. "Geneviève told me herself and I almost fainted when she did!"

Roderick scratched his head. "I don't understand."

"Brother-in-law, are you okay?" Stepping forward, Karma peered at him like a specimen under a microscope. "You've been acting strange ever since you returned from Madrid two weeks ago, and I'm worried about you."

"Love can do that to a guy," Duane joked. "And trust me, Roderick's got it bad."

Ignoring his brother, Roderick raised his voice to be heard over the noise in the room. "When did you speak to Geneviève, and how did you get her cell phone number?"

"I didn't. I saw her in the foyer and introduced myself." A proud smile curled her lips. "It's not every day I get to meet my shero, and I wasn't going to let the opportunity pass me by."

It took a moment for her words to sink in, and when Roderick glanced over his shoulder and spotted Geneviève standing in the foyer with his parents, his mouth fell open. Seeing her was a shock to his system, and he feared his legs would give way. Looking striking in a one-shoulder, mustard-colored dress, gold accessories and stilettos, Geneviève took his breath away, and his heart soared to unimaginable heights.

"Bro, snap out of it. Quit staring at Geneviève like a deer in headlights and go talk to her."

Roderick wanted to take Morrison's advice, but his leather Armani shoes were glued to the marble floor. He tried to speak, but his lips wouldn't move.

"Get going." Duane shoved him toward the hallway. "This is your big chance, so don't screw it up. We're counting on you."

Snapping out of his mental fog, Roderick marched through the corridor, reaching the woman he loved in four quick strides. He knew everyone was watching him—his friends, his family and the professional photographers his mother had hired for the party—but he took Geneviève in his arms anyway and kissed her. He couldn't help himself, couldn't resist his flesh. She tasted better than he remembered. He put one hand on her hip, the other on her cheek, and devoured her lips. Forgot about everyone else and focused on pleasing her. "Am I ever glad to see you," he whispered against her mouth .

"I know. I can tell."

Whistling, Roderick caressed her hips. "Wow, that was some kiss."

Geneviève winked. "You're welcome."

"I can't believe you're here. You should be in Philly, maxing and relaxing at your estate."

"No, I should be right here with you." Her smile was sad. "I came here to apologize. I shouldn't have accused you of selling me out to the press, or betraying my trust…"

His eyes narrowed. He spotted Reagan at the other end of the hallway, and his niece was waving with such gusto it looked like she was fending off a bee. Behind him, he heard his parents whispering to each other, and Roderick wished they'd return to the party instead of listening in on his private conversation, but before he could ask them to leave Geneviève spoke, and the words died on his lips.

"I made a mistake, and I hope you can find it in your heart to forgive me because I'm absolutely crazy about you, and I want to be your girlfriend."

His mother oohed and aahed as if she were watching the most romantic movie of all time, and answered on his behalf. "Of course Roderick can forgive you. You're only human, and it's obvious you love my son very much, and that's the best news ever!"

Roderick loved his parents, but he wanted them to

disappear. Wanting privacy, he considered taking Geneviève into the media room, but he knew Viola would follow them so he stayed put. He held her tight, inhaling her floral perfume, and his thoughts returned to the night of her final concert in Madrid. Seeing Geneviève fall onstage had been the most terrifying moment of his life. He'd wanted to help her, to protect her, and from now on he would. He was going to be her ally, her biggest supporter, and would do everything in his power to keep her safe. He'd been given a second chance with the Philly beauty, and he wasn't going to blow it.

"Roderick, there's no pressure." Geneviève spoke in a quiet voice. "We'll take things slow, but if the stress that comes with dating a pop star becomes too much for you and you decide you don't want to be with me just tell me the truth. I'm a big girl. I can handle it—"

"That's not going to happen. You're the perfect woman for me and I don't want to lose you again."

"I've been a mess ever since you left the cabin, and every time I think about the things I said to you that morning I feel sick to my stomach…"

Holding her close, Roderick stroked her hair, her neck and shoulders. He didn't care that everyone at the party was watching them with wide eyes and gaping mouths. He'd been given a second chance with Geneviève and he wanted her to know how much he loved her, even if he had trouble saying the words.

"I should have listened to you instead of kicking you out." Geneviève reached out, and slowly caressed his cheek with her palm. "I let my emotions get the best of me, and I'm sorry."

"You're not the only one to blame for our argument," he said, meeting her gaze. "I should have been honest with you about the promotion and my desire to transfer to the LA office, but it never occurred to me we'd hit it off, let alone fall in love, yet that's exactly what happened."

Her face lit up. "You love me?"

"Of course I love you. You're smart, witty and ridiculously funny and I couldn't imagine being with anyone else. You're it for me, Gigi, and I love you with all my heart."

To prove it, Roderick kissed her tenderly on the lips. A finger jabbed his shoulder, over and over again, and he cranked his head to the right. His dad flashed a thumbs-up, but his mom was giving him the stink eye, and Roderick knew she was upset.

"Son, enough," she scolded in a shrill voice. "You know better than that. You'll have plenty of time to romance your beautiful girlfriend later." Viola adjusted the neckline of her gold sequined dress, then swept a hand toward the great room with dramatic flair. "Geneviève is a guest in our home, and you will treat her with the utmost respect. Get her a glass of champagne, show her around our estate and introduce her to the rest of the family."

"With pleasure," he answered, wearing a broad smile. "I'd love nothing more."

"And I love you, Roderick Miles Drake."

"Of course you do. There's a lot to love!"

Geneviève laughed, and it was music to his ears.

"I don't know what the future holds, but I love you and want to be with you for the rest of my life."

"Roderick, I feel the same way. You're everything I could ever want in a man, and I'm proud to be your girl." Closing her eyes, Geneviève pressed her mouth against his. Cheers, whistles and applause exploded around the room, and Roderick knew his friends and family were still watching them. It didn't matter. He was 100 percent focused on pleasing Geneviève, and he wasn't letting her go until he had his fill of her, and there wasn't anything his mom could do about it.

Deepening the kiss, Roderick inclined his head and held her close to his chest. Joy flooded his body, making him feel like the happiest man alive, and love filled his heart to the brim. He'd found his soul mate, the woman of his dreams, and as they stood in the foyer gazing longingly at each other, there was no doubt in his mind that they'd make beautiful music together.

* * * * *

"What are you doing?" she asked. Her hands gripped his strong arms.

"Hugging you." His voice was a sexy whisper. His head lowered. His lips stopped right before they touched hers.

Erin's heart hammered. The tips of her breasts tightened against the planes of his chest. Excitement simmered in her veins. The heat in his eyes could have melted iron.

"Kissing you?"

She could pull back now, and he'd let her go. He'd say goodbye, walk away and never bring up what happened again. Will was a ladies' man, but he wasn't a jerk. If she didn't want his kiss, he'd accept that.

She knew what she wanted. It wasn't due to the fun of the night, the look in his eye or two glasses of wine. The soft plea in his voice when he'd asked. The smallest hint that he was just as eager for their lips to touch as she was. That was what busted her defenses. Erin lifted on her toes and pressed her lips to his.

Synithia Williams has loved romance novels since reading her first one at the age of thirteen. It was only natural that she would one day write her own romance. She is a 2017 RITA® Award finalist and a 2018 African American Literary Awards romance nominee. When she isn't writing, Synithia works on water quality issues in the Midlands of South Carolina while taking care of her supportive husband and two sons.

Books by Synithia Williams

Harlequin Kimani Romance

A New York Kind of Love
A Malibu Kind of Romance
Full Court Seduction
Overtime for Love
Guarding His Heart
His Pick for Passion

Visit the Author Profile page
at Harlequin.com for more titles.

HIS PICK FOR PASSION

Synithia Williams

To my husband and best friend, Eric. I love you.

Dear Reader,

This is the last book in my Scoring for Love series. If you've been here since the start, thank you for taking this journey with me. If this is your first book in the series, I hope you enjoy it and decide to check out the other books. There are many layers to friendship, and you never know what can tip the balance in a friendship. In *His Pick for Passion*, I explore what happens when a platonic friendship becomes romantic and how that can affect relationships with others. I got the idea for this story after an after-hours conversation with coworkers. Which proves inspiration can come from anywhere. I hope you enjoy Will and Erin's road to happily-ever-after. Be sure to sign up on my website, www.synithiawilliams.com, to get updates on the next steps in my writer's journey.

XOXO,

Synithia W.

Chapter 1

"She's the only woman who's ever told you no. That's why you're being difficult."

Will Hampton paused in the middle of putting the diamond Cartier watch on his wrist while holding his cell phone between his right ear and shoulder. He was ready for a night out in Chicago after his team, the Jacksonville Gators, won their basketball game the night before. The team headed back to Jacksonville afterward, but he'd stayed in town to attend a party and hopefully hook up with supermodel Vanessa Collum.

Or at least, those were his plans before his sister called him with this nonsense.

Will clasped his watch closed and straightened, holding his cell phone in his hand. "Kelly, what are you talking about?"

"You don't want to do me this one favor because Erin

is the only woman who doesn't fall over in a dead faint when you smile at her," his sister continued in her accusatory tone. "Come on, Will. She just moved to Chicago six months ago, and I know she doesn't know anyone. She's sitting at home, alone, on a Friday night, bored to tears and wishing she'd worked up the nerve to ask out the guy in her office."

Will snorted. "I can't imagine Erin asking out any guy." Not that his sister's longtime best friend would be afraid to ask a guy out, but more that she'd be too focused on doing her own thing to chase after a man who wasn't confident enough to ask her out. He'd overheard enough of her conversations with his sister about how she wanted a man who wasn't afraid to approach her.

"Erin's trying to come into the new millennium," Kelly said with a bit of a laugh. "This guy is interested, but he's hesitating because they work together. Or at least that's what I've gathered from what she's told me about him. Regardless of him, she's relatively new in town, alone and most likely bored. You're there and it'll only take you two minutes to drop in and make sure she's okay. Then you can run off with that supermodel you're trying to hook up with and be on your merry way."

"I can guarantee you Erin doesn't want to see me. She doesn't like me that much."

Something he'd accepted a long time ago. Erin liked men who were serious. Dependable. He'd recognized early on he wasn't that guy.

"She likes you." He could hear the but in Kelly's voice. "She just doesn't think you're very…datable."

"Which means she doesn't like me."

Datable, though. Did that mean Erin had considered dating him? The thought brought a small smile to his lips.

"Does it matter? She likes you well enough. She's my best friend, and you two could always talk about basketball. Come on, Will, just go check on her. She sounded a little down when I talked to her earlier. I want to make sure she's okay."

Will sighed heavily, though it was mostly for show, and checked his watch. "Where does she stay?" He could swing through real quick just to do his sister this favor. Erin was her best friend, and even though he doubted Erin would want to see him, it would ease Kelly's mind.

He hadn't seen Erin since she'd visited their family last Christmas. They'd talked a little about the Gators' season but that was the extent of their conversation. Erin never lingered when it came to talking to him. He never pressed for more of her time.

"Thank you, Will!" Kelly's appreciation oozed through the phone. "I'll text you her address. She's going to be happy to see you."

"No, she's not. She's going to cut her eyes at me. Look at me like I'm lacking something, then send me on my way."

Erin wasn't mean, but she was no-nonsense. Always focused on her next step for success. He sometimes felt as if he weren't working hard enough when she was around. That his accomplishments on the basketball court were trivial, even though Erin, a former athlete, loved basketball as much as he did.

Kelly laughed. "Dang, Will, must every woman you know fall at your feet? Aren't you getting enough play from professional basketball groupies? Does my best friend have to drool when you walk in a room, too?"

Will tugged on the collar of his shirt. "I ain't saying all that."

"But you do love the attention of the ladies. Erin is cool. She just never fell for your lines."

Will checked his reflection in the mirror and ran a hand over his newly trimmed beard. "That's because I've never tried them on her," he teased.

His sister's deep belly laugh smacked the smile right off his face. "Oh my God! You've got me crying." She hiccupped and giggled some more. "Seriously, don't embarrass yourself. Just check on Erin. Let me know she's okay and then move on to one of the other women who fall for your silly lines. Call me after you see her, okay?" Another chuckle. "Never tried them on her. Boy, bye."

The end of the call cut off his sister's merriment. Will stared at the phone for several seconds. His words hadn't been that funny.

His phone vibrated, and a text from his sister popped up with Erin's address. According to the map feature on his phone she didn't live too far from his hotel. He texted his friend who was throwing the party Vanessa was attending and told her he'd be a few minutes late, then headed out of his hotel room to the driver waiting for him downstairs.

On the way through the lobby, his sister's laughter nagged him. He frowned and avoided eye contact with the people in the hotel who may have tried to stop him and ask for an autograph or a quick picture. He didn't typically shun the attention he got as a professional athlete. He loved being in the league. Loved being at the top of his game and especially loved the fans.

Fans cheered if the team was winning or losing. They sent emails of encouragement, tagged him and his teammates in pictures on social media of them rocking their Gators gear, and met the team at 3:00 a.m. after a win on the road to support them. But at the moment, he was too distracted by the way his sister outright laughed at him.

He slipped inside the car waiting for him in front of the hotel. Sure he'd never tried to hit on Erin, but that was because he'd always assumed Erin wouldn't entertain his interest. He was used to landing on his feet. Erin had the ability to knock him on his ass the same way she'd done in that one pickup game they'd played when they were ten years old. She'd demand more of him, and as Will's father liked to point out, he was a one-trick pony. Outside of basketball, there wasn't much people expected out of him.

What if he was wrong? What would happen if he let Erin get a glimpse of what he'd considered off and on over the years? If he showed her he was interested in her as more than the girl he'd played ball with as a kid or his sister's best friend?

Man, don't get any bright ideas. Stick to what you know. Women like Vanessa. Easy. No expectations.

Will arrived at Erin's apartment complex and asked the driver to wait. He'd check in on her, call Kelly and let her know Erin was okay, then make his way to the party. No foolish ideas of hitting on Erin.

He knocked on her door, then shoved back his sleeve to check the time. He had another twenty minutes to get to the party if he hoped to convince Vanessa to leave with him and see the hit show *Slam!* playing in town.

The door to Erin's apartment flew open. The annoyed twist to Erin's full lips meant she wasn't surprised to see him.

"I knew it!" she said. "I told Kelly I didn't need to be checked on."

Will stood frozen. His brain forgetting how to breathe. Since when had Erin gotten all of those…those curves?

Okay, it wasn't as if he hadn't noticed Erin was stacked. He was a man, and a curvaceous woman could inadvertently trigger the male radar, but he'd never seen Erin's curves on display. His sister's introverted best friend was opinionated, confident and occasionally funny, but she tended to be reserved with the way she dressed. The woman before him did not look like the reserved lady he was used to.

The dress she wore fit her ample breasts like a glove; the snug waistline accentuated her hips, then flared out to stop midthigh. Her thick dark hair fell in deep waves to her shoulders. She'd always been cute. When he caught her smiling—usually at someone else—he'd occasionally wondered what her soft body would feel like beneath his hands. Okay, more than occasionally. But she'd never stopped him cold like this.

Erin lifted her arm and snapped her fingers. Not quite in his face; she was too short for that. Five six or so, average height, but compared to his six-foot-six-inch body she was tiny.

"Hello! Earth to Will. Are you done with your inspection?"

The direct question spoken with a hint of amusement broke the spell faster than her snapping fingers. "Where are you going?"

The question came out more demanding than he'd wanted. The hint of humor in her face quickly evaporated to the irritation she threw his way more often than not.

That's what made him always think twice before hitting on Erin. He didn't understand why he seemed to get on her nerves quicker than anyone else. He treated her with the same level of respect he did with Kelly. Hell, he'd even stepped in and been her date to the high school military ball when her jerk of a "boyfriend" had canceled at the last minute. Yet she still treated him like there was an invisible wall between them.

"Out," she snapped back. "Why?"

"I came to check on you."

She waved a hand. "No need. Like I told your sister, I'm good."

She was more than good. She was fine as hell. His eyes lowered and automatically his gaze swept over her. The V neckline of the sexy black dress she wore gave a peek at the swell of plump breasts. His crotch stirred.

Will shifted uncomfortably. What the hell? Was he actually reacting to Erin?

"I'm here, so can I at least come in?"

He had a few questions. He *was* here, so he might as well do his job and check in to make sure she was okay. That she wasn't seeing anyone not worth her time and all that.

Yeah, that's the reason.

Erin huffed and rolled her eyes, but she stepped back so he could enter. Damn she smelled good. Lush and fruity. His mouth watered.

"You going out?" he asked.

"That is what I just said." She closed the door, then led him farther into her place.

Her apartment was nice, an open floor plan with plenty of space and a view overlooking downtown Chicago. The furniture was modern in style—no extra cushions or overstuffed couches for Erin. Everything in perfect alignment and order, but her space still felt welcoming. The pictures of her family on various shelves and colorful abstract art on the wall balanced the sharp lines of the furniture.

"I'm meeting a coworker at this new bar with a few other people."

He heard the trace of nervousness in her voice and saw the spark of excitement in her eyes. She was looking forward to going out. "So, who is this guy?"

She glanced at him over her shoulder as she led him to the kitchen. "Who said there was a guy involved?"

"Who do you think?"

She snapped her fingers and wrinkled her nose. "Dang, Kelly!" She pointed to the fridge. "Want some wine?"

Will laughed and leaned against the counter next to her. "Sure. So, who's the guy?"

She pulled out a bottle of pinot grigio. She put the bottle next to him on the counter and pushed his hip. "Why?"

Will fought to ignore the flash of heat her playful touch ignited as he slid out of her way. "Because I'm checking on you like my sister asked. Is this guy worth your time?"

She rolled her eyes and opened the drawer he'd blocked. "Will, you really can stop with the questions. Kelly knows the guy is cool and it's not like you care." She pulled out a corkscrew and uncorked the wine.

"Of course I care." Way more than she'd ever know. "You're my girl."

The corner of Erin's full lips tilted up. She opened the cabinet and pulled out two glasses. "I'm your sister's girl."

Will took the glass of wine she handed him. "Come on. Humor me. Is he cool?"

She sighed and tried to hide a smile by taking a sip of her wine. "Yes. He's cool. This isn't really a date. More like us hanging out with some friends."

"Not serious then?" Satisfaction breezed through him like a cool fall wind. He chose not to explore why he liked hearing that so much. "Where are you going? Maybe I can drop you off."

"No need," she said. "I'm scheduling for a car to pick me up."

"So he's not picking you up?"

"Once again, not a date."

"Still, if I were hanging out with you for a 'not date'—" he made air quotes with his fingers "—if I really wanted things to turn into something more, I'd offer to pick you up. Show up with flowers. Open the door for you as you got in my car."

He'd slid closer to her. He took a sip of the wine and got lost in the dark pools of her soft brown eyes.

Erin sucked in a quick breath. Blinked and looked away. "That's because you're good at running game. It's not about game with Jared."

Will scowled. Is that all she thought of him? Well, he couldn't blame her. He was about saying and doing all the right things to get on a woman's good side.

That wasn't the way he thought of Erin. Everything he would say and do to be closer to her would be different. She wouldn't accept anything less. He couldn't imagine giving her anything less.

Her cell phone rang before he could correct her. She crossed the room and pulled the phone out of a small red handbag.

"Speak of the devil. It's Jared." She threw him a happy smile.

Will's lips stretched with what he hoped looked like encouragement. He sipped his wine and tried not to let his gaze travel over her curves in that sexy dress while she answered.

He could use this as his exit. He'd checked on her and everything was well. She had plans. Technically, his reasons for stopping by were satisfied. Still, he waited.

"Oh no, I'm sorry to hear that." Erin's brows drew together.

Will's ears perked up. That did not sound promising.

Erin shook her head. "It's no problem… I understand. We'll get together another time."

Will put his glass of wine down. Was this jerk really canceling on her? Somebody better be dead because any other excuse wasn't good enough. If this guy could see her now. In that dress. Then he wouldn't be canceling this date.

"Call me later," she said. "Let me know how things turn out… Okay… Bye, Jared." She ended the call and sighed. "Looks like I don't have to go out." She let out a weak laugh.

"I heard. What happened? An accident?"

She ran her fingers through her thick hair. A sign of frustration of hers. "No. He had a leak in his apartment. Something about a pipe under the sink."

"Oh really?" Sounded like bull to him.

"Really." She glanced around, then down at her dress. "Guess it's Netflix for me after all."

The disappointment in her voice twisted his gut. He

pushed away from the counter and crossed over to her. "It doesn't have to be," he said. "You can hang with me."

"Oh no. I'm not going to some crazy Hollywood party."

"We're in Chicago. Not Hollywood." He pointed to the view of the city outside her window.

"Doesn't matter. Celebrities mean a Hollywood-like party."

Will thought about the group gathered for the party. Other athletes, supermodels and a few television stars. She had a point. "Okay, no party. I've got tickets for the show at the CIBC Theatre. We can do that."

Her eyes went wide. "Wait a second. You've got tickets to *Slam!*? Those are the hardest tickets in town."

He felt like he'd just learned he was the only man who could save the planet from attacking aliens. "I do."

"And you don't have a date? I don't believe it." She propped a hand on her hip.

"I thought about picking up someone at the party."

She chuckled and cocked her head to the side. "You can just pick up a date that easily?"

He rubbed his chin. "Well, I don't mean to brag."

Erin poked him in the chest. "Good grief you're conceited."

He wrapped his hand around her slim wrist. "Is that a no?"

Her pulse fluttered against his fingers. She didn't pull away from his soft grasp. An almost-playful look came to her eye. "It's a fact."

Heat simmered between them. Sizzling and popping like corn kernels in hot oil. Will slid closer to her.

Erin shook her head. She cleared her throat, broke eye contact and slid back. "You know what? I stood in line for hours and still didn't get tickets. I'll put up with you for a few hours to see that."

Her words didn't dampen the pleasure in his chest. He didn't care about missing the party or the interest of Vanessa. Hanging with Erin seemed a lot more fun.

He held out his arm. "Then let's go."

Chapter 2

Erin joined the rest of the theatergoers who jumped to their feet and clapped at the end of the performance. The critically acclaimed show lived up to the hype and more. Will had definitely come through for the win on this.

She hadn't expected him to enjoy the show as much as her. But he was on his feet clapping just as enthusiastically. Will was the last person she would have guessed to be the one to turn what would have been a depressing night of cookies and Netflix after being stood up into one of the best nights she'd had since moving to Chicago.

Then again, maybe he was exactly the right person. This wasn't the first time he'd come through for her. Or the first time she'd appreciated him being there.

"People didn't lie," Will said as they exited the theater with the crowd. "That show was damn good."

He directed her away from the crush of theatergoers

toward the sleek black car waiting on them. He didn't touch her, but that didn't stop her body from being acutely aware of his nearness. The strength and pull of him made her gravitate closer to his side.

"It was," Erin agreed. "Thank you for taking me. I didn't mean to spoil your plans to take someone a lot more fun than me."

"Don't be silly. I have fun with you."

Will smiled at her in that way he had of making her feel beautiful and amazing. He didn't intentionally steal her breath away. Will was like that. A charmer through and through.

A charmer with rich chestnut skin, obsidian eyes brightened by his sparkling personality, and a meticulously cut beard surrounding sensual lips. Will was the guy women fantasized about and men wanted to hang out with.

Erin broke eye contact. "Since when do you have fun with me?"

The cold Chicago air sliced through her coat and up the hem of her dress. She shivered and shoved her hands in her pockets. Will stepped closer and placed his hand on her lower back. Simultaneously blocking the wind and radiating heat.

She started to pull away, but it was cold as crap out there and Will was tall and warm.

"Remember when I took you to the military ball in high school? We had a lot of fun."

"That was fifteen years ago," she said. "We haven't hung out since."

The driver opened the car door for them. Will's hand on her back clung to her coat, stopping her from getting into the car. She met his eyes, and he raised a brow.

"Whose fault is that?" he asked in a low, seductive voice.

A flicker of disappointment and hurt crossed his handsome features. There and gone in a blink of an eye. Erin's pulse jumped. She wanted to touch him. Press her hand against his chest and ask what the flicker in his gaze meant.

Instead of doing either, she slipped in the car. They both knew the answer to the question. She was the reason they hadn't hung out since.

Will was too charming. Too handsome. Too easy to fall for if you didn't know he didn't take anything seriously including relationships.

Will was two years older than her. That night when her boyfriend had bailed on her, he'd skipped a party to take her to the military ball. By then he was an impressive college player and son of a former league champion who was well on his way to the pros. Yet he'd given up a night in town with his friends to save her from embarrassment.

When he'd walked her to her door at the end of the night he'd wrapped her in his arms and surrounded her in warmth and the seductive cloud of his expensive cologne. She'd been floating on a cloud of joy from the fun they'd had and squeezed him tight, but when he'd pulled back the smile she'd expected wasn't there. He'd looked at her as if he couldn't believe he was lucky enough to hold her in his arms. Dark eyes lowered to her lips and she'd known with everything in her that he was going to kiss her. She'd jumped out of his arms as if he'd gone up in flames. She'd grown up watching Will go from girlfriend to girlfriend as quickly as he changed basketball shorts. She'd refused to be another casualty in the William Hampton war on female hearts.

Will slid into the car next to her. Close enough for her to feel the gravitational pull he radiated like the moon, but not close enough to touch. "So, what do you want to do next?"

She wasn't surprised he'd moved on from the topic of them hanging out. Will didn't stay on one topic for long.

"I think I'll just go home."

"You can't go home now. The night is still young." He looked so damn sexy as his brows drew together and his lips pursed in a disapproving frown.

Midnight had come and gone. The night was hardly young, but she wasn't tired. Her body still buzzed from the excitement of the show.

"I don't typically hang real late." Even as she said the words she realized how dull she made herself sound.

It wasn't as if she was against staying out late; she'd just spent the years since college trying to climb the corporate ladder. Her dreams of playing basketball professionally died with an injury in high school. Now she dreamed of being an executive at Global Strategies, one of the top marketing firms in the country. Her after-midnight activities typically involved drafting proposals and working on client projects.

Will leaned back and stretched his long legs in front of him. "Well, I'm not ready to go back to my hotel and sit around."

"You could still go to that party."

He shook his head. "Nah, not in the mood for that, either." He turned and met her eyes. "Let's grab something to eat. Then I'll take you back to your place."

She was hungry. They hadn't eaten before the show,

and honestly, she really wasn't ready to go home. "I'm down for that."

He grinned as if she'd just made his night. Her stomach flipped. She tried to ignore that. She had to ignore her body's reactions. If she didn't realize he treated all women like queens she'd begin to think his enthusiasm was just for her.

"I know just the place."

He took her to a late-night bistro near Mariano Park. Erin had never been there before, and thought they'd need reservations. Will not only knew the best spots in whatever city he traveled to, but was well known enough to get immediate seating.

They were given a private booth in the back, and once they were settled, Will started talking about old times. The days when she and Kelly would torment him during their dance marathons whenever Erin slept over. How they'd played basketball together as kids.

He ordered a bottle of wine with their food. After her second glass she relaxed and forgot about keeping her guard up with Will and just enjoyed his cheerful personality.

"So, this job, you like it? Kelly said you're only in town for a few months."

Will had moved closer to her while they talked. He faced her, one arm rested along the back of the booth behind her, and the elbow of his other arm was on the table. His humor-brightened eyes were trained on her the entire time.

"I do like it. I moved to Chicago to work closely with the executive team. I'm trying to make partner, and being here gives me better access to the upcoming projects and puts my work right in front of the other executives.

I'll be in Charlotte in a few weeks for All-Star Weekend because we're doing several launch parties there."

Erin had done everything she could to be considered for the partner position. Taken the hardest jobs, traveled wherever they needed her to go and worked extra hours to ensure her projects never got behind schedule.

Basketball had once been her life. After her injury, getting the best grades and finding success in other arenas had taken over. She was competitive by nature, and fighting her way to the top was how she fed that need.

"You travel a lot. Don't you get tired of that?"

"You travel a lot, too. Do you get tired of that?" she tossed back.

Will rubbed his beard and chuckled. Her eyes dropped to his full lips. The bottom one plumper than the top. His teeth too perfect. She smiled; he'd gotten veneers after losing a tooth his senior year of high school. Knowing about that imperfection reminded her how much she really knew about one of the league's biggest stars.

"Sometimes," he admitted surprisingly. "The good thing is knowing I've got a place to go back to. My house is my sanctuary."

"Your sanctuary? I wouldn't have expected you to use that word." She lifted the glass of cabernet and took a sip. The full-bodied wine was smooth as it glided over her tongue.

"Why not?"

"Because you're such an extrovert. I wouldn't expect you to need a sanctuary."

Will laughed low and deep. She felt the rumble all through her body. Most definitely in the spots aching for touch. "Everyone needs a sanctuary. But I love what I do. You know that."

"It's all you've ever wanted to do." Basketball was the one thing Will was consistent with. The one thing he hadn't lost interest in over the years.

"Watching my dad in the league only made me want to be just as good as, if not better than, him. I love everything about playing ball, but yeah, occasionally I like to chill at home."

"Do you chill with anyone in particular?" Well, damn. She hadn't meant to say that. At least not in the flirty, I'm-digging-for-information way in which the words had come out.

The subtle shift in Will's eyes from playful to predatory made her stomach clench. He went from friendly best friend's brother to the man who drew in women with a crook of his lips that she knew he was.

"No one in particular," he said in that noncommittal way players everywhere perfected. "What about you? Things serious with you and that guy you were going out with?"

Not currently, but she'd hoped they might turn into something. Her coworker Vivien and Kelly had finally boosted Erin up enough to ask Jared out. She'd been crushing on him hard since starting in the Chicago office.

She mimicked his shrug. "Not yet, but I'm excited about seeing where it'll go."

The light in his eyes dimmed for a second. He took a sip of his wine, finishing the little bit in the glass before turning to her again. "Oh really? You haven't changed your mind after he bailed on you tonight?"

Jared's canceling at the last minute had sucked. That didn't mean she wasn't interested in going out with him again one day. "He mentioned us getting together later this weekend. Besides, I can understand if he had a pipe burst in his apartment that he'd need to take care of that. I like Jared because he's just as driven as I am. I've dated other guys who didn't understand my commitment to my job. They always wanted me to give up my goals to spend more time with them. Jared isn't like that. He works just as hard as I do."

"Sounds…fun," Will said with a sarcastic twist of his lips.

Erin shook her head. His sarcasm rolled off her easily. "It's like if you'd only been around women who wanted you to give up basketball, and then you meet a woman who loves the sport as much as you do. I doubt you'd change your mind after one canceled date."

"I've met a few women who really love basketball." He lifted his hand and took a lock of her thick hair between his fingers. "There's only one of those women who I'd want a real chance with."

His eyes locked with hers. His eyes saying a lot of things she wanted to believe. He couldn't possibly mean her. But the spark of interest and desire in his gaze made her wonder.

"You say that as if you haven't tried to have a chance with her."

He continued to play with the ends of her hair. "I haven't, but maybe I will." Before she could ask who the woman in question was, Will shifted in the seat. He let go of her hair, bent his elbow and rested his head on his closed fist. "I've had fun hanging out with you tonight."

She let go of the fantasy that he could be talking about her and moved with the subject change. "Yeah, me, too."

"You never did reply when I asked about why we don't hang out more often."

Because my heart's racing right now just having you

this close to me. "Come on, Will. When would we hang out? You're off playing basketball and partying most of the time. We see each other when I visit your family over the holidays."

"And?" He sounded like her reasons weren't legit.

"And...and what? Tonight you did Kelly a favor and checked on me. Then bailed me out after I was jilted. Again," she mumbled under her breath.

Will pushed the hair behind her ear. The blunt tips of his fingers brushed her cheek. Electric sparks flew across her skin. Her nipples tightened.

"And just like before," he said softly, "I think any guy who stands you up is a fool."

She waited for the smile. The spark of amusement that would let her know he was trying to make her feel better. None of that was there. He looked dead serious, and that made her breathing hitch.

Dark eyes dropped to her lips. Erin pulled her bottom lip between her teeth. His pupils dilated before his gaze lifted to hers. Passion swirled in the obsidian depths. He leaned forward ever so slightly.

Erin cleared her throat and backed up. She looked around the restaurant for the waiter. "Man, it's getting late. I think they're ready to close. We should probably get ready to go."

He opened his mouth as if to argue, then nodded. Will offered to pay, but Erin insisted since he'd done more than enough by taking her to see *Slam!*.

They were quiet on the car ride back to her apartment. Only an occasional comment on the cold weather and Will confirming he'd fly back to Jacksonville on Sunday. Everything was normal and abnormal. A hum of awareness simmered between them. A subtle shift she wanted to pretend wasn't there.

Was she being a fool, or had Will been about to kiss her? Not a sweet, innocent, hey-we're-friends kiss. But a steal-your-breath, make-your-body-yearn, soul-stirring kiss. She'd gotten the same feeling that night he'd taken her to the military ball. When he'd hugged her a second too long and squeezed her a smidge too tight. When he looked as if he really saw her. As if she weren't just Kelly's best friend who hung around all the time or some random woman he was trying to seduce.

Will insisted on walking her back to her door. She turned and faced him before going inside.

"Well, thanks for a fun night, Will," she said. "I really had a great time."

Will placed a hand on the doorjamb next to her. He was close enough for her savor the scent of his cologne and see the remnants of what she hadn't wanted to label as desire in his eyes. "Maybe we can hang out the next time I'm in Chicago."

"Maybe." He kept watching her. His eyes intent and serious. Her stomach fluttered in a way it never had when Jared stood close. She held out her hand. "Good night."

He looked at her hand, and the corner of his lip tilted up. "I can't get a hug?"

Her heart somersaulted. She'd hugged Will before. Every Christmas when he came home, and she attended their family Christmas party. He went around the room and hugged everyone there. Then there were the quick one-armed hugs he'd given her when they briefly crossed paths while she was with Kelly. There was no reason this hug should be different.

"Sure," she said in a fluttery voice.

She opened her arms and leaned in her upper body for what Kelly would call a "church hug"—just shoulder contact, no full-body touching. Will's arm wrapped around her waist; the other pressed into her back. His hand glided up her spine until his fingers bracketed the base of her neck.

"What are you doing?" she asked. Her hands gripped his strong arms.

"Hugging you." His voice was a sexy whisper. His head lowered. His lips stopped right before they touched hers.

Erin's heart hammered. The tips of her breasts tightened against the planes of his chest. Excitement simmered in her veins. The heat in his eyes could have melted iron.

"Kissing you?"

She could pull back now, and he'd let her go. He'd say goodbye, walk away and never bring up what happened again. Will was a ladies' man, but he wasn't a jerk. If she didn't want his kiss he'd accept that.

She knew what she wanted. It wasn't due to the fun of the night, the look in his eye or two glasses of wine. The soft plea in his voice when he'd asked. The smallest hint that he was just as eager for their lips to touch as she was. That's what busted her defenses. Erin lifted on her toes and pressed her lips to his.

Chapter 3

Will pressed Erin's back against the door to her apartment. She was soft, and warm, and tasted like wine. She smelled delicious, like strawberries and vanilla. Her curves cushioned his body and made him want to snuggle into her and never get up.

He hadn't planned to kiss her. Hadn't planned to flirt with her, but he hadn't expected to have so much fun with her, either. To laugh and joke with her while they reminisced about old times. To have her look at him with the fire of passion in her beautiful eyes.

He pulled away from her addictive mouth and ran light kisses over the soft skin of her jaw. "Can I come in?"

God, was that him? He sounded needy and almost desperate. The pulsing of the blood in his veins along with the swelling of desire between his legs had him feeling desperate. He wanted to get closer to her. Kiss her more. Touch her.

"I don't know…" Her hands clutched his sides. When his lips grazed her neck, her head fell back.

"For coffee." He ran a hand up, then down, her back and lower to caress the softness of her ass.

He kissed her again and her body trembled. He knew he was waging an unfair war, but damn if he could help himself. He was obsessed with kissing her. Her lips were plump and pillow-soft. Her delectable scent made him want to lick every single part of her. Discover if her breasts were just as sweet.

This time when he pulled back her mouth followed his as if she couldn't bear to let him break the kiss. Her eyes opened and were glazed with desire.

"Just coffee," she said in a husky, passion-laden voice.

His heart jumped. He forced himself not to grin like he'd won the finals. "Thank you."

She slowly turned and pulled the key out of her purse. He couldn't help himself. He had to touch her. His hand rested on her small waist. He pushed her thick hair aside and kissed her neck as she unlocked her door.

"Will!" she said with a shocked giggle.

He grinned and kissed her neck again. This time letting the tip of his tongue dart out against her skin. "What?"

Her door opened, and she moved out of his arms. Immediately he missed holding her. He closed the door and locked it, then followed her into the kitchen. She went straight to the coffee maker and pulled one of the individual coffee pods from a chrome rack next to the machine.

"I've got Sumatra, breakfast blend and chocolate-raspberry," she said, twirling the rack. Her voice thick and trembling.

Just looking at her made him want to pull her back into his arms. Her hair fell in a thick curtain to right below her shoulders. The sexy dress she wore cinched in her waist and highlighted her hourglass figure. Her calves looked sculpted from the finest stone, the muscles taut from the high-heeled shoes.

Will strode up behind her and placed his hands on her hips. "You are so damn sexy."

"You're just saying that because we kissed." Her voice trembled a little. He heard the doubt in her tone. She didn't believe him.

"I'm saying that because it's true."

"You never called me sexy before." She pulled one of the chocolate-raspberry coffee pods out of the rack and lifted the top of the coffee machine.

"That doesn't mean I haven't thought it before."

She scoffed and put the coffee in the machine. Will pushed her hair aside and kissed her neck again. Her body had tensed. He wanted her soft and warm again.

"I first noticed how sexy you are that day you beat me in basketball back in high school. You wore those tiny purple shorts and that damn racerback yellow top. That was also the first time I realized basketball shorts could drive a man wild." He ran one hand around to rest on her belly and gently pulled her against him. "That's when I first noticed your curves. Another time was when you were helping Kelly study for some test. Your hair was pulled up in this messy ponytail, you had a pencil stuck in it, and you kept biting your thumb whenever you were trying to concentrate. I couldn't stop looking at your mouth. All of the things I imagined your mouth doing to my body made me hard as a rock." He brushed his hand over her lower lip. They parted, and her breathing stuttered. "I won't even talk about the night of the military ball. That short, dark blue dress with the halter top. You know I wanted to kiss you at the end of the night. Don't you?"

She sucked in a breath, then nodded. Will smiled and kissed her shoulder. Her body was soft again. She leaned back into him.

"Last summer was the most recent time," he continued. The memories flowing like water spilled from a cup. "His birthday party. You made my dad laugh. He doesn't laugh much since Mom died, but whatever you said brought tears of joy to his eyes. Your eyes sparked with intelligence and compassion. I thought you were beautiful. I still think you're beautiful."

Erin quickly spun and faced him. Her eyes serious, her lower lip between her teeth. She watched him for several seconds and shook her head.

"Are you playing with me? Please don't play with me. We've known each other too long."

He cupped her face in his hands. "I'm serious."

"This will change everything. Do you really want to chance that?"

Right now. At this very moment. He didn't want anything else except to taste her lips again. How things changed could wait until tomorrow. He meant every word he'd said. Had looked and wondered what it would be like between him and Erin on more than one occasion. This was no game to him. No test to see if she was attracted to him.

"Yes. I do." He lowered his head and kissed her deeply.

Erin was tumbling down a rabbit hole she'd never escape from, but she couldn't seem to make herself care. Will's kisses were incredible. Soft and sweet one second. Deep and demanding the next. Like a thief he snatched her breath, and like an experienced criminal he made her crave her body's reaction.

With one swift movement, he lifted her and placed her on the counter. Erin wrapped her legs around his waist. Their mouths never leaving each other. The brush of his beard increasing her arousal. His strong hands stroked up and down her thighs. Squeezing and massaging them with expert fingertips. His hips pushed forward. The thick ridge of his erection rubbed against her core until she was soaking wet.

He reached behind her and slowly lowered the zipper on the back of the dress. She didn't want slow. Slow gave her too much time to think about what she was doing. That this was *Will* kissing her. Will turning her blood into steam with his expert touches. Impatiently, Erin pulled her arms out of the sleeves and let the dress bunch at her waist. She shoved his coat off and onto the floor. Her hands worked at the buttons of his shirt. Will jerked the shirt off and tossed it aside as if he was just as impatient as she. The undershirt beneath was gone next.

His chest was a masterpiece of muscles and tightly coiled hair. Her fingers played in the rough strands. The tips of her fingers ran light circles over his flat nipples. Will shivered. His hands tightened on her thighs. She grinned, enjoying how responsive he was to her touch.

His answering smile told her she'd pay for teasing him in the most decadent way. Then his face became serious. He looked at her and she feared he would see everything she'd tried not to acknowledge about her feelings for him. Her eyes lowered to his mouth. Her lips parted, and she leaned forward. Will's fingers buried in her hair. He tilted her head and kissed her harder. His tongue caressing and claiming her as if they were old lovers reuniting.

His other hand reached behind her and effortlessly unfastened her bra. She slid the bra to the floor. The hairs on his chest tickled her sensitive nipples. She rubbed her chest against his. Reveling in the decadent feeling.

Will pushed her back. Her hands spread against the counter and her chest thrust forward. Then he had one breast cupped in his hands and his lips closed over the tip. Pleasure exploded like a ton of C-4, setting her body on fire. Her gasps and whimpers echoed in the otherwise silent kitchen. Will's soft, satisfied moans accompanied them. Long fingers gently squeezed and toyed with the tip of her other breast. Erin groaned and threw her head back. When his hand left her breast, she barely got out her sob of complaint before it slipped beneath the hem of her bunched-up skirt. His exploring fingers hesitated for a second at the waistband of her underwear.

He lifted his head. Heavy-lidded eyes filled with desire devoured her. "No turning back?"

She shook her head. Was he kidding? A marauding army couldn't pull her out of his arms right now. Not when she'd melt into a puddle and evaporate into nothing if he didn't keep kissing her. "No turning back."

He tugged on her underwear. Erin lifted her hips, and he ripped them from her body and tossed them over his shoulder. Then his fingers were there, parting her slick folds and teasing the most sensitive nub on her body with nimble fingers. Her body twitched and tightened. Heat flooded her veins like a flamethrower.

Her legs spread farther. Reaching between them, Erin hastily yanked his pants open. No longer thinking and just going with instinct. Her hands dived into his underwear and eagerly clasped around his length. Will's shudder echoed through her. He was the perfect size. Thick and long enough to make her core sing in anticipation. She stroked him and licked her lips. He kissed her with less control than before and gently bit her bottom lip.

"Please tell me you have a condom," she moaned.

"Back pocket," he ground out. He sounded just as desperate as she felt.

He reached into his pocket. Pulled out the protection and was covered and pushing deep into her in record time. They both cried out as he filled her. Deep, hard and oh so perfect. Erin grabbed his solid shoulder with one hand and supported her weight with the other. Will held on to her hips with a desperate grip and made her call out his name right there on her kitchen counter with long, hard strokes.

They came together quick and fast. Years of curiosity, anticipation and mutual desire erupting in an orgasm that made everything in her shake. Shatter. Succumb.

Before their breathing returned to normal, he gently lifted her off the counter. His lips brushed across her ear. "Bedroom?"

She pointed a limp hand in the direction of the bedroom. Will carried her inside and to the bed. Gently, he pulled back the covers and lay with her. Their breathing slowly calmed. She dozed off but woke a short time later to his hands on her body.

This time he moved slowly and more deliberately. He covered every inch of her body with kisses and brought tears to her eyes with pleasure so intense she didn't think she could take it. Will settled between her legs and whispered in her ear. "I don't think I'll ever get enough of the taste of you." Then he sank deep into her and brought her to another orgasm that scattered her thoughts to the edges of the universe.

She fell asleep again, and when she woke up an hour later with him beside her, regret and uncertainty crept around the edges of her mind. As if he sensed she was about to freak out, Will came to her. He wrapped her in his strong arms and kissed her until she clung to him.

"No turning back, remember," he whispered into her ear. Then worked her up into such a frenzy that she shoved him onto his back and took control. Losing herself in the sensual feel of him until she collapsed spent, again onto his chest.

Every time she swore she was done, that her body couldn't possibly take any more pleasure, he proved her wrong. With kisses, touches and caresses he made her lose all inhibitions. And in between he covertly captured pieces of her heart as they talked quietly about her job, his hope to coach one day and all the times they'd wondered over the years what being with each other would be like.

When he finally let her drift into a deep sleep near 6:00 a.m., she had a smile on her face. She was wrapped in Will's arms. The last place in the world she'd ever expected to be when she'd woken up the previous morning.

"I never thought I could be this happy," she murmured into his chest before she fell asleep.

And she was happy. Until she woke up late in the morning and the only sign of Will was a note on her nightstand.

Had an emergency. I had to leave early. Last night was cool. TTYL.
-W.

Chapter 4

Erin wished the entire night was just a bad dream. She went over every second in her head searching for signs she might have missed that Will was playing her for a fool. He *had* looked at her as if she were the only woman in the world. Something special *had* happened when they kissed.

Hadn't it?

He could have really had an emergency. One that prevented him from waking her to explain before he'd left. Not sneaked out because he was ashamed, regretful or disgusted by what happened.

She made coffee; the K-Cup she'd put in the machine the night before sat unused, and she tried not to think about the reason she never made the coffe.

Hard to not think of that when her body was still deliciously sore. She'd showered and put on pajamas, but she wasn't in the mood to leave her apartment. She wouldn't

call him, either. Demand to know why he left. Ask piti-
fully when…if he would be back.

She picked up her phone and called Kelly. Will mentioned an emergency, which meant Kelly should have
information.

Kelly answered after four rings. "Hey, what's up?"

"You didn't have to send Will to check on me," Erin
said. *Hey, I spent the night being turned out by your
brother* didn't seem like a good greeting.

"Sorry. I couldn't help it. You seemed nervous," Kelly
said, not sounding the least bit apologetic.

"I wasn't nervous. We were just hanging out." She
had been very nervous and excited about going out with
Jared. Now she could barely picture his face. Damn, Will
and his magic stick!

"With a guy you have been checking out for weeks,"
Kelly teased. "I knew Will would help snap you out of it."

Understatement of the century.

"So, how was it? Was he good?" Kelly asked eagerly.

For a second Erin's face burned as she thought about
how damn good Will had been. But quickly shook her
head. Kelly wouldn't be talking about that. "What?"

"Jared. Your date. Was he okay?"

Erin let out a sigh of regret. "No. He canceled." Things
would have gone so much better if he hadn't canceled.

"Oh no! That sucks. Please tell me you didn't spend
the night eating cookies and watching Netflix."

Definitely not that. She should have done that instead. "Actually, Will helped me out. He had tickets to
Slam! and took me to see the show. Instead of a boring
night in, I had…a lot of fun." She swallowed hard as her
body heated. Her nipples tightened as if Will were still

there waiting to give them attention, and desire spread between her legs.

Kelly was quiet for a few moments. "Really? That's… surprising."

"Why?"

"He was looking forward to meeting up with some model at a party later. He couldn't wait to hook up with her."

Erin's stomach clenched. "He didn't mention a model, just a party."

"Oh wait," Kelly said as if she just had a terrible thought. Dread lacing her voice. "He didn't try to hit on you?"

Erin's stomach clenched. "Why would you say that?"

"I was giving him a hard time about not wanting to check in on you because you're the one woman who doesn't turn into a puddle when he smiles at you. He knows you don't fall for his lines. Then he was all, 'That's only because I never really tried.' Please tell me he didn't try."

Erin's world tilted and spun; she felt sick. More than nausea. A soul-deep infection she wasn't sure had a cure. *Because he never really tried?*

"He tried," Erin said, infusing her voice with but-I-wasn't-that-stupid tone. She rubbed her forehead.

Kelly laughed. "Oh my God. I wish I could have seen his face when you shut him down. I told him you wouldn't fall for his mess. Was he really dumb?"

One of them had been. "Yeah…really stupid. What kind of idiot does he take me for?" She forced a chuckle. Her eyes burned.

Oh, he took her for an idiot. One he'd taken three

times. Four if she counted the way his mouth had made her come.

"Girl. I'm so glad you're smarter than that." The relief in Kelly's voice made Erin's cheeks burn. "You know how Will hit on my college roommate. Homegirl swore she was all in love with him and then they were done in less than a month. Even worse, she fell for his 'we can still be friends' line. I don't know what Will did to her, but she's still sending him Christmas cards. Even though she won't talk to me." Resentment crept into Kelly's voice. "That's why I know you're my friend, Erin. You aren't crazy enough to jump in bed with Will and hate me because he played you. Other women may fall, but you're my girl. Always there for me and not to get a piece of my brother, who followed in my famous father's footsteps. I won't lose you because Will doesn't know how to commit."

Erin looked up at the sky and prayed for a lightning bolt to strike her immediately. No, she needed a time-traveling device and the lightning bolt to strike her when Will kissed her at her door. She could never tell Kelly what happened, and what happened could never happen again. If Will had been up-front, not fed her all those lies about the times he'd wanted her over the years, she wouldn't feel like a fool. But he had. He'd played her, and even though she knew he was never serious, she'd fallen for the lines. No, she'd damn near pushed herself into his arms. She could never trust him again.

"Don't worry about that, Kelly. Losing me to your brother is something that will never happen."

Will checked his watch and tapped his foot on the floor of the Gators' auditorium-style conference room.

He was tired from basically no sleep and catching a last-second flight back to Jacksonville to rush home. The Gators' public relations director had sent every member of the team the message to return, which was followed up by messages from Coach Simpson to get their asses back here immediately.

For the hundredth time he wondered if he should have woken Erin up and explained before leaving. For the hundredth time he knew he hadn't been ready to face her. Something happened last night. Something more than just amazing sex. Something easy to not think about when she was in his arms, but much harder to face the next day.

He felt like he'd run into an electric fence. Zapped to the depths of his soul. Being with Erin made him want to stay wrapped in her arms forever. Which brought to mind ideas of forever. Which then sparked a need to run a thousand miles away. He had to sort through his feelings, what he wanted next, the ramifications of having the one woman who would expect more from him than a casual affair in his bed.

He shifted irritably in his chair. A large hand slapped his shoulder. Will glanced up as his teammate and friend Jacobe Jacobs moved to the seat next to his.

"Any idea what's happening with this?" Jacobe asked.

Will shook his head and got his mind off the mess he'd left in Chicago. "No clue. Just the same cryptic summons home that you got."

He glanced at the rest of his team filing into the room. As always, disappointment weighed him down. They'd lost one of the key members of the team last year when Kevin Kouky retired. Will understood why Kevin had stepped away from playing, but the loss was felt every time the team was together. Kevin had been one of the oldest members of the team, which meant his experience had also set him up as a leader. A role that no one had yet to fill.

There was another teammate Will didn't see after everyone entered the room. "Hey Isaiah, where's Mike?"

Isaiah Reynolds had taken the other empty seat next to Will. Isaiah glanced around the room, frowned and shrugged.

"No idea. I haven't talked to him since the game on Thursday," Isaiah answered.

That was surprising. Isaiah and Kevin had been close friends, and Mike, who'd tried to come in and fill the space Kevin left, so much so he'd damn near campaigned to be listed a team captain, had also jockeyed to be Isaiah's new best friend.

Isaiah shook his head. "I would have thought he'd be the first one here."

"You're right about that," Jacobe said. "He's been trying to get on the good side of all of the upper management."

Further conversation was interrupted by Coach Simpson and the head of public relations entering the conference room. The faint hum of conversation ended, and everyone looked to Coach. His grim expression sent dread through Will's body.

"I want to thank you all for coming so quickly today," Coach said in a strong, booming voice. "The news is going to hit this afternoon, but we wanted to get the entire team here together before the media circus started."

Media circus? Will looked to Jacobe and Isaiah, but they wore the same confused expression as him. A rumble went through the room. Questions about "what news?" rose to the top.

Coach Simpson held up his hand and silenced everyone. "Last night Mike Smith was at a party. An argument started, and a fight ensued. One person was killed. Mike was arrested and will be charged with murder."

"What the f—" Will's outburst was cut off by similar loud exclamations from the other members of the team.

Will looked around the room. His head spinning. Mike was extra, but he was levelheaded on most days. Not only that, he was a key component of the team. Murder? Had the guy really killed someone?

"Quiet down." Coach's sharp voice cracked like a whip through the noise. The questions lowered to a low grumbling. "I know you've got questions. We've all got questions. Questions I can't answer. The team has controlled the story for now, but it's going to hit in a few hours and the media are going to eat it up. That along with some of the other incidents related to the team in recent years have made management question the way this team is handled."

Jacobe sat up straighter. "What's that supposed to mean?"

"It means," Coach answered, "they don't think you have good leadership." He held up his hand as the rumblings began again. "Stop it. It doesn't matter right now. We can't hide the facts. We've had fights on the court, fights between teammates and incidents of indiscretion in the news. There isn't a lot we can argue about the behavior of the players on this team."

Jacobe and Isaiah both shifted uncomfortably in their seats. They weren't the only guys who'd had situations come up over the past few years. There were a lot of guys going through life changes, and some of those changes were messy and complicated. Just what the media loved to eat up.

"Are they getting rid of you, Coach?" Will asked. The true question on everyone's mind.

"That's what I'm trying to stop. And it's why I have Rebecca here from PR. We've got a plan, one you aren't going to like, but if you want to make this team successful after all the changes we've had, then I suggest you shut up and listen."

Rebecca Force stepped forward. Will should have known things were bad if she was called in. Rebecca only showed up when there was a problem that couldn't be fixed with just a well-worded statement and a few public appearances. Will's stomach sank. He wasn't going to like this.

"The team is going into a soft lockdown," Rebecca said. "Which means no parties, no clubs, no travel that isn't sanctioned or approved by the team. There will be a series of events scheduled for the Gators that will focus on conflict resolution, building successful working relationships and communication, along with team-building exercises."

Several teammates protested. Will wanted to join in. No travel unless sanctioned. He needed to get back to Chicago. He hadn't figured out what would happen with him and Erin, but he owed her a face-to-face conversation. Not just a phone call.

"I'm sorry, guys, but this is where we're at," Rebecca continued. "Obviously, we've got some things we need to work out internally and externally. The Gators organization is committed to meeting the needs of our players, coaches and staff. We are a championship organization, and if we want to remain a championship organization, then we have to act like one."

Will raised a hand. "How long will this last?"

"Effective immediately," Rebecca said. "We will see how things go over the next few weeks before All-Star Weekend. Then we'll review the lockdown after that. If we need to keep it in play until the playoffs, we will."

"I know this is hard," Coach jumped in. "But one of our guys is accused of murder. Murder. That's serious. This isn't something to play around with, and we don't need any other situations to pop up this season. Not if we want another win. If you don't like it, then you need to think about the reasons why."

Several guys spoke up. Complained about plans they'd made, the loss of their freedom, how they shouldn't be punished for Mike's mistakes. Will heard and understood every protest. He also understood the position the team was in. He enjoyed his lifestyle as much as anyone else, but he also wanted another ring. The championship trophy.

"Guys, settle down," Will called out. He stood and faced the rest of his team. "Yeah, I know this sucks, but they're only talking about until the All-Star Weekend. After that, maybe this thing with Mike will die down."

"Yeah, but they're restricting our travel. I've got ladies waiting on my visits," Tyler Jenkins said, brushing imaginary dirt off his shoulder.

"You think I don't understand?" Will said, pointing to his chest. Tyler and the rest of the guys laughed. "Look, guys, we're trying to make it to the playoffs. We're two-time champions. I don't know about you, but I want number three."

He held up three fingers. A rumble of agreement

went through the group. Will shrugged and looked at his teammates.

"This thing with Mike is going to be a shitstorm. We've got to work together, focus on winning, not get caught up in what happens when his trial starts. Let's just see how the soft lockdown works, and then we'll go from there after All-Star Weekend." Will turned and looked at Coach and Rebecca. "Right?"

Rebecca smiled and nodded. "Right."

Coach's brows drew together, but if Will wasn't fooling himself he swore there was also pride in his eyes. "You're right."

"All right," Will agreed. He looked back at the team. "Let's do this."

The meeting ended soon after. Rebecca stuck around to answer more questions. Both Isaiah and Jacobe bumped fists with him.

"Good speech, man," Jacobe said. "If I didn't know better, I'd say you sounded like a coach."

Will grinned and lightly tapped Jacobe's shoulder with his fist. "Just trying to settle things down."

The team slowly began to file out of the room. He had been trying to settle everyone down, but there was one thing Will couldn't walk away from. If there was a snowball's chance in hell that Coach would let him get back to Chicago to talk to Erin, he had to try to take it.

Will caught Coach Simpson before he left the locker room. "Coach, this team-sanctioned travel. How do I get approval for that?"

Coach's gray brows drew together. "You put in a request first through me, and if I agree then I run it up through PR for final approval."

Will rubbed his hands together. Thinking about the

best way to request a travel excuse after just getting the rest of the team to accept the lockdown. "You see, I've got to get back to Chicago."

"What for?"

"There's this woman…" *And what happened between us last night is something that changed my world and I need to know why.*

Coach shook his head before Will could finish speaking. "Hell no. I'm not approving travel so you can go get laid."

"It's not like that."

"Then what is it like? Unless something changed in seventy-two hours you were not in a serious relationship and were looking forward to a weekend in the arms of supermodel Vanessa Collum, am I right?"

Will ran a hand across the back of his neck. "Yeah, but something did change. I ran into an old friend."

"No. You work your player magic another time."

"But she won't understand."

"Then make her. You're the one who always has the women eating whatever you dish up." Coach slapped his shoulder. "Look, Will, the way you got the team to calm down speaks a lot. They wouldn't have accepted that speech from a lot of members of the team."

"I didn't do anything special. I'm looking out for the team."

"And that's what makes a great leader. Someone who looks at the big picture and can help people get to the end goal. Will, I was going to tell you this later, but the thing with Mike messed up the announcement. The votes are in and you're the person chosen to lead the Eastern Conference team All-Star Weekend."

Will stumbled back as if Coach had pushed him. "There has to be a mistake. I'm no leader."

Coach raised a brow. "Are you sure? Because the way you settled the team says otherwise." He squeezed Will's shoulder again. "You can make up with your lady friend later. Today, lead by example. Show the team you're not just words."

Will watched Coach walk away with a mixture of frustration, disappointment and elation. Leader of the Eastern Conference team. That position was a voted position. He never would have thought other players, players not on his team, would think he was the best choice. Despite all the work he'd done toward the championship win last year. He'd only scored the winning shot, that was all. He wouldn't have gotten the MVP vote if it wasn't for that.

Still, he was honored. He would have to lead by example, and for once he didn't mind giving up something. He only hoped Erin understood.

When you meet her, it'll hit you like a two-ton bull and you'll know she's the one.

The words his dad had told him when Will asked how he'd known their mom was the woman he'd marry. His dad had played four seasons in the league before meeting and settling down. He'd been happily married and faithful for twenty-eight years. When his mom died unexpectedly, his dad had spent the first year in a depression and the past year partying like he had before his marriage.

He hadn't believed his dad when he'd said he'd know when he met the right woman. Until last night. When he'd felt like he'd been hit by a two-ton bull.

Could Erin really be the one? After all the years of knowing her?

He left the conference room and slipped into one of the quieter meeting spaces. He pulled out his phone and called Erin.

"Hello, Will." Erin's voice was cold and unwelcoming.

Will frowned. He'd expected something a lot warmer in her greeting after the night they'd had. "Erin, hey, did you get my note?"

"I did."

"Look, this team emergency is bigger than I expected. It'll hit the media in a few so I won't go into the details, but I'm on lockdown. I can't make it back to Chicago."

"Oh, you were planning to come back?" she said, as if the idea were novel.

"Yeah, I was coming back."

"I thought you had achieved your goal and were done with me."

"My goal? What are you talking about?"

"You know what you told Kelly. That you could seduce me if you really tried. You won. No need to return."

Damn! He balled a fist and pressed it against the wall. He'd forgotten all about that conversation with Kelly. "Last night wasn't about that."

"Sure it wasn't, Will."

"Erin, I'm serious. Last night was special. You can't tell me you didn't feel that."

"What I can tell you is that last night won't ever happen again," she said in an even, fury-filled voice. "You've gotten what you wanted. You were able to seduce me with wine and a few lies."

The cold fury in her voice was like a knife in his gut. "Those weren't lies."

"Don't try to smooth this over. I know what you're

about. I knew what I was doing. Part of life is making mistakes and having regrets."

"Don't regret what happened." He didn't regret what happened. Couldn't possibly think of regretting it.

"Don't call me anymore, Will," she said at the same time.

He felt as if he were trying to grasp smoke in his hands. He could feel her slipping away with every crisply spoken word. "Come on, don't be that way."

"And you don't pretend as if you want something serious with me. I was foolish enough to fall for your lines last night, but I'm not that foolish today. The only thing I ask is that you don't tell Kelly. I don't want anyone to know about last night. I know you'll lose bragging rights, but maybe you can at least be decent with me on that."

"Erin, wait—"

"Goodbye, Will. Lose my number."

She ended the call. Will stared at his phone. He tried to shake off the loss he felt. Tried to reassure himself that he, Will Hampton, ladies' man and perfect playboy, wasn't feeling a sharp pain in his chest.

He shook off the feeling. He'd get her back. This wasn't the end. It couldn't be. Not when he'd finally recognized the jewel who'd been sitting right in front of him for years.

Chapter 5

Erin arrived in Charlotte, North Carolina, for All-Star Weekend ready to rock. Global Strategies was working with Mountain Brewed, a craft beer company with a large following in the Midwest that wanted more national recognition. She'd worked her magic to get them prime sponsorship spotlights throughout the weekend. Her deal included name placement, an event endorsed after-party and their name as the official sponsor for the slam-dunk contest.

Her efforts had impressed her boss and the other executives. She was a little impressed with herself. She'd busted her butt over the past several months to broker a deal to snag the sponsorship spots. Her goal had been to prove she had what it took to be promoted to executive, and if the weekend went well, she'd have just that and more.

She maneuvered her way through the crowd in the

back of the Spectrum Center, where all of the contests and games related to the weekend were being held. As she walked through the crowd of sponsors, players and workers she tried not to think about running into Will.

Seeing him was inevitable. He was the captain of the East Coast team, for crying out loud. What she wasn't going to let happen was allowing seeing Will to distract her from her ultimate goal: rocking this sponsorship deal. No getting caught up in any sensual spell he tried to pull.

If he even wanted to try. He's already proven he could get you in bed.

She pushed the humiliating thought aside as she spotted the producer for the televised contest and Gary Price, the CEO of Mountain Brewed. She placed her hand on Gary's shoulder to get his attention.

"Are you all set?"

As the sponsor of the contest, Gary was allowed to go out on the court during one of the breaks, wave at the crowd and throw a quick plug for Mountain Brewed.

Gary nodded and grinned. His family waited just to the left of him. They would get to go out on the court, too, and they practically buzzed with excitement. "All set. I wasn't sure you'd be able to work out this sponsorship deal, but you did."

"All I want is to make Mountain Brewed a household name. After this weekend is over, it will be."

Gary beamed. The producer touched his headphone, then pointed toward Gary. "We're ready. Let's go out."

Erin held back and watched them walk into the arena. She went to one of the televisions mounted on the wall to watch. She preferred being behind the scenes making sure everything went smoothly.

Once again she hoped this worked out for her career

plans. She loved traveling for her job, but a part of her was also ready for the stability that came with being an executive. Sending other reps out to broker the deals while she handled even larger clients through the home office.

"I was hoping to see you here."

The hairs on the back of Erin's neck stood up. An unwanted shiver went across her body. Her mouth dried out as delicious tingles prickled her most private spots. She looked upward and took a deep breath. She hoped her heavy sigh sounded irritated to him and not like the fortifying breath she needed before seeing him again.

Crossing her arms beneath her breasts, Erin slowly turned and faced the inevitable. She had to fight to keep her face neutral. The man was too damn good-looking. He was in the east coast colors of blue and white instead of the Gators' green and gold. Impossibly strong muscled arms and legs on display. His beard neatly trimmed and a seductive spark in his eye.

"I was hoping to avoid you," she said in an attempted go-screw-yourself tone of voice.

Her tone must have been convincing, because some of the cocky spark in his eye vanished. "You're still mad at me?"

How could he even think she wasn't mad at him? "I'm not mad. I just never want to speak to you again, and wouldn't mind pushing you off a very steep cliff into a river of starving, angry crocodiles below."

He cocked a brow. "That sounds pretty angry."

"What do you expect when you basically lie to get me into bed with you?"

Any hint of seduction left his eyes. His gaze was sure and steady as it met hers. "I didn't lie. Everything I told you that night was true." He took a step forward. "I can't stop thinking about you."

Dammit, why did he have to sound sincere and look at her with those perfect brown eyes? Or stand close enough for her body to react to the pull of his? She straightened her back and her shoulders. "Well, I've stopped thinking about you."

"Give me a chance to explain."

"There's nothing to explain. Kelly told me more than enough."

"My conversation with Kelly had nothing to do with what happened that night. I made love to you because I wanted you." He slid even closer. Blocking out the noise and movement of the other people in the arena. "And you wanted me, too."

Had they turned up the heat to incinerate? Because her body felt as if she were standing on the edge of an active volcano. She swallowed hard and narrowed her eyes into the don't-F-with-me glare she used when people tried to scam her on contract negotiations.

"What I might have wanted that night doesn't matter because everything that happened was based on a lie. A bet you had with yourself to see if you could get me in bed. Well, you did. Congratulations." She reached up and patted his shoulder in a patronizing gesture. His very solid shoulder. She quickly pulled her hand back. "You can move on and quit pretending it meant more to you."

She moved to walk away on that high note. Will moved with her. His fingers touched her elbow. They were rough and warm. Sparks of electricity popped across her skin.

He leaned in. "That night meant more to me than you'll ever know."

He looked genuine. Sounded truthful, almost desperate for her to believe. The yearning in his eyes made it hard for her to breathe. She forced herself to remember the conversation with Kelly. His need to prove he could get her in bed. The hastily written note. The fact that he hadn't bothered to come see her in the weeks since it happened. Just calls and texts she'd ignored before blocking his number.

She stepped back so his hand fell away. "If that were the case, you wouldn't have run out the next morning."

"I had an emergency. You heard about what happened with Mike. They called all the team back for that."

She had. The Gators had issued a statement. Something along the lines of the team not condoning violence of any kind and sending prayers for the family of the victim, but none of that had anything to do with what happened between them.

"And you couldn't even wake me up and tell me? I open myself to you. We do things some married couples probably don't do to each other, and you just skip out with a note."

For the first time, he looked embarrassed. "I…"

"Whatever. Save that for someone else."

"But Erin—"

"Hey, Erin, I've been looking all over for you."

Erin nearly sagged with relief when Jared called her. She quickly turned and smiled brightly as he walked up. He leaned in and kissed her quickly before sliding his arm around her waist. Will frowned and leaned back. Erin tried not to feel weird. She could date whomever she damn well pleased after the stunt Will pulled.

"I was just finishing up," she said.

Jared grinned and held out a hand. "Will Hampton,

I'm a big fan. I met your sister earlier today. She's great. I told Erin that's pretty cool she grew up knowing you."

"Not that cool," Erin muttered.

"Yeah…" Will pointed to Jared, then Erin. "You two…dating?"

She lifted her chin and glared defiantly. "Yes, we are."

Jared had called the day after Will left and asked her for a do-over after canceling on her that ill-fated night. Just the two of them. Seeing no reason to deny, she'd agreed. She'd refused to let the pain of Will's betrayal keep her from living her life.

Will cocked his head to the side and stared at Erin. "It's like that?"

Her cheeks burned. The fact that a hint of guilt tried to creep into her conscience made her want to kick him in the shins. She forced the guilt away. Ignored how much memories of their night together pushed to be released in her brain. Remembered instead the note, Kelly's words, the fact that Will Hampton wasn't serious about anything.

"Yes. It is," she said simply. "Goodbye, Will. Come on, Jared. Gary should be done now."

Jared looked between her and Will, then his arm tightened around her waist and they walked away. She ignored the heat of Will's gaze boring a hole in her back the entire time.

Chapter 6

Will found his sister first thing the next morning thanks to her ever-so-helpful online check-in at one of the brunch spots near her hotel. She wasn't far from where he and other players participating in the All-Star Weekend were staying, so he dressed and walked the few blocks to meet her. Along the way he stopped occasionally to sign an autograph or take a picture with a fan. Since Kelly was an early riser it wasn't too crowded on the streets and he wasn't bombarded.

When he entered the restaurant, he wondered briefly if Erin was with her. His pulse jumped in anticipation, with a hearty mix of frustration. Their reunion hadn't gone as he'd expected. He'd hoped time would have cooled her anger and allowed her to listen to his explanation. An explanation he'd left in dozens of voice messages. Guess she didn't listen to any of those.

When he spotted Kelly alone at a table near a window,

sipping coffee and scrolling through her phone, disappointment made his shoulders slump.

Will waved at the hostess and walked over to his sister. Kelly looked up from her phone and grinned. "What are you doing here?"

Her smile was as bright and sunny as the red-and-orange sweater she wore with dark jeans. He didn't know a time when Kelly didn't wear bright, happy colors. Not only did the colors suit his sister's sienna complexion, they were the perfect match to her outgoing personality. The sunshine of the family. That's what their dad called her.

Will bent over and hugged her before pulling out the chair opposite her. "Coming to see you."

"How did you—"

"You check in everywhere on social media." He held up his own cell phone.

Kelly nodded, then shrugged. "Gotta let people know where I am in case I turn up missing."

"Anyone who tries to steal you will return you within the hour."

Kelly stuck out her tongue, but laughter sparkled in her eyes. She flipped the long bangs of her chin length bob out of her eyes in a perfect I'm-cute-and-I-know-it arc before meeting his gaze. "What do you want with me? Make it quick, because I'm meeting someone."

"Erin?" he asked expectantly.

Kelly shook her head. "No, she has to work this morning. Getting things ready for the after-party tonight, and I think her group is also sponsoring some other event today."

"Good."

Kelly raised a brow. "Good? Why is that good? Are you trying to avoid her?"

"Because I need to talk to you about her." He leaned forward, resting his elbows on the white tablecloth. "What's up with that guy she's here with?"

For a second confusion clouded his sister's dark eyes. Then they cleared up and she cocked her head to the side. "Who, Jared?"

"Yeah, Jared," Will said his name as if it were a fatal disease. The guy who'd stood her up that night they'd slept together. The guy who absolutely did not deserve Erin.

Kelly wagged a manicured finger. "Why are you screwing up your face like that? Jared is a nice guy."

"He looks like a chump to me. How long have they been seeing each other?"

Kelly crossed her arms and leaned back in her chair. "About a month."

"A month? Nah, that can't be right." They'd slept together four weeks ago. She'd said she and Jared weren't serious. She wouldn't have lied about that.

"Again. Why do you even care?" Kelly's eyes widened. She slowly sat up and shook her head. Holding up a hand as if she needed to stop traffic, she glared. "Oh no. Don't tell me you're on that crap again."

Will shifted uncomfortably in his seat. "What crap?"

"The 'I could get with Erin if I wanted to' crap. Will, she already turned you down once. Are you trying to get embarrassed again? Especially when you are *literally* in a city with hundreds of women who showed up just to hook up with a famous basketball star."

"I don't care about those women," Will replied. "And I'm not on any crap, and who says she turned me down?"

Kelly's brow furrowed. "She did. She told me you

tried to hit on her and she sent you on your way. That is what happened, right?"

Will looked away and scratched his chin. He'd forgotten Erin didn't want Kelly to know. He'd called Kelly when Erin shut him down after their night together. Fired up and ready to go off on his sister for telling Erin he'd lied to her, but quickly realized Erin had kept what happened between them a secret. Probably because she didn't want Kelly to think she'd fallen for a game. When game-playing wasn't what he was doing.

He couldn't get Erin out of his mind. Couldn't stop thinking about that night. He'd even talked to his dad about how he felt without revealing who the woman was he was thinking of.

Son, when it hits you it hits you. You've just got to figure out if you're hit because she turned you away, or because you're really feeling her.

His dad treated Erin like another daughter. Will was positive his dad would give him a hard time if he knew she was the woman he was thinking about.

"Wait one damn minute," Kelly said in a low voice. "Did something happen?"

He avoided eye contact. "No."

Kelly's napkin hit him in the face. "I can't believe you. Erin? Of all people you had to go after my best friend?"

Will tossed the napkin aside. "It wasn't like that."

Again, the manicured finger of accusation pointed between his eyes. "You always say that, but then I end up losing a friend because you move on. Really, Will, why her?" She sounded genuinely hurt.

"Listen, I'm telling the truth. I went to check on her that night, and then that *Jared* guy called and canceled.

I just wanted to take her to a show and make her smile, but then one thing led to another and—"

"You accidentally took your clothes off and screwed my best friend?" She looked as if she wished there was something harder than a napkin she could toss at his face.

"Nah, not like that. You know I've always liked her."

"I know you're attracted to her. You're attracted to every woman with curves and a cute smile, Will. But you know Erin is my best friend. She's not like my college roommate or the coworker I just hung out with occasionally. Erin is the person I tell my secrets. My right hand. The one I count on above everyone else outside of my family, and now you're playing around with her."

"I'm not playing around with her. I really like her. What happened with her...well, I can't stop thinking about her." He reached across the table and placed his hand over Kelly's. He took a deep breath and forced out words he never though he'd say. "I think she could be the one."

Kelly stared at him for a second, then she jerked her hand back and rolled her eyes. "You are so full of crap, Will. You only want her because she ignored you for weeks and is dating someone else."

His face burned with embarrassment. Here he was, revealing to his sister something he'd been scared to think about, and she dismissed him so easily. Was it really that hard to believe he could be serious about what he felt for Erin? "You don't believe me?"

"Hell no," Kelly said with a don't-play-me-for-a-fool glare. "I don't believe you because you change your mind about everything about as fast as I blink. You can't stick to anything outside of basketball. Erin will be fun for you, then you'll move on to the next woman and I'll be minus a best friend." Kelly pounded her fist on the table. "Keep your penis away from my friend, understand?"

Will drew back. She really thought she could order him to stay away from Erin. He loved Kelly, and he understood her concerns, but what he'd felt with Erin was something he knew was more than a one-night stand. If he didn't try he'd regret walking away for the rest of his life.

Before he could argue, a tall man in light gray slacks and a dark blue pullover walked up. "Hey, Kelly, sorry I'm late."

Kelly turned away from Will and grinned. "Tyrell, hey, no problem. My brother kept me company for a few minutes but he's leaving now."

Will tamped down the need to finish his argument. Now wasn't the place. Kelly was having a knee-jerk reaction. He'd give her time. Eventually, she'd come around once she realized Erin wasn't just a passing hobby for him.

He slowly rose to his feet and shook Tyrell's hand before looking at Kelly again. "This conversation isn't done."

"Oh, it's all the way done." Her face grew serious, pleading. "Please, Will. For me, don't do this."

Instead of answering, Will turned to Tyrell. "You two have a good breakfast."

He walked away before Kelly could snap back with something smart. Kelly's pleading look and insistent demand that he stay away from Erin rang in his ears as he made his way back to the hotel. An earworm that made him regret seeking out his sister in the first place.

How was he going to convince Erin and Kelly that what happened between them had nothing to do with the conversation he'd had with Kelly two months ago? Nothing to do with trying to get a woman who'd turned him down back in his bed. Nothing to do with his no-strings-attached dating history. There was something there between him and Erin. He wasn't sure what. Wasn't sure if the something was long-lasting, but it was something he hadn't experienced before. And he'd experienced a lot of women.

He respected his sister, but this wasn't something he could give her. Erin had stirred emotions in him he couldn't ignore. Instinctively he knew he was right. Just like when he was in the middle of a game, and he stopped overthinking plays and just went with the flow of the play, his teammates, the opponents. Instincts took over and helped him make game-changing plays. He trusted his instincts. He wasn't going to ignore them now.

Chapter 7

The after-party's official start time was nine, but Erin knew people wouldn't start showing up in full force until after eleven. That didn't stop her from making sure everything was prepped and ready to go for the few who would show up on time to snag a table, chair or place at the bar that wasn't already reserved.

Jared came up behind her and placed his hand on her hip. "Everything looks great. You did a fantastic job."

"Thank you," Erin said with a satisfied grin on her face.

She had to agree. The club they'd chosen for the after-party was one of the hottest spots in town. Multiple DJs would keep the party going all night. Mountain Brewed had a variety of its craft beers on tap, along with a few cocktails inspired by the brand. The beers were free to those with tickets to any of the weekend's events. There were also special gifts for the VIP sections, and more prizes would be announced to partygoers all night.

Jared pulled her closer and kissed her cheek. "You're going to be a shoo-in for the executive position."

She leaned away from his kiss and surveyed the surroundings. "I don't like to count my chickens before they hatch." Though a part of her knew that if this night went off without a hitch she would be the top contender. She'd even heard rumors that several players participating in the weekend planned to attend the Mountain Brewed party.

She really hoped one of those players wasn't William Hampton.

"Count them," Jared said, squeezing her hip. "You deserve, it baby." He kissed her cheek again. "I'm going to check on the caterers again."

Erin smiled as he walked away. The damp spot where he'd kissed her created an unnerving cold sensation that made her want to swipe at her cheek. She waited until he'd slipped into the kitchen before she did that.

What was wrong with her? Ever since bumping into Will she'd been hyperaware of all of Jared's annoying little habits. She didn't want to think about the reason why. Comparisons only made things worse. Why was she comparing Jared to Will anyway? They were completely different. For one thing, Jared wasn't a lying jerk who'd said nice things only to get her into bed.

Everything I told you that night was true.

Why had he looked so genuine when he'd said the words? Sincerer than she could have expected. Sincere enough to make her wonder if maybe she'd jumped to conclusions. Or maybe she was being delusional and falling into his trap again.

"Well, this place is fantastic." Kelly's voice.

Erin grinned and turned to face her friend. "It is, isn't it?" They hugged each other.

The sunny smell of Kelly's perfume enveloped Erin. When they pulled back, she gave her friend a quick once-over. Kelly was stunning in a strapless red dress. "What are you doing here so early?" Erin asked. "I didn't expect you to show up until later."

"I wanted to talk to you before you get too busy," Kelly said.

"Okay, let's go to the bar. You can tell me what you think of the signature drink."

They hooked arms and strolled over to the bar. Erin ordered two of the cocktails. Neither she nor Erin was a craft beer drinker. Once they were settled on the bar-stools, Kelly faced Erin and frowned.

"Why didn't you tell me you and Will slept together?"

Erin froze with her drink halfway to her mouth. She closed her eyes and pictured her hand slapping the back of Will's perfectly faded head. "He told you that?"

She couldn't believe he told Kelly. Why? Was he trying to embarrass her further?

Kelly shook her head. "No, but I can read a lie in Will's face from a mile away."

She opened her eyes and met Kelly's worried gaze. "Why did you ask him if we slept together?"

"Because he came to me this morning asking a lot of questions about you and Jared. When I told him to back off, he felt some type of way about that. That's when I put two and two together."

"What two and two is that?" She wasn't volunteering this information willingly.

"That when he came to see you a month ago, and tried

to hit on you, that you two did a lot more than just go to see *Slam!* Apparently, he slammed into you."

Erin rolled her eyes. "He didn't slam into me." He'd slid in to her. Nice and hard. Over and over.

Heat spread through Erin's body. Kelly raised a brow. Erin looked way and took a long sip of her drink.

"Please tell me you aren't still hooking up with Will?"

Erin slammed her drink onto the bar. "No! Not at all."

"Then why is he all worried about who you're seeing now?"

"Because I told him it would never happen again. After you told me what he said, I knew he was just playing a game." A game he denied playing.

Everything I told you that night was true.

Kelly studied her. "So there's really nothing there?"

There was something there. Erin just planned not to acknowledge it. "Nothing at all. We had a fun night, I got caught up in the moment, and one thing led to another. It was just sex on my end, and once I realized what he was up to, then it wasn't even that."

"Why didn't you tell me?"

"Because I didn't want you to think I was silly for sleeping with him. And he is your brother. It's kind of awkward."

"I don't care if you sleep with Will," Kelly said. "Not really. I know sex can really be just sex." She reached over and placed her hand over Erin's. "I just don't want to lose my best friend to him."

Erin placed her hand over Kelly's. "There is no way you're losing me to Will. It's not even a competition. Believe me, nothing is ever going to happen between the two of us again."

Kelly watched her for a few long seconds before her

face relaxed and she smiled. "Good." Kelly raised her glass. "To after-parties and getting the promotion."

Erin raised her glass. "To getting the promotion."

They clinked glasses and took a sip. Erin meant everything she'd said. Nothing else was happening between her and Will. She wasn't going to fall for his games again. There was no way he could be serious about anything, least of all her. They'd grown up together; wouldn't she have gotten some hint over the years if he was attracted to her?

There was that night of the military ball.

That night didn't count. But as the party began to go into full swing, and Jared pulled her onto the dance floor one last time before things became too busy, all she could think about was how Jared's hands on her hips didn't make her heart race the way Will's hands had.

When Will arrived at the Mountain Brewed party the club was lit. He would have liked to have gotten there earlier, but after the activities of the day he'd had a full evening of press-related events. Not to mention the team clearance allowing him to attend the party hadn't come through until late.

The soft lockdown was in full effect. Mike had been charged and the trial date set. The team scrutiny from the media had come as expected. Stories about the various publicity nightmares they'd faced over the years. Though the lockdown irritated Will and several other teammates, he understood the reason behind it even more. Right now, the Gators needed only positive attention in the media.

Will didn't want any drama tonight. Now to convince Erin to talk to him without pissing her off. He'd tried calling and texting her all day. No response. He needed her to listen and hoped she understood. He owned his mistakes, and leaving without telling her had been wrong. He hadn't been ready to face what happened between them. Something special started that night they were together. Special enough to keep him thinking about only her in the weeks since. Tonight, he wanted her to at least hear him out. Her boyfriend *Jared* be damned.

He searched through the crowd for her. Pausing for the occasional selfie with fans both male and female at the party. There were several other players who attended. He'd heard plenty of people talking about the Mountain Brewed party. Every mention of the brand she represented reminded him just how dedicated and driven she was. He did not deserve someone like her, but he was selfish enough to try.

Eventually, he spotted Jared. He stood in a corner, one hand on the wall, as he talked to a woman in a black jumpsuit who leaned against the wall. Jared glanced over his shoulder quickly before turning back to the woman who was not Erin. They smiled at each other, flirtation apparent in her eyes. Jared ran a finger down the woman's cheek, and she slipped a piece of paper into his pocket.

Will frowned. What the hell was going on with that? This guy couldn't be that much of a jerk to hit on another woman at Erin's party. Could he?

Will stalked right over to them. "Jared, you seen Erin?"

Jared jerked and straightened. He turned quickly and looked guiltily at Will. "Will, hey, what's up?"

The woman wrapped a hand over Jared's biceps. He shook her touch away.

"Why don't you tell me?" Will said, looking at the woman. He held out a hand. "Will Hampton."

"I'm Iris," she said with a grin.

Will shook her hand, then looked back at Jared. "Looks like you two are pretty close."

Jared shook his head. "Actually we're…"

"Not as close as I hope we get later," Iris cut in.

"Oh really?" Will tilted his head to the side. "I wonder what Erin would have to say about that."

Jared's eyes widened. "Come on, man. No need to pull Erin into this."

Apparently, he really was that much of a jerk. "Why not?"

Jared shrugged. "You know how it is. It's a guy thing. Monogamy is good in theory, but hard in practice." He tapped Will on the chest. "What Erin doesn't know won't hurt her."

Will saw red. His hands clenched into fists. He wanted nothing more than to punch Jared's teeth all the way to his stomach. "No, you see, what Erin doesn't know and eventually finds out about will hurt her. And as her friend, I'm not going to stand around and watch you try to play her."

Will turned away. Jared grabbed his arm. "Hey man, you can't just rat me out."

Will jerked his arm away. "I can, and if you grab me like that again I'm going to embarrass your ass in front of Iris, Erin and every other woman here."

Jared puffed up his chest. "What the hell is wrong with you? I thought you'd understand."

"Understand what?" Erin's voice cut in.

Will spun around. Erin stood there with her arms crossed. For a second, he was struck speechless. She wore a fitted black dress with a low V-cut neckline and a hem that stopped right above her knees. Sky-high heels accentuated her legs, and her thick hair fell in a smooth, sleek curtain to her shoulders. Damn, she was breathtaking.

Then he realized her eyes were shooting daggers at him. "Why are you looking at me like that?"

"Why are you trying to pick a fight with Jared?"

"Me pick a fight? I came over to ask this sucker if he'd seen you, only to find him getting some other woman's number."

Her eyes widened. She looked from him to Jared, who shook his head so hard it was a wonder he didn't scramble his brain.

Jared rushed forward. "Baby, he's lying."

"Check his left pocket if I'm lying," Will said.

Iris wrapped a hand around Jared's waist. "No need to check. Hell yeah he asked for my number."

Pain flashed in Erin's eyes. She looked from Jared to Iris, then to Will. Will reached for her, but she lifted a hand and stepped back. "To hell with all three of you." Then she turned and hurried away.

Chapter 8

With stealth and determination, Erin got through the rest of the party without bumping into Jared or Will. Kelly gave her a few looks a couple of times that asked if Erin was okay. She always smiled and kept it moving. Lord knew there was enough going on at the party to keep her busy and distracted from the fact that she'd been played for a fool. Again. And to make the realization even more mortifying, Will had witnessed her embarrassment.

She was mad at Jared. Mad at him for being just another jerk, but when she took half a second to stop and think, she realized she wasn't hurt. She'd never considered Jared to be *the one* but shouldn't she feel a little more disappointed he'd gotten another woman's number at her party?

By the time the party wound down after 2:00 a.m., Erin had kicked off her shoes as she went over the follow-up details with the club owners. Despite Jared's being a total douchebag, and the told-you-so look in Will's eyes after ratting Jared out, she was happy with the results of the party. That was all that mattered. She was here to do a job, and she'd done the job successfully.

After finishing up her conversation with the owner, Erin walked through the now mostly empty club to the side door. She waved at the bartenders and other workers cleaning things up and thanked them for their hard work when movement at one of the tables caught her attention. She turned and gasped as Will stood and strolled toward her. He was dressed in a trendy suit. The coat slung over his shoulder with one hand. He'd rolled the sleeves of the white shirt up to his elbows and unbuttoned the top buttons.

"What are you still doing here?"

"I'd think the answer to that question would be obvious," he said. He moved closer until only a few inches separated them. "I'm waiting on you."

Her shoes were still off. In her hands. Which made him tower over her. She yearned for the height. To be on a more even playing field. Will unnerved her enough already without her being reminded of his height. The way his body surrounded her in a cocoon of pleasure. How solid and firm every part of him was.

Erin slid back a step, then pushed her hair behind one ear. "Why are you waiting on me?"

"Because we need to talk."

"No, we don't. I've said everything I need to say." She turned to walk away.

Will's long stride put him right beside her. "Well, then you can listen to what I have to say."

He followed her down the hall to the side door leading to the back parking lot, where her car was parked. Erin stopped at the door to put her shoes back on. Will used the opportunity to stand in front of the door. Blocking her exit.

Erin got her shoes on, then crossed her arms. "Haven't you done enough tonight?"

"You can't be mad at me for what that fool did."

"You should have stayed out of things."

"No, I shouldn't have. If I'd stayed out of things you'd still be dating a cheater. You deserve better than that."

"Yeah, I deserve a guy who lies to get me in bed."

She moved to push him out of the way. Will held his hands in front of his chest and widened his stance. "I didn't lie to you." He sounded frustrated. "Why won't you believe me?"

"Because I know you, Will. I grew up watching you go from girl to girl then woman to woman. Why should I believe I'm different?"

Lightning-fast hands grasped her waist and he pulled her close. Dark eyes burned into hers. Hot and serious but also pleading. "You are different. You know me. Not the professional athlete people see on television, or the fun guy the media portrays. You've seen my struggles. You told me to keep trying when I struggled to keep my grades passing in college and Dad told me not to worry because I was going to play ball professionally. You had the audacity to correct my free-throw shot after I'd been drafted." His eyes softened along with his grip on her waist. "You wrapped your arms around my shoulders the day my mom died in the hospital and let me cry."

Her heart broke again at the memory. Kelly consoling their father, who'd been devastated. Will, trying not to break down. His body shaking with suppressed grief.

She'd sat and pulled him against her. He'd crumbled instantly. Her heart had twisted with the agony of the family's pain.

Will pressed his forehead to hers. His voice lowered. "You've seen parts of me no one else has ever seen. Just because I've been blind in the past doesn't mean I am now. I see you. The smart, determined, take-no-prisoners woman you are. That's the woman I want."

Erin shook her head. Her heart wanted to believe him. Her head fought back. The guy she'd secretly had a crush on for years couldn't possibly mean what he was saying.

"Will, I don't want to be a fling," she said softly but firmly. "You can't just walk away when things get tough."

He lifted his head and met her eyes unflinchingly. "I was wrong for not waking you before I left, but the only reason I walked away last time was because of the team meeting. We're on lockdown. I should be back at the hotel now, but I had to see you. I had to know you were okay. I had to be sure that asshole didn't break your heart."

She looked into his dark eyes. "He isn't the one capable of hurting me."

The same determination she'd seen in his face before an important game filled his eyes. The look she knew meant he was ready to bring his A game. "I promise I won't break your heart."

She pressed her hands against his chest. She should push him away. This was Will. Just as she knew parts of him hidden from the world, he knew parts of her. He could hurt her so much more than anyone like Jared ever could. Walking away right now would be the smartest thing.

Her fingers curled into the material of his shirt. "I want to believe you," she whispered.

His heart pounded beneath the muscle of his chest. Tension seeped out of his body, as if he'd been waiting anxiously for what she would say next. "Then let me show you that you can believe me. Let me try to be the man you deserve."

Her head jerked up. Hope and fear swirled inside her. He kissed her before she could say anything else.

His kiss thoroughly sucked the air from her lungs. Her hands clung first to his shirt before flying up to wrap around his neck. Her heart sprinted with each sexy sweep of his tongue. Will's hand plunged into her hair; the other played along the taut muscles of her back. Time meant nothing. Getting caught by the workers at the club meant nothing. The only things she was aware of were the heat of his body, the yearning in her veins and the possessive way his hands held her.

The hand on her back gripped a handful of her dress. Cool air brushed the back of her legs as the hemline rose. Erin wanted the dress off. Wanted to feel his naked body hot against hers. Wrap her hands around the hard length of him and relive all of the pleasure he'd given her that one brief night. The press of his erection against her belly proved he felt the same. The urgency of his kiss was just as hot and desperate as hers.

His hold on her hair tightened just enough to send a rush of excitement through her. He slowly pulled her head back, then ran light kisses across her jaw. "Come back to my hotel."

The low rumble of his voice made her body tremble. Her chin lifted and lowered automatically. The need to be back in his bed drowned out every other thought in her head. Her breasts ached. Her sex throbbed. She wanted to drag him to the floor and get the edge off right now.

Reality hit right then like a fifty-mile-an-hour car collision. She was ready, after just a few minutes, to jump in bed with him again. If she went to his room she'd be right back where she was a month ago. Did she want that? Yes. Did she believe him? Kinda. Was she ready to trust him?

She shook her head. "No."

Will's kisses stilled. He raised his head and met her eye. "Why not?" No accusation or anger. Curiosity and the same sexual frustration she fought colored his tone instead.

"I need time to think. Time to process. This wasn't supposed to happen."

"Stop thinking about what's supposed to happen and think about what you want to happen."

Another image of him dragging her to the floor. Or pressing her against the wall. Then there was the back seat of the car.

Erin shook her head and scrambled out of his arms. Will's hands slowly released her. "I want to believe you," she said. "I want to think you're really ready for a relationship because, Will, I'm a relationship type of woman. I'm not asking you for marriage or forever, but I am asking you for a commitment, monogamy, honesty." He opened his mouth and she covered whatever he was about to say with her hand. "You need to think about this, too. You might think you're ready, but you need to be sure this is what you want. Even if we're only together for a short time. For that time, I've got to be the only one. You can't lie to me. Make sure that's what you want, too."

His body relaxed. She dropped her hand. His brows drew together. She saw the battle in his eyes: automatically say what she wanted to hear against the realization that this time there would be more of a commitment than the "no turning back" they'd stated before. She'd made him really think about what she was asking him to do, which meant she was right to have stopped him.

Tell that to her body, still buzzing with the need to say yes and follow him to his hotel room.

"If you really mean what you say, then call me tomorrow." Erin slipped around him and pushed open the door. "Otherwise, let's just pretend none of this ever happened."

Chapter 9

Will had exactly ninety minutes before he had to be back at the stadium to prep for the All-Star Game. As the elected leader of the team he couldn't be late, and had reiterated their coach's advice to spend the time between practice and the game relaxing, meditating or sleeping in order to be ready. Instead, he'd hired a car and was on a mission.

He was going to check on Erin.

He'd tried calling her, but not surprising, she hadn't answered. He'd gone by one of the Mountain Brewed sponsored events, but she'd put one of her employees in charge. Jared was nowhere to be seen. When he'd called Kelly to low-key investigate what Erin was up to, his chatty sister hadn't disappointed him. She'd said Erin wasn't feeling good after the night before and had stayed in her room.

Immediately concerned, Will was going to make sure

she was okay. He'd thought about what she said. Any other time, any other woman, he would have moved on. A woman putting a claim on him wasn't something he went for. There were too many women and too much fun to be had to be nailed down with just one, but being nailed down by Erin did not make him want to skip out early on the relationship. The second she'd said what it would take to be with her, he'd known he wanted to try.

How hard could a relationship be anyway? If you were into the person, then being with them should be easy. They'd talk, have sex, have fun hanging out with each other. A relationship would be like their night in Chicago except instead of just for a night it would be like that every day. What could possibly go wrong?

He was going to ace this boyfriend thing. He got out of the car and bounded into Erin's hotel. Kelly let it slip where Erin was staying, but he didn't have her room number. He tried to work his magic at the front desk, but the hotel clerk refused to give him Erin's room number.

"I'm sorry, sir, but we do not give out our guest's room numbers. You are not listed as one of the guests staying in the room."

Will gave the woman one of his signature smiles. "Yes, Ebony, I understand," he said, using the name on the tag pinned to her uniform. "But I've got to talk to her about this party they're doing for us."

Ebony shook her head. "I can't go against policy. I could lose my job."

He had no argument for that. He wasn't going to ask her to risk her job. "Give me a second. Let me try to call her again." He pulled out his cell phone and dialed Erin's number.

He didn't expect an answer. She'd been ignoring his

calls and texts ever since she'd believed he'd lied to her. So when she did answer on the second ring he was momentarily stunned into silence.

"Hello? Will?"

He snapped out of his shocked surprise. "Erin, what's your room number?"

"Why?"

"Because the lady at the counter won't give it to me." He smiled at Ebony, whose scowl softened from frustrated to mildly annoyed.

"You're here? At my hotel?"

"Yes, so what room are you in?"

"Why are you here?"

"Kelly said you weren't feeling well. I came to check on you."

"To check on me?" She sounded skeptical.

"Yes, to check on you. Now I've only got ninety minutes." He looked at his watch. "More like seventy-five. Will you let me know your room number so we can talk?"

She hesitated again. He worried she wouldn't agree to see him. "If you don't I'm just going to knock on every door in this hotel until I find you."

Ebony opened her mouth to argue. Will put a finger to his lips and shook his head.

Erin sighed. "Fine. I'm in room five fifty-three."

"I'll be right up." He hung up the phone and grinned at Ebony. "I was only teasing." Kinda. He winked, then hurried to the elevator.

His heart pumped furiously as the elevator made its ascent. What was wrong with him? Why was he getting nervous about seeing Erin? He'd dated before. Dated exclusively a couple of times; this wasn't any different.

Except it was completely different. Before, he'd known when things wound down he'd be able to charm his way out of the relationship and still keep the woman as a friend. With Erin, if things wound down, what would their relationship be like afterward? If he screwed this up, would he lose her in his life completely, and worse, would his sister lose a best friend?

"Then don't screw this up," he muttered as the elevator doors opened and he made his way down the carpeted hall to Erin's room.

Let things play out. Wait and see, and if things started to waver, he'd do what he always did—maneuver the situation so the woman broke things off with him. He'd never cheated or become an asshole, he just knew how to subtly become emotionally unavailable until the woman decided to move on. He then accepted the breakup amicably and they remained friends. Except the idea of manipulating Erin made his stomach churn.

He knocked on her room door. It swung open immediately. Erin stood on the other side, dressed in gray sweats that tapered at her trim ankles and hugged her hips. A fitted Mountain Brewed T-shirt clung to her full breasts and slim waist. She'd pulled her thick hair out of her face with a colorful scarf. The rest of her hair hung loose to her shoulders. No makeup that he could tell. She was absolutely delicious.

"Hey," she said hesitantly.

Her eyes met his. Questioned what he wanted. Why was he there? One wrong word and he knew she'd turn him away.

"Can I come in?"

She licked her full lips before stepping back. "Sure." Will entered and waited while she closed the door.

Her room was actually a one-bedroom suite. Her laptop and files of papers were spread on the table next to the mini kitchen. Through a door he could see her unmade bed. His dick tightened with the thought of lying with her on those sheets. He turned away from the bedroom.

This was not about sex. The sex was outstanding, but he didn't want her to think that was all he was interested in.

"So, what's up?" she asked. She stood in front of the television. Away from him. Old reruns of the sitcom *Martin* played in the background. The volume up enough to hear but not loud enough to distract from their conversation.

"How are you feeling?"

"I'm fine. I just had a headache. All the noise, smoke and…stuff from the night before."

"I was worried about you."

"No need. I'm working." She pointed to the papers on the table. "And planned to still make it to the game tonight."

"Good." He rubbed his hands together. Nervous in an unfamiliar way as they inched closer to what he'd come here to say. "I'd like for you to have the reserved seats I set aside for family."

"Isn't your family going to have those seats?"

"Yes, but come on, you're practically family."

Something flickered in her eyes. She lowered them before he could make out what. "I am, I guess. Don't worry about me. I have seats with Mountain Brewed."

To hell with sitting with her client. Didn't she understand what he was saying? No other woman had sat with his family at one of his games. "I'd like for you to sit with my family."

"Why?"

He took a deep breath. Planted his feet so that he wouldn't shuffle from one to the other like a scared kid. "I thought about what you said last night, and I'm in."

"You're…in?" She crossed her arms under her breasts, pushing them up.

Will nodded. "Yes. All in. Relationship, monogamy, the whole deal. Let's do this."

The excitement, joy, jubilation he'd expected didn't come. Instead she eyed him as if he'd just ordered a burger at a pizza parlor.

"Have you thought this through? I mean, you aren't really known for the serious relationships you've had."

"That doesn't mean I can't be serious when it counts. And Erin, you count." He walked over and uncrossed her arms. He laced their fingers together. "I can't get you out of my mind. I've been out there. I've played the field. I don't want to play anymore. I want to grow up, and I'd like to grow up with you."

"What about Kelly? She doesn't want us together."

He didn't give a damn about what his sister wanted. Kelly had nothing to do with this, but he understood her concern. Kelly was her best friend. "Kelly only said that because she thinks I'll hurt you."

"Will you hurt me?"

Will tugged on their joined hands until she came closer. "I promise I'll never hurt you. I only want to make you laugh. I never want to make you cry."

Her eyes softened along with her body. Her brows drew together. He could see the fight on her face. Two sides of her in open combat. One telling her to believe him, the other ready to run and hide. He didn't give the latter a chance to counter.

He lowered his head and kissed her, and her soft lips parted and welcomed him in. A tremor, fast and unexpected, racked his body. He felt shaken and freed all in one. When her arms inched up around his neck and her body pressed into his, he was lost.

He didn't want to act as if he were starving for her. But the urgency to have her in his arms pushed for release like a Black Friday mob. She teased him with sweet, soft sweeps of her tongue and drove him mad with the low feminine noises she made, as if he was just as addictive to her. He wanted to throw her over his shoulder, carry her into the next room, rip off her clothes and really make a mess of the sheets on that king-size bed.

He wasn't that guy. He couldn't lose his cool. Couldn't let her know how much she drove him crazy. She pushed her hips forward against the stiff rod of his erection. Will's control snapped.

Reaching down, he lifted her into his arms. She let out a little yelp of surprise. His mouth covered hers in a scorching kiss, and he marched straight for the bedroom.

Will's hands never left her body. Erin closed her eyes and savored every caress. They undressed quickly. Clothes flying to random corners of the room. He turned her to face the bed, swept the hair over her shoulders and ran soft kisses down the side of her neck.

Erin's head fell to one side. Pleasure took over every other sense. She didn't want to overthink this. Didn't want to focus on what she should do when she knew what her body wanted to do. What her heart wanted to do.

Will's large hands cupped her breasts. With slow, sensual strokes he circled her nipples with the tips of his fingers. Making them hard, aching points. Erin's lungs struggled to suck in air. She pushed her chest forward. Silently begging for more.

The soft bite of Will's teeth on her neck came when he finally gently pinched the tips of her breasts. Erin's body shook. Her knees edged out until her legs were spread.

"Touch me," she whispered.

"I am touching you." Will's deep sensual voice in her ear. He ran his tongue across the outer edge.

Erin's fingers dug into his thigh. "Please."

One hand left her breast and trailed down her body to gently part the slick folds of her sex. "Like this?"

"I hate you."

His fingers slid easily across her wet heat. "Doesn't feel like you hate me."

One long finger pushed deep into her. Erin's mouth fell open. Her hips undulated back and forth. Grinding on his fingers in tandem with the teasing pulls of his fingers on her breasts. Will kissed along her neck. Softly pulled on her ear with his teeth. Pushed forward so she felt just how much he enjoyed what he was doing to her.

She shattered much too soon. Pleasure and loss sweeping through her. She wanted more than what he'd given her, but she'd already begged once. With the shattering release came the realization of how easily he'd made her body melt in his arms.

She pulled out of his embrace and lay on her side facing away from him. Was this what it was going to be like? Will kissed her, touched her, and she became dough he could shape into whatever he needed?

He slid up behind her. His body solid and warm behind hers. Without a word, he gently pushed her onto her back. Erin kept her eyes lowered. Unsure even with herself what she felt in this moment.

His lead lowered, and he kissed her slowly, hesitantly. When he broke the kiss, they both were breathing heavily. Will rubbed the tip of his nose against hers. She lifted her lids and met his dark gaze.

"I'm not going anywhere. I meant what I said. Trust me. Please."

His voice held just as much plea as hers had a few minutes before. With his eyes he begged her to let go. To believe in what they were doing. Believe in him.

Erin reached between their bodies and took his length into her hands. She spread her legs until he could settle between them easily. "No turning back," she whispered.

She positioned him at her opening and Will pushed in one decadent inch at a time. He lowered his head and kissed her deeply. The relief as real in his kiss as the shiver that went through his body.

"No turning back," he said against her lips.

Then his hips shifted and touched that perfect spot deep inside her. She'd laid out her standards and he hadn't shied away. He was here. He wanted to try. That's what she clung to as he made her body explode in a shock wave of pleasure.

Chapter 10

Erin sat with Will's family during the All-Star Game. They weren't surprised when she joined them. In fact, Kelly and Mr. Hampton pretty much assumed she would join them anyway because she was so close to the family. She let them go with that assumption.

She hadn't talked to Kelly after her quick, wonderful afternoon with Will. Now that she wasn't wrapped in his arms and only concentrating on the feelings between them, she worried about Kelly's reaction. Erin had chosen to let go of her fears and trust Will. That didn't mean Kelly would be happy with the decision. The last thing Erin wanted was for her relationship with Will to ruin her friendship with Kelly. Her oldest and closest friend in the world.

"So, Erin, Kelly tells me you're doing big things," Calvin Hampton said, breaking into her thoughts.

Calvin and Will were similar. Both tall, though Calvin

had at least two inches on Will. They had the same dark brown skin, piercing eyes and devastating smile. Calvin also had gray only at the temples, which gave him a sexy, sophisticated air. Erin respected him as much as her own father, who'd worked as Calvin's accountant for years.

Though many women still threw themselves at Mr. Hampton, Erin could never see him in a sex object kind of way. He was Kelly's dad. The guy who'd informally coached her with Will in basketball before she'd hurt her knee. He was like a second dad, which made her worry about how he'd take it when she and Will made their decision public. She didn't want to lose her connection with either of them.

Too late to think through the what-ifs now, Erin.

She dunked that thought and answered Calvin's question. "I'm trying," she said. "I've been working really hard on this Mountain Brewed campaign. It's gone better than expected, which means—" she held up her right hand with her fingers crossed "—when I get back I should be offered the position on the executive team."

"You ever thought about opening your own advertising agency?" Calvin asked. As usual, he was always promoting creating income that wasn't solely tied to the whims of someone else.

"I have, but for now I'm happy with working where I am. I love what I do. Having to deal with the business side of things is not my idea of fun."

Just the thought of handling benefits packages, payroll and accounting was enough to make her break out in hives. Erin wanted to focus solely on projects and making her clients' businesses household names. Maybe one day she'd open her own firm, but for now she didn't want to add that extra stress in her life.

"Going into business for yourself isn't as bad as you think," Calvin said. His eyes were still on the game, but he leaned to the left where she sat next to him and spoke up so she could hear him over the crowd. She knew that even if his attention was on Will on the court, he was also in tune with their conversation. "If you can't handle the books then look at getting a good business partner who can handle that for you." He pointed toward the court. "It's like I tell Will all the time. You need to have a backup plan."

Erin's eyes zeroed in on Will. He ran down the court. A teammate threw him the ball. He focused on the left side of the basket, but deftly passed the ball behind him to an open man on the right who easily scored three points. The crowed cheered. Erin grinned.

Kelly lightly elbowed Erin. "Dad's about to start his lecture again." She wasn't as into the game as Erin and Calvin. Kelly enjoyed the perks of growing up the daughter of a professional basketball player, but the perks were about as far as her interests went. Erin knew she was only here to support Will.

"And why shouldn't I?" Mr. Hampton asked with a quick glance at Kelly. "I keep telling you kids you need to make the necessary plans to be secure when you get older. Invest in yourself. Find ways to make your money work for you."

Erin remembered one of her and Will's late-night chats when he'd spent the night with her in Chicago. He'd briefly mentioned investments he'd made in various businesses over time. "Doesn't Will invest?"

Calvin waved a dismissive hand. "He does, but not wisely. His head is too in the clouds. He can't calm down and focus on one thing."

Calvin's quick dismissal of Will's investments irritated Erin. It wasn't the first time Calvin had done that. He seemed to always push Will to expect less and rely solely on his skills as an athlete. "He mentioned wanting to take a more active role in team leadership," Erin said. "He's talked about maybe coaching one day."

Mr. Hampton laughed as if she'd told the funniest joke. He even took his eyes off the court and patted her shoulder. "Coaching? Will?" He shook his head. "My son is good at basketball, but he's not coach material. Not at all."

Erin clenched her jaw instead of telling Mr. Hampton that he was being ridiculous doubting Will. How could he so easily dismiss his son's ability? He'd been voted captain of the Eastern Conference team, for crying out loud. That wasn't given to someone who didn't show some type of ability to lead.

She could understand some of Calvin's reservations. She had grown up around Will. He did jump around a lot. But when it came to basketball he absorbed everything he could. Will listened to everything his dad told him about basketball and adapted the way he played based on his father's feedback. He'd done the same with coaches. Will learned what worked and was disciplined enough to follow direction. He knew how to correct, and he also knew how to rally his teammates, so they could correct themselves. The man knew the game.

"I don't know, Daddy," Kelly said, sounding defensive. "I think he'd be okay. If he really wanted to do it. Will doesn't give up when he wants something."

Mr. Hampton laughed again. "He doesn't give up when he wants to do something fun or if he wants to be with a woman. That's about all of the dedication he can provide."

The conversation was interrupted by the buzzer for halftime. Erin and the rest of the people in the VIP lounge cheered. Some people drew Calvin aside for conversation, and that was the end of the discussion about Will's abilities as a basketball coach someday. After halftime they focused on the game.

When the game ended, Erin stayed with Kelly and Calvin as they traveled to one of the smaller jazz lounges, where they'd meet Will. He'd told her earlier that the team had already approved this outing since he'd be with his family.

With each passing second, she grew more nervous and agitated. The time for the truth had come. She had to tell Kelly and Calvin about her and Will, yet she couldn't summon the words. She wanted Will there with her, so they could present a united front. She couldn't handle their looks of disbelief, or worse, pity, because she'd fallen into the trap. She and Will were serious. They'd have to get used to it.

She glanced at Kelly at the bar. Sipping on a drink and flirting with a guy while Mr. Hampton signed autographs at the other end of the bar. What if Kelly thought she'd betrayed their friendship by not telling her up front? She wasn't ashamed about being with Will. There was no reason why she shouldn't tell her best friend.

"Kelly, I need to tell you something," Erin said.

Kelly glanced over her shoulder at Erin. "Now? I'm kind of busy." She motioned her head toward the guy.

"Well, this is kinda important."

The volume of conversation at the door increased. The air buzzed with an electric heat. He was there.

Erin turned, and her gaze connected with Will's. The corner of his sexy mouth lifted, and a joyous light sparked in his midnight eyes. Erin bit her lower lip, but that didn't stop her own smile from taking over.

Bypassing the women trying to get his attention and the men holding up their hands for a high five, he came straight to her. The grin on his face bigger than she'd ever seen. His stride purposeful. All because he'd seen her.

She didn't have time to think about how his focus on her might look to others. She was caught up by his apparent happiness to see her. The questions about their relationship were irrelevant. She wanted to be with this man. He wanted to be with her. That was all that mattered.

Will strode right up to her, swept her into his arms, and kissed her in front of everyone in the nightclub.

"So how long has this been going on?" Calvin's concerned voice asked.

After the initial shock of him kissing Erin in the middle of the party, his dad had maneuvered them to their VIP section. There wasn't much time before fans, other celebrities and guys who'd played with his dad eventually invaded their VIP section. He was usually excited about the attention he and his father got when they were in a room together. One of the league's best players and his superstar father. Not today. The distractions would prevent him from making his point. He was ready to try to have what his parents had before his mother's death.

Will wrapped his arms around Erin's stiff shoulders. They sat next to each other on one of the leather couches. His dad and Kelly sat on the other. His dad's expression was a mixture of shock and concern. Kelly, on the other hand, simmered with silent fury. Her arms were crossed tightly over her chest.

"A few months now," Will answered.

Kelly's eyes widened. "Months?" She turned betrayed eyes on Erin. "You told me there was nothing going on between you two. That there wouldn't be anything between you."

He didn't think it was possible, but Erin got stiffer. "There wasn't. This hasn't been going on for months. Not really." Erin focused on his dad as if she couldn't bear the accusation in Kelly's eyes. "Will and I connected with each other about two months ago, but it wasn't until yesterday that we made the decision to be together."

"Yesterday?" Kelly seemed to choke on the words. "I asked you what was going on yesterday and you said nothing. You lied to me."

Erin scooted forward on the chair. "I didn't lie."

Kelly held up a hand when Erin started to speak again. She grunted and turned her head away. The pained look on Erin's face brought the first feelings of guilt to Will. He didn't regret being with Erin, but he would regret if this decision came between her and Kelly.

His dad shook his head. "So yesterday you two decided it was time to be a couple. Son, what are you doing?"

Calvin asked the words as if Will had said he was quitting football to pursue a career selling ice to polar bears. As if Will couldn't be trusted to make a sensible decision. Will's cheeks heated. He hated when his dad talked to him that way, because it almost always made Will question his decisions. Maybe he couldn't get better grades. Maybe he wasn't focused enough to lead a team.

"Do you have a problem with me being with Erin?" Will asked.

His dad's doubt about Will's ability to take something

seriously wasn't as surprising as his dad's apparent concern about Will and Erin being together. Erin was like family. He knew his dad loved, respected and admired Erin almost as much as his own children. When Kelly had shown no interest in basketball but was best friends with a girl who loved the game, his dad had welcomed her into the fold. Will had expected his dad to be happy about the news. Happy to see Will with a "good girl" with a "smart head" on her shoulders, as he'd always described her.

"Of course I don't have a problem with Erin," Calvin said, affronted. "You know Erin is like family."

"Then what is the problem?"

"I'm concerned because I do care about Erin. Are you both sure you know what you're doing?" Calvin's worried gaze snapped to Erin. "Erin, you're a smart woman with a lot going for you. You deserve to be with someone who'll appreciate you."

Erin sucked in a breath. Her body stilled, and she jerked back. The words were like a kick to the balls.

Someone who would appreciate her? He did appreciate her.

"What the hell is that supposed to mean?" Will asked before Erin could respond. He didn't bother to conceal the anger in his voice. "What makes you think I won't appreciate her?"

"Will, come on, we both know you're nowhere close to being ready to settle down." The words slid off Calvin's tongue as easily as he rattled off basketball statistics. Confident and without a hint of doubt.

"I'm not asking him to settle down," Erin said quickly.

"Then you're okay with him seeing other women?" Calvin countered.

Erin shook her head. "No."

"I know my son. He's not ready to be in a committed relationship."

"I am when it comes to Erin. I know what I'm doing," Will cut in, defending himself. "You weren't much older than me when you met and married mom. You didn't hesitate to step up and be the man she wanted you to be. You said you knew the instant you met her that she was the one."

"That is true, but you've known Erin all of your life. You've had years to step up and be with her. Now you're caught up in the newness of a 'connection' and you're ready to say the woman you've ignored for years is suddenly the right woman for you. I'm sorry, but I'm having a hard time buying it."

Erin placed a hand on Will's stiff knee. She squeezed lightly and looked from his dad to his sister. "I know this is a shock. I know this is going to take some adjustment, but I believe Will. I trust him. Because he's known me for years I believe he also respects me. He wouldn't say he wanted to be with me if it wasn't true."

Warmth spread through Will's chest. She trusted him. He'd worried after leaving her today she'd change her mind or wonder if she'd made the right decision. Instead she gave him something more than just a defense against his family's concerns—she gave him her trust. Something he never wanted to violate.

"Kelly, please don't be angry with me," Erin pleaded. "This won't change anything between us. You're still my best friend and always will be."

"Even if he breaks your heart?" Kelly shot back.

"No matter what happens between me and Will, I

know his actions have nothing to do with yours. I'm going into this with my eyes wide open."

His dad studied them again, then shrugged. "I've said my piece. You both are adults and can make your own decisions. If you're happy we're happy." He looked at Kelly. "Aren't we?"

Kelly rarely argued with their dad. Will saw how much she wanted to keep up the fight, but Calvin had deemed this battle over. Will knew they had a long way before he won the war.

Kelly slowly uncrossed her arms and sighed. "Fine." She glared at Will. "I hope you know what you're doing."

Erin spoke up first. "Come on, Kelly. I don't want to lose my best friend over this."

Kelly's face softened when she focused on Erin. "Neither do I."

Erin nodded toward the bar. "Let's get a drink, okay?"

Will knew that was code for "let's leave the guys behind and talk." Kelly nodded and stood. Will rubbed Erin's back. She squeezed his knee again. Silently telling him she had this. Then stood.

He watched them walk away. Noticed how several of the men in the club had their eyes on them. He'd noticed that before. The way his sister and Erin drew the eyes of men. He'd always felt protective of them both. Always kept an eye out to step in if a guy got out of line, though typically both women were more than able to handle themselves.

This was the first time he'd felt a whisper of jealousy. A possessiveness he wasn't used to. Not in a way that made him want to walk with Erin and push off any guy who turned her way, but a new strange feeling that Erin was his to protect now. Guys could look all they want, but at the end of the day she would return to him. He liked the feeling.

"You do look like you've got it bad." His dad's voice broke into his thoughts.

"What do you mean?"

"The way you're looking at her. It's different."

"Different how?"

His dad grinned and leaned back in his chair with his arms spread over the back. "You think I haven't noticed the way you looked at Erin like you wanted a piece of her?"

Prickles of heat darted along his cheeks and neck. He'd never been embarrassed to talk about sex with his dad. His dad had given him "the talk" early and with no sugarcoating. The idea of his dad knowing he'd checked Erin out over the years was embarrassing. He'd thought he'd hidden those feelings.

"I didn't think anyone noticed."

Calvin laughed. "Son, I see everything. I noticed, but you've got a little bit more than lust in your eye tonight. Just remember what I taught you. Let her down easy. Make her think it's her idea when you're ready to move on. I like Erin, and I don't want you to break her heart too bad."

Before he could answer that he didn't plan to break her heart at all, two veteran ballplayers came over to talk and catch up with his dad. Within minutes their spot was the place to be, and Will was caught up in the stories of what it was like when they'd played "real ball" before ballplayers got soft. He let the conversation with his dad drift to the back of his mind to be dealt with later.

Champagne flowed; people laughed and joked. The crowd grew. His dad drew lots of beautiful women.

Young and old. Seeing his dad go back to playboy after a year of mourning their mother gave Will mixed feelings. On one hand he was glad his dad had shaken the cloud of mourning that had hovered over him for so long. On the other hand, he couldn't put the man who'd been nothing but a faithful husband and father and the man who played women like a game of chess together.

If this was what his dad was like before he'd met Will's mother, and he'd walked away from being an unrepentant bachelor to dutiful husband for love, then Will knew he could do the same. He could be the man Erin deserved.

He glanced around searching for Erin. She hadn't come back to VIP, and he'd gotten so caught up in the stories and fun his dad drew that he hadn't checked to see how her talk with Kelly had gone.

He spotted her by the bar. Smiling, he headed her way when one of the women in their section stepped in his way. Will held up his hands to avoid bumping into her. She slipped her hand in his. Sliding a small piece of paper into his palm.

"Call me," she said with a grin.

Will balled the paper in his hands. "You know what, I've got to go find my lady."

The woman raised a thinly arched brow. "You've got a lady? Since when?"

He didn't like how surprised she sounded. Was his being in a relationship that unheard of? "Doesn't matter when. All you need to know is I'm not interested."

He stepped back from the hand she tried to run up his thigh. He didn't want her touch, but he was also human. A woman's hand that close to a certain part of his anatomy might cause an automatic response. He turned away from her skeptical smile and looked back at Erin. A guy had come up and started talking to her. A guy he didn't recognize. Erin smiled during their conversation, but she didn't look engaged.

He quickly worked his way through the crowd to her side. When he walked up, he slid a hand up her back to gently clasp her shoulder. He didn't care if he interrupted the conversation as he leaned in and pressed a soft kiss to the back of her neck.

"Let's get out of here," he whispered in her ear.

Her body shivered and melted beneath his hands. She turned soft brown eyes up to him. "Finally remembered I'm here," she said with a small smile.

He searched her face for any type of hurt behind her teasing. She hid her feelings well, but he saw the flicker of uncertainty in the quick way her lower lip slipped between her teeth and back out.

"I'm sorry. You know my dad draws a crowd. I started talking and lost track of time."

He vaguely realized the guy who'd been talking to her had slipped away. Will quickly slid into the place the man had occupied next to Erin. He dropped his hand from her shoulder to lightly grasp her waist.

"And what's in your hand?" She lifted his hand that still held the scrap of paper.

Will's hand popped open. He tossed crumpled paper onto the bar. "Nothing important."

"I saw her slip you her number."

"And you also saw me ball it up." He nodded to the crumpled paper. "I don't want her number. I also can't stop random women from trying to give me their numbers, but what I can promise you is that I'll never keep them." He met her eyes and hoped she saw the vow in his gaze. "I'll never call them. I'll never do anything to disrespect you. No turning back, remember?"

Her face softened. The worry in her gaze finally drifted away. "Okay."

Relief swept through him. "How did it go with Kelly?"

Erin took a deep breath and shrugged. "It went okay. She's not happy. She thinks you're going to break my heart and that I'll hate her, but I told her not to worry. I asked her to trust me."

"And what did she say?"

"That it's my choice. She agreed to back off. I don't think she likes it, but she's agreed to accept it."

Will nodded. Good. He'd talk to Kelly more later. Even if their dad didn't believe Will could be sincere, he wanted Kelly to understand. He wouldn't give up Erin for Kelly, but he wanted his sister to trust that he wouldn't break her best friend's heart.

Erin's hand squeezed his knee. "Did you really want to get out of here?"

He would have stayed longer. Enjoyed the party. Listened to his dad and the older players reminisce about the good old times, but with her hand on his knee and the warmth of her touch spreading up his thigh to a very welcome hardening of his anatomy, the idea of being alone with her was a lot more appealing.

"Your room or mine?"

She slipped off the stool and pressed her curves into his, and Will knew he'd leave any party when Erin looked at him like that. "Yours."

Chapter 11

When the International Auto Show chose Jacksonville, Florida, for the location of its next exhibition, Erin had immediately signed on to oversee the event marketing and promotion. Now, as the auto show grew near and the project would mean spending several weeks in Jacksonville, Erin was glad she'd taken the assignment.

After the success she had during All-Star Weekend, she'd gotten the expected promotion. Her life had been a whirlwind in the two months since. Now, as she sat in her office looking at tickets to Jacksonville, her toe tapped, and she hummed a happy tune. Even though she'd seen Will the weekend before, she was ready to be with him again.

"Someone's in a good mood."

Erin looked up from her laptop and grinned at her colleague Vivien standing in her doorway. "It's the end of the day on Wednesday," Erin replied. "Which means we've passed the halfway point. Of course I'm happy."

"I guess this has nothing to do with you getting to spend several weeks working on the auto show project in Jacksonville where your handsome and successful boyfriend lives?" Vivien teased.

Erin pursed her lips. "Hmm…he does live there, doesn't he?"

Vivien shook her head. "You aren't fooling me. I know you're excited to go. You two hardly see each other."

"That's not unexpected when we're both busy," Erin said with forced casualness.

It was true they barely saw each other. Between the team lockdown, his frequent games and her getting up to speed with the new position, their time together was limited to snatched weekends, video chats and one quick hookup when they'd both been in New York.

Despite the distance, things were still going well. Will showed no signs of being restless about their relationship. There were no reports of him out partying with a different woman on his arm every night. She liked to believe that was due to them dating and not the team lockdown. She was happy and couldn't believe she was happy with Will.

"True, but you have to admit it'll be great when you're both in town. Have you told him?"

"I told him I was going to be in Jacksonville, but not for how long. I didn't realize the show would turn into also scouting other clients so we can possibly open another office in the city."

That little nugget had come after this morning's team meeting. The company CEO wanted to expand their reach in the southeastern United States. An office in Jacksonville, with two professional sports teams, a strong port system and plenty of businesses, was an ideal location. Erin was ecstatic about the idea of spending more time in Will's city. She hoped he would feel the same.

"After this morning's team meeting I've spent the day on the phone with the Jacksonville Chamber of Commerce and the Florida tourism department. This auto show will bring in people from all over the world, and there are a lot of plans to be made. I'm booking a flight now to travel down for the rest of the week to meet with the head of the convention center and ensure there is enough space to accommodate."

Vivien's eyes widened. "You should surprise him. Show up at his doorstep in nothing but a trench coat and heels."

"And you've obviously watched too many movies. I am not the trench coat and heels type."

"Doesn't mean you can't try it. Keep things spicy."

"We've only been dating four months. Things are spicy."

Vivien shrugged. "Maybe so, but a guy like Will gets all kinds of erotic offers. You've got to make sure you're always a step ahead of the groupies." Vivien's phone rang. She pulled it out. "Gotta take this. Let's go to lunch when you get back, okay?" She answered the phone and was out of Erin's office before she could reply.

Her words lingered long after. Vivien knew what she was talking about. Her boyfriend played hockey professionally. They'd been together for over a year and Vivien always updated Erin on the myriad wild and freaky things she did to keep things interesting in their relationship. Erin had considered Vivien's stories entertaining, and a bit impressive—such as the blow job during a movie premiere without getting caught by the

Hollywood stars—but Erin didn't think she'd have to go through that much just to keep Will interested. Would she?

When they were together the sex was hot and amazing, but it was also pretty standard. Hotel rooms, in a bed. That one time on the floor. Would he eventually get bored with her and tempted by a woman who could make love to him while hanging upside down from a ceiling fan?

"Now you're being ridiculous," she muttered to herself.

She picked up the phone to call Will before she let her doubts blossom into paranoia. Every time they talked he sounded happy to hear her voice. She'd tell him her trip was extended. They could spend more time together. All would be well, and she'd realize Vivien's suggestion was the exception, not the rule.

When he answered, she heard female laughter and music before he spoke. Her heart jumped. A sick churning started in her stomach.

"Erin! Hey, baby, what's up?" He sounded happy she'd called.

"Hey, where are you? There's a lot of noise in the background."

"Yeah, sorry about that. Kevin's in town with his wife. I decided to invite him and some folks over for a quick get-together. Give me a second—I'll go inside."

She listened as he told someone he was going in. Relief swam through her. She hadn't met Kevin or his wife, but that explained the voices. The guys Will hung with most on the team were all married now. The female laughter could have come from any one of those women.

"Hurry back, sexy," a woman's voice said, loud enough for Erin to hear through the phone.

Will chuckled. "Nah, take that over there to Rob. Didn't you hear me say my lady was on the phone? Not interested."

Erin couldn't make out the woman's response, but her tone sounded pouty and petulant. That definitely was not one of the wives. She tried to tamp down her jealously and worry. Whoever she was, he had pushed her away.

That doesn't mean she won't try again. Mystery woman is there. I'm not.

"Hey, I'm back," Will said.

"So, who's calling you sexy and telling you to hurry back?" she asked immediately. She hated the jealousy that edged into her voice.

"Rob brought over some people when I made the call about Kevin being here," Will said, sounding annoyed. "If I would have known I wouldn't have invited him over."

"Oh." She didn't know what else to say. Well, she did. *Kick out Rob and that thirsty woman immediately*, but that wasn't the best response. Irrational, jealous girlfriend wasn't what she was going for. Will said he would be monogamous and give her what she wanted. She was going to trust him.

"Look, don't even think about her." His voice lowered to warm silk on the other end of the line. "You're the only woman for me. I miss you like crazy. I even asked Coach about another travel approval so I can get up there and see you during our bye week after you leave Jacksonville."

She snapped away the thoughts of the woman who was still at the party in her man's house and focused on what he'd said. He was trying to see her. He missed her. They were secure.

"No need to do that."

"Why not?"

"I'll be in Jacksonville for more than a few days. I'll be there several weeks. Maybe longer." She quickly filled him in on the plans to scout out the area for more clients and to open an office.

"That's what I like to hear. Do you know how great having you here is going to be?"

His unveiled enthusiasm made her insides warm. "I have a pretty good idea. It'll be nice to see you more often. I'm searching for flights now, and after that, I'll start looking for a temporary place. The company has agreed to subsidize housing for me."

"No, no subsidized housing. Stay with me."

Erin stopped scrolling through the flights on the computer. She sat back in her chair, then rotated it to look out the windows at the city. "What?" Her heart drummed in her chest.

"You heard me," he said, sounding even more excited. "I've got more than enough space, and I'd love to have you here with me."

"Will, that's a big step. We've only been dating a few months."

"But we've known each other for years. We know everything there is to know about each other already. I said I'm in and I mean it. If you're here I want you with me."

"What if you get tired of me being around?"

"I won't. I'm going crazy not being able to see you more often now. Pick your flight and come straight here. No hotels. Let me make love to you in my bed. The way I want to." His voice lowered to an octave that made her hot and slick.

"If you're sure," she said in a low, shaky voice. They were really discussing doing this.

"More than sure. Now book that flight and get your ass down here as soon as possible. I can't wait to have you in my arms again."

"Why is that?"

"Because just the idea of you here in my space, my bed, has me hard as hell."

She laughed and shifted in the seat. Her body aching to be next to his. "I'll be there tomorrow."

"Good. I'll be more than ready to see you."

When the call ended she was just as wound up for him as he sounded. She searched for the earliest flight she could with a grin. The idea of Will, hard and wanting, made her nipples hard and breasts tingle.

Hurry back, sexy.

The purr of the unknown woman's voice whispered through her head. While she was wet and ready here, mystery woman was there. Erin clicked the earliest flight listed and thought about tomorrow. Not about her boyfriend, hard and ready right now in his home with a woman who'd called him sexy.

"I never thought I'd see the day Will Hampton avoided getting some ass," Kevin said with a laugh.

Will shook his head as he walked back into his kitchen where his friends Kevin, Isaiah and Jacobe finished drinking their beers as they sat around the island. His quick get-together to welcome Kevin home for a visit had grown way more than he'd expected. He'd invited a few of the guys from the team, not just his friends. He hadn't expected Rob to bring not only his current fling but one of her friends.

"She's not the one I want," he said to Kevin.

"It's true," Jacobe said. "Will's in a committed relationship now."

Kevin's brows rose to his hairline. "Say what? I'd heard rumors, but I didn't believe them."

Will laughed and stood next to them at the island. "Why didn't you believe them? You three settled down. If that can happen anything can happen."

Isaiah slid a beer across the counter toward him. "Me settling down one day was never in question."

That was true. Isaiah was the first guy Will met who couldn't wait to find a wife. He'd never been into the groupies or playing the field.

Will nodded. "Yeah, but you falling head over heels in love with Angela instead of your perfect pick was unexpected."

Isaiah had been in a long-term on-again, off-again relationship with his college sweetheart. His friend had sworn she was the woman for him, but Will had seen from the start that they had a convenient relationship. Not a love match. Will had seen a love match firsthand with his parents. He could recognize the signs.

"Passion picks better," Isaiah said with a grin and a wink.

The three other men laughed and clicked glasses. Will couldn't agree more. The passion between him and Erin was proof enough that being with her was the right choice. The more time they spent together, the more he knew he was entering the territory his father warned him about. The land of no return. When you knew you'd met the woman you wanted to spend the rest of your life with.

"Your sister's best friend, right?" Isaiah asked.

"Erin—you all met her during one of the All-Star Weekends," Will replied.

Kevin's head tilted to the side. "What changed? You've known her forever. Now you're ready to settle down."

"I didn't say I was ready," Will said. "But I can tell there's something different with her. Something that makes me want to try to be that guy."

Isaiah laughed. "What guy?"

"That guy like you guys. You know. The whole thing. Movies on the couch. Date night. Always and forever type stuff."

His three friends exchanged looks. He didn't miss the doubt in their faces. Doubt they quickly hid behind smiles and congratulations.

Will put down his beer and braced his hands on the island. He was ready to hear the truth. "All right, why do you three find it so hard to believe what I'm saying?"

Jacobe spoke up first. "It's not that we find it hard to believe. None of us were exactly ready to fall in love and be where we are now."

He knew that. All of his friends had had their plans, and when they'd first started playing together their plans hadn't included being happily married to the women they were with now. "So what's different about me?"

Jacobe continued. "You've never shown interest in long-term relationships. Ever. The three of us, well, we'd been there before we finally bit the bullet. You on the other hand…well, you've not only dodged the bullet, but you knew how to manipulate the bull's-eye."

Will laughed at his friend's accurate description. He had avoided any semblance of a long-term relationship. He also hadn't wanted to step up and try to have more until Erin. "I don't know. I can't say I'm even on the right track with Erin, but it feels right. I've got to at least try. I just need everyone to understand I'm committed. No one wants to believe I can be faithful."

Isaiah tipped his beer bottle toward Will. "Well, you've never had a girlfriend before."

Will's shoulders straightened. "I've dated."

Kevin shook his head. "Casually dating isn't the same as having a girlfriend. You've never been exclusive with a woman."

"And there's nothing sexier than a man who's committed," Jacobe said. "You don't know how many women hit on me just because I'm in a relationship."

Isaiah's eyes widened. "Right! It's like I get more women hitting on me now."

Will thought about Donna, the insistent woman Rob had brought with him. She'd caught him right after he'd gotten off the phone with Erin. Right when he'd been hard and thinking about Erin's soft body next to him in his king-size bed upstairs. An erection and a willing woman was usually all he needed. Six months ago, he would have pulled Donna into a room and accepted everything she had to offer. A quick fling with no strings.

For an instant his body had gone on autopilot and he'd nearly reached for her when she'd pressed against him and cradled his obvious erection in her hand. He'd pushed her away instead. Then joined the party and avoided her the rest of the afternoon. But that instant of autopilot reaction had scared him.

"So you guys still have women trying to get you in bed?" In the back of his head Will knew that was true. He just had never paid attention. The guys were always with their women when they were out in public.

"All the time," Isaiah said, exhausted.

"More than I like," Jacobe grumbled.

"It's annoying as hell," Kevin muttered.

"How do you handle it?" Will asked. "The pressure to…you know…be faithful?"

"There is no pressure," Isaiah said. "I don't want those women. I only want Angela. The choice is easy."

Will bumped Isaiah with his elbow. "Okay, I expect that from you." He looked at Jacobe and Kevin. "What about you two? Neither of you is as noble as Isaiah."

Isaiah chuckled and sipped his beer. "I'll take that."

Jacobe and Kevin laughed. Jacobe spoke first. "It's about the same for me. Yeah, the women who hit on me are sexy and tempting, but I think about what I'll lose versus what I'll gain from a night with a woman. After that the choice is easy."

"You just have to make sure everyone understands the choice is easy for you," Kevin added. "Someone is always going to try to test you. Just make sure you don't fail the test."

Will studied his beer and let his friend's words sink in. He thought he was doing a good job letting the world know he was with Erin. His social media feed was filled with pictures of them together. He wasn't out partying like he used to. The team lockdown helped with that. He turned away women who tried to hit on him. He'd just keep doing what he was doing. Eventually, everyone would understand he wasn't living the bachelor life anymore.

The conversation moved to other things. His thoughts wandered back to the split second of autopilot. Thank God Erin would be in Jacksonville tomorrow.

Chapter 12

Instead of having him pick her up from the airport, Erin told Will she would meet him at his place. He had practice today, and she needed to make a pit stop before going to his home. She stopped at one of the hotels near the airport and quickly exchanged the jeans and blouse she'd traveled in for a black-and-pink lace bra and panty set, black leather heels, and a trench coat.

Vivien's idea to show up in nothing but underwear and a trench coat sounded less ludicrous the more Erin thought about the random woman calling Will sexy. Maybe she was being neurotic, but she'd seen the logic of Vivien's suggestion. Spontaneity was the spice of life, right? There was nothing wrong with keeping things exciting between them. Any time the idea that at four months she was already anxious about keeping things spicy made her worry about her future with Will, she forced her concerns to the back of her mind.

She hurried out of the hotel and back to her car. She kept her head low and avoided eye contact as the desk clerk called for her to have a nice day. Even though nothing was visible beneath the trench coat, she couldn't shake the feeling that everyone looking at her knew she was nearly naked beneath and was on her way to try to surprise her man.

Her heart raced the closer she got to Will's place. When she stopped at the gate that blocked his driveway so he could buzz her in, she worried he'd think her attempt at being sexy and spontaneous was silly. The thought almost made her turn around and get dressed. The idea that he'd be overwhelmed by desire when he saw her and press her right against the wall next to his front door and make her say his name in multiple languages…well, that brought a smile to her lips and sent warm prickles across her skin.

"Good, you're here," Will said through the intercom. "I was beginning to worry. Come on. I can't wait to see you."

His eagerness made the pressed-up-against-the-wall fantasy seem even more likely. Surprising him at his door dressed in nothing but lingerie and a trench coat was a very smart idea.

She left her bags in the car and skipped up the steps, as much as she could skip in six-inch heels. The added height meant her curves would press even more perfectly against Will's body. Just the thought of his hands squeezing her ass, his lips along her neck and shoulders as he ripped the underwear from her body, turned her blood into lava.

After ringing the doorbell, Erin unfastened the coat's belt. She quickly unbuttoned the thin coat and placed her hands on her hips with the edges of the coat pushed behind her hands. She popped one hip to the side and assumed what she hoped was a seductive pose. With a deep breath, she waited. Her heart pounding and breaths shallow. She couldn't wait to see the look on his face. The mixture of surprise and desire in his eyes.

The lock on the door clicked as he unlocked it. Erin sucked in a breath and pasted a smile on her face. The door swung open and she thrust her breasts forward.

"Surprise!"

The woman who answered gasped. Erin's jaw dropped. Her face burned as if the sun were right below her skin. Mortification mingled with the shock flowing through her system.

Erin jerked the coat closed. "Who the hell are you?" The words were rude, but at the moment she didn't give a damn about being polite.

The woman, young with long dark hair, wore cutoff jean shorts and a white button-up shirt tied in a bow in front, which gave a peek at her perfectly sculpted abs. She pressed a hand to her well-endowed chest and shook her head.

"I'm sorry, I'm Juanita, Mr. Hampton's housekeeper," she said in a low, throaty voice that would have put Marilyn Monroe to shame. "He asked me to answer the door for him."

"His housekeeper?"

Will had a housekeeper? Well, of course he had a housekeeper. She couldn't imagine Will cleaning his own toilet. Her eyes swept over Juanita's curves, thick, tousled hair, wide brown eyes and pouty lips. She couldn't picture Juanita cleaning toilets, either.

"Yes, I've worked for him for two years now. You must be Erin. I'm pleased to meet you." Juanita smiled and held out her hand. The smile appeared genuine, but it didn't quite reach her big brown eyes.

Erin shook Juanita's hand. Her other clutched the coat together. Her embarrassment barely cooled. "Likewise," Erin murmured. "Where's Will?"

"He's upstairs," she said. "I just finished making up his bed. He likes to tangle the sheets," Juanita said, batting long lashes and trying to look innocent.

Erin didn't like her. "Does he?"

"Yes. He can be really messy. I spend a lot of time working in his bedroom."

Okay, this chick was going to have to go. Erin stepped into the house. Forcing Juanita to step back since the woman was obviously not going to invite her inside anytime soon. "Well, I'll be staying, so I can help tidy up and you can focus on other areas of the house. The bedroom can be my territory."

Juanita quirked a brow. "He likes the way I handle things in there."

"Maybe so, but I'm handling *everything* in there from now on."

Juanita's fake friendly mask dropped for a second. A flash of challenge crossed her features before she covered it up with a smile. "Whatever you prefer. I'm here to serve Mr. Hampton however he needs serving." The last was said with a saucy twist of her full lips.

Erin's eyes narrowed. Was she going to have to check Ms. Juanita? She opened her mouth to tell Juanita to stop playing games and put her cards on the table when Will came in the entranceway.

"Baby, you're here." His grin was brighter than a dozen diamonds in sunlight. The complete joy in his face stole her breath.

He rushed forward, swept her into his arms and spun her around. Erin yelped, then laughed. Completely caught up in his excitement. He pulled her close and stopped her greeting by kissing her so deeply and intimately her bones melted like candle wax. Her arms wrapped around his neck; her body melded with his. The world became nothing but his lips against hers, the strength of his embrace, the heat of his desire.

Juanita loudly cleared her throat. Erin had forgotten her that quickly. Will slowly broke their kiss. He pressed his forehead against hers and smiled.

"Yes, Juanita?" Will asked without breaking eye contact with Erin.

"Did you need anything else, Mr. Hampton?"

Will shook his head and kissed Erin again. "That'll be all. Thanks again. See you in a week."

"I can come earlier. It's time for me to work on the baseb—"

"Yeah, sure, whatever," Will said, cutting her off. He hefted Erin up. Her legs spread and straddled his waist.

Without another glance at the disappointed housekeeper, Will carried Erin quickly up the stairs and to his bedroom.

"I think you upset Juanita," Erin said, grinning.

"I don't give a damn about upsetting her. You're here." He kissed her again. When he lowered her back to her feet, she was taller than he expected. Frowning, Will stepped back and looked her over from head to toe. The trench coat was open; the sunlight glinted off the pink lace underwear. His eyes darkened with desire. "You came here wearing this?"

"I flashed the wrong person when the door opened."

"Then I will make sure I always answer the door when you're expected."

He jerked the coat off her shoulders. Erin shook her arms until it fell to the floor. He nearly ripped her underwear as he lowered to his knees to pull them down. Erin kicked them to the side. Warm hands grasped her waist and his eager lips pressed against the soft curve of her stomach. Erin sucked in a breath. Her hand clung to his wide shoulders. Her knees felt as stable as sand.

Reaching behind her, Erin unhooked her bra and tossed the scrap of material to the side. She let out a sigh of pleasure as her breasts were unbound. Will's tongue grazed across her stomach, dipped into the sensitive hollow of her navel, then lightly brushed across the soft dips at the tops of her thighs. When he rose back to his feet, she hopped up and wrapped her arms around his neck and pulled him close for another searing kiss. The brush of his shirt against her bare nipples sent waves of pleasure through her, but that wasn't enough. She wanted to feel the rough hairs of his chest against her breasts. Have his legs tangled with hers. Run her fingers over the taut muscles of his body.

"Get naked now," she murmured against his lips.

"You don't have to tell me twice," Will said with a smile that made her body erupt into thousand-degree flames.

She helped him tug off his shirt. Thankfully he wore basketball shorts that were easy to pull down. Her eyes widened, and her heart skipped a beat when his erection popped free as he lost the shorts.

"Is the lack of underwear in anticipation of me?"

"Erin, I've wanted you in my arms from the moment I last let you go." There was no teasing in his eyes. His voice was serious, deep and edged with a need that made her heart ache.

She willingly went to him. "I'm in them now."

Will engulfed her with his embrace. Until there was nothing on earth except his body against hers. His lips took away her ability to speak. His caresses turned her body into one huge nerve ending that reacted only to his touch. When they landed in a tangle of limbs on the bed she grabbed and clawed at him. Pulling him closer in a fit of urgent need.

He pushed between her legs, spreading her thighs so he could settle heavily between them, then entered her in one hard, deep push. They both cried out. His hand tangled in her hair and lifted her head off the mattress so he could kiss her. The urgency buzzing between them created a frantic pace. The wave of release crashed over her almost instantaneously.

"Yes, Will. Yes, Will. Yes, Will," she moaned over and over as her nails dug into his back.

His body tensed, shuddered, then shook as he followed her over the cliff. He buried his face in her neck. The soft bite of his teeth pressed into her shoulder.

"Why are you biting me?" she asked breathlessly.

"Because," he said, sounding just as out of breath as she did, "I wanted that to last longer, but you felt—" His hips pushed forward. "*Feel* too damn good."

Erin grinned and squeezed around him. "Good thing I'm here all night."

Will groaned low and let out a sultry chuckle. "And for many nights afterward." He lifted his head and looked into her eyes. His face serious. "I'm glad you're here."

Her heart danced, and she couldn't hold back the grin that took over her lips. "I'm happy I'm here, too."

Chapter 13

William wasn't surprised to find Erin in his home gym the next morning. She was an early riser. Often in the gym or out running to start her day. Back in high school they'd even worked out together a couple of times. Her drive to push herself to the limits, test her endurance so she could be a better ballplayer, was something he had admired and wished several of his teammates possessed at the time.

When he'd learned she'd been injured during her senior year and had to give up her dreams to play in college he'd felt bad. Not that he pitied her. Erin had an unbreakable spirit, but he hated that the opportunity to see how far she could have taken her drive had been cut short. He wouldn't have been surprised if Erin had played for a championship team in college or gone on to play professionally afterward either in the US or abroad.

He strolled over to one of the weight benches and

watched her as she jogged on his treadmill. He sipped a cup of coffee; the one he'd made for her he sat next to him on the bench. She glanced at him, smiled, then lowered the setting on the treadmill, taking her from a run to a brisk walk.

"Hey," she said. "About time you got up."

Will grinned and sipped his coffee. She was sexy as hell. A thin sheen of sweat made her brown skin glow. Her thick hair was pulled back in a ponytail that swung jauntily with each of her movements.

"If you wouldn't have worn me out so much last night I might have gotten up earlier."

"Well, I can't really apologize for that."

"I wouldn't expect you to." He pointed to the treadmill. "How long have you been on that?"

"About forty-five minutes," she said. "I'm about to finish up and maybe do some light lifting."

"You still go all out in the gym, huh?"

She shrugged. "Some things are hard to give up. I've always liked working out. It helps me clear my mind."

He nodded understanding what she meant. "Does your knee bother you?" He noticed the compression sleeve on her knee.

"Sometimes, but it hurts worse when I'm inactive. I have exercises I can do to keep it strong."

"Do you still play?" He hadn't seen her play in years. Matter of fact, he hadn't heard her talk about playing.

Erin shook her head, her stride steady on the treadmill. "Not really. I joined a rec league a few years ago, just to do something different for exercise, but other than that, I don't really get on the court."

"You can play with me."

"And beat you like I used to?" she teased.

"You beat me one time," he said, raising his hand to block her words. "And I had the flu."

Erin laughed. "You had the flu a week before, don't get it twisted."

"I was weakened."

"I still beat you."

She focused back on the news program playing on the flat-screen on the wall above his row of cardio equipment. He considered getting on the bike to warm up a little. He had to leave in two hours for team practice, and he typically warmed up there. Working out in his home gym would be a lot more fun with Erin there.

"Can I ask you about Juanita?" Erin said.

Will frowned. Thrown off by that question. "Juanita? What about her?"

"How long has she worked for you?" Erin continued to look at the television screen, but he doubted she paid attention.

"Her mother owns the cleaning service and was the one who originally cleaned my place. After she got sick two years ago, Juanita took over."

"Do you know she wants to sleep with you?"

The idea was so ludicrous Will laughed. "No, she doesn't. She has a boyfriend."

Juanita was cool. The way she tucked his sheets in the corners of his bed, tight but not too tight, was perfect. She left snacks or sandwiches for him on days he had practice. Sure, she was sweet, but she'd never come on to him. He'd never tried to come on to her. She was too close for comfort. With access to his home. He liked her cleaning style and had never considered messing that up by sleeping with her.

Erin didn't look amused. "Having a boyfriend doesn't

mean she doesn't want to sleep with you. You should have heard what she said."

He dropped the smile and gave Erin his attention. "What did she say?"

"She says you like the way she makes up your bed. That you work her hard in that room. Or something like that."

Will chuckled, Erin glared, and he forced down his amusement. "I am particular about the way I like my room set up. She knows that."

Erin stopped the treadmill. She stepped off and grabbed the towel hanging on the rail. "I don't think that's what she meant." She sounded irritated.

"What else could she mean?"

"She made it sound like you two were sleeping together."

Will shook his head. "No. Not at all. I haven't touched her. Never have. Never will."

"Are you sure? I mean…if you have you can just—"

Will put his coffee mug down and stood. "Erin, I'm telling you the truth. There is no way I'd ask you to live here while you're in town if I was sleeping with my housekeeper. I've got too much respect for you and too much faith in what we're trying to do. I promise you, I won't have you around women I used to date or had any type of relationship with. I would never put you in that type of situation."

She nodded but still looked unsure as she pulled her foot behind her toward her backside and stretched. Will placed one hand on her waist and used the fingers of his other to tip her head up.

"Believe me. Juanita is just my housekeeper. Nothing more. If you don't believe me or if you don't want her around just let me know. I'll fire her."

Erin shook her head. "No. No, of course I believe you. Don't fire her. Maybe I read too much into what she said."

"I'm serious. If she says anything you think is out of line let me know. I want you to be comfortable here."

She smiled and her body relaxed. "I can't believe we're really doing this."

Neither could he, but he couldn't find an ounce of regret with his decision. "No turning back, right?"

"No turning back."

"Good." He quickly swept her up and over his shoulder before she realized what he was doing. Her shriek of surprise and hitting his back made him grin.

"Will. What are you doing?"

"Taking you back upstairs."

"Why?"

"Because I've got one hour and you look too damn sexy in those workout clothes for me not to make love to you at least one more time."

Chapter 14

After a successful meeting with the convention center bigwigs followed by a good meeting with the visitors' bureau, Erin decided to treat herself to a mocha latte. She was excited about how the expo was coming together. There was a lot more work to do, but nailing all the final details was crucial.

She went to a bakery Kelly had told her about the last time she was in town. She hadn't spoken to Kelly since arriving, but since Kelly didn't work far away she pulled out her phone to call and surprise her friend. Maybe they could meet up.

She opened the door to the bakery while also dialing Kelly's contact info. She pressed the phone to her ear and walked to the counter.

"Erin?" Kelly's voice, but not through the phone.

Erin spun and grinned when she saw Kelly sitting near a window. "Hey! I was just calling you."

Kelly jumped up and ran over to hug Erin. "What are you doing here?"

"Getting a mocha latte."

Kelly slapped Erin's arm. "In Jacksonville. Not in this bakery."

Erin laughed. "Here for work. I'll be in town for several weeks preparing for the auto show and scoping out a few potential clients."

Kelly beamed. "That's great! We can hang out."

"I know." Spending more time with her best friend was another bonus to being in Jacksonville.

"Where are you staying? You know what, it doesn't matter. You can bunk with me instead of a hotel."

"Oh. I'm staying with Will." An inexplicable shiver of guilt went through Erin. She'd been so excited to spend time with Will, and distracted by the woman talking in the background, that she'd forgotten to tell Kelly about her trip to Jacksonville.

"He knows you're here?" Kelly sounded affronted by the idea of her brother knowing before her.

"Yes. He offered when I told him yesterday."

Kelly's head cocked to the side. "You called him before calling me?"

The hurt in Kelly's voice sharpened the spiral of guilt in Erin's midsection. She hadn't meant to hurt her feelings. "I thought he'd be happy to know I'd be in town."

"You didn't think I'd be happy to know? I mean I am your best friend. Or I thought I was." Kelly crossed her arms.

Erin placed a hand on Kelly's stiff arms. "You are. Of course you are. Really, Kelly. Don't be upset."

"I'm not mad. I'm just…" She sighed and waved a

hand. "I don't know. I guess it makes sense. Calling your man first. He's more important."

"That's not true. You are just as important."

"Well… I'm not giving you orgasms," Kelly said wryly.

Erin cringed and placed a hand over her face. "Can we please not talk about Will and orgasms."

Kelly pulled Erin's hand down. "Why not?"

"He is your brother and it's weird." She and Kelly always talked about their relationships and the good, bad and ugly sexual encounters they'd had over the years. She had no desire to discuss Will's abilities with his sister.

"You're right. That is kind of weird," Kelly agreed. She bared her teeth and cringed. They both laughed.

Relief washed over Erin as they both relaxed. Though Kelly had said she would respect Erin's wishes after All-Star Weekend, it had taken several weeks afterward for Kelly to really accept that Erin and Will were dating. She'd had plenty of snide remarks whenever Erin mentioned Will. So much so Erin had stopped bringing up anything related to her and Will when she and Kelly spoke.

"Do you know how long you're staying with Will?" Kelly asked. "After you two do what we aren't talking about then you can stay with me."

"I'm not just staying with Will for a night or two. He wants me to live with him while I'm here."

Kelly took a few steps back. "Wait, move in, move in? Already?"

A couple entered the coffeehouse. Erin and Kelly moved out of the way. Erin followed Kelly to the table she'd occupied before. That gave her a few minutes to prepare for the upcoming conversation. Kelly accusing them of moving too fast or saying Erin wasn't thinking straight.

"We are moving in together while I'm here," Erin said once they were seated at Kelly's table.

As expected, Kelly's disapproval came swiftly. "Isn't this too soon?"

"I thought the same thing, but this feels right. I miss him so much when I'm not with him. We've known each other forever. It's not that big of a step."

"Spoken like Will," Kelly said dismissively. "Those are his words, right?"

They were, but Erin felt the same as him. At first, she'd been skeptical and worried she was too optimistic about the way things were between them. Then there'd been the way he'd looked at her yesterday. The joy on his face. He was just as invested as she was.

"They're my words, too."

Kelly was unfazed by Erin's admission. "Oh no. Please don't tell me you're going to fall for Will's line?"

"It's not a line. Or a scheme. We're in this. We're finally going for what we'd been too afraid of before."

Kelly looked ready to argue, then she held up a hand. "You know what? I'm staying out of it. Do you. Be happy."

There wasn't an ounce of sincerity in Kelly's declaration. Erin decided to ignore that. She wanted to move on and focus on the good part of being in town with her best friend. Not spend the weeks she was here arguing about her relationship with Will. "Thank you."

Kelly rubbed the back of her head. "Now you have to deal with Juanita." The casually spoken words hit with a mighty punch. They weren't dropped unintentionally.

A sick feeling churned in Erin's stomach. "The house-keeper?"

Kelly sighed and nodded. "Yes. She's obsessed with Will. Always trying to make him happy and comfortable."

She was irritated at Kelly for "casually" mentioning Juanita, but she asked the question she knew her friend wouldn't lie about. "Have they…you know? Slept together?" She didn't want to doubt Will. She wanted to believe he hadn't lied to her, but Will was used to having his way. He may have thought not telling her about any involvement between him and Juanita was easier than dealing with the truth.

"I don't know, I haven't asked."

"Oh." Erin was not relieved.

"But I do think if they haven't it's not because she doesn't want to. The way she fawns over him." Kelly crinkled her nose. "Disgusting,"

"He offered to fire her for me."

Kelly's eyes widened. She leaned forward. "What? Really? Why?"

She saw no reason to lie. If she wanted to know how much of a pain Juanita was going to be she'd rather find out sooner rather than later. "I got the feeling she wanted me to think she'd slept with Will. He said he never touched her. Then offered to fire her."

Kelly considered the words and took a sip of her coffee. "If he wasn't my brother I'd say it's weird to fire someone you haven't had an inappropriate relationship with."

"You would?" That thought hadn't crossed Erin's mind. When Will made the offer she'd taken it as him trying to make her more comfortable in his home. Had it just been a way for him to get her off his back?

"Yeah. Get rid of the other woman before she causes problems. But he is my brother," Kelly said with what Erin guessed she thought was a reassuring smile. "Sounds like he's trying to get right. No more games."

Erin tried to return the smile, but her lips felt stiff. "No more games." She got up and ordered her mocha latte. When she joined Kelly again they talked about other things. Kelly's job, the progress with the auto show. The entire time Erin smiled and laughed, but still thought about Will and his sexy housekeeper.

Chapter 15

Three weeks later, Erin tripped over her shoes as she entered the smaller of the two closets in Will's master suite. She landed on her hands and knees with a thud. Pain shot through her old injury and her body like a fiery harpoon.

With a groan, she rolled over and eyed the shoes. The heels she'd worn the day before and a pair of sandals from the day before that. She looked from the shoes on the floor to the neat row of shoes sitting on the rack in the closet.

She gritted her teeth and swallowed a curse. Pulling herself off the floor, she picked up the shoes, threw them onto the rack, then stormed out of the closet. She marched to the bathroom and pounded on the door.

Will swung open the door quickly. A towel was wrapped around his trim waist. The smell of his body wash drifted out. Erin's skin immediately prickled with awareness. She almost forgot why she'd marched over after seeing his naked chest.

"What's wrong?" Will asked.

She lifted her gaze from his chest to his confused eyes. "I tripped over my shoes in the closet."

He raised a brow. "Okay…did you hurt yourself?"

"Yes, as a matter of fact I did. I landed on my bad knee."

Concern replaced the confusion in his gaze and he lowered his eyes to her knees. "Are you okay? Do you need me to get you something?"

"The only thing I need is for you to tell Juanita to stop throwing my shoes right in the door of my closet."

The confusion returned to Will's face. "What?"

"She throws my shoes right in the door of my closet. I've asked her not to do that because I tripped last week, but she's still putting them in there."

"I asked her to put your shoes up for you."

"What? Why?"

Will went back into the bathroom and picked up a brush. "Because you leave them all over the house. Mostly in the entryway, but other places, too. I almost tripped."

She was momentarily stunned. She did tend to take off her shoes wherever she wanted. Remembering where a pair were when she was running late in the mornings was a frequent source of frustration, but that frustration had always been hers alone. She didn't think about changing the habit when she moved in with Will. "Why didn't you say something to me?"

He shrugged and brushed his hair. "Because Juanita cleans up the house. So I asked her to pick up your shoes for you."

She didn't need Juanita being the solution to any problem Will might have with her. "If you have a problem with me then you discuss it with me. Not her."

"I didn't discuss a problem I had with you with her. I asked her to add picking up your shoes to her list of things she does around here." His voice was calm.

"Then why is she just leaving them in the door of my closet instead of putting them on the shelf? They're right where I would trip on them."

"I'm sure it was an accident." Will dropped the brush and picked up his toothbrush.

"An accident? I specifically mentioned asking her not to put my shoes there because I tripped before. She did it again. She doesn't like me."

The truth she'd been more certain of in the past three weeks. Juanita hadn't said anything specifically to Erin, but she let her know in subtle ways. She poured out the coffee after Will fixed a cup but before Erin got coffee. She'd accidentally washed one of Erin's dry-clean-only shirts. Made a seemingly innocent comment about how if Erin would allow her to clean up the bedroom it would help Will sleep more comfortably. A dig at how Erin wasn't straightening the room up to Juanita's standards. Nothing she'd done was outright mean, but Erin felt the unwelcoming undertone in all of Juanita's reactions.

Will scoffed and spread toothpaste on the toothbrush. "Come one, Erin. Juanita just told me she likes you."

"And you believe her when I'm telling you she doesn't?" What else was the woman supposed to say? *No, Mr. Hampton, I'm jealous and hating on your girlfriend?*

"Of course I do. She has no reason not to like you." He brushed his teeth.

"She has a very good reason not to like me."

"Like what?" he said around the toothbrush.

"She wants to sleep with you. She hates that I'm here. I'm cock-blocking her. And by that, I mean literally blocking her from your cock."

Will's shoulders shook with laughter as he continued brushing his teeth. Erin got an overwhelming urge to pound him over the head with one of the shoes she tripped on. "This isn't funny."

Will finished brushing, rinsed his mouth and then wiped it with a towel. "Yes it is. Juanita is not interested in me."

He walked out of the bathroom. Erin let him pass and followed him to his larger walk-in closet. "Are you blind? The woman prances around here in cutoff shorts and midriff shirts, calling you Mr. Hampton in her Hello Kitty voice, while flipping her hair and pushing out her breasts."

Will chuckled again and flipped through the color-coordinated rows of shirts in his closet. "Hello Kitty doesn't have a voice."

"Will you stop pretending this is a joke? I'm serious. Why do you want to ignore what's blatant? She's interested in you. You can't tell me she's never hit on you."

Will pulled down a dark blue shirt, then turned to the rows of already-pressed pants. "I can tell you she's never hit on me. Just like I told you I've never slept with her nor would I put you in a position to be in this house if I had. Will you stop looking for problems that aren't there? I offered once, and I will again. You want me to fire her, I will." He pulled a pair of pants from a hanger. "I'd be more than happy to if it meant never having this conversation again," he murmured with annoyance.

Erin crossed her arms over her breasts. She did not like Juanita. Did not believe the woman had no interest in Will. She couldn't figure out why Will was so oblivious to the way the woman eye-screwed him every time he walked in a room. She was trying to believe him. Trying to not become a jealous, insecure girlfriend who let Will's past play into their future.

Will walked over to the sock drawer and opened it. Erin frowned. "Are you going out?"

He looked at her with surprise. "We're going out. Remember?" Her frown must have been his answer, because he sighed heavily. "It's Isaiah's wife's birthday. He's throwing a small dinner party for her at the new nightclub downtown. I mentioned it to you yesterday."

"Oh crap, I'd forgotten all about that," Erin said, slapping her forehead. "Do we have to go?"

"Yes. Isaiah is my boy. He's excited about throwing Angela a party. I told him we'd come."

"I'm swamped with work. I've got to get the updated proposal back to my home office and the coordinators with the auto show tomorrow. I have to work on that tonight." Plus, her knee throbbed, and she was exhausted from the busy day.

Will's eyes narrowed. "Or do you just not want to go out again?" The emphasis was on *again*.

"Again? Why do you say it like that?"

"Because you never want to go out. All we do is sit in the house every night."

"We go out. We went out on Saturday."

He held up a finger. "One night out of the entire week."

"Most people go out on weekends. During the week I'm busy and tired. I can't go out every night."

"I'm not asking for every night, just a few nights."

"I'm not telling you to stay in with me," she shot back. "I'm not trying to hold you prisoner or anything. If you want to go out, then go. I'll be perfectly fine here alone."

He pushed the drawer back in forcefully. "Now you're making its sound like I'm abandoning you."

"No, I'm not. I seriously couldn't care less if you went out without me while I worked. I'm not going to sit here crying because you're not with me."

He jerked as if she'd slapped him. "Good. Stay here. Work. I'm going to Angela's party."

"Fine. Have a great time. I'm going to put up the shoes your housekeeper just dropped in my closet, ice my knee and get some work done."

She spun as gracefully as she could with a sore knee and hobbled to her closet. She waited, for what she wasn't sure. She pulled out pajamas and went into the bathroom to take her own shower while Will dressed for the party. They didn't exchange words as he prepared to leave.

He was gone when she got out of the shower. Erin pushed back her disappointment. The hurt and anger over a fight that had erupted out of nowhere. She was left feeling unhappy and alone, something she'd never felt before. Tears pricked her eyes, but she squeezed them shut and swallowed her emotions.

"Crying is stupid. This entire situation is stupid. You should just go back to Chicago and work from a distance."

That thought didn't make her feel any better. She pushed the fight and thoughts of the fun Will was having at a birthday party without her from her mind. She focused on the proposal and getting the wording straight, instead of wondering how many single women would be at the party. Single women who would be more than happy to keep Will company while his girlfriend stayed home to work.

He came home four hours later. She was still working on the proposal. She sat in the middle of their bed. Her laptop out and notes from her meetings spread around her. She'd put on pajamas and tied her hair up. She glanced at Will as he came in the room. He stopped at the door and stared at her.

She broke eye contact first, looking back at the laptop, and tried to pretend as if she hadn't been watching the clock and wondering if he'd get home before midnight.

"How was the party?" she asked.

Will crossed the room and dropped on the bed. With a sweep of his arms he pushed aside her laptop and pulled her close. The smell of cigar smoke and alcohol mingled with the spicy scent that was his.

"The party was awful because I spent the entire night thinking about you and wishing you were with me." He nuzzled her neck.

Erin wanted to push him away. Wanted to hold on to the anger from earlier, but his lips found the sweet spot along her collarbone, and her body relaxed. She'd missed him. "I'll go next time."

"I'll talk to Juanita about the shoes." His hand burrowed beneath the covers, found her legs and caressed her thighs. "I'm sorry about earlier. I don't like fighting with you."

Erin opened her thighs. His eager hand quickly lifted to the soft spot between her legs. "I'm sorry, too."

He kissed her deep and hard. Then made love to her so

thoroughly the only thing Erin could think about was the pleasure she found in his arms, and the joy in knowing it didn't matter who was at those parties or how much they may want Will, because he'd come home to her arms.

Chapter 16

"Have you talked to Dad?"

Will looked away from the television to Kelly sitting next to him on his couch. His sister had come over to hang out with him for a little bit while the carpets were being cleaned at her place. They'd passed the time in his media room watching a movie and finishing off the cherry slushies Kelly had brought with her.

Erin was working late. Again. Making deals as she worked on the final details for the auto show that weekend.

"I haven't talked to him since last week," Will answered. "Why?"

"He's throwing a party at his place next weekend. He wants us to come by."

Will stretched out his legs and rested his feet on the coffee table. He ignored the urge to check his watch and wonder how much longer before Erin got home. "Another party?"

Kelly laughed. "Yep. Another party. He's pretty much confirmed you got your party boy gene honestly."

"Yeah, but he's about to outdo me. He's having something at the house almost every weekend now." Will didn't have people in and out of his place like that.

"Well, you know Dad. He doesn't like to be left alone."

Concern replaced Will's humor with the situation. Their dad had been a phenomenal basketball player. Famous, successful and the life of every party. He'd loved their mom and was devoted to her for every minute of their marriage. Until she'd died, Will had always considered his dad the rock of their family. After his mother died it became clear really quick that their mother had been the rock, the glue and the protective shield.

Calvin was lost, depressed and withdrawn without her during the first year after his wife's death. Then, suddenly, he'd jumped right back into the limelight. Taking full advantage of his prior celebrity status. Attending parties, dating different women and surrounding himself with people. Will loved his dad, but he missed the stable role model he'd once been.

"It's like he's someone else," Will said. "I didn't think he'd come around. Then I saw him laughing with Erin last year and I thought maybe he'd get a little better. I just didn't expect…"

"What, for him to act like a frat boy?" Kelly said.

Will shook his head. "That about sums it up."

"I think Dad just doesn't know how to be alone. This is just another phase. He'll snap out of it." She sounded optimistic.

Will wasn't as confident. "But what if he doesn't? You

know there are a lot of crazy people out there. I don't want him to get caught up in something stupid."

Kelly drew back and gave him an admiring look. "Just listen to you sounding like a worried parent. He's a grown man who's been around longer than we have. He can see something stupid coming from a mile away."

"So you aren't worried about this new take-life-by-the-horns, party-hard attitude he's taken on?"

"No, I'm not," Kelly said.

"Why not?"

"Because I'd rather he be out and about, talking to people and living his life, instead of sitting in the house depressed." Her brows drew together. "Dad depressed was scary. You know that."

Will sighed and rubbed his head. "Yeah... I know." That didn't mean he liked the way their dad went from mourning to life of the party overnight. Their dad still grieved for their mom. Will could barely imagine the pain he must be in. Just the idea of something happening to Erin made him break out in a cold sweat. His parents were married for twenty-eight years. His dad had to be hurting.

Will looked at his watch. This was the hard part about living with Erin. Worrying when she worked later than expected. "Erin should be home soon."

Kelly shifted on the couch and faced him. "Are you really okay with her living here?"

"Of course I am. I wouldn't have asked her to move in if I didn't want her here."

"You've never lived with a woman before. It has to be something to get used to."

They were both used to having their own space. They'd spent the first month just getting used to having someone always around. Strong personalities led to the occasional spat. That was to be expected.

"It is," he said. "But we're working through things."

"Things like what?" Kelly asked.

Will thought about the past few weeks with Erin under his roof. He loved having her with him every day. Sleeping next to her. The way her body curled up against his beneath the covers. Talking to her about the plans for the day while they drank coffee after working out together in his gym. All of that was great.

"Uh-oh," Kelly said, leaning closer. She pointed a finger at his face. "You're frowning. Why are you frowning?"

"I'm not frowning." He relaxed his features. Maybe he'd frowned just a little bit.

"Oh now." Kelly waved her finger. "Spill. What's wrong?"

Will ran a hand over his beard. "It's just…when she gets home she's usually really tired. Which means even though I'd like to take her out to dinner or go hang out with some of our friends, she's not really into that."

"Well, she is a homebody. You know she doesn't like hanging out like that."

"I know, but we've spent nearly every night here. I love my place, but sometimes I'd like to go out."

He'd like to pamper her. Give her a chance to relax and enjoy herself after a long day of work. Erin was a homebody. He wasn't, and he was still getting used to that.

"What else?" Kelly prompted.

For a second, he hesitated. Kelly hadn't been happy about him and Erin, but she knew Erin admittedly better than him in some areas. His sister could help him figure this all out. "She leaves her shoes around the house."

Kelly's brows rose. "Come again?"

"Wherever she takes them off, she leaves them."

"Are you saying she's sloppy and makes a mess?"

"No, not like that. Just her shoes. She kicks them off right at the front door and then walks away. Then she frantically searches for them every morning because she forgot where she kicked them off. So she picks another shoe, then there are multiple pairs by the door. I asked Juanita to bring them back up to our bedroom and put them in the closet, and that turned into an argument with Erin."

He was still confused about that one. He'd thought he was being helpful by asking Juanita to help organize Erin's things. True to his word, he'd talked to Juanita about putting Erin's shoes on the rack. Juanita had apologized profusely and at one point Will thought she might cry. He hated when people cried.

Kelly turned back to the television. "How is she getting along with Juanita?"

Kelly's question was asked too innocently. Which meant she'd already had an idea about how Erin and Juanita were getting along. "I don't get what's up with that. Neither of us is here when Juanita comes in to clean. Do you know Erin thought I was sleeping with her? Can you believe that?"

Kelly shook her head and pressed a hand to her chest. "I can't. Anyone who knows you, knows you wouldn't sleep with the woman cleaning up your house. That's too close to home."

Will dropped his legs from the table and swiveled to his sister. Finally, someone who understood what he'd been trying to say. "I know. Much less put her in that type of situation. I thought she'd believed me, but I don't think she does."

Kelly patted his knee. "Just be patient. You know Erin likes to have her way. She's also got a jealous streak."

"Erin? I never saw her as the jealous type."

"Well, that's because you never talked to me about her and her boyfriends before," Kelly said sweetly.

"Boyfriends? What boyfriends?" He vaguely remembered Kelly offhand mentioning guys Erin dated, but honestly he hadn't thought anyone had been serious.

Kelly rolled her eyes. "Don't act like no other man was interested in Erin before you. She dated, and she gets jealous easily. Keep that in mind if she, you know, starts to act a little clingy." Kelly squeezed his knee with the word *clingy*.

The word sent chills up Will's spine. Erin clingy? He couldn't picture it, but then again, why would she immediately assume he and Juanita were lovers after only one conversation with the woman? Did she really have a jealous streak he never noticed before?

Clingy, homebody, jealous. Okay…maybe they could work through that. If Kelly was right about Erin, and he had no reason not to trust his sister, as long as he didn't give Erin any reason to act on those feelings they wouldn't cause any drama in their relationship. He wasn't about drama. He'd just work hard to make sure Erin understood he was interested only in her.

And what if she doesn't believe you?

That was a question he didn't want to think about answering.

Chapter 17

"Wow, so Will Hampton is really going to settle down?" The woman's words were accompanied by a round of disbelieving chuckles.

For what felt like the hundredth time since arriving with Will at his dad's party, Erin had to force to keep the smile on her face. She joined in with the round of strained laughter coming from the small group surrounding them. The same bemused amusement from everyone who acted utterly shocked by the idea of Will Hampton in a committed relationship. What's next—could humans breathe under water?

Will's arm around her waist stiffened. Apparently, he, too, was tired of the jokes and snide comments. He pulled her closer to his side and met her gaze. The tension around his smile eased, and his face softened the way they always did when they made eye contact. As if he knew he could get through all the comments and the doubts as long as she believed in him.

Erin returned his smile. Shoved down her annoyance and own concerns when faced with so many people questioning what was between them. She squeezed him back with the arm she had wrapped around his waist.

"I am," Will said, still looking into Erin's eyes. "I finally realized what was in front of me all these years. No more playing the field for me." He looked back at the woman in the group, Jocelyn, who'd made the comment. "I'm a one-woman man."

Jocelyn raised a brow and studied Erin as if she were a newly discovered species. She probably did deserve a place on the new and incredible discoveries list. The rare woman who could make a playboy give up his bachelor lifestyle and become a one-woman man. Women from all corners of the globe would come and marvel at this rare sight.

And maybe you're being a bit melodramatic.

"I knew it would happen one day." Oliver Parker, the son of one of Mr. Hampton's longtime friends, glanced between Erin and Will. Oliver was around the same age as Erin and Will. He'd been around them growing up and had hung out with Will sporadically when they were younger.

"How did you know that?" Erin asked, surprised.

Oliver shrugged. "Just a feeling I had. You two never acted like you noticed each other, but it was obvious you did. Will was at every one of your games back in high school and could rattle off all your stats before you could. You knew every girl Will dated and could give Kelly the rundown on her the second Kelly bothered to notice Will was dating someone new."

Erin's face burned. Had her interest in Will's dating life been that obvious back then? She'd said she paid attention because she wanted to know what type of girl fell for Will's practiced lines so easily. Guess she only had to look in the mirror to find out.

Will ran his hand up her back. "Guess you're right, Oliver. I did always pay attention to what was happening with Erin. See, baby, we were meant to end up here."

He kissed her forehead. A murmur of approval went through the previously disbelieving crowd. Well, except for Jocelyn. She still examined Erin as if she held the secret to life.

Erin smiled and pulled away. "I'm going to grab a drink."

Will's brows drew together slightly. She saw confusion blossoming in his handsome face. Erin smiled and tried to reassure him with her eyes that everything was okay before she hurried away. Oliver's belief that she and Will would eventually end up together bothered Erin.

She'd been obsessed with the various girls Will had hooked up with. He'd only been interested in how well she did on the basketball court. For a guy who'd become a professional basketball player with aspirations to coach one day, that wasn't exactly a sign he'd been romantically interested in her.

Had everyone known she'd had a crush on Will? Had they all seen the feelings written on her face and expected her to fall into his arms one day? If so, why did that bother her so much?

He said he'd always been interested in you, too. What if he was just waiting on the right time to hook you?

She was halfway to the bar, weaving her way through the multitude of guests at the party, when a warm hand grasped her waist a second before she was pulled back against Will's solid body. She couldn't suppress the grin on her face as he lowered his head and kissed her neck as he hugged her tight.

"Your basketball scores weren't the only thing I noticed," he whispered in her ear. "They were just the only things I could talk about with Oliver or anyone else without giving away that I was paying too much attention to my sister's best friend."

She turned and wrapped her arms around his neck. His hands rested on her hips. "Are you saying you had more lurid thoughts about me back then?"

"You don't know half of the lurid thoughts I had about you." He lowered his head and kissed her quickly. "I just never thought you would take me seriously."

"Why not?"

Uncertainty replaced the playful look in his eye. "No one takes me seriously unless I have a basketball in my hand. My grades were mediocre because I had a hard time focusing in school. I was barely passing. Everyone knew I was only getting by because I could play ball. So I became the guy everyone liked hanging around with so they'd focus on how cool I was instead of how stupid I was."

Erin's hands gripped his shoulders. She scowled at him. "I never thought you were stupid. Don't you ever say that again."

"You also didn't think I was the smartest guy out there. You've always had your stuff together, Erin. Your grades were outstanding. When you hurt your knee, you didn't have to worry about college because everyone knew you'd get an academic scholarship. You took the blow like a champ and turned an injury into determination to succeed elsewhere. You're smart, successful and driven. People listen when you talk. I never thought a woman like you would—"

She placed a finger on his lips. "Don't say a woman like me would be with a guy like you. Will, you are smart. Maybe a little unfocused at times, but I never mistook that as stupidity. And you are the guy people love to be around. You're charming and charismatic, and you have a genuinely good heart. If you would have shown interest… I wouldn't have backed away."

"The one time I showed interest, you turned away."

The night of the military ball. The night after she'd overheard him and a few other guys on the boys' basketball team rank the girls in school and rank her somewhere toward the bottom. The "cool" girl. The one you'd sleep with, but she made a better homegirl than anything. She'd never told anyone about overhearing that conversation. It had been too humiliating. Actual confirmation that she was indeed at the bottom of the list of girls whom boys were interested in. In high school that had hurt like hell.

"Do you remember the day before the military ball? When you and some of the other guys from the team were helping set up for the dance?"

Will frowned and escorted her out of the crowd of people bumping into them to one of the walls. "Yeah, what about it?"

"Well, I was helping set up, too."

"I know. I saw you there."

She licked her lips and took a deep breath. "But you didn't see me as I got supplies out of the closet and you and the other players walked by…ranking the girls at the school."

His eyes became distant as he searched for the long-ago memory. Then his face cleared, and he cringed. "Erin…"

She shook her head. "It's okay. I knew that was the way most of the guys looked at me. The way most guys still look at me. So when you tried to kiss me, I thought you were just being nice. I knew I'd read more into it than was really there, so I turned away."

"Damn, Erin, I didn't mean it like that. I was a senior. I thought they'd laugh if they knew I was crushing really hard on a sophomore."

Erin laughed and rolled her eyes. "As if your teenage ego wouldn't survive."

"The frailty of teenage ego shouldn't be underrated or scoffed at."

Her smile softened. "I know that now. But it still makes this—" she pointed at the two of them "—hard to believe sometimes. It still feels like I'm falling hard for the really popular guy and one day he's going to decide he's had a fun time but now it's time to move on to something else."

She lowered her eyes and clamped her mouth shut. Instantly hating she'd let that piece of insecurity out. She was never vulnerable to someone else. Especially a guy. Now here she was giving Will the road map to break her heart.

"And I feel like the dumb jock who finally got the smartest and prettiest girl in school to realize there's more to him than sports. I feel like I have to make sure you understand there is no one else for me. That I'm serious, but I'm afraid you'll lose faith in me like everyone else and walk away."

Her eyes shot up to his. No trace of deception in his

face. Her heart hammered, and her chest tightened with an emotion she knew it was too soon to acknowledge. Yet it was still there. She loved him.

She met his eyes. Ran her fingers over the rough hairs of his beard. "I won't lose faith in you, Will."

"And believe me, Erin, I won't decide to move on to something else." He brushed a hand across her cheek.

His eyes heated and swirled with such ferocious passion she couldn't breathe. Long fingers pushed into her hair and pulled her head back. She lifted on her toes and closed her eyes. Her entire body ached for his kiss.

"Will you two get a room already!" Kelly's voice interrupted. "No, scratch that. Since this is Dad's house and you probably could find a room."

Erin opened her eyes. The same disappointment flowing through her cooled the flames of passion in Will's eyes. They smiled. His eyes promised to finish what they started later, and her body shivered.

"I was just going to get a drink," Erin said. She pulled out of Will's arms and faced her friend.

Kelly eyed them with exasperation. "Then I'll take you. You've barely spent a second with me at this party." She reached over and took Erin's hand in hers. "Sorry, Will, but I'm taking my friend."

Will raised a hand. "As long as you bring her back."

Kelly raised a brow. "I'll think about it." She pulled on Erin's hand. "Come on, I want to introduce you to someone."

Erin waved at Will over her shoulder as Kelly pulled her away. "Who do you want to introduce me to?"

Kelly shook her head. "No one. I just wanted you to come outside with me. There's a DJ and I want to dance, but no one has started dancing yet."

Erin laughed and followed Kelly. If anyone loved dancing as much as Kelly did, it was Erin. For as long as she could remember she and Kelly were often the first two people on the dance floor at any party. Then they stayed out there until the lights came on. She and Kelly hadn't gone dancing in months. She'd much rather have fun with Kelly than listen to another person ask if she and Will were exclusive.

"Then let's get this party started," Erin said.

The party ended at three, so Will and Erin found a room and stayed at his dad's place. The next morning, Will left Erin sleeping in the bed and went downstairs in search of breakfast. He spotted his dad sitting outside. His head back soaking in the early morning sun's rays, dark shades on his eyes and his feet stretched out in front of him. Will grabbed two bottles of water and went outside to join his dad.

"That was some party," Will said.

His dad's lips spread in a grin, but he didn't lift his shades or sit up. "It was. I still know how to throw a good party."

"Yes, you do," Will replied with a smile. Already, a crew cleaned up the confetti and other trash from the backyard. They wouldn't come into the house until after noon. That way the cleaning wouldn't disturb the family.

"Did you and mom throw parties like this before you had us?" He remembered some sedate dinner parties, the occasional New Year's bash, but nothing frequent or elaborate.

"Nah. I gave all this up when I met your mother."

"You must have missed it."

"Why do you say that?" Calvin asked.

"Well, you've gone right back to having parties. I figured you must have missed doing this."

"I didn't miss this at all. In fact, I never thought I'd have a reason to fill my days and nights with strangers again. Your mom was supposed to be my company for the rest of my life."

The pain in his dad's voice made Will's throat tighten. "We're here for you, Dad. You don't have to fill your life with strangers."

Calvin reached over and patted Will's knee. "I appreciate that. But you kids have your own lives. I don't want you babysitting me."

"It's not babysitting. We care about you. Remember that. If you need us, just give a call. You don't have to do all this."

His dad nodded, but Will didn't consider the gesture an agreement.

"Erin still asleep?" Calvin asked.

"Yeah. She and Kelly were on the dance floor all night. Just like old times, huh?"

Kelly and Erin would have two-person dance parties during their frequent sleepovers. He used to tease them about being danceaholics, but he also enjoyed watching them. The joy on his sister's face. The way Erin would let loose and enjoy herself in a way she rarely did.

"It was," his dad said. He turned his head in Will's direction. "How long are you going to keep stringing her along?"

Will jerked back. "Who, Erin? I'm not stringing her along. I'm serious about her."

His dad scoffed and flipped his wrist. "I don't believe it."

"Why not? It's like what you had with Mom."

"No, it's not." Calvin said flippantly. "What I had with your mom was special. It was instantaneous. The moment I saw her I knew she was the one. You can't say that about you and Erin."

"Just because I can't say that doesn't make it less real. She's different."

Calvin glanced at Will over his shades with an I'm-not-convinced smirk on his face. "She grew up and into her curves. She's not the shy, serious, young ballplayer you used to know. Now you've noticed she's female and your body woke up. That's all."

Will sat up straight. He gripped the bottle of water in his hand. Angry frustration coursed through him. "Dad, why do you always dismiss my feelings like that? Like I can't be serious about anything?"

"I don't dismiss your feelings. I've just raised you and know you better than you know yourself. You're not ready to settle down. You shouldn't play around with Erin like this."

Will pointed to the trashed backyard. "If you were living like this before you met Mom then you weren't ready to settle down, either. I'm sure people doubted your intentions, too. I'm more than just a ballplayer who wants to sleep around and party."

His dad grunted. Will clenched his teeth. "I'm serious. I know my life right now is temporary. I get ten, maybe twelve good years in the league. I'm on year eight. I've got a few more and then there's the next step. I want to coach, I want a family, I want kids."

His dad sat up quickly. He winced and placed the heel of his hand on his temple. "Kids…have you gotten Erin pregnant?"

A wave of panic washed over him. "No! I mean kids

in the future. Not kids now." He shuddered and shook his head. The idea of diapers and baby food while he was still in the league sent a wave of fear through him. He was just getting the hang of being in a relationship and warming up to the idea of him and Erin being forever. Kids would complicate things. "All I'm saying is I know what I want when I retire. I've got a plan."

"And you've made Erin another step in your plan. Find a good girl to get hooked so you can settle down with her when you're ready."

"It's not like that. I lo—I like her. A lot."

He stopped himself from saying *love*. He didn't want to give his dad another thing to question him on. The feelings he had for Erin were strong, different and potent. Yeah, he had occasional concerns about how they fit together. The frustrations he'd aired to Kelly hadn't gone away. But outside of petty frustrations and the occasional argument, things between them were good. Nothing compared to seeing her at the end of a day. Having her look at him as if he could achieve anything.

His dad laughed and patted his knee again. "See, son, you can't even say you love her. That's how I know this is just another fling. You want to meet a good woman and have a family one day, cool, I believe that. Just make sure you don't hurt Erin along the way. I like that girl. I wouldn't want Kelly to lose her oldest friend because you're testing a theory."

"What theory? I'm not testing a theory." He stood, tired of the conversation with his dad. "I'm going to prove to you and everyone else that I'm serious."

Calvin pulled off his shades and eyed Will warily. "Hold up. Don't you go and do something stupid."

Just like his dad. Automatically assume any decision

Will made would be the wrong decision. "The only thing I'm going to do is prove to you and everyone else that I'm not to be underestimated. I know what I'm doing with Erin. It doesn't matter what you think. The only thing that matters is how she feels about me."

He turned and marched back into the house. Erin entered the kitchen at the same time he did. She took one look at him and concern filled her expression.

"What's wrong?"

He didn't want to rehash the conversation with his dad. That only brought back memories of the surprise on everyone's face last night. The incredulous laughs and are-you-hearing-this side-eyes thrown around whenever people heard he was in a real relationship.

Erin crossed to him immediately. He placed his hands on her hips. "No turning back, right?"

"Of course? Why?"

"Clear your calendar for next weekend," he said.

"Why?"

"Because I'm taking you out of town."

Chapter 18

"I am so glad you convinced me to do this."

Will smiled and took Erin's hand in his. They lounged on chairs overlooking the Caribbean at the private island resort Will booked for them as promised. Before getting lost in playoff frenzy, this quick weekend away was just what they needed.

Though Coach and the rest of the upper management hadn't wanted him to take off so close to the playoffs, he'd pleaded his case and convinced them the likelihood of him getting into any trouble on a secluded private island with his live-in girlfriend was about as likely as aliens invading. He and Erin needed this quick weekend away. Between the games and her late nights working, they'd barely spent quality time together. Once the playoffs started things would be worse. He wanted to reconnect with her before they were pulled further apart.

"I know what I'm talking about sometimes," he said.

Erin turned on her side in the lounge chair. Sunlight glinted off her golden-brown skin. As secluded as they were, she'd opted to go topless. He had no problems with that.

"I'm going to be so behind when we get back."

Will brought her hand to his mouth and kissed her. "Nope. You are not doing that. No thinking about how things will be when we get back. This weekend is just about us."

Erin nodded and ran her fingers through the hairs on his beard. "You're right. No thinking about work or the playoffs," she said. Her finger trailed across his lower lip. "What are we going to do to keep our minds off of all our responsibilities back home?"

His lips spread as he took in her luscious curves covered in nothing but sunlight. His dick swelled. "I'm thinking lots of time naked, wrapped in each other's arms, with the sounds of the waves in the background."

Erin grinned and rolled over onto her back. She raised an arm over her head, pushing up her breasts and making his mouth water. She lifted a hand and bent her finger in a come-here motion. Will eased out of his chair and onto his side next to her.

"I'm okay with that," she said in a warm, husky whisper. "But are you sure you'll be able to keep my mind off work?"

He placed a hand on her hip and squeezed. "Is that a challenge?"

She lifted one shoulder. "Just a serious inquiry."

Will kissed along her shoulder, then lightly bit her neck. He breathed in deep. Savoring the scent, taste and feel of her. He'd bring her here every year. "I'd like to think I'd be able to keep the woman I love distracted enough to not think about work."

Erin jerked back. The movement startled Will. Her eyes were wide as she studied him. "The woman you… love?"

His pulse pounded like ocean waves during a hurricane. He'd let that slip out. His plan was to tell her how he felt tonight during the romantic dinner he'd planned. Not blurt out the words while they sunbathed. But he couldn't bring himself to take them back. His dad's doubts had plagued him in the days since the party, but Will knew what he wanted for his life. When he'd tried to imagine building something with another woman, he couldn't.

He brushed the back of his hand across her cheek. "Yes. The woman that I love."

"You love me?"

He pressed his forehead against hers and ran his hand along the sun-warmed skin of her thigh. "There's no other woman on this island who I'm going to be spending most of my time making love to, is there?"

She took his face in her hands and kissed him soundly. Will shifted onto his back and pulled her body on top of his. When she lifted from the kiss, the smile on her face was radiant. "I love you, too."

The relief he felt was palpable. He hadn't realized how much he'd worried about her reaction until she said those words. "Do you?"

"Yes." She kissed him again.

The tips of her breasts brushed his chest. Will ran a hand up and down her back. *Don't get distracted now. Ask her.* "Do you love me enough to take a full-time position in Jacksonville?"

"What?"

"I want to make this living-together thing permanent. Not just temporary. Will you move to Jacksonville and live with me?"

Hesitation cloaked her eyes. "I don't know. I mean, yes, I want to, but my job is in Chicago."

"You said they may open an office here since they're doing so much business here."

"That's true, but nothing is set in stone. We already have an office in Miami. They may consider Orlando or Tampa for the next office."

"Push for Jacksonville. Push to stay here."

Erin sat up. Her fingers trailed along his chest. Her brows drew together as she considered his offer. "I can bring it up, but I just made senior executive. I can't control where the company ultimately ends up."

"And if they don't end up here, what are you going to do? Move back to Chicago?" Forget about trying to make things work with him?

She blinked several times as if the question caught her off guard. "I guess so."

He shook his head. "How will we work if you're in Chicago?" He sat up, and Erin scrambled to get off him. He stood and paced toward the ocean.

"We worked before. We can do it again."

He turned to face her. "We barely saw each other before. Even with you here we barely see each other. That's why I planned this trip. Now you're saying you're willing to go back to Chicago if your company doesn't open an office here."

"Will, things are still early in our relationship. I can't say I'm ready to completely give up my life in Chicago and move here."

"Why not?" he asked, frustrated.

She jumped up from the chair. Her eyes were bright with her own emotions. "Because everything is happening so fast. We're happening fast. What if…"

"We don't make it? Is that what you were going to say?"

She shook her head. "No. I don't mean it like that."

"Then how do you mean it? Do you not trust what we've got can last?"

"I want it to last. I really do, and I love you, but Will, I can't tell you right now that I'm ready to give up my apartment and quit my job if they don't open a Jacksonville office. You're asking me to give up my entire life."

"I'm not asking you to give up your life. I'm asking you to build a life with me. I'm asking you to be with me long term. I'm asking you to be my partner. My wife."

She staggered back. "Wife? You want to marry me?"

The other big question he'd decided to ask her at dinner tonight. The one thing that would prove to her and everyone else he was ready for the next step in his life. "Why else would I ask you to live with me for good? I'm serious about us, Erin. I thought you were serious, too."

He moved to walk back into the beach house. Erin grabbed his arm. Her eyes danced with confusion and hope. "You're serious? You want us to get married?"

"Yes."

"But I didn't think… You never said anything about wanting to get married."

He slipped his arm around her waist. "Because before we got together, marriage wasn't something I'd considered. Marry me, Erin. Let's make this official and show everyone we're serious about each other."

"Will, this is… I mean…what about…"

"Forget about all of the excuses you're going to come

up with. Just tell me what you want. Tell me you want
to be with me. That you love me." He brushed his lips
over hers. "That you'll marry me."

The battle in her brain played out across her features.
A frown, a smile, a shake of the head, an uplift of her
lips. Then her eyes met his. Excited and happy. A little
unsure. But her next words made him rejoice. "I will."

Chapter 19

I will.

As soon as they'd returned to Jacksonville, Erin had second-guessed her decision. Not because she didn't love Will. She did. He was fun and and went with whatever impulse struck him. Like the last-minute trip to the Caribbean before the playoffs.

She loved spontaneity. Isn't that what all women mentioned at least once in a relationship? For their man to be more spur-of-the-moment with romance? Will was that, and that was exactly the reason why she wasn't sure about her decision.

He wanted her to give up her life and trust they would be together forever. She wanted forever with him. But was she being foolish? What if he woke up a week, month or year from now and decided he'd tried marriage and it wasn't for him? Where would that leave her?

They'd just finished their morning workout. Getting

up at 5:00 a.m. to work out in his home gym after a fantastic weekend on a private island with him had been harder than she'd expected. But in true Will fashion, he'd jumped up at the first blare of the alarm clock and dragged her out of bed with him. She'd come upstairs to make their post-workout breakfast smoothies before they showered and she went to work and he to practice.

She entered the kitchen and stopped. Juanita stood at the counter, the blender running and the protein powder and frozen fruits they used for the smoothies next to it. Her hips twitched in her cutoff shorts as she hummed to herself. Erin gritted her teeth and took a long, deep breath. Juanita had stopped dumping her shoes in the front of the closet after Erin said something to Will. She also had made no other snide or potentially inappropriate remarks since then, either. Juanita was being nice, so she was trying to be nice.

The blender stopped and Juanita continued her humming as she poured the smoothie mix into a tall clear cup.

"Good morning, Juanita," Erin said.

Juanita's shoulders stiffened, but when she turned to face Erin she wore a big, bright smile. "Morning, Erin. How was your workout?"

"It was good." Erin pointed to the blender. "You didn't have to do that. I was just about to make the smoothies."

Juanita shrugged. "It was no big deal. I knew you both were down there, and I decided to help out. I know Mr. Hampton starts preparing for the playoffs this week. I like to make things easier for him."

Well, aren't you helpful. Erin bared her teeth in a tight smile. "That's nice. I can take over from here."

"I'll just make the coffee and then I'll get started on the other things I need to work on."

Will came into the kitchen behind Erin. He placed his hands on her shoulders and kissed her cheek. "You've made the smoothies already?"

"No, Juanita did that."

Will looked at Juanita. "You didn't have to do that."

"I know you're about to get busy. I added flax seeds to your smoothie. The extra protein will help out."

Will squeezed Erin's shoulders and grinned. "Thanks, Juanita. You always know how to take care of me."

Juanita brushed a lock of dark hair out of her face and smiled sweetly. "I always try to take care of you, Mr. Hampton."

Erin just barely stopped herself from rolling her eyes. "Flax seed, huh? I've never had that in a smoothie. I'm looking forward to trying it."

"Oh, I didn't put any in your smoothie," Juanita said. "You don't need the extra nourishment the way Mr. Hampton does."

Of course you didn't. "No big deal. You're probably right."

Juanita picked up the two glasses with smoothies and brought them to Erin and Will. Her hips seemed to sway with an extra flare as she crossed the room. Erin stopped herself from snatching the cup from the woman. Juanita's eyes were trained on Will as he took his cup. Their fingers brushed during the exchange. The corner of Juanita's mouth tilted up, and she lowered her lashes to look quickly away.

Erin glanced up at Will. He seemed focused entirely on the smoothie. Had she missed something? Did Will and Juanita just have a moment, or was she being paranoid again?

"I was thinking about telling Kelly today," Erin said quickly.

"Telling Kelly what?" Will asked, then took a long sip of the smoothie. He licked his lips, nodded and stared at the cup. "This is excellent, Juanita."

"I'm happy you like it," Juanita said in what was two decibels up from a purr, before turning and sauntering back over to the coffee machine.

Erin gripped the cup in her hand. "That you asked me to marry you. That we're getting married."

Will's eyes lit up. "You are?"

"Is it a secret?"

"No, of course not, but I was worried you wouldn't want to tell people."

"I want everyone to know. There's no reason for us to keep this secret." She took a sip of her smoothie. Damn if it wasn't delicious. She wasn't going to tell Juanita that, though.

Will cupped her face in his free hand. His smile was like a beam of sunlight straight to her heart. "Then tell her. Tell everyone. My mind is made up. You're the only woman for me."

He lowered his head and kissed her deeply. Erin leaned into him. Her body burned for more contact with his. Passion erupted in her veins until she thought she'd burst into flames.

A cry followed by a crash rang through the kitchen. Erin and Will jumped apart. They spun toward Juanita, who was frantically peeling off her shirt.

"Juanita? What are you doing?" Will asked.

"Ow, ow, ow," Juanita chanted, jumping from foot to foot. "I spilled coffee on myself. It's hot." She spun toward them and placed a hand on her chest. A large red splotch spread out over her breasts. Breasts that weren't hidden by the now-wet lace clinging to them. "Am I blistering?"

Will's mouth opened, closed, then opened again. His brows raised as Juanita stuck her chest out for inspection.

Erin stepped forward. "No. You aren't blistering, but you should go put a new shirt on. I'll grab some ice."

"I'm so sorry about the mess." Juanita pointed to the broken coffee mug and spilled liquid on the floor.

"Don't worry about it, just go get a new shirt," Erin said.

Juanita nodded. She didn't cover herself or seem the least bit shy about standing there nearly topless in front of them. "Okay, I'll clean this up when I get back."

She hurried from the room. Her cheeks nearly as red as her chest. Will watched her go.

"You didn't check to make sure she didn't burn herself too badly."

Erin slapped his arm. "Are you crazy?"

"What?" He rubbed his arm.

"She did that on purpose."

"Why would she do that?"

"Because we were kissing."

"Are you saying that she doused herself with scorching hot coffee just because I kissed you?"

She saw it creep into his eyes. Doubt, frustration, the here-we-go-again look. Erin couldn't do this anymore.

"You have to let her go."

"I thought you didn't want me to fire her."

"Nope, now she has to go. Today was too far."

"I'm not firing her, Erin. She spilled coffee on herself."

"On purpose, and then stripped so you could ogle her breasts."

He waved his hands in front of him. Just like a guilty man searching for the truth. "I didn't ogle."

"You couldn't speak," Erin said between clenched teeth.

"Because I was surprised."

She rolled her eyes and threw up her hands. "You're ridiculous. Is this what our marriage is going to be like? You're going to hire sexy housekeepers and take up for them every time they do something to hit on you?"

"She didn't hit on me. Damn, Erin, will you stop it with the Juanita-wants-you stuff? She spilled coffee. She immediately went to change." He looked at his fitness tracker on his wrist. "I've got to get ready for practice. You check on Juanita and make sure she's okay before you go."

He tossed her one last disappointed look before shaking his head and leaving the room. Erin glared first at his retreating back and then the coffee on the floor. If it was an accident, then why did Juanita automatically have a change of clothes ready?

Chapter 20

"Girl, you know he's so used to women falling all over him that he's oblivious," Kelly told Erin.

They were sitting in Kelly's favorite coffee shop. Erin had called Kelly and asked her to meet for lunch. She couldn't shake her irritation from this morning. She was sure Juanita had spilled the coffee and stripped on purpose. But Juanita had come to Erin after Will went upstairs and apologized.

I'm so sorry. I didn't mean to cause any problems between you and Mr. Hampton. I really am happy for you two. He deserves to be happy.

Erin had felt foolish after Juanita's apology. Had she overreacted? Was she letting her own doubts about her and Will cause her to sabotage their relationship? What if he was right and Juanita wasn't interested in him at all and she'd been looking for signs of a problem that weren't there?

"You think?" Erin asked, poking at the tomatoes in the prepackaged salad sold at the coffee shop. "Maybe she really did accidentally spill coffee on her shirt."

"Really, Erin, who spills an *entire* pot of coffee down the front of their shirt? Did she trip?"

"No."

"Did the pot jump from the coffee maker and attack her?"

Erin laughed. "I don't think any of Will's appliances are cursed or possessed."

"Then how could she have spilled coffee? I think you're right. Especially since you said she was already pulling her shirt off as soon as you two kissed."

"Will thinks I'm overacting. He says I'm acting jealous. I'm not a jealous, possessive person. He knows that. Why would he think that?"

Kelly shrugged and lowered her eyes. "I don't know. Maybe he's used to that with some of the other women he's dated. Will used jealousy as a sign to end things quickly. He could be getting cold feet about this entire relationship thing and is ready to call it quits."

Erin frowned and thought about their time on the island. "You think?"

Kelly reached over and placed her hand over Erin's. "This is why I was concerned when you two started dating. I didn't want him to treat you like he does every other woman he deals with. I don't want his dumb behind to ruin our friendship."

Erin pulled her hand back. "If he wanted to end things or was having doubts, he wouldn't have asked me to marry him."

Kelly fell back in her seat. Her eyes bulged like swollen cotton balls, and her jaw unhinged. "What?"

That wasn't exactly how Erin planned to reveal the news, but she couldn't get down with Kelly's assumption.

"That's the other reason I asked you to lunch." She grinned. "Surprise, we're really going to be sisters."

The happiness she'd hoped would sprout over Kelly's face didn't come. Disbelief warred with frustration and disappointment. The fight was quickly replaced with a moderately pleasantly surprised smile, but Erin had seen it. Kelly wasn't happy about this announcement.

"He asked you to marry him. Like, legit get married?"

Erin nodded. "He did. He wants me to take a permanent position here in Jacksonville so we can be together."

"He just told our dad he wasn't ready to get married."

"I don't know what changed."

"What changed is Will had another spontaneous, let's-do-this idea. He's not thinking this through."

"I thought you'd be happy for me. For us?"

"I am... I mean." Kelly frowned and looked at the sandwich she'd barely touched. "Erin, you're my best friend. I only want you to be happy, and you deserve to be loved. Are you sure Will is the right guy for you?"

Erin waited for the doubts that had plagued her ever since Will asked to rise up. For the fear she was making the wrong decision, or that Will wasn't serious about them. But in the face of Kelly's doubt she realized she wanted to be with Will. She wanted to stay with him. To wake up beside him. To encourage him to reach for the goals he never thought were possible. Will had spent so much time surrounded by people who only saw the surface and didn't expect much more from him. He was so much more than a basketball player. She wanted to be there for every victory and to lift him up after every failure.

"He is the right guy for me. And I know I'm the

right woman for him." This time she took Kelly's hands in hers. "Kelly, this won't change anything about our friendship. You'll always be my best friend. The sister I never had. My maid of honor."

Kelly's eyes softened, and the corners of her lips tipped up. "You want me to be your maid of honor?"

Erin rolled her eyes. "Girl, please, you know you're my maid of honor. We planned our weddings when we were twelve. Nothing's changed."

Kelly held up a hand. "Please tell me you've finally gotten over the burgundy and green colors."

"What's wrong with burgundy and green?"

"They're atrocious colors! You should have outgrown that. No ugly colors."

"They aren't ugly. They're perfect."

Kelly shook her head. "You're hopeless. I hope this wedding is at least a year away. That'll give me plenty of time to try to convince you to pick more tasteful colors."

They laughed and the tension between them evaporated. Erin let Kelly steer the conversation to other things, but as they talked Erin couldn't shake the memory of the frustration and disappointment that had flared in her best friend's eyes.

Erin finished the day meeting with the public relations director for the local hospital system about handling their new marketing campaign. The meeting had gone very well, and Erin was confident she'd be able to secure their business for the next account.

She smiled as she left the hospital and walked with a skip in her step toward her car. Securing the hospital's account, along with the marketing for two new trade shows coming to the area, would go a long way toward proving the company needed an office in Jacksonville. She was also pursuing other accounts to make the deal even sweeter.

Her cell phone rang just as she got to her car. She pulled it out of her purse and looked at the screen. Her boss's number.

"Hey, Roxanne," she answered, and unlocked her car.

"Hi, Erin, do you have a second?"

"Yes, I just wrapped up the meeting with the hospital."

"Good. How did it go?" Eagerness crept into Roxanne's voice.

"Really well. I think they'll consider us for their marketing campaign. I'm going to put together a proposal and get it to them early next week. I think we'll be really close to justifying opening the Jacksonville office."

"Any headway on getting marketing business from the Gators?"

"Not yet. I haven't approached them. I'm working other leads. But I am going to meet with the PR team for the Jaguars next week."

"When next week?"

"Tuesday, I believe. I have to check my calendar."

"Okay, but can you get back to Chicago by the end of next week?"

Erin opened her car door and tossed her purse over to the passenger seat. She then leaned one hand on the top of the car and held the cell phone to her ear with the other. "End of the week? Why?"

"Well, we're keeping it under wraps, but since you're a part of the senior executive team I can let you know. We're working out the details of a merger with the Noble Group."

Erin's jaw dropped. The Noble Group was one of the

largest marketing firms in the country. They had offices all over the United States and in several countries around the world.

"Are they buying us out?" A company that large could buy them if they wanted to, but she would expect Roxanne to sound more upset if that were the case.

"No. This started with discussions several months ago. They really became more interested after you knocked things out of the park with the auto show. They've seen the work we can do. A merger will benefit everyone."

"Wow. This is a lot to take in."

"I know. That's why we need you here. We want all the senior executives here in the home office to discuss details if we go through with this. Can you be here?"

"Yes, of course I can be there."

"Great. Let me know when you book your flight. We'll plan the meeting for the following morning. Also, plan to stay for at least a few weeks. Will that throw off any of the deals you're currently working on?"

Erin thought about the upcoming meetings next week and the proposals she had to put together. "I do have a few other tentative dates on the schedule. If we can send one of the senior project managers down here they may be able to handle some of the details while I'm in Chicago. You know, this is really a good example of why we need the Jacksonville office."

"Forget the Jacksonville office. If we get this merger you're the front-runner for the Chicago office."

Erin was flabbergasted. "Chicago? *You* run Chicago."

"But I'm trying to get to New York. You know that's where my parents are. If things work out, I'll be moving to the New York office and turning things here over to you."

"Roxanne, I can't believe you'd recommend me. I've only been senior executive for a few months."

"But your dedication to this company goes back long before you were promoted. You've proven yourself. I couldn't think of anyone better to handle the office."

Erin grinned and accepted the compliment. Taking over the Chicago office would be a dream come true. Especially if they merged with the Noble Group. But her perfect dream job would jeopardize everything she and Will had planned for.

Chapter 21

"Hey, Will, can you stick around for a second?"

Will, Jacobe and Isaiah stopped talking and faced Coach Simpson. The team had just completed practice and Coach had worn their asses out. Will was looking forward to nothing more than sitting in the steam room, showering and getting home to Erin.

Their argument that morning had weighed on him all day. He didn't believe for a second Juanita was coming on to him, but he was tired of the tension she inadvertently caused in his relationship with Erin. He was going to have to let her go.

"Anything wrong?" Will asked.

"Just need to talk to you for a second."

Will looked at his friends. "I'll catch up with you guys in a second."

They both nodded, exchanged curious looks, then

headed off the court with the rest of the team. Will pushed back his frustration with being singled out to stay behind. He'd hoped to get a second to talk to Jacobe and Isaiah about what was happening with him and Erin. And to tell his two closest friends that he was getting married.

"What's up?" Will asked after turning back and facing Coach.

"Come with me to my office."

Will frowned but nodded. He followed Coach through the hall, past the locker room, to the office he occupied. Unease crept up his spine the entire way. What in the hell was this about? He'd followed all of the rules of the lockdown and had cleared everything with upper management before doing anything outside the lockdown rules.

Will was too anxious to sit in one of the chairs in Coach's office, so he leaned against the table near the window. "Is everything okay?"

"Don't look so nervous. I haven't asked you in here to deliver bad news."

"Okay," he said slowly.

"I want you to know that you did a great job as the captain for the Eastern Conference team during All-Star Weekend. I haven't had the chance to talk to you about that."

The words on Will's tongue died on his lips. He couldn't even remember what he'd planned to say. Coach's compliment threw him completely for a loop.

"Um…thanks."

Coach chuckled and leaned back in his chair. "You don't have to sound so surprised. You've really stepped up in the past few months. Starting with your acceptance at putting together the team for the All-Star Weekend and by setting a good example during the team lockdown."

"I understood the reasons for the lockdown."

"I know, but you helped the rest of the team understand the reasons. You calmed their concerns and took up for the organization. You really stepped up and showed your leadership ability."

Will grunted and shrugged. "I don't know about that. I was just being a team player."

"Don't wave off what I'm saying. You really have been a true leader. More so since Kevin retired. I've heard some of the guys on the team talking about voting on a new team captain before the playoffs. Your name has come up."

Will pushed away from the wall and sat in the chair across from Coach's desk. "They're considering me? Why?"

Sure, he'd been captain during All-Star Weekend, but that was All-Star Weekend. Fun weekend. Not serious games that counted. He wasn't full-time team leader material. He was the guy who gave his teammates a good time. The person they could count on for a few laughs, but that was about it.

"Because you're the guy who won us the championship last year."

"I hit the last shot."

"But you also scored twenty-two points and had twelve rebounds and twelve assists. You were the MVP of the game. This year, you've performed in every game as if it were a playoff game. You've stepped in to be not only the best player on the team, but also the one others know they can come to."

"I wasn't asking for extra attention."

Coach laughed. "Will, you always get extra attention. The media love you. You're on social media all the time." He held up a hand before Will could interrupt. "But you don't use your million followers just to promote foolishness. You bring attention to causes. You stand up for people who are being discriminated against. And you give pretty good tips on the best places to eat."

Will chuckled and rubbed his jaw. "That's just because I believe in that stuff. I don't do it for attention."

"That's what makes you a great leader."

"Why not Jacobe or Isaiah? Wouldn't they be better as captain?"

Coach shook his head. "I disagree. Jacobe has settled down, but he's still a bit of a hothead on the court. Isaiah is one of the leaders on the team, but he's not the one the rest of the guys naturally gravitate toward."

Will thought about what Coach said. He knew he was a great ballplayer, but a leader of the team? Could he be the one the rest of the guys looked up to?

"I know you want to be a coach one day. This is a good step toward that. Show people you can help lead a team, and when you're ready to move on to the next step in your career, you've already proven yourself."

"Why are you telling me this?"

Coach leaned forward and rested his arms on the desk. "Because I know you tend to shy away from responsibility. I don't know why, but I don't think you should shy away this time. I'm with this team for the long haul. We've come a long way, and we've got a long way to go. I've watched you improve and grow into your abilities. I believe you can do this, regardless of what you may believe. Stop doubting yourself. You can do this."

Will thought about Coach's words for the rest of the day. Dozens of thoughts and revelations went through his head. He'd wanted nothing more than to pull Jacobe and Isaiah to the side and ask them what was up, if Coach was mistaken, and tell them about himself and Erin, but the locker room hadn't been the right place. Everyone was still hyped up and excited about the playoffs. The right time hadn't presented himself.

So when he walked through the door of his home and saw Erin's red heels where she'd obviously kicked them off near the door, he smiled and picked them up. It didn't matter if the time hadn't been right to talk to his friends. His lady was here. He could talk to her. That was something he didn't think he'd ever get tired of.

He found Erin in the kitchen. Her tablet in one hand, the other hovering over the handle for the microwave as the seconds ticked down. She looked up from her work when he walked in. Will held up her shoes.

She cringed. "Sorry, my feet were killing me."

He chuckled and looked down at her red-painted toenails. Then his gaze traveled back up her smooth legs until the edge of the skirt of her business suit stopped his perusal.

"I'd be happy to take care of more than your feet."

He placed her shoes on one of the chairs at the table and crossed over. He wrapped one arm around her waist and pulled her lush curves against his. He kissed her softly, reveling in the way she leaned into him.

"I like the sound of that." She leaned back and smiled. "What's got you in such a good mood?"

"I got good news today."

The microwave beeped. The reminder to take the food out. He let Erin go so she could remove the frozen meal she'd heated up.

"I did, too," she said. "You go first."

She peeled back the plastic on the small tray, and the smell of orange chicken filled the kitchen.

"Don't eat that. Let's go out for dinner. Or order something in."

"It's already heated."

"And throwing away a frozen dinner is not that big of a deal. Besides, if we both got good news, then we should go out and celebrate."

He slid away the tray of frozen preservatives and pushed it farther down the counter. He loved Erin, but he did not understand how she could eat those things.

Erin held up a hand and shrugged. "Fine. Let's go out, but first you have to tell me your good news."

"Coach pulled me aside after practice today. With Mike's arrest and conviction, we're out prospects for a team captain," Will said. "Coach Simpson thinks the guys will suggest me before we go into the playoffs. They say I'm a leader on the team."

Erin's eyes widened, and she grinned. "I hate to say I told you so."

"Since when do you hate saying that?"

Her brown eyes sparkled, and she shrugged. "You're right. I love saying it. I told you so! Will, you have to stop listening to what your dad says. You're a natural leader. You just have to accept that."

He placed his hands on her hips and pulled her forward. "I know that. It helps having someone on my side to remind me to get out of my own head."

"I'll always be ready to snap you back to reality."

"That doesn't scare me nearly as much as it should," he said with a laugh. He kissed her again. He couldn't get enough of her lips. The feel of her. He hated that he'd taken this long to finally step up and accept the way he felt about Erin.

"Now my good news," she said.

"Shoot."

"Our office is considering a merger with Noble Group. Which means a promotion for me."

Will lifted her up by the hips and spun her. She gripped his arms and laughed. "That's awesome."

"I have to go back to Chicago next week to meet with the other executives and discuss the merger. It's not final, but if we can come up with a game plan moving forward, this could be great for my career."

"How long will you be in Chicago?"

"A few weeks at least."

He nodded. "That's good. It'll give you time to pack your stuff and close out the lease for your apartment."

The excitement in her eyes diminished. "I won't have time to deal with all of that. Besides, that can come later."

Later when? She'd said she wanted to marry him. Which he took meant she was ready to give up her apartment in Chicago and move in with him. But he didn't want to ruin their good news.

"That's cool. We'll work it all out later. I'll miss you, so let me know as soon as you'll be coming back."

"You sure you'll be okay while I'm gone? Who's going to feed you frozen meals while I'm out?"

"No one, thankfully." He was about to say that Juanita used to stay late and sometimes make meals for him, but that brought him back to this morning.

"And another thing. When you get back, Juanita will be gone."

Her eyes widened. "Why? If it's about this morning…"

"It's about more than this morning. I want things to

be good between us. This is going to be your house, too. If she makes you uncomfortable, then she has to go."

"She only makes me uncomfortable because she wants you."

He shook his head. "None of that matters. I'll let her go at the end of the week."

Her brows knit together. He saw the need to argue warring in her eyes. Then she took a breath and nodded. Maybe she didn't want to ruin their night, either.

"You're right. Let's go out and celebrate."

Chapter 22

Will was sitting in the team conference room scrolling through an Instagram feed on his phone when Jacobe came up beside him.

"You and that phone, man. What are you looking at now?" Jacobe slid into the seat next to Will.

"Engagement rings," he answered. He stopped on a picture of a huge five-and-a-half-carat diamond ring. "Is five carats too big, or too small?"

"Depends on the woman. Some like huge rings, some like smaller ones. Why are you looking at engagement rings?"

He looked up and met his friend's eyes. "I asked Erin to marry me."

"What? When?"

"The other week when we were on vacation in the Caribbean."

"Why didn't you tell me?"

"When I got back things were hectic. Coach told me about the captain thing. Then there was the hustle of getting Erin back to Chicago. Then I thought, why tell everyone when I haven't even given her a ring. I'm going to surprise her with it when she gets back next week."

"Marriage. Man, are you sure? I mean, you two haven't been together that long."

"You weren't with Danielle long before you asked her to marry you. And don't give me the 'you two knew each other in college' spiel, either. I've known Erin almost my entire life. We finally hooked up. She's the one I want."

Jacobe nodded and rubbed a hand across his jaw. "I can't argue about any of that. If you're sure she's the one you want to marry, then, hey, who am I to judge? I wish you both the best."

Will relaxed, unaware that he'd gone stiff as he'd waited for Jacobe's reaction. He hadn't told his dad. He already knew what Calvin's response would be to the news. *She's a nice girl. You'll only disappoint her.* Kelly had lit into him right after Erin went out of town. Accusing him again of stealing away her best friend and threatening to kill him if he broke Erin's heart.

"I appreciate that," Will said. "Everyone isn't happy about the arrangement."

"Who isn't?"

"My sister, for one."

"I'd think she'd be happy. Her best friend is now a part of the family. Isn't that a dream or something women have?"

Will laughed. "I don't think so. It's my own fault. She and her college roommate were close. I got in between that."

The one quick hookup that hadn't ended as neatly as

he'd liked. Kelly's roommate had taken her anger about her and Will ending out on Kelly. Her sister had lost a friend, but even before the breakup Kelly had complained. Saying her roommate no longer wanted to hang out with her and how she couldn't trust her with her secrets because she'd just spill them out to Will later.

"This thing with Erin is different, though, right?" Jacobe asked.

"It is, but she doesn't see that."

"Then you'll just have to prove her wrong."

"I hope so. Hey, Kelly is having a get-together at her house this Friday."

"You know we can't party." Jacobe pointed to Coach Simpson and Coach Grey entering the conference room with a few other members of the team. They were meeting to go over film from the first playoff game. The Gators won, but it had been a tough fight. "We're in the middle of the playoffs."

"Not a *party* party. Just hanging out. A few friends, everything chill and low-key. Erin is out of town. I'm getting bored at home alone."

"Juanita isn't offering to keep you company?"

Will scowled. "Why would you say that?"

"Because that woman looks at you like you're a piece of meat. I'm surprised you didn't have any trouble with her after Erin stayed with you."

"You think she's interested?"

"Honestly, I thought you'd been hitting that for a long time."

"Why didn't you say anything?"

"You don't kiss and tell, and I get my kicks in my own bedroom."

"Well I'm not sleeping with Juanita, never did and

never will be. I let her go last week. She was causing Erin to feel uncomfortable."

"I'm not surprised. That's for the best. Don't let anyone up in your place that makes your lady uncomfortable."

Coach Grey and Coach Simpson faced the now-full conference room. Isaiah came in and sat on Will's other side. The postgame meeting had begun, so Will pushed aside everything except what they needed to do next to keep winning. But he couldn't help the relief in knowing he'd made the right decision by firing Juanita.

"Are the rumors true?"

Erin looked up from her laptop on her desk in the Chicago office to Vivien in the door. She raised a brow. "Is what true?"

Vivien looked over her shoulder before coming into Erin's office and shutting the door. "The big M-word?"

Erin's heart picked up a beat. M-word. Marriage? How did Vivien find out? "Who told you?"

"Well, there's only one reason all of the company senior executives are meeting every day. And I saw some of the executives from Noble Group slip into one of those meetings. So, it is true?"

Erin's one fear was replaced with another. Word of the merger wasn't supposed to spread. Employees got panicky and started jumping ship if they thought their jobs would be cut.

"I can't say anything."

Vivien plopped down in the seat across from Erin. "Just tell me if I should start looking for another job."

Erin shook her head. "Of course not. You're one of our

leading project managers. *If* the company were considering a merger, then I would fight to keep you on board."

Vivien's shoulders relaxed. "That's a relief."

"But I need you to not feed into any gossip about a merger. That spooks people. We don't need that to happen. Not right now."

Vivien nodded. Vivien putting things together and figuring out what many of the executives were talking about wasn't a surprise. She was intuitive and usually picked up on things faster than others. Erin trusted her not to run and spread word of anything she learned.

"You know if this merger happens Roxanne is going to hightail it back to New York," Vivien said. "She wants nothing more than to be back home." Vivien's eyes widened. "That means you would be perfect for the Chicago office!"

Erin couldn't help but laugh at the way Vivien's brain worked. "Once again, *if* that happens then we'll see. Besides, I'm not sure if I want to take over the Chicago office."

A wave of nausea hit her. Erin frowned and reached for the pack of saltine crackers next to her mouse and pulled one out. She munched on the cracker, then downed it with some water.

"Why not?" Vivien asked. "This makes perfect sense."

Taking a deep breath, she felt the nausea return to a low simmer in her stomach and focused on Erin. "Will wants me to live with him permanently. He's talking about marriage."

"Is it because you're pregnant?"

Erin choked on the cracker. Tears came to her eyes and she placed a hand on her chest as she coughed.

"Pregnant?" she croaked. She picked up the water bottle and took a sip. She shook her head. "I'm not pregnant."

"Then why have you been eating saltine crackers constantly for the past week?"

"I've been feeling sick." She held up a finger. "But this morning I realized the half-and-half in my fridge is expired. I threw it out and expect to feel fine tomorrow."

Vivien raised a brow. "Are you sure? You're also kind of glowing."

"I am not glowing. That's a pregnancy myth anyway. I have never seen a pregnant woman glow. Most of the time they look miserable."

"My sister glowed when she was pregnant." Vivien pushed the hair over her shoulder. "I plan to glow when I'm pregnant."

Erin shook her head. "I am sick because of bad dairy, and if I am glowing it's because I'm happy. Things are going great personally and professionally."

"Still, it never hurts to take a test."

"I'm on the pill."

"And you're not too busy to ever forget to take it?"

There was that time while they were on vacation. She'd forgotten three mornings in a row, but had taken three as soon as she remembered, then prayed that it balanced everything out. Besides, she and Will used condoms. Sometimes.

"I see by your expression that I'm right."

"I'm not pregnant."

Vivien gave her an if-you-say-so look. "Fine. You know, it'll be good for you to not be pregnant anyway."

"Why is that?" Erin picked up another cracker and ignored Vivien's pointed look.

"Because a baby would make you actually consider

his offer to move down there and give up a great opportunity to run the Chicago office."

"Marrying Will would be just as great."

"Men talk about marriage all the time, but there still isn't a ring on your finger." Vivien stood. "*If* this merger happens and *if* they offer you the job, just think about what you're giving up if he is only talking about marriage and not serious."

Erin had nothing to say to that and nibbled on more crackers as Vivien left her office. The nausea hadn't lessened up. She felt even more sick after her conversation.

It's bad dairy. That's all.

She looked at the bare finger on her left hand. Will had asked, but he hadn't made an announcement or told anyone as far as she knew. And he was the king of announcing big things on his social media accounts.

Erin glanced back at her calendar. Kelly was having a party this Friday. Erin had planned to surprise Will and show up. She'd told Kelly to keep the secret. Deciding to give her friend the heads-up this time since she'd been so upset when Erin hadn't initially told her she was coming to town.

She'd talk to Will this weekend. Tell him about the opportunity to run the Chicago office. Find out if he was serious about them, or if marriage was just another spur-of-the-moment idea he'd had.

She ran a hand over her stomach. *Bad dairy. Please, God, let it be bad dairy.*

Chapter 23

William arrived at his sister's place early. The team was scheduled to practice first thing next morning, then fly out for the next playoff game that afternoon. He was worn out after a grueling afternoon of running drills with the team. He wanted to go straight home and fall asleep, but Kelly had called and asked if he was still showing up. Unwilling to disappoint his sister, he stopped and picked up some of the apple turnovers she liked and a twelve-pack of beer.

He had no plans to drink, but he knew Kelly would appreciate it.

She opened the door after he rang the bell. Loud music blared from inside and mingled with the sounds of voices. "Will, you made it!" she said with a grin.

Will frowned and looked over her shoulder at the dozens of people inside. "Kelly, this is more than a small get-together."

She shrugged. "I know. You know how things balloon out of control."

"I'm tired and probably not the best company for a party."

She waved off his words and took the box of apple turnovers out of his hand. "Just stick around for a few minutes or so. You can't leave right after getting here."

He sighed and followed his sister inside. He recognized most of the people at the party. Several of Kelly's friends he'd hung out with. The guy she'd started dating that he'd met during All-Star Weekend. Some of her co-workers were there, too.

He trailed behind her on the way to the kitchen. Stopping to smile and greet some of the people there along the way.

"You need help with anything?" he asked Kelly once they reached the kitchen.

She shook her head and put the apple turnovers on top of the fridge. "I've got it."

"You know those are for the party," he said.

She shrugged. "I smell them through the box. They're my favorite, and I'm not sharing." She came over and wrapped him in a quick hug. "That's why you're the best brother ever."

Will chuckled and hugged her back with his free arm. He still held the twelve-pack of beer in his other hand. "You're tipsy."

"That doesn't mean you're not the best brother."

He hoisted the beer onto the island in Kelly's kitchen. "I really am only going to stick around for a few minutes. I've got a long day ahead of me."

"I completely understand. Give me an hour and then feel free to slip out."

"Deal."

"Hey, Mr. Hampton."

Will let go of his sister and spun around. Juanita stood in the door of the kitchen. The very last person he ever expected to find at his sister's house party.

"Juanita? What are you doing here?" He looked from her to his sister.

Juanita pointed to Kelly. "I was invited."

Shock warred with angry frustration. "Excuse us a second." He took Kelly by the arm and pulled her into the mudroom next to the kitchen. "Why is she here?"

"Okay, look, it's not that big of a deal," Kelly said. "I ran into her at the grocery store the other day."

"You don't grocery shop. You order your groceries."

"I don't order all the time. And I just needed to pick up a salad mix. I do know how to enter a grocery store."

He held up a hand. "Whatever, get back to why she's here."

"I saw her in the produce aisle. She was crying, so of course I went over to check on her. She said you fired her, and she wasn't sure why. You're her biggest client and she was worried you were going to blacklist her to others."

Will jerked back. "I would never do that."

"Well, she doesn't know that. I tried to tell her that, but I also didn't have the heart to say Erin made you fire her because she was jealous."

"Erin didn't make me fire her."

Kelly raised a brow. "Really?"

"I fired her to make Erin more comfortable."

"Sounds the same to me."

"That doesn't matter," Will interrupted. "That still doesn't explain why she's here."

"I'm getting to that if you let me finish," Kelly said

with an eye roll. "Anyway, I told her you would be here tonight. I figured if she heard from you that you weren't going to blacklist her she'd be okay."

"You invited her here for me?" This was unbelievable. He wanted to strangle Kelly.

"Not *for* you. For you to talk to her. That's all. Just get it over with. Let her know you'll give her a good reference and all that."

"I told her that when I let her go."

"She didn't believe you."

Will rubbed his forehead. "Fine. I'll talk to her. Then I'm out. You don't get an hour from me after pulling this crap."

He turned Kelly by the shoulders and ushered her back into the kitchen before she could argue. He was already tired, and this wasn't making things any easier. Juanita waited for them in the kitchen. She anxiously twisted her hands in front of her as she watched them return.

"Juanita, I just want you to know—"

"Can we talk somewhere quieter?" Juanita said. "I don't want anyone to overhear me beg for a good reference." She pushed her hair behind her ear. Her big eyes were sad and glistened with unshed tears.

Guilt churned in Will's gut. *Damn!* He'd never meant to make her cry. "Sure, we can go in the mudroom."

He motioned with his head for her to proceed him. Juanita smiled and wiped her eyes quickly before scurrying toward the room. Will glared at Kelly. His sister raised her hands and shrugged before mouthing *sorry*.

Yeah, he bet she was sorry.

He followed Juanita into the small space. The tears still glistened in her eyes.

"Look, Juanita, I don't know what you think, but I'm

not going to blackball you. Okay? If you need a reference, I'll have nothing but good things to say about you."

"But you weren't happy with my service? I thought I gave you everything you needed."

"You were great, but it was just time."

"Why? Did I do something wrong?" She frowned. "It was the coffee day, wasn't it?"

"Things were a bit…tense between you and Erin. I can't have that in my home."

"Erin didn't want me there?"

He wasn't going to use Erin as the excuse for why he fired her. He'd made the decision and he was sticking by it. "I didn't want tension in my home. Erin and I are getting married. We deserve a fresh start."

"Is it because she knows how I feel about you?" Juanita stepped forward.

Will's neck snapped back. "Come again?"

Juanita sighed and ran her fingers through her hair. The movement stretched the material of her shirt. He took in what she wore. A button-up blouse with a deep V-neck, short skirt, heels that almost made her as tall as him.

"I knew it. I've tried to hide the way I feel about you, but she saw it from the start."

The walls in the mudroom seemed a lot closer than they were before. "The way you feel about me?"

Her eyes widened, and she pressed a hand to her chest. "I thought you knew?"

"Why would I know? You've never said anything."

"You were always nice to me. You'd let me stay late and make dinner for you. All the comments about how good I took care of your bedroom."

"I was just being nice."

She stepped even closer. The scent of her perfume surrounded him. Nearly choked him. "Well, now you know. I can't walk away without telling you how I feel."

"Juanita, I'm with Erin. That's not changing."

"She isn't right for you." Her hands went to the buttons of her shirt.

Will slid back, but bumped into the shoe rack behind him. "Hold up. What you think doesn't matter. I love her."

"That's because you haven't given us a try," she said flippantly. "Think about it. You think you want her because she was under your nose for years and you didn't go for her. Well, the same is true with me. And I promise you, I can love you so much better than she can."

Will was too stunned to even think. What was going on? This had gotten out of control too fast. Before he could say anything else, Juanita pushed him. He fell back until his butt hit the top of the wooden shoe rack. Juanita had her shirt open and jumped onto his lap in a second. Her knees settled on either side of his hips, her breasts pressed into his chest.

"Hell no," he protested.

His hands went to her waist at the same time her mouth smashed into his. She'd caught him off guard and took full advantage. Her tongue pushed past his lips, invading his mouth with the taste of strawberries and cigarettes.

Anger and disgust rolled through him. He should have fired Juanita the second Erin said she didn't trust the woman.

A sharp cry at the door made Juanita pull back. They both turned toward the sound. Will's entire body froze.

The devastated look on Erin's face made him want to claw out his heart.

Juanita wrapped her arms around his neck and grinned. "I told you he liked the way I took care of him."

With a shake of her head, Erin turned and ran away from the door. Kelly stood in the spot behind where Erin had stood. Her eyes wide as she looked at Will and then in the direction Erin had run.

Not giving one damn about Juanita, he pushed her off his lap. Ignoring her cry of surprise, he hurried out of the mudroom.

Kelly grabbed his arm. "Will, what the hell? What are you doing?"

He jerked off Kelly's grip. "Not now, Kelly."

He hurried after Erin, but by the time he got outside she was already in her car and driving off. Will placed his hands over his face and kicked the wall. How the hell was he supposed to fix this?

Chapter 24

Erin didn't go back to Will's place. She knew that would be the first place he looked for her. She didn't book an immediate flight back to Chicago, or call her parents and schedule an impromptu visit home. Instead, she got a room at a hotel near the airport and spent the night alternating between crying and raging.

When her eyes popped open in the darkened hotel room her memories wouldn't even give her a few minutes of ignorance. A vision of Will with his hands cradling Juanita's hips while she straddled his lap and they passionately kissed flashed across her vision so clearly it might as well be projected on the hotel ceiling. She closed her eyes, but of course that didn't help.

She yearned to spend the rest of the day in that bed. Hiding from the ramifications of yesterday. Hiding changed nothing. She couldn't afford to drown in pain. She wasn't that person. She had to be strong. Her hand rested over her stomach. New pain sliced through her chest. She had new responsibilities now.

Slowly, she sat up and got out of bed. She pulled out clothes for the day, showered and put on her makeup before taking a steadying breath and turning on her cell phone. The phone lit up like the Vegas Strip. Numerous calls, texts and voice messages.

She deleted Will's. She wasn't quite ready to hear his excuses. She called Kelly after seeing her friend's last text.

Call and let me know you aren't in a ditch.

The corner of Erin's mouth twitched with that. It was something she would say. Her friend picked up after the first ring.

"Erin! Thank God, where are you?"

"I'm in a hotel room."

"Which one?"

"I'm not telling you. You'll tell him." She didn't want to see him.

"No, I won't. He's not with me and I haven't seen him since he ran out of here last night looking for you. Now tell me where you are. I need to see you for myself and make sure you're okay."

The denial sat on the tip of Erin's tongue. She wanted to see Kelly. Needed her friend's shoulder to lean on. If anyone would understand it would be Kelly. Even if her understanding came with an *I told you so*.

"I'm at the Aloft near the airport," Erin said.

"I'll be there in thirty minutes. Meet me in the lobby. I bet you haven't eaten anything."

She hadn't, so she didn't argue. Thirty minutes later

Erin and Kelly sat at one of the tables in the hotel lobby. Juice, bagels and fruit spread before them that Erin didn't want to touch. The constant nausea she lived with made her want to turn away from all food. Too bad she couldn't do that.

She picked up a bagel and hoped it would be easy on her. "So, what did he say after I left?"

She hated that the first thing she wanted to hear was Will's reaction. Was he angry at her? Relieved his relationship with Juanita was finally in the open? The least bit sorry things were over?

"He was pretty upset," Kelly said. "More than I expected him to be."

"Why, because I didn't stick around and give him the chance to sweet-talk me into forgiving him?"

Kelly winced, then shook her head. "More like… hurt."

Erin snorted. "I guess that's a new feeling. He's never had a woman run away from him before."

Kelly picked up an orange and twisted it in her hands. "I'd agree with you, but this was different. Erin… I think he was hurt because you were hurt."

Erin rolled her eyes, then blinked back the tears that tried to escape. She would not feel bad for him. This was all his fault. "To hell with his hurt. Kelly, you were right. All along. I never should have believed him. Will isn't the type of guy to settle down and be serious about anything. Much less a relationship."

Kelly reached across the table. "Erin, I—"

"No, let me finish. From the start you warned me this would happen. The truth is, I didn't want to believe you. I've had a crush on Will for as long as I can remember. I never thought he would be interested in me. Not seriously anyway. So when he said all those things about how he's wanted me for years, too…" She sighed and rubbed her temple. "Well, I let myself believe in fairy tales."

"There's nothing wrong with believing in fairy tales," Kelly said.

"There is when it comes to a guy like Will." Erin shook her head and swiped at her wet eyes. "I'm such an idiot." She looked in her lap, pressed a hand to her abdomen, and shook her head. "A royally screwed-up idiot."

"Erin, it's my fault," Kelly blurted out.

Erin's head popped up. "How is this your fault? Did you put Juanita on Will's lap?"

Kelly shook her head but didn't look away. Guilt swam in her eyes. "No, but I might as well have. I… Well, you know I wasn't happy about you two together. So I played up your insecurities a bit. I told you Will was unreasonable and set in his ways, and may have let Will think you were possessive and jealous."

Erin shook her head. Kelly's confession rattled around in her head along with disbelief. "Why would you do that?"

Kelly twisted her hands. "Because you're my friend. You've always been my friend. The stuff I tell you I don't tell anyone else. And if you're with Will, that means you'll start telling him."

"That's not true."

"I've lived it before. And even if you don't want to tell him you'd eventually let stuff slip. Remember the situation with Alec a year ago."

Erin clenched her teeth. "Yes." Kelly's ex-boyfriend, who hadn't taken their breakup lightly. He'd tried to kidnap her and restrain Kelly in his apartment. Kelly had gotten out and called the police. Alec was now living in jail in Nevada for different charges.

"You swore to keep that between us because we both know Will and my dad would have done something stupid. Will didn't need to get in trouble and jeopardize his career because Alec was a real idiot. I handled the situation, and no one got hurt. If that happened again…"

"Let's hope nothing like that happens again," Erin cut in.

"My point is that I have secrets I don't want my family to know about, and you keep my secrets. If you're Will's wife…then you can't keep my secrets."

"That's really messed up for you to think you couldn't confide in me because of my relationship with Will. I'm not your college roommate. We've been friends since we were kids. You know me well enough to trust me to always have your back."

"I know. And I'm sorry."

Erin shook off Kelly's sorry. Her guilt and confession didn't make last night go away. "Nothing you said to either of us should have pushed Will to kiss Juanita. And from the looks of it they were about to do a lot more."

"Okay, here's where the really messed-up stuff comes in." Kelly sighed and straightened her shoulders. "I invited Juanita to my house. I knew Will would be there, and I knew you were showing up early."

"What?" Erin's voice was high and sharp. A few people in the lobby glanced their way. She didn't care. Why would she invite Juanita to her house? Kelly didn't even like Juanita. Did she?

Kelly held up a hand. "That's not all." She licked her lips and took a heavy breath. "I might have slightly encouraged Juanita to take a shot with Will. I told her you were the only reason he fired her. When they were back there, it was under the pretense of Juanita wanting a good reference. Will didn't initiate anything. Honestly, he told her he was with you and that he wasn't interested."

"Then how the hell did she end up on his lap?" Her anger with Kelly, Juanita and the entire situation heated her voice.

"She pushed him down and jumped on him." Kelly raised a brow. "Homegirl was insistent. Will had just said no. I think he was pushing her off when you came in and saw what happened."

"Why didn't you tell me the truth then?" Erin asked. "You let me leave."

"It all happened too fast. You were there, then you both were running out. Then there was the hurt in Will's voice. When he called me this morning, he begged me to ask you to talk to him. To let him explain." Kelly leaned forward and gave her a pleading look. "Erin, he's never begged me for anything. He really loves you. I messed up and I'm sorry."

"You're sorry? For playing us both. Kelly, what hurts more than you playing us is you thinking my relationship with Will would affect the type of friend I am to you. I don't agree with a lot of the things you do, but that doesn't mean I'll tell your secrets. And please believe that it doesn't matter if I was with Will or not, if you ever get in another situation like you had with Alec and I felt your life was in danger, I'd tell them. You handled Alec and told me about it after the fact. If I had known before I would have told because I care about you and don't want to see you get hurt. Me dating Will wouldn't have changed that."

Kelly reached over and placed her hands over one of

Erin's. "I know. I just had flashbacks of losing friends before. I'm sorry, and if you hate me forever I understand, but please, at least talk to Will. He's really upset, and even if you don't work things out you've got to clear the air."

Erin leaned back in her chair. She pulled her hand from under Kelly's. She wasn't sure how she felt. Kelly may have manipulated their concerns, but in the end they hadn't trusted each other. If they were really in love shouldn't she have taken the time to confront Will and find out what happened instead of jumping to conclusions? Shouldn't he have known not to go in that room with Juanita because of what Erin suspected?

She didn't know the answers. Maybe love didn't have a thing to do with their reactions in that moment. As much as she wanted to avoid facing what was next, she couldn't.

Erin straightened her shoulders and looked at Kelly. "I have to talk to him regardless of what I feel."

"Because you want to try to work things out?"

Erin shook her head. "No, because I'm pregnant."

Will barely made it through team practice the next day. He went through the motions. Worked the plays and even forced some level of conversation out, but as soon as they finished he showered and was out of there.

He'd given Coach some excuse he couldn't even remember about why he needed to fly separately the next day instead of with the team tonight. He was pretty sure Coach read the lie on Will's face, but trusting him, had agreed. Will had to be on a plane at five the next morning or else he wouldn't be allowed to play.

Which meant he had less than twelve hours to find Erin and convince her to take him back.

His cell phone rang as he walked to his car. His dad. Will cursed and considered not answering. In the end he relented. "Dad, hey, what's up?"

"I hear you're the new Gators team captain," Calvin said with a bit of surprise and disbelief. "Why didn't you call and tell me?"

"Because it's not that big of a deal," Will answered. He put his gym bag in the back of his car and leaned against the side.

"It is a big deal. You talk a good game about wanting to be a coach one day. Being a leader of a team is a good first step. See, that's what I mean. You don't take stuff seriously. Otherwise, you'd know what an honor it is for your—"

"Dad, I get it. I know it's a big deal. I'm actually very proud and honored they chose me. I know that this will help prepare me to be a coach one day. I've even talked to my coaches about mentoring. So you can save the lecture."

"Hold up. Where's all this anger I'm hearing coming from?"

"From years of you thinking I can't be anything but a ballplayer. You telling me that I'm not smart enough or focused enough. I know I take an interest in a lot of things, but if something's important I've never dropped the ball. You can at least give me some credit for that."

Several seconds of silence passed. "You're right. I'm sorry. I just didn't want to push you into anything."

Will rubbed the bridge of his nose. "Pushing and encouraging are two different things. You never encouraged me, Dad."

"I have encouraged you."

"Only in things you thought I could handle. If things

were hard, then you told me to back away. It's like you think I'm irresponsible or stupid."

"I don't think you're stupid." His dad's voice sounded weary. "Listen, Will, growing up, I wasn't the best student out there. In fact, a lot of people called me an idiot. So I became good at basketball. I made it to the pros and became the guy everyone loved. No one cared about my IQ if I won games. I told my coach that I'd like to coach basketball one day, and he laughed at me. Said I should focus on what I was good at. So I did. I focused on ball-playing and partying. Then your mother came, and I focused on being the best husband and father I could be. I didn't want you to feel the same disappointment I felt."

Will's anger deflated. He'd had people tell him the same thing. Underestimate his abilities. He understood how much that hurt, but if he ever had kids he would rather tell them they could fly to the moon than have them doubt themselves. "I look up to you more than anyone in the world. To me you can do anything, Dad. To hell with your old coach. But just because you weren't encouraged that doesn't mean you should discourage me."

"I know. Old habits are hard to break. Look, Will, I called because I'm proud of you. You're doing things I didn't think I could do, and I want you to know that. I'm going to try to do better. I'm don't want to be the dad who doesn't support his kids. I guess I let that drop after your mother died. I'm still trying to figure out what to do next."

"The only thing I can tell you is to do what makes you happy. Don't feel like you have to go back to the person you were before you married Mom. Not unless you really want to do that."

His dad chuckled. "That's the thing I'm still trying to figure out."

Will checked his watch. He needed to find Erin, but he didn't know where to start. Maybe Kelly would know where she was by now.

"Dad, one other thing. Did you ever…did Mom ever think you were interested in other women?"

"Why?"

"It's Erin. This woman kissed me yesterday. A woman Erin thought was interested in me."

"Apparently she was."

Will rubbed the bridge of his nose. He'd been so blind. "Yeah, I figured that out much too late. Now I've got to fix this."

"Are you sure you want to fix this?"

Will thought about it. The look on Erin's face when she'd thought he'd betrayed her. The disgust he'd felt as Juanita threw herself on him. The foolishness hanging over him for not listening to Erin all the times she'd warned him about Juanita. He'd been arrogant and hardheaded when he didn't believe her.

"I do. I love her. I asked her to marry me."

The sound of his father sucking in a breath preceded several seconds of silence. Guess that was a lot to process. "Look, I don't know what's going on with you and Erin now," Calvin said. "But I will answer your question. Yes, there was always someone trying to get with me, but I made sure your mom knew she could trust me. Don't put yourself in a situation that will give her a reason not to trust you. And if you really love her, and you're serious, then fight for her, but you also have to be ready to accept if she doesn't forgive you. You can't make a woman stay who doesn't want to stay."

The pain in Erin's eyes flashed across his mind again. He wasn't sure if he'd be able to say anything to make her trust him again. "That's what I'm afraid of."

Erin waited to go to Will's place until after his plane was supposed to leave the airport. She'd avoided his calls. She was prepping herself before seeing him.

Kelly's revelations cleared him of her original concerns. That he'd been sneaking around with Juanita all along. Still, other fears crept in to take the space left behind. Did she really trust Will? Could they really be right for each other if they'd so easily let Kelly's interference affect them?

Then there was the biggest complication of all. Will didn't want kids. Not while he was still playing basketball. While she had no doubt he'd take care of their child, she didn't want to see the flicker of disappointment go across his face when she told him. That split second where he would regret the situation before putting on a brave face and asking her what she wanted to do.

She wanted this baby. The idea of Will grudgingly taking on the role of father made her worry the pregnancy would only drive a bigger wedge through their relationship.

The house was empty when she arrived. She bypassed the kitchen and went upstairs. All of her stuff was there. She'd pack and get back to Chicago as soon as she could. She'd tell him after the playoff game. Then they'd deal with what was next.

She walked into the bedroom and froze. "Will?"

He stood by the window. His arm pressed against the pane as he looked out. At the sound of her voice, he spun and faced her.

"What are you doing here? You're supposed to be traveling with the team."

He hurried across the room. He held out his arms as if to pull her into them. Erin crossed hers and stepped back. If he held her, she'd forget about all the concerns that still plagued them.

His hands dropped. He rubbed the back of his neck. "If I'm not on a plane at 5:00 a.m. then I can't play."

"You shouldn't have risked your ability to play. You're the leader of the team."

"I don't care about the game right now. How can I care about that when you're thinking the worst? Erin, I didn't kiss Juanita. I know it looked really bad, but that's not what happened."

"I know."

He jerked back. Confusion clouding his face. "You do?"

"I talked to Kelly this morning. She explained what happened and a lot more."

Erin pushed past him and sat on the edge of the bed. She told him what Kelly had revealed. When she finished talking his shoulders were rigid and his hands balled into fists.

Will paced back and forth in front of Erin. "I can't believe she did that. I'll never forgive her."

"You will because she's your sister. I don't like what she did. I understand her twisted logic, but that's not what's really bothering me."

"Then what is, because I don't get her logic and I'm pissed." He stopped and faced her. "Erin, you have to understand I've never been interested in Juanita. I should have listened to you from the start."

"But that's the thing. You didn't listen to me because

you believed what your sister said. We don't really know each other. We don't really trust each other. If we did, we wouldn't have let someone come between us so easily."

"Because the person who came between us was someone we trusted." Will lowered to one knee in front of her and took her hand in his. "I'm not saying we can't trust our family, but when it comes to our relationship we have to trust each other more. No more letting others influence what we think. If we have a problem with each other, or a situation we're in, we talk to each other."

"Are you saying you're not going to talk to your friends anymore?"

He shook his head. "I'm saying no matter what advice others may try to give us, what's between us is between us." He squeezed her hand. "Erin, I love you. I want to be the person you count on. The person you know will always be there for you."

Erin's heart swelled, but she pulled her hands away. "There's something I need to tell you. I don't think you're going to like it."

"What is it?" He straightened his shoulders as if preparing for a blow.

Erin lifted her chin and met his eyes. "I'm pregnant."

Will's eyes widened. He looked down at her stomach as if he could see their child growing. Then back up to her face. The brightest grin spread across his face. He snatched her into his arms and squeezed her.

"Oh my God! I'm going to be a father."

Erin pushed back and looked at him. Was he serious? But she saw no doubt on his face. "You're happy? You always said you didn't want kids while you still played."

"I didn't think I did, but hearing this…" He cupped her face in his hands. "Erin, I couldn't be happier. I want a family. You are my family. I want to marry you. I want kids with you. I want forever and old age with you."

Her head spun. She placed her hands on his broad shoulders. Steadying herself even though she was sitting still. "Wait…are you for real? I mean… I thought…"

His brows drew together. "You didn't think I wouldn't be happy, did you?"

"I wasn't sure."

"Are you happy?"

"Yes." She didn't hesitate. "I want this child."

He slid closer and placed his hands on her hips. "Do you want to raise this child with me?"

He sounded so unsure. So afraid she would walk away. Erin placed her hand on the side of his face. "I love you, Will. This is new, and sudden, and scary, but…" She ran her fingers through his beard. Stopping him from speaking when the uncertainty in his eyes increased. "I wouldn't want to take this step with anyone but you."

His shoulders relaxed. He leaned forward and pressed his forehead to hers. "I promise to do everything in my power to prevent another situation like last night. I never want to see that look in your eyes again."

"I promise to hear you out before jumping to conclusions. You're right. If we're in this, then we talk to each other. Trust each other."

Will lifted his head and met her gaze. His eyes were soft, warm, happy. "Love each other."

Erin grinned and placed her lips against his. "I can get down with that."

Chapter 25

"Eight pounds, twelve ounces!"

Will accepted the hugs and back-pounding after he announced the weight of his son to the waiting room full of people. His dad, Erin's parents, Kelly, Jacobe, Kevin and Isaiah along with their wives all filled the space. There were no other people in the waiting room. Though Erin called it a drastic waste of money, he'd rented out the entire floor. There would be no pictures of his family leaked to the media on this day.

"When can I see her?" Kelly asked, pulling back after nearly strangling him with her hug.

"She's in recovery," Will said. Erin had to have a cesarean and had gotten through the procedure like a champ. "The doctors will come and let us know when she's moved to her room. But Little Will is already in the nursery."

"Then why am I still talking to you?" Kelly asked, and rushed past him.

She was quickly followed by Erin's parents and his friends' wives. He laughed as he watched the rush to see the baby.

"Get used to that," Kevin said. "Once babies come, no one wants to see you anymore."

Will grinned and shook his head. "Just means my boy is loved."

Isaiah slapped Will on the shoulder. "Will Hampton is a father. Congratulations, man. I'm happy for you and Erin."

"I appreciate that," Will said. "And congrats to you and Angela. I hope things go well with her pregnancy."

Isaiah's face brightened with pride and love. "Thank you. Our kids will get to play together."

"That's going to be crazy," Will said, shaking his head. "I never thought I would want to be here, but now that I'm here I wouldn't change a thing."

"Before we all start crying," Jacobe chimed in, "can we go see the baby now? For his sake, I hope he took after his mom."

Will pushed his friend's shoulder and handed them cigars, and they joined the group of family and friends hanging around watching his son through the nursery glass.

His son!

Man, he'd never get tired of that.

Later that night, after all of their family and friends had left, Will sat on the edge of Erin's hospital bed and watched as she nursed their child. His heart was so full of love, contentment, fear about being a good parent and excitement about watching his kid grow up.

He brushed the hair away from Erin's forehead and kissed her softly. "I love you so much."

She grinned up at him. Her eyes still tired from the surgery but also bright with happiness. "You're only saying that because I had your baby."

He chuckled and kissed her lips. "I'm only saying that because it's true."

Erin chuckled. "Did you see the way Kelly kept checking on him? She's going to spoil him worse than our parents."

"Kelly should spoil him. Because of her we almost didn't make it."

Erin sighed but didn't argue. He'd forgiven his sister, but he no longer trusted her with the secrets of his and Erin's relationship. She and Erin were good, and he was glad their friendship had survived.

She laid her head on his shoulder. "Can you believe we're here?"

"No," Will said. He couldn't keep his gaze off the beautiful, perfect face of his son. "I never would have thought I would be here, with you, this happy."

"Do you regret it?"

"Not a second. Do you regret it?" he asked hesitantly. "Moving to Jacksonville?"

She tilted her head back to meet his eyes. "You know I don't."

"You wanted to run the Chicago office. Your career was the most important thing to you. Now…"

"Now I'm an executive running the Jacksonville office, a wife and a mother. I wouldn't change anything."

A small knot of worry released in Will's chest. He'd gone to the farewell party they'd thrown for her in Chicago. Watched as the people sincerely wished her well and expressed how much they wished she were staying in their office. Saw the hint of sadness in her eyes. She still had the job and traveled to Chicago and New York when duty called, but she wasn't at the center of things. He'd worried a part of her regretted marrying and moving in with him.

"You sure?"

"Positive. I love you, Will. I've loved you ever since that night I was afraid to let you kiss me after the military ball, even though I wouldn't let myself admit how I felt. I'm the lucky one because I actually got to marry the only man I've always wanted."

Will wrapped his arm around her shoulder and pulled her in close. His eyes burned. His throat was thick with emotion. He doubted anything, not winning the championship every year, coaching a championship team or being inducted into the Hall of Fame, would ever make him feel this happy ever again.

"No turning back?" he whispered against her forehead.

Erin snuggled close to him. Their son made a gurgling noise that brought smiles to both of their faces. She placed her free hand on his thigh and squeezed. "No turning back."

* * * * *

Soulful and sensual romance featuring multicultural characters.

Look for brand-new Kimani stories
in special 2-in-1 volumes starting March 2019.

Available May 7, 2019

Forever with You & *The Sweet Taste of Seduction*
by Kianna Alexander and Joy Avery

Seductive Melody & *Capture My Heart*
by J.M. Jeffries

Road to Forever & *A Love of My Own*
by Sherelle Green and Sheryl Lister

The Billionaire's Baby & *The Wrong Fiancé*
by Niobia Bryant and Lindsay Evans

KPST0319

Get 4 FREE REWARDS!

We'll send you 2 FREE Books plus 2 FREE Mystery Gifts.

Harlequin® Desire books feature heroes who have it all: wealth, status, incredible good looks... everything but the right woman.

FREE Value Over $20

Savion Monroe's serious business exterior hides his creative spirit—and only Jazmin Boyd has access. Beautiful, sophisticated and guarding a secret of her own, the television producer evokes a fiery passion that dares the guarded CEO to pursue his dream. But when she accidentally exposes Savion's hidden talent on air for all the world to see, will he turn his back on stardom and the woman he loves?

Read on for a sneak peek at
Forever with You,
the next exciting installment in the Sapphire Shores series by Kianna Alexander!

Savion held on to Jazmin's hands, feeling the trembling subside. He hadn't expected her to react that way to his question about her past. Now that he knew his query had made her uncomfortable, he kicked himself inwardly. *I shouldn't have asked her that. What was I thinking?* While his own past had been filled with frivolous encounters with the opposite sex, that didn't mean she'd had similar experiences.

"I'm okay, Savion. You can stop looking so concerned." A soft smile tilted her lips.

He chuckled. "Good to know. Now, what can you tell me about the exciting world of television production?"

One expertly arched eyebrow rose. "Seriously? You want to talk about work?"

He shrugged. "It might be boring to you, but remember, I don't know the first thing about what goes on behind the scenes at a TV show."

She opened her mouth, but before she could say anything, the waiter appeared again, this time with their dessert. He released her hands, and they moved to free up the tabletop.

"Here's the cheesecake with key lime ice cream you ordered, sir." The waiter placed down the two plates, as well as two gleaming silver spoons.

"Thank you." Savion picked up his spoon. "I hope you don't mind that I ordered dessert ahead. They didn't have key lime cheesecake, but I thought this would be the next best thing."

Her smile brightened. "I don't mind at all. It looks delicious." She picked up her spoon and scooped up a small piece of cheesecake and a dollop of the ice cream.

When she brought it to her lips and slid the spoon into her mouth, she made a sound indicative of pleasure. "It's just as good as it looks."

His groin tightened. *I wonder if the same is true about you, Jazmin Boyd.* "I'm glad you like it."

A few bites in, she seemed to remember their conversation. "Sorry, what was I gonna say?"

He laughed. "You were going to tell me about all the exciting parts of your job."

"I don't know if any of what I do is necessarily 'exciting,' but I'll tell you about it. Basically, my team and I are the last people to interact with and make changes to the show footage before it goes to the network to be aired. We're responsible for taking all that raw footage and turning it into something cohesive, appealing and screen ready."

"I see. You said something about the opening and closing sequences when we were on the beach." He polished off the last of his dessert. "How's that going?"

She looked surprised. "You remember me saying that?"

"Of course. I always remember the important things."

Her cheeks darkened, and she looked away for a moment, then continued. "We've got the opening sequence done, and it's approved by the higher-ups. But we're still going back and forth over that closing sequence. It just needs a few more tweaks."

"How long do you have to get it done?"

She twirled a lock of glossy hair around her index finger. "Three weeks at most. The sooner, the better." She finished the last bite of her cheesecake and set down her spoon. "What about you? How's the project going with the park?"

He leaned back in his chair. "We're in that limbo stage between planning and execution. Everything is tied up right now until we get the last few permits from the state and the town commissioner. I can't submit the local request until the state approval comes in, so…" He shrugged. "For now, it's the waiting game."

"When do you hope to break ground?"

"By the first of June. That way we can have everything in place and properly protected before the peak of hurricane season." He hated to even think of Gram's memory park being damaged or flooded during a storm, but with the island being where it was, the team had been forced to make contingency plans. "We're doing as much as we can to keep the whole place intact should a bad storm hit—that's all by design. Dad insisted on it and wouldn't even entertain landscaping plans that didn't offer that kind of protection."

She nodded. "I think that's a smart approach. It's pretty similar to the way buildings are constructed in California, to protect them from collapse during an earthquake. Gotta work with what you're given."

He blew out a breath. "I don't know about you, but I need this vacation."

Don't miss Forever with You
*by Kianna Alexander, available May 2019
wherever Harlequin® Kimani Romance™
books and ebooks are sold.*

Love Harlequin romance?

DISCOVER.

Be the first to find out about promotions,
news and exclusive content!

Facebook.com/HarlequinBooks

Twitter.com/HarlequinBooks

Instagram.com/HarlequinBooks

Pinterest.com/HarlequinBooks

ReaderService.com

EXPLORE.

Sign up for the Harlequin e-newsletter and
download a free book from any series at
TryHarlequin.com.

CONNECT.

Join our Harlequin community to share
your thoughts and connect with other
romance readers!
Facebook.com/groups/HarlequinConnection

**ROMANCE WHEN
YOU NEED IT**

HSOCIAL2018